RAMSAY SOUGHT
HIS LONELY BED.

He had learned that a lovely face oft hid an evil heart. When it came time to take a wife, he would choose one with plain features and average form; one who did not turn men's wits to jelly.

Ramsay tightened his fists and closed his eyes against the acid memories.

So he would stay home and forget how her chin jutted just so, as haughty as a queen's, while in the depth of her azure eyes there seemed to be an everlasting flicker of fear that—

"Damn!" he muttered, and turned his face to the pillow.

But he couldn't forget how her hair gleamed in the firelight, how her delicate body felt against his arm, and how, when they kissed, he felt as if her very soul spoke to his. Not of certainty and pride, but of fears and doubts and a small slip of a lass who needed him like none other.

Other **AVON ROMANCES**

LOIS GREIMAN

The
HIGHLAND ROGUES
FRASER BRIDE

AVON BOOKS
An Imprint of HarperCollinsPublishers

AVON BOOKS
An Imprint of HarperCollins*Publishers*
10 East 53rd Street
New York, New York 10022-5299

First Avon Books paperback printing: April 2001

Avon Trademark Reg. U.S. Pat. Off. and in Other Countries, Marca Registrada, Hecho en U.S.A.
HarperCollins® is a trademark of HarperCollins Publishers Inc.

Printed in the U.S.A.

10 9 8 7 6 5 4 3 2 1

The Prophecy

He who would take a Fraser bride,
these few rules he must abide.

Peaceable yet powerful he must be,
cunning but kind to me and thee.

The last rule, but not of less import,
he'll be the loving and beloved sort.

If a Fraser bride he longs to take,
he'll remember these rules for his life's sake.

For the swain who forgets the things I've said
will find himself amongst the dead.

Meara of the Fold

Chapter 1

Scotland
In the year of our Lord, 1534

"We are nearly there. There is no need to fret, Pearl," Anora whispered, and nudged the mare deeper into the woods.

In the late night gloaming, mist billowed up in dancing waves of ghostly silver. No sound broke the silence, naught but the soft hiss of dew slipping from bending bracken. High overhead, tattered clouds skittered past a bloated blood red moon, and from an unaccountable distance, an owl called, boding ill. But Anora of the Frasers had no time for age old superstitions. No time for fear.

"Only a moment ago I saw a tower just past the

highest hill. We shall find help there; I am certain of it. Surely once the lord learns of the Munro's intentions, he shall champion our cause and—"

A scratch of noise sounded from behind. Anora jerked about in her high backed saddle, but nothing alarming met her gaze though she searched the gloom for some seconds.

"Truly, Pearl," she said, turning back, "you are such a nervous ninny sometimes. I told you, there is no one following us."

Beneath her, Pearl flicked an ivory ear at her mistress' trembling tone.

A rustle of noise sounded again, closer this time. Anora spun about, heart thumping in the tight confines of her chest. "Who comes?" she demanded, but her only answer was the whisper of alder leaves overhead.

Hard edged seconds ticked by before Anora turned forward and nudged Pearl again. "As I said, we are alone," she whispered, and shifted her eyes sideways, searching the darkened woods. "All alone. And therefore . . ." Off to the right, a chipmunk scolded and scampered up the skeletal remains of an ancient oak. Anora's stomach flipped and righted. "Safe," she finished, but just at that instant, a horse whickered.

Pearl stopped of her own accord, head turned, ears pricked forward, and every muscle taut.

"Who goes there?" Anora called.

For a moment nothing moved, and then, like a frightful dream, a charger stepped from the shadows. As dark as sin he was, and upon his back sat an armored warrior. Black chain mail covered the rider's chest and a dark helmet hid his face.

In the muffled silence, Anora could hear her own breath, harsh in the stillness.

"Who are you?"

The shadowy warrior said nothing. Instead, he reached down and with slow deliberation drew a sword from his scabbard. Muted moonlight caressed the curved edge of the blade, gleaming from point to hilt, and for a moment Anora remained frozen, mesmerized by the dancing light. Then the charger bent his great neck and pranced toward her with cadenced steps. The warrior raised his sword and with that movement the glimmering reflection on the blade turned from gold to blood red.

Jarred from her torpor, Anora rasped a prayer and clapped her heels against the mare's ivory barrel. Sensing peril, Pearl leapt into a gallop. Trees rushed past like ghostly sentries. They snatched at Anora, snagging her hair as she bent over her mount's straining neck. Was the warrior still there? Did he follow?

Curling her fingers into the mare's mane, she twisted about to peer into the darkness behind.

Nothing. They were safe, but . . .

No! There he was again, bounding around a copse of trees. Silver steam billowed from his charger's nostrils like smoke from a dragon's maw. Moonlight gleamed with wicked zeal along his unsheathed blade.

Terror ripped up Anora's spine. She twisted forward again, but just as she did, hands reached for her.

She screamed and jerked away. Pearl plunged at the pull of the reins, whipping her mistress sideways. The clawing hands retreated into nothing more than reaching branches, but Pearl's sharp movement had unbalanced her rider. Digging in with her knees, Anora grappled for control, and the panicked mare pivoted around another tree and leapt at the last instant to avoid a log.

For a moment Anora was suspended in nothingness. There was naught beneath her but air, and then she landed, crooked in the saddle but still astride. The reins had been yanked from her grasp, but her fingers tangled again in the mane and she held on for dearest life.

Where they headed she did not know, but they were racing downhill at a frenetic pace with branches whipping past her face and rocks tripping them at every turn.

A prayer burned through her soul, but there was no time to finish the frantic plea, for they were twisting again. Her knee struck a tree. She gasped in pain but held on, leaning back now against the speed of their descent, hoping only for continued survival as the world whipped past in a haze of fear and darkness.

Wind roared in her ears, rushing up from . . . no, not wind; water. They were nearly at the end of their descent. Once in the river, she would gain control, head upstream, lose her pursuer, and . . .

But in that instant of hope, Anora saw the log looming before her. Ordinarily it would have been no great feat to leap the thing, but the woods were dark, the mare panicked, and her take off late. Still, she soared valiantly. Anora's breath stopped, and for a moment it seemed as if time stood still. A dozen errant memories flitted through her mind like wind chased clouds: Evermyst's dizzying heights, Isobel's gentle laughter, Meara's gruff voice—and then suddenly the world jolted back into motion.

Pearl's cannons struck wood, and then they were falling. The earth spun toward them like a falling top. Anora heard her own rasp of fear, felt her head strike the earth, and then, like an odd, distorted dream, blackness settled over her.

Ramsay MacGowan was beginning to tire of his younger brothers' bickering.

" 'Tis raining," Lachlan said glumly.

"And I suppose that, too, is me own fault?"

If Gilmour's mood was deteriorating with the weather, Ramsay could not tell it by his jovial tone. It was one of the things that annoyed him most about his younger brother. He was always happy.

"Aye, 'tis your fault," Lachlan grumbled, and hunched his brawny shoulders irritably against the rain. He was only slightly older than Gilmour, but their personalities could hardly have been more different. Lachlan's dour demeanor matched the weather, and suited Ramsay's own less than jovial mood quite nicely.

" 'Twas not my idea to chase after some mythical Munros," Gilmour argued. "As I recall, 'twas you, brother, who was so eager to find trouble where there was none."

"If Munros be creeping about MacGowan land, I want to know of it," Lachlan said.

"Yet we searched for a week and a day with naught but blisters on our arses to show for our troubles. Lucky for you I have friends at Beauly Manor."

"And had you not dallied so with—"

"Not again about the fair Agnes," Gilmour insisted. "Truly, brother, 'tis not me own fault that she prefers me over—"

"Prefers you!" Lachlan snarled, turning about to glare past his dripping tam. "She hardly prefers you.

'Tis simply that she could not be rid of you. 'Ahh, me Agnes . . . ' " he crooned, reenacting last evening's performance, " 'your eyes are like the brightest star. Your—'."

"Eyes!" Ramsay snorted, and huddled deeper inside his woolen high collared cloak. The eldest of the trio, Ram knew better than to become involved in his brothers' foolish quarrels. But Gilmour had already turned his ungodly smile in his direction.

"What say you, Ram?"

" 'Tis naught," Ramsay said. Rain dropped off the ends of his narrow braids, dripping onto his shoulders with drumming regularity.

"I thought you said 'eyes.' "

"Your hearing has long been suspect," Ramsay rumbled. Irritation trickled down his neck like the unceasing rain drops.

"Humph," Gilmour said. "Yet I was certain you spoke. Did you not hear him speak, Lachlan?"

"Indeed I did. He said 'eyes.' "

Gilmour nodded. "Just as I suspected. And did he say it with a certain . . . disdain?"

"Aye, he did," Lachlan agreed soberly.

"You ken why that is, do you not, brother?"

"I do. He is ruined."

Gilmour nodded. "Aye. Ruined. And you know why."

"I do indeed. 'Tis because of a certain maid."

"By the name of Lorna."

"She broke his heart, you ken." Lachlan sighed.

"There was a time she could do no wrong."

" 'Tis true." Lachlan stared forward, gazing moodily into the oncoming rain. "I remember well when our worldly brother saw no shame in waxing eloquent on the beauty of a woman's eyes."

"A time when he could take pleasure in the company of a bonny lass."

"When he would not ridicule the innocent."

"When he—"

"Innocent, me arse!" Ramsay growled.

"What say you?" Gilmour asked, wide eyed. His head was bare to the driving rain, but he seemed unaffected.

"Do you impugn me Agnes' innocence?" Lachlan asked.

"Methinks he does," Gilmour stated. Though there was disbelief in his tone, there was a devilish sparkle in his eye. Even his damned golden haired horse looked happy.

"Shut up, the both of you," Ramsay said, looking straight between Gryfon's black tipped ears. They were unequal in length and pinned in perpetual vexation against his neck.

There was silence for an entire blessed heartbeat before Gilmour spoke again. "What does he know of innocence, since he has been so horridly burned by his own misjudgment of the fairer sex?"

"Me Agnes *is* innocent," Lachlan said.

"Certainly she is."

"Truly?" Ramsay said, speaking against his better judgment. "Then pray tell, where did she spend the night, Mour?"

Gilmour's lips twitched, but he spread his fingers across his chest in a display of abject innocence and said, "However would I know, brother? 'Twas you who was ogling her bosom."

"Ogling—" Lachlan began, outrage already building in his voice.

"Aye," Gilmour said, nodding emphatically so that water fell in fat droplets from his golden hair. "Though I meself cannot imagine how he could wrench his gaze from her bonny smile, her beautiful eyes, her innocent—"

"The lass," Ramsay said, careful to keep his tone flat, his expression impassive, "is about as innocent as me claymore."

Lachlan growled; Gilmour grinned.

"Why do you imagine she wore such a revealing gown? Might she have been too warm during these damp autumn days? Do you think, mayhap, that she did not realize her bosoms were tucked up under her chin like heaven in the flesh?" Ramsay glowered at his brothers. "Is that what you think, lads?"

"As for me, I barely noticed," Gilmour said, lifting an innocuous hand palm up. "But 'tis the fashion, I suppose. Nothing more."

" 'Tis seduction!" Ramsay stated. "Nothing less."

"Seduction!" Lachlan hissed.

"Are you about to let him defame your Agnes like—" Gilmour began, but in that instant something snagged Ramsay's attention. It was just a shadow amidst shadows, but with it came a prickle of unease.

"Quiet," he ordered softly, and the others immediately fell silent. "Do not turn yet, but I think we are not alone."

"Explain," Gilmour said, his voice as low as Ramsay's.

"Where?" Lachlan asked.

"To our left and a little ahead." Ramsay paused, not allowing Gryfon to turn his hirsute head and warn the rider that he had been spotted. "Do you see it?"

"Aye. A warrior," Lachlan replied. "Goodly sized. Black mail and ventail astride a dark horse. A stallion, I think. Mayhap a five year old—"

"Christ, man," Gilmour groaned. "We do not need to know the steed's name. Is he alone?"

There was a moment's delay, but not the slightest movement of Lachlan's head. "I see no others."

"Are you certain?"

For the first time in several hours, Lachlan grinned. "We'll know when we confront him."

"Confront him!" Gilmour scoffed. "You know what that means, don't you, Ram?"

"Aye," Ramsay said, and shifted his shoulders ever so slightly to feel the pleasant weight of his claymore against his back. "It means that our wee brother's spoiling for a fight."

"And you know how disagreeable he gets when he does not get his way," Gilmour said, still watching the road ahead.

"There is nothing worse than a disagreeable brother," Ramsay said, and with that, spun Gryfon toward the left. Had Lachlan not done the same they would have collided. Instead, they lunged in unison into the trees.

For one heart pounding instant the dark shadow stayed where it was, then it turned with the speed of light and leapt away. They charged after like hounds behind their prey, but in a matter of minutes they knew they had failed.

"Where the devil did he go?" Ramsay growled.

Lachlan glowered into the distance. "I do not care for this."

"I rather dislike it meself when people disappear into nothingness," Gilmour agreed, steadying his steed.

"If he wished us no harm, why did he not declare himself?" Lachlan wondered.

"Mayhap my reputation as a swordsman preceded me," Gilmour said.

"And mayhap he was following someone," Ramsay countered, and cued the bay to the left. Gryfon ground his teeth and irritably flicked his tail as he turned.

The other brothers urged their taller horses alongside. "Tracks," Gilmour said. "Two sets. Heading breakneck toward the burn."

"Aye, and the second is the warrior's."

"Are you certain?" Gilmour asked, but Lachlan didn't deign to answer. "So he was following someone. But was he friend or foe?"

"Foe," Ramsay answered, moving his green plaid aside to slip a short blade from inside his bull hide boot. "But he lost his quarry. Thus he returned to their tracks to find him."

Pulling his own blade from its sheath, Lachlan dismounted and turned to face downhill. " 'Tis only right, then, that we find him first."

The rain made the trail difficult to follow, but the brothers were in their element. Lachlan crouched low over the uncertain trail while Ramsay rode to his left and Gilmour to his right. A MacGowan did not grow to manhood without learning to protect his own.

Never were their eyes still as they wended their way through the misty rain, only to turn back and try again and again.

A log lay across their trail. They skirted it, wary of everything, for the sound of the water below drowned all else. But soon they were at the bank of the burn, and there the hoofprints halted.

Gilmour glanced once more to his right, making certain no one watched them. "What now?"

"We guess which way. Right or left," Lachlan said, gazing over the rumbling water, but Ramsay was already turning his mount downstream.

"Left," he said. " 'Twas where the warrior came from."

"A good thought."

"Aye. He is estimably wise," Gilmour agreed. "What a pity Lorna ruined him so when—"

"Do not start up—" Ramsay began, but stopped in an instant, for he'd noticed green velvet just visible beneath a scattering of twigs and leaves.

"What is it?" Gilmour asked as Lachlan drew his dirk.

"The quarry," Ramsay said, nodding toward the figure nearly hidden between a fallen log and bending bracken. "It seems we have found him."

Spinning his mount about, Gilmour galloped toward the body. Lachlan followed, but Ramsay remained where he was, scanning the woods for any hidden danger. When none presented itself, he kneed his cantankerous steed back up the hill, stopping just as his brothers knelt before the fallen rider.

Silence filled the woods. Tension cranked his gut tight.

"Tell me," he said finally, unable to see for himself. "Is he dead?"

Lachlan was silent as he checked for a pulse, but finally his voice broke the quiet. "Nay. The lad yet lives. There's a bump on the back of his head, but no blood that I can see and—"

"The *lad*." Gilmour's tone was disbelieving as he

gently turned the body over. "Bloody hell, brother, 'tis little wonder Agnes showed you no interest. You're slow as a skewered turnip."

"What's amiss?" Ramsay asked.

Gilmour glanced up at his elder brother with a grin. "Either I am mistaken, and I never am, or . . . *he* is a *she*."

Ramsay was afoot in a second, beside his brothers in an instant.

"Nay. He's—" Lachlan argued and swiped aside the plaid tam that covered the victim's head. A tangle of flaxen curls tumbled across his brother's arm. "A lassie!" he hissed.

"Aye," Gilmour said and ran his fingers gently across a smudged cheekbone. "And as bonny as the sunrise."

"A *lassie*," Lachlan repeated.

"With a warrior on her trail," Gilmour said.

"The warrior!" Lachlan rose slowly to his feet, shoulders bunched forward like an angry bull. "He did this to her."

"But why?" Gilmour rose beside him to peer into the woods.

"And where is he now?"

"Gone. And we'd best be, too."

"Aye." Lachlan tightened his fists and gazed down at the unconscious form. "Fetch me mount, Mour, and hand her to me when I am astride."

"You?" Gilmour scoffed. "Were she a side of mutton, I would consider allowing you to take her home. But she's a lassie, and I am undoubtedly the man for the job."

"You jest," Lachlan said.

"You mistook her for a lad, brother."

"Which has naught to do with me ability to carry her."

"What if you mistake her for a stone or a twig or a . . . an apple core and discard her along the way?"

"You'll be keeping your wayward hands to yourself, Gilmour, or by the saints, I'll—"

"Sweet Almighty!" Ramsay said, and pushing his brothers impatiently aside, lifted the girl into his arms, and strode for his horse.

Chapter 2

❦ "**T**he warrior, was he a Munro?" Flanna asked.

The brothers were closeted in the solar with their parents, the notorious laird and lady of Dun Ard.

"I know not," Lachlan answered. "We gave chase without delay." Ramsay watched him pace across the woven carpet and onto rough timber. "But he eluded us."

"Eluded how?" 'Twas their father who spoke, christened Roderic but generally called the Rogue by those who knew him well.

Lachlan shrugged, giving a single lift to his heavy shoulders. He had inherited their grandfather's bulk, while Ramsay had inherited . . . what? His mother's cautious skepticism, perhaps. He glanced at her and almost smiled. She was known as the Flame of the

14

MacGowans—and the only woman able to keep the Rogue on a leash.

"I know not," Lachlan was saying. "One moment he was there, and the next . . ." He blew out a sharp exhalation. "Gone."

"Gone?" said the laird and lady in unison.

"I know you think our Lachlan has lost his wits," Gilmour said, one hip cocked against a tall leather trunk. "And in the light of the news that he could not tell that yonder sleeping beauty was a lassie, well . . ." He shook his head, candlelight shining off his wheat toned hair. "I can understand your feelings, but truly the warrior did seem to vanish into—"

"Were it not for me, you would never have left Dun Ard at the outset and the lassie would still be lying out there alone and unsheltered," Lachlan said.

"And were it not for me, you would be calling her Angus and challenging her to a wrestling—"

"We'd best learn where she belongs soon," Flanna interrupted. "Before 'tis too late."

The room went silent with her unsaid words.

"She'll come to," Lachlan said. "Surely she will."

"I pray you are right," Flanna said. "But until then, we would be well advised to inform her clansmen of her whereabouts."

"How do we find her kin?"

"Surely someone has missed her," Roderic said. "She is a bonny lass, and . . ." His words faded to a halt as he glanced toward the Flame. "So I am told."

His bride of near thirty years raised a single brow at him. "You have not noticed for yourself, then?"

"Of course not, me love," he said and grinned as he took her hand. " 'Tis Gilmour who has brought me reports."

"I see. So you think her comely, Mour?" Flanna asked.

"Aye." His smile matched his father's almost to perfection. "But not half so bonny as you, Mother."

She chuckled, as though she'd heard a hundred such lies and was not inclined to believe a single one of them.

"But nearly as pretty as Gilmour," Lachlan said.

Flanna laughed aloud, and though Gilmour sent a scathing glare in his elder brother's direction, humor lit his eyes.

"And what of you, Ramsay?" Roderic asked. "You have been unusually quiet. Do you not find her comely?"

Ramsay shrugged. He would rather listen to the others banter than to join in himself. Since returning from Edinburgh some months ago, he found Dun Ard changed somehow . . . and yet he knew that it had not changed at all. It was only his perception that had been altered. His parents had always been devout and loyal leaders of the clan MacGowan. His brothers had always bickered. The Flame had always adored the Rogue and had that adoration returned a hundred fold, but perhaps Ramsay had not appreciated it before, had not realized how rare and precious a thing they shared. Not until Lorna, he thought, and turned his mind aside, careful to keep his expression impassive.

"I suspect she is bonny enough," he said.

"Bonny enough?" Lachlan snorted.

"She has the face of an angel," Gilmour argued. "Me Mary is the very embodiment of purity and grace. 'Tis simply that Ram—"

"Mary?" said three voices in unison.

Gilmour canted a grin at them. "The lass needs a name; I have come to call her Mary."

"Whyever—" Lachlan began, but Ramsay interrupted.

"As in the sainted mother of God," he said, and rose irritably to his feet.

The solar went silent.

"Something peeves you, Ramsay?" Flanna asked.

He shot her a glance. They had a connection, he and his mother, and he had no wish to lie to her. But if the truth be told, something did bother him, though he did not know exactly what it was.

"Nay, nothing peeves me, Mother," he said. " 'Tis simply that . . ." He paced, following much the same course Lachlan had, past the rarely used gittern and lute. While the Flame of the MacGowans was adept with a bow and downright devilish with a dirk, she was unexceptional in the more ladylike arts. Mayhap that accounted for her lack of coquettish behavior. Ramsay had expected to find that same forthright quality in other women, and been disappointed.

"Simply what?" she asked now.

"We know nothing of the woman," he said. "True, she may be as saintly as me brothers suspect, but perhaps she is the opposite."

"You're daft!" said Lachlan.

"He is," Gilmour agreed casually. "He is daft."

"And what, pray tell, has made you decide that, brothers?" he asked, keeping his tone level. "The fact that I think a bonny face might hide an evil heart? What if she were old and crotchety with a wart on her nose and a balding pate? Then might she be evil?"

"Certainly," Gilmour said.

"Of course," agreed Lachlan.

Ramsay glowered, though he tried not to. "Mother, talk to them."

But she was smiling and the Rogue was chuckling out loud.

"Me thinks 'tis a bit early to decide whether she be sinner or saint," Flanna said. "Mayhap we could wait until she awakens, at least. Don't you agree, me sons?"

"Aye," Lachlan said.

"I'm willing to wait forever for her to awaken, if need be," Gilmour replied.

"And you?" Flanna asked, looking at Ramsay.

Having shoved his emotions neatly back out of sight, he shrugged. "It matters little to me what her temperament proves to be. I only hope that she is not a spy."

"A spy!" For a moment he thought Lachlan might actually launch himself across the room at him. Lachlan, after all, had always been prone to sharp flashes of temper. He remained as he was, however, though his square hands ground to fists. "Your time at court has turned your brain soft. The lass could no more be a spy than I could be a . . . a . . . rotting parsnip."

"I've oft wondered about the similarities," Gilmour murmured, straightening from the trunk.

"And why not?" Ramsay asked, ignoring him. "With sentiment turning against the French every day, there may be any sort of trouble brewing against us. Remember, brothers, Norman blood does flow through our veins."

"She is no spy," Lachlan said and Ramsay shrugged.

"Then perhaps she's—"

"Hold!" Flanna's voice rang against the stone wall,

her eyes gleaming nearly as bright as her auburn hair in the light of the nearby candles. " 'Tis not our place to determine what she is just yet. Not until we learn *who* she is."

"She is no—" Lachlan began, but Flanna raised her hand for silence.

"Gilmour, I've a mission for you. You will travel to Braeburn and ask if perchance they are missing one flaxen haired maid."

He nodded. "Aye, Mother, though I am loath to leave the fox to guard the hen house."

She stared at him quizzically for a moment, then turned to her husband. "He is your son," she said, asking for an explanation.

"Methinks he refers to Lachlan as the fox," Roderic said.

"Ahh." She turned back toward her third born son with a raised brow. "Never have I heard my ancestral home called a hen house before, Mour. But rest assured, I've a task for your brother as well.

"Lachlan, you will attempt to find the warrior—" she began, but Roderic shook his head and she turned toward him. "Nay?"

"Send our Lachlan to find the man who may have wished the sainted Mary harm?" He shrugged, laughter in his eyes. "Methinks 'twould be best if the warrior retains the ability to walk when he is brought to our fair keep."

She nodded. "Lachlan, *you* will ride to Braeburn and inquire about the maid. Gilmour, you find the warrior. And Ramsay . . ." She turned toward him, her eyes slightly narrowed as she examined his face. "What of you, my son?"

He resisted the urge to squirm under her gaze. It seemed like a lifetime that she stared at him, but finally she spoke.

"You will find the maid's mount."

"As you wish, Mother," he said with some relief for her averted gaze.

She smiled. "Good. With God's grace, by the morrow we will know the maid's true identity."

"She is no spy," muttered Lachlan, eyeing Ramsay.

He shrugged. "A heretic, then. Or a murderess, or—"

"A heretic!" Lachlan rasped.

"A—" Gilmour began, but Flanna rose abruptly to her feet.

"Quiet!"

"A *murderess*!" Gilmour snorted.

Roderic rose beside his wife. "Lads," he said, his voice deep. "Your lady mother called for silence. Surely you've no wish to upset her. She might . . . swoon."

"Aye," said Gilmour wryly. "And I might suddenly burst into a hundred wee pieces, like a shattered mug, but I rather doubt it."

"Are you saying your mother is less than the epitome of fragile femininity?" Roderic asked.

Silence spread over the room like spilled ink. The brothers glanced nervously at each other and away.

"Well, Father," Gilmour said finally. "Malcolm of Ryland does still bear that scar."

"Aye," Lachlan added. "And I think mayhap Haydan the Hawk could have defended himself without Mother's assistance."

"Scars," Roderic said, as if dismissing such an inconsequential topic. "How can you speak of scars in the presence of me fair bride? Look at her. Is she not as delicate as a spring blossom?"

Flanna lowered her eyes and lifted one hand delicately toward her bosom. A little eyelash batting and she would have fit into the queen's entourage like a cog into its niche, but not a soul there seemed wont to mention the disparity between her reputation and her demeanor.

"No comments?" Roderic asked finally. "Very well, then. What have you learned here, lads?"

"Not to trust Mother's innocent expressions?" Gilmour murmured. Lachlan grinned, then cleared his throat as he glanced away.

"What say you, Mour?" Roderic asked.

" 'Tis naught."

"I was quite certain you spoke, so tell us what sage wisdom you have learned from this day."

Gilmour clasped his hands behind his back and spoke like a chastised lad. "Not to judge truth on mere appearances?"

"Well said." Roderic grinned as he kissed his wife's hand, then placed it upon his arm. "Try to remember that as you go forth."

"Aye, Father," Gilmour promised.

"I shall," Lachlan agreed.

They failed.

Twenty-four hours later, Ramsay stood in the doorway of the infirmary and listened to his brothers with a mix of resignation and humor.

"Her eyes are sapphire," Gilmour said.

"You do not know the color of her eyes," Lachlan argued. "Just as you do not know her name."

"Unless I am wrong. And I never am . . ." Gilmour smiled wistfully as he gently squeezed the hand of the woman who slept on the mattress between them. "Her eyes are as blue as the heavens from which she was sent to me."

"To *you*," Lachlan scoffed.

"Certainly to me. Who else . . ."

Ramsay let their words filter into nothingness as he watched the girl. By virtue of her silence alone, she seemed far more intelligent than his two rambling brothers.

Her face was nearly round, saved from being babyish by her pointy little chin. Against her ivory cheeks, her downy lashes seemed almost dark, though they were truly no darker than her hair, which was the rich hue of summer barley. It was as long as his arm and as luminous as the morning sun. 'Twas little wonder, really, that his brothers were daft over her. It was a hard won lesson, to learn to separate a woman's looks from her soul, and if one was to judge her by her face . . . well . . . the word "saint" did come to mind.

But strangely, it was her hands that fascinated him. They were so slim, so refined and pale and delicate. Placed together on the coverlet, they made it seem almost as if she were praying, and in a moment they twitched ever so slightly, as if moved by her own supplication.

Aye, she seemed angelic, perfect, a tiny slip of bliss sent to earth in the form of a woman. But he had known perfection before, had spent sleepless nights waiting to know it again—to hold her, to beg her for one more kiss, knowing he shouldn't, knowing she was too pure, too good. Only to find . . .

"I'll not have you saying that sort of thing about the lass," Lachlan said. His voice was low, challenging. All humor had fled from his tone, but far be it from Gilmour to care about that note of warning.

"Just because she's an angel doesn't mean she does not possess the same desires and needs of other women. It doesn't mean she will not want me," Mour said, and carressed her cheek with his knuckles. "But you are right: an innocent should not hear such words. I must keep me thoughts to meself."

"As well as your hands," Lachlan said, and knocked the other's arm aside. "Or I'll see you tossed arse first from the infirmary."

Gilmour laughed as if genuinely surprised. "Please tell me you do not think to have her for yourself, brother."

Lachlan's eyes narrowed. "And why not?"

"Because you ... well ... you ..." Gilmour flipped his hand up and down as if encompassing his brother's entire being. "An angel does not belong with an ogre."

"And neither does she belong with the devil."

"Truly, Lachlan, she is much too refined to be had by the likes of you. Look at that angelic face," Gilmour said, and once again stroked his fingers up her cheek. "Look at that—"

But in that instant the angel awoke. Her eyes flew open. "Unhand me," she growled.

"You're awake!" Gilmour's eyes widened.

"Praise be!"

She jerked her gaze to the right at the sound of Lachlan's voice. "Touch me, either one of you, and I swear by the living God I'll see you cut and quartered before the dawn."

Chapter 3

A nora remained very still. Where was she? Had the Munro caught her? Or—

The warrior! He had chased her and she'd run. Panicked. She knew better than that, better than to show fear.

"They *are* blue."

She snapped her gaze to the man at her right. He was dark, broad, powerful. She'd learned long ago never to trust a powerful man.

"What?" she asked, her voice hoarse.

"Your eyes," he said. "They are blue."

"Mary?"

She swept her attention to her left. The man there was fair haired, winsome, ungodly handsome. She'd learned long ago never to trust a handsome man.

"What did you call me?" she asked.

"Mary. 'Tis the name I gave you whilst you slept, for I imagine you look like the sainted mother of Christ."

Flattery. She let herself relax a smidgen, but she couldn't be careless, for oft those who spoke of saints were the antithesis of holiness themselves.

"You needn't worry," said the fair haired man, "for we will not harm you."

"Nay," agreed the other, his voice deep and earnest. "Indeed I will guard you with me very life."

She carefully soothed her voice to one of schooled refinement. "Where am I? Who are you?"

"You have come to Dun Ard, the high fortress." The fair haired man smiled easily. "We be the brothers MacGowan. I am called Gilmour, and yonder broad pillar is Lachlan."

The MacGowans! Even in her home in the far north, she had heard of them.

"Lass?"

"Aye?" She stilled the rapid beat of her heart and raised her chin a notch.

"Your name . . . 'tis not Mary by any wee chance, is it?"

Perhaps there was new hope here, for they were strong men with a powerful clan behind them. But her uncle had seemed a likely protector too, until he had heard her troubles. Then his charity had withered like a winter pear and his true nature showed through. She would not so easily share her troubles again. She would learn what these men could do for her and act accordingly. In this world of shadows and travails, the truth was highly overvalued, while a lie, often—

"Lass—"

"My apologies," she murmured, knowing she had

waited too long to answer and now had no more time to consider the matter. "Aye. I am Mary."

"Nay." 'Twas the broader of the two who spoke. "It cannot be."

"Indeed it is," she said and tried a tremulous smile in the direction of the one called Gilmour. The effort made her head throb, but her course was set. "Tell me, my laird, how did you know? Could it be that you are not only bonny, but gifted also?"

"Gifted?" he asked, and leaning forward, reached for her hand.

Her stomach pitched, and she was tempted almost beyond control to pull out of his reach, but she forced herself to allow his touch.

He took her fingers gently in his hand and raised them to his lips.

"Nay, lass, I had no gift, not until you appeared like an angel—"

"*Mary.*"

The word came from the far end of the room. Anora lifted her gaze, realizing in that instant that she had been careless. Too careless. 'Twas not just the two brothers who shared this space with her. There was another man, a dark haired fellow with deep set eyes and a solemn expression. Two small braids were pulled back from his well sculpted face, and his mouth, though generous, was set in a hard line.

She watched him approach her bed. He was neither as tall as the one brother nor as broad as the other, and yet he seemed bigger than both somehow, making them appear harmless by comparison.

"Your name is Mary?" he asked.

"Aye." She held her breath. It was a foolish act. He

was only a man, after all, but her hand was shaking in Gilmour's palm so she pulled it swiftly to her side. " 'Tis. And thine?"

"What an amazing coincidence," he said. "That you should bear the very name me brother gave you. Where might you hail from, Mary?"

Her mind spun. She dared not reveal that she was from Evermyst. But where? Someplace far away. Far— she was running out of time. Too slow. Too—

"Lady—"

"Levenlair," she said.

He canted his head at her. "Levenlair?"

She should have chosen another castle. One not so well renowned. A fictional one, mayhap, or—

"I've heard of such a place," he continued, "though I know little of it. Far to the north, is it not?"

"Aye, 'tis." She fidgeted with the blanket for an instant, then forced her fingers to lie still. Only a foolish child would squirm under a man's gaze and as a lass she'd learned the penalty for foolishness. Better to use her greatest defense against him. After all, arrogance was free. "Me father was laird of that fair castle."

"Indeed?"

"Aye," she said, and pursing her lips, gave a slight nod. "And what of you?" His hair was shoulder length and thick as a stallion's mane. The color of a bay steed, it hung in glistening waves just past the shoulders of his simple saffron tunic. But 'twere his eyes that held her attention. They were a piercing indefinable hue and as brooding as a king's. "You must be a servant here. How fortunate, for I am quite parched. Fetch me a horn of something. Wine, preferably. Mulled, but not too hot."

For a moment the room was silent, and then Gilmour laughed, but she dared not take her gaze from the other.

"Ahh, Mary," Gilmour said, and nudging a stool forward with his foot, seated himself close by her side. "Awake for only a moment and already you can see a man's true place in the world."

She pulled her attention away with an effort and pinned it on the fair haired brother. "Your servant is woefully obstinate, I fear, for he is still here."

"He is like that at times."

"In truth, lass," said the one called Lachlan, "Ramsay is not a servant, but the eldest of us five brothers and heir to Dun Ard."

"Oh." She fluttered her lashes downward lest they see the lie in her eyes. "My apologies, of course."

"Nay," said Lachlan. "Indeed, lass, 'tis we who must apologize."

"You?" she asked and raised her gaze to his. She did not like to be surprised, and yet she was.

"Aye," he said, his expression as solemn as a stone. "For we failed to keep you safe."

"But you did not even know I was here."

"We should have."

Now, here was an overdeveloped sense of duty. She liked that in a fellow, so long as he kept his distance. "Nay, good sir," she said demurely. "You are very kind and very gallant, but 'tis surely not your fault that I was attacked."

"Attacked?" Lachlan's tone was angry, but his eldest brother's was smooth, urging caution when he spoke.

"We saw no sign of an attack."

She swept her gaze to his face, knowing her eyes

would look as blue and innocent as a babe's. "Surely you did not think I was traveling alone from my home in the north. I was with my entourage when we were set upon."

"Entourage! Where——" Lachlan began, but Ramsay interrupted again.

"When was this?"

His demeanor was unruffled, his tone level, but his eyes. . . . He knew something and was fishing to learn more, to catch her in a lie.

" 'Twas some days ago," she said. "North of——"

"The Munros." Lachlan's voice was low, and suddenly his dirk appeared in his hand. " 'Twas the Munros who set upon you, wasn't it?"

Her heart jumped against her ribs. She should have seen this eventuality, should have known they would have heard of the Munros' passage through their land. Should have guessed the conclusions they would draw.

"I . . ." She stared at him. "I do not know. I . . . am not from these parts."

Lachlan shook his head and took a step nearer. "The Munros do not live hereabouts either. Surely——"

"You have not heard of them?" 'Twas the suspicious brother who spoke, as if he were dissecting her every word. "How strange. They too are from the north. I thought every Scot knew of their doings. Most especially the daughter of the powerful laird of——"

She moaned. The sound creaked weakly from her lips. She fluttered her fingers to her brow and let her head fall back against the downy pillow.

"Mary!"

"Lass! Are you——"

"What be you lads doing in here?" rasped an old

voice, and suddenly Gilmour was brushed aside and an old woman appeared. Gray eyes widened in surprise. "Lass, you've come to."

Anora said nothing, but moaned again, working for the perfect amount of pathos.

"All right then, lads. What have you done to her?"

"I was but passing by when I saw the lass was alone," Gilmour said, "and since you were absent, I thought it best to check in on her."

"Check in on her, you say." The woman tsked as she felt Anora's brow. "Ach." She smiled, making her face crinkle like old parchment as she touched the backs of her fingers to her patient's cheek. "Poor wee lassie—having to wake up to the likes of these three rogues, eh?"

"I assure you, we did nothing to alarm her," Lachlan said.

The old woman dropped her gaze to the dirk he held. "What, then, were you doing, lad? Teaching her the feminine art of battle?"

Gilmour laughed. " 'Tis true, me brothers are sadly inept with the fairer sex, Elspeth. But I did nothing to cause her the least bit of alarm. Indeed—"

"Nothing?" scoffed the old woman, and snatching his arm, steered him toward the door. "There hasn't been a day since your birth that you haven't caused a bit of alarm. And that goes for the both of you." She grabbed Ramsay's arm en route. "Now go, the lot of you, and don't be bothering the lass again until I say she be ready for company."

She closed the door firmly behind them. For a moment the room seemed enormously quiet, and then she chuckled.

"Ahh." She tsked as she approached the bed. "Me

apologies, lass. They must have given you a start." Her fingers felt cool against Anora's cheek as she swept back her hair. "But then again, there be nastier faces to wake up to. Truth be told, they set me own heart to fluttering, and me their nan since the day they were birthed. 'Tis shameful, I know. But Lachlan's brawn, and me Ramsay's . . . ach, but I do go on, and here you be with an ache in your head pounding like a war drum."

"How did you know?"

"About your head?" She chuckled as she turned away, and in a moment she was back, a steaming kettle in her hand. " 'Tis me job to know, lass, for I've been trained by the healer herself."

"The healer?" Anora watched the gnarled hands pour water into a horn mug and then dip, quick and efficient, into a leather bag. In a moment she was mixing dried herbs into the brew. There was something soothing about the way she moved. Something that reminded her of Meara's ways.

"The healer." Elspeth said the words with reverence. "The Lady Forbes. The lads' auntie, she be. Each one of them has been patched up by her ladyship herself. 'Tis said there be magic in her hands. And mayhap there is, for not one of them . . ." She sighed dreamily. "Well, a lass could do worse than to be bound to any one of the three, hey? Their father has earned a dukedom, and their lady mother . . ." She paused, her eyes alight. " 'Twas she who brought me here many years since. She who drew her sword against . . ." She swallowed hard and frowned for a moment, but finally she went on. " 'Tis enough to say that the lads have their mother's fire. Aye," she said, nodding sagely. "Their mother's fire and their father's strength. 'Tis nothing they cannot best if they put their backs to it."

Anora glanced toward the door, her mind spinning.

"Here now, lass," said Elspeth, pressing the horn to her lips. "Drink this down. 'Twill set you to dreaming, it will. But you'll feel the better for the rest."

"So what be your name, me wee one? I've not seen you about Evermyst before. Mayhap you've been hiding from the spirit, too?"

The girl said nothing, for she could not. Indeed, her heart was beating too hard for her to speak.

"The quiet sort." The Munro laughed, nearly blocking out the sound of the sea that she so loved. His beard was bushy, as red as rowan berries, and it set to quivering with his mirth. " 'Tis me favorite type of maid. Come hither, lass."

She shook her head, setting her droopy coif to waggling as she backed a step away.

"Relax, lassie. Have you not heard? I'm to be the new laird of this keep soon. 'Twould be wise of you to make friends whilst you can, eh? Before your mistress returns. Come hither."

Her legs were shaking and her hands, pressed against her soiled gown, felt damp with fear. "Please, me laird," she whispered, "me lady has been good to me and I've no wish to displease her."

"Displease her?" He laughed again. "So you think your mistress will be unwilling to share me?"

"I . . . I only know that—" she began, but in that moment he leapt.

He was ungodly quick for a big man. She tried to twist away, tried to escape, but there was no hope. His hand closed like a giant claw around her arm and she was swung toward him.

"There now, no need for fear, lass. I only—" His words
stopped, ending in a hiss of surprise as his eyes widened,
then narrowed. *"Who are you?"*

*Her muscles ached with tension, and her lungs cramped
with fear.*

"Who the devil are you?" Reaching up, he snatched the
drooping coif from her head. Golden tresses fell unencum-
bered to her waist, and without the dowdy headdress every
inch of her face was visible. *"Witch!"* he rasped and yanked
his sword from its sheath.

"Nay!" Anora awoke with a gasp, one arm covering
her face, but no blade descended to end her life.

'Twas a dream. Just a—

But no. She knew better. 'Twas a harbinger of things
that might be.

She must return to Evermyst! Immediately.

The floor felt cold against her bare feet, but she
barely noticed, for already she was running, racing
through the doorway toward the stairs.

Her mind spun. She must find Pearl. Leave Dun
Ard. Head north. There was no time to delay, no time
to stop, and no time to avoid the man who loomed before her. She struck him full on and fell, tumbling backward. Her feet scrambled as she tried to regain her
balance, to escape, but he was already reaching for her.

"Nay!" She tried to twist away, but he pulled her
back.

"Relax, lassie," he said, and she froze. The words of
her dream quivered like a spent arrow through her
mind. In the darkness she could not see her captor's
face, but she knew him.

"Munro," she whispered.

"Who are you?" he asked.

"Let me go!"

"And why should I?"

She was shaking, straining away from him. "Let me be. You are neither peaceable nor beloved," she rambled wildly.

"What's that?"

She froze at the sound of his voice, for it was not raspy and hoarse, but smooth and bonny and surprised.

"Who . . ." She tried to stop her shaking, to see through the gloom. "Who are you?"

Silence again, then, "I believe I asked that first."

"I am . . ." She couldn't remember her lies. They were becoming twisted in her mind, melded with her frantic dreams. Where was she? *Who* was she?

"Are you well, lass?"

"Aye, but I must—" She must what? Run into the night like a demented banshee? She realized suddenly that he was leading her away like a lambkin on a string, and yet she could not seem to resist. The blackness of the hall receded beneath a distant glimmer of light. They turned a corner and he glanced toward her. His eyes struck her, soulful and intense. His hair, tossed as if by restless sleep, shone like polished mahogany in the tallow light. He was not the Munro. He was Ramsay MacGowan, but he'd said the words spoken in her dream, and—

"Mary," he murmured. His breath fanned her cheek. His chest was bare and dark. It was as broad as a boulder and sculpted with mounded muscle and tugging sinew. Against her arm, his hand felt as powerful and unyielding as the rough timbers beneath her feet.

Power. 'Twas what she needed to win the day. 'Twas

what she craved, and 'twas here, right before her, if she could but harness it. And why could she not? Aye, he had seemed distrustful and distant at their first meeting, but that was in the full light of day. All men changed with the coming of darkness. That she had learned long ago. With an effort, she stilled the tremor in her hands. All her life men had admired her, had praised her golden tresses, her soft skin, her feminine form. Those attributes had gained her little but hardship so far, so it was surely time to collect on them. She was hardly above using her physical features to gain her ends, and MacGowan was hardly above feeling the bite of desire. That was a potent force indeed, but she would not be the one to pay the price this time.

"Ramsay," she whispered. " 'Tis you."

"Aye," he said. His tone was quiet, cautious. "But why are you here?"

"I . . ." she turned her eyes sideways, forcing herself to be calm, to remember her mission. "I had a dream," she whispered, and moved marginally closer.

"A dream?"

"Aye." Her voice was only a wisp of sound in her own ears. "Aye. 'Twas most . . . most . . ." She broke off.

"Lass, you are shaking." He leaned slightly closer. His breath smelled of sweet wine, and when he slipped his arm around her back, she was able by dint of sheer will to keep from drawing away. "But you needn't worry," he said, and stroked her hair lightly.

"Nay. Not whilst you are here," she said, and forced her eyes to fall closed. " 'Twas you I dreamt of."

The stroking stopped, but she refused to look up to determine his mood.

"Not the one who frightened you, I hope."

"Nay." She paused, holding her breath as if ashamed to say the next words. "The one who saved me."

She heard him draw a deep breath and then his hand moved again, but slowly, as if he were thinking. "How clever of me," he said.

"Aye," she murmured, and grasping his arms in shaky fingers, pulled herself closer so that her nipples touched his chest through her borrowed night rail. They tightened on contact, sending a tingling warning through her system. But she had no time to decipher warnings. "Clever and brave and ultimately chivalrous."

"You took quite a blow to your head, lass. Are you certain you are not mistaking me for someone else? One of me brothers, mayhap?"

She forced a tremulous smile. "Nay, my laird. I am a fine judge of men. You are not the ogre you pretend to be."

In the darkness, she watched his brows rise toward the line of his hair. "I am ever so happy to hear it," he said. "But now I wonder, if you judge me so kindly, why you were afraid just moments ago?"

"I thought you were . . ." A bearded face flashed through her mind. She jerked at the image, then realized the opportunity that came with the fear and pulled herself closer to Ramsay's warm chest.

"What is it, lass?"

She loosened her grip and eased back a scant half an inch. " 'Tis naught," she breathed. "Only the dream."

His gaze never wavered from her face. "But in the dream I saved you, did I not?" he asked, and eased his arm down her back, circling her waist.

Panic rose in her throat. Too close, her mind

screamed. But she must play the game. All she held dear depended on it. "Aye," she said, and remained as she was, in the circle of his arm. "You did."

"Then surely I deserve a kiss," he murmured, and suddenly his lips were against hers.

Her heart slammed into her ribs and her hands shook, but she allowed a moment's touch, just the slightest flash of flesh against flesh before she pushed him away. He retreated the slightest distance, but she dare not fight him, lest he guess her mood. Instead, she lowered her eyes and fought a silent battle with the terror.

"Mary," he whispered, his arm still around her. "Me bonny Mary."

"Aye?" 'Twas all she could do to force out that single word, to remain where she was.

"You kiss like an innocent, sweet lass," he said and she forced herself to glance up through her lashes at him. "But . . ." He touched her chin, locking his gaze on hers. "You lie like a wanton."

Chapter 4

"**W**hat!" She reared away from him. In the darkness, her eyes looked as wide as a child's. The innocence was a lie, of course. But against his arms her hands trembled, and for an instant he was tempted to pity her. To learn her past. To right the wrongs.

History, however, had taught him better than to give in to temptations. The price was more than he was willing to pay.

"You lie," he said simply. "And quite convincingly, I might add."

"Whatever do you mean?" She tried to pull away, but he kept his arm wrapped loosely about her back so that her upper body was slanted slightly away from him. The light from the tallow candle behind her shone through the thin fabric of her night rail. Her breasts, small and soft and hopelessly enticing, seemed to glow with an iridescent light of their own.

He had always had a weakness for glowing breasts, he thought wryly. Pulling his gaze from the sight with a hard effort, he snapped his attention to the conversation at hand.

"The Munro," he said simply. Arousal lowered the timbre of his voice to a rumble, and he resented both the desire she caused and the proof of its existence.

She was staring up at him again, her eyes ungodly wide, her delicate body all but naked to his gaze. Beneath his plaid, his clueless arousal nudged toward his belt, and he scowled at its stirrings.

"Wh—who?" she murmured.

He managed to laugh. His wick had the sense of a drowning cow; it could do little more than bob to the surface. But his mind could learn from old wounds, and despite the sight of her breasts, the touch of her skin, and the sweet curve of her bottom against his arm, he remembered the pain of feminine lies.

"The Munro," he said, feeling the words come a little more easily, though his hard desire refused to subside. "You said his name quite clearly."

"I did not," she gasped.

"Aye, lass, you did. When you so cleverly collided with me, you uttered his name."

She stared at him for a moment longer and then she laughed. He felt her relax a smidgen in his arms. "I fear your hearing is not what it might be, good sir." She turned slightly. Her breast brushed his arm, burning on contact. Against his conscious will, his muscles contracted, and she drew smoothly from his grip while he struggled for composure. But it had been some

months since the pressure in his groin had been re-
lieved and hard edged desire and clear-headed thinking made rare bedfellows indeed. "What did you say,
then?" Crossing his arms against his chest with hard
won nonchalance, he watched her wander toward the
light.

"I said, 'Let me go.' "

Munro. Let me go. They did share a certain similarity,
but he canted his head with noncommittal brevity and
rested his shoulder against the wall.

" 'Twas not I who ran into you, lass," he reminded
her, "but the other way about. I was merely attempting
to keep you from hurting yourself. Which brings me to
the most logical of questions: why were you fleeing
down the hall like a frightened hare?"

"I told you, I dreamed a dream."

"Aye," he said, his tone evidencing the doubt he
felt. "The dream in which I saved you."

She did not try to deny it, but raised her sharp little
chin and stared at him in the wavering candlelight.
"Tell me, my laird Ramsay, is it all women you dislike,
or just me in particular?"

He refused to let her see his surprise. "I fear you do
not judge men as well as you think, lass. For I do not
hate women at all."

"Oh?" The hint of a smile played across the pink
bow of her lips. He had always had a weakness for
pink bows . . . and lips. "Angry, then."

"What?"

"Are you angry at all women, or just me?"

"Is there some reason I should be angry at you?"

She shrugged. Her nipples caressed the gossamer
fabric of her gown, but he refused to notice. Refused to
be aroused. Refused to feel breathless. "Nothing comes

to mind, sir. Thus I think you must be peeved with all of the fairer sex, and I wonder why that might be?"

Because women were supposed to be nurturing, loving, kind, when instead . . .

He jerked his mind back to the situation at hand.

"Methinks you are trying to lead me away from the original topic," he said. "I asked about your dream."

She shrugged. He knew better now than to let his gaze drift even the slightest inch from her face.

"I dreamed that my people were in trouble," she said.

"And you thought to race back through the night to save them?"

"They are my kin," she said simply.

" 'Twould be rather foolhardy of you to endure such a dangerous journey alone, would it not?"

"What choice do I have?"

He stared at her for a moment and then laughed. "I am certain you know exactly what choice you have."

She raised a brow at him and for a moment he saw a spark of anger flash across her delicate features. "Mayhap you overestimate my intelligence," she suggested, her tone as cool as spring water.

"Nay. I doubt that," he said. " 'Tis me brothers. The two of them would trot grinning through the fires of hell for the privilege of making fools of themselves for you."

"Fools of themselves?"

"Did I say fools? I meant, they would trot through hell for the privilege of escorting you home."

"Oh?"

"I fear they are quite smitten," he said in brief explanation.

"But not you."

He raised a placating hand, palm outward. "Me apologies, lass. But you cannot expect to have every man swooning at your feet."

"I see. So you are above . . ." She turned slightly, as if searching for the perfect words. She was standing very close to the candle now. Close enough, in fact, that he could see the dark circles of her nipples through her kindly gown. "Swooning?"

His groin tightened with painful urgency, but he wrested his gaze back to her face and his thoughts back to the conversation. "Again, I apologize."

She laughed, and somehow the sound only made the ache in his groin more insistent, for this was honest humor. No subterfuge, no simpering; a forthright from-the-gut laugh that seemed incongruous coming from her baby soft lips.

"So tell me, MacGowan, are you immune to all feminine charms or just my own?"

"I fear there is no way to answer that without insulting either me or thee," he said and she smiled.

"Please, speak freely."

"I am as attracted to women as the next man."

"Ahh," she said, and turned to pace slowly along the wall. Her night rail hugged her thighs as they moved, and though there was little more to see than the outline of her delicate form and the flicker of her tiny feet below its hem, the moment seemed hopelessly erotic. "So what is it about me that you find unbecoming?"

He watched her. "Dishonesty."

"What?" She stopped in mid stride.

"I have little use for lies."

"Is that it, then?" she asked. "Does the fact that you have decided—wrongfully, I might add—that I am less than truthful, turn you away from me?"

"I have no fondness for women who manipulate men to gain their own ends."

"And is that what I am doing, MacGowan?"

" 'Tis what you are trying to do, though I don't know why or how."

"Am I so deceitful?"

"Aye, I think you are."

"Then mayhap there was no dream. Mayhap I knew you were here and ran into the hall with the express purpose of finding you thus."

He rolled his back against the wall to watch her pace before him.

"Mayhap I calculated just how I would look with . . ." She tossed her head at the candle. Golden light flickered in the tangled mass of her glorious hair. "With the light at my back and my night rail so thin." She pressed it to her abdomen, stretching the fabric tight across her bosom so that it fell in a V between her legs. "Mayhap I thought myself irresistible."

He wrestled his gaze from her hand, forced it past her breasts and locked it on her face. His own felt hot. "Mayhap you did."

"So . . ." She stood directly before him now, her tiny feet nearly touching his, her face raised. The laces of her gown lay open, caressing her breasts and showing the smooth lawn of her ivory throat, and he swallowed hard. "Mayhap I hoped to seduce you."

He said nothing.

Their gazes melded and desire flared like a smithy's fire in his gut.

She leaned a fraction of an inch closer, her lips slightly parted, her eyes half closed.

"But there was a dream, Sir Angry," she said. "There was a dream and you saved me from its terrors."

"Did I?" 'Twas no easy task to force the words past his stuttering lips. 'Twas more difficult still to make them sound nonchalant.

"Aye, you did. And for that I give you this."

She rose on her tiptoes. He felt the brush of her breath against his cheek, felt her nearness like an onslaught to his senses, and then her lips touched his. Lightly, like the stroke of a butterfly's wing, they caressed him. He closed his eyes to the rushing feelings and tightened his fists, keeping them resolutely by his sides, but there was little hope of restraining other parts of his anatomy. Though he remained where he was, his erection pulsed against her.

Eyes wide, she halted the kiss abruptly. He slowed his breathing with a determined effort and held her gaze.

"My good sir." Her voice was cool and she watched him from beneath lowered lids, like a consummate seductress. Yet her hands were clasped together like a lost child's. "I fear 'tis you who is the liar." And turning away, she disappeared down the hall.

Ramsay sat quietly near the door of the solar.

"So you did not find the warrior who was following our bonny Mary?" Roderic asked, turning toward Gilmour.

"Nay." Mour took a bite from the scone he'd charmed out of the kitchen maids and scowled. "Even his tracks disappeared."

"Disappeared?" Lachlan scoffed and fiddled with his knife. "Like a puff of smoke?"

"Nay," Gilmour said. "Like a ghost."

"You should have sent me after all, Da," Lachlan

said. "I fear me brother was in too big a hurry to return to the infirmary to follow the trail."

"Unlike you, brother, who certainly has not been mooning about waiting for a single word with the lass," Gilmour said.

"I but worry that you'll wear her out with your constant—"

"And what of you, Lachlan?" Flanna interrupted. "What news from Braeburn?"

"None, Mother," he said, "but 'tis of no import now, surely, for the lass is awake and has told us herself whence she hails."

She paused for just a moment. "Of course. Levenlair was it not?"

"Aye. Her entourage was attacked and she was left to fend for herself." A muscle jumped in Lachlan's jaw. "I think I will take it upon meself to look for the warrior this day."

"A fine idea," Gilmour said. "As for me, I have business here in the keep."

"In the infirmary, more like."

"Nay," Gilmour insisted. "I've no such plans. Surely such a delicate thing needs her . . ."

Ramsay's thoughts drifted away.

Aye, the lass did look to be a delicate thing; but beneath that satin soft skin there was probably a core of iron. She hardly needed *his* help. He'd been a dolt last night. Aye, and worse. Why he'd been unable to sleep, he didn't know, or why his restless feet had then taken him in the direction of the infirmary. After all, he wasn't attracted—

Well, mayhap he was somewhat attracted, but only because his wick was a hopeless hound. His head wasn't the least bit intrigued. He should have stayed away. Shouldn't have touched her. Shouldn't have talked to her. Shouldn't have questioned her honesty. After all, what did he care if she lied? What did he care that she had the voice of a queen, the eyes of a wanton, and the hands of a wee, frightened lass? What did he care that he could not tell which she truly was? He had no intention of getting involved with her. He didn't like her, wasn't interested in her, didn't plan to—

"Mary!"

"Mary!"

The dual gasps startled him out of his reverie, and he jerked his head up just in time to see her curtsy in the doorway.

"My apologies, my lairds. My lady," she said. "I've no wish to disturb you, but a servant said I might find you here."

"Mary," Lachlan said, stepping toward her, "you should be abed."

"Aye," Gilmour agreed, and pressing past his brother, reached for the girl's hand where it rested on the door jamb. "Come, I'll escort you back to the infirmary."

"I must not." Her voice was soft yet firm, but when she pulled her hand against her skirt, it was with unbridled haste. She was fully dressed in the indigo gown they'd found her in. It had been washed and repaired and made her appear only marginally more sturdy than the nightgown had. "Though I thank you for all your help and hospitality, I fear I cannot stay any—"

"Cannot stay!" Gilmour cried.

"What?" Lachlan chimed in.

"I must return to my home."

"Surely you cannot—"

"Not so—"

"My sons—" Flanna sent them each a withering glance. "Shall we let the lass speak, or shall we bind and gag her before carting her off to abide in the infirmary forever?"

Lachlan cleared his throat. Gilmour grinned sheepishly.

"Come in, Mary of Levenlair," Roderic said.

Ramsay filled his starving lungs with air as she glided across the floor. Not a glance did she spare him, as if last night had never been.

Flanna smiled at her. "There are many things I could ask you, young Mary," she said. "What brought you here. Where you were bound. Who troubled you. But mostly I wonder, however did you escape Elspeth's watchful eye?"

"I am quite well and have no need—" she began but Flanna interrupted her.

"So you sneaked away."

From his place beside the door, Ramsay saw the girl's face color. Like a harmless lambkin, she looked—all soft and pale and helpless.

"I believe your Elspeth thought me asleep, my lady," she admitted quietly.

"Ahh, I see. And why did you feel such a need to hurry from your bed?"

"I must return to my homeland immediately." She paused for a moment. " 'Tis my old nurse. Her health is not good. Still, she insisted I travel to my cousin's during her travail, but I did not plan to be gone so long, and now with the further delay . . . I must return home today."

"Today!" 'Twas Lachlan who could no longer remain silent. "Surely not."

"I've no wish to seem ungrateful for all you've done, and no wish to ask for more, but . . ." She paused. "You haven't by chance found a white palfrey running loose, have you?"

"Lass," Gilmour said, "truly, you cannot take on such a grueling journey at this time. If you are so concerned about your nurse, we could certainly send Lachlan to see to her health."

Ramsay rose. "So it is a white steed I should be searching for?" he asked.

"Aye." She turned toward him. "A bonny mare with an unruly mane and a crimson saddle pad. There's been no word of her, then?" Her voice was cool, her chin raised at an indifferent angle, but her hands . . . once again they seemed to be at odds with her words, for they gripped her mended skirt with tenacious ferocity.

"Nay. No word thus far," Ramsay said, and lifted his gaze from her hands to her face.

She loosened her grip abruptly, as if caught in the act of something disgraceful, and let her velvet skirt swirl to the floor. "Well, there is naught to be done for it, I suppose. She is only a steed, after all. I must away without her."

"Surely you cannot think to go alone," Flanna said.

"I would not ask more from you than you've already given. Indeed . . ." Her sky blue eyes swept sideways, encompassing Lachlan and Gilmour, but somehow missing Ramsay entirely. "It seems I owe you my very life, but I must leave immediately."

"Surely not."

"Not alone, at any rate," Lachlan said, and shifted

his weight slightly, so that his solid form was balanced between wide spread feet.

"Aye," Gilmour agreed. "I shall escort you."

" 'Tis I who shall go," Lachlan corrected, but his brother shook his head as if saddened.

"Truly, brother, there is none I would rather have at me back than thee as I accompany the fair lass to her home in the north. But Mother needs you here."

"And though she is eager to be rid of the likes of you, I fear I must disappoint her," Lachlan argued. "For 'tis I who shall escort the girl."

"Nay. I—"

"Lads!" Flanna interrupted. "Mayhap it would be best if you did not speak of me as if I were not here."

"My apologies."

"So sorry," Lachlan murmured.

"Aye," she said and glanced at one, then the other, before turning her gaze to Ramsay. "And what of you, my son?"

He pulled his gaze from the girl's face. Something had coiled hard and fast in his stomach, but he shrugged with deliberate nonchalance. "If my brothers manage to refrain from killing each other, I am certain she will be quite safe with the two of them."

Flanna raised her brows. Roderic rose beside her. "The *two* of them?"

"Together?"

" 'Twould mayhap be more than the lass had bargained for," Flanna opined.

"That I doubt," Ramsay said, his tone as dry as his soul.

"What say you?" His parents turned in unison toward him.

He could feel the girl's gaze shift in his direction as

well, but he kept his attention focused on his parents. "I am certain the lass will be safe with me brothers to protect her."

"Aye." Flanna held him in her gaze for a moment longer before turning to their guest. " 'Tis decided, then," she said finally. "Preparations for the journey will begin immediately. You shall return to Levenlair with Lachlan and Gilmour, as well as a serving maid and additional guards."

"You are too kind," Mary murmured, curtsying as she did so and ignoring the rumbling disagreement that had already begun between her two escorts.

"Nay," Roderic said. "We only wish to keep you safe until you reach your home."

Aye, Ramsay thought, watching her from beneath lowered brows. But who would keep them safe from her?

Chapter 5

❦

"And what of Bully?" Anora asked.

"What's that?" Gilmour turned toward her. They would be leaving in the morning, but he had arrived at her door some minutes before, asking if she would like a stroll in the gardens. She had accepted with ladylike grace. It had not been a difficult task to divert his attention past the sun washed arbors to the greens beyond. There, not fifty rods from Dun Ard's drawbridge, a host of men trained for battle. Ten score, perhaps more, but the vast number did nothing to throw them into chaos. They trained in perfect precision, well armed, well organized, well mounted, with a broad and impressive captain at their helm. She had noticed him before, had even inquired about him, for a well trained army was one of the things Evermyst needed most. True, her warriors' armor needed mending, their claymores sharpening, and their bows restringing, but first and foremost, they needed the kind of confidence and skill that could be taught only by a leader such as Dun Ard's broad captain of the guard.

"Bully," she said, glancing away from the captain and up through her lashes. "Will he be accompanying us?"

"Bull—oh," Gilmour said and laughed. "You mean Bullock."

She joined in the laughter, making the sound as light as feather down and carefully self effacing. "Bullock," she said, and glanced once more toward the hillside. The man was as broad as a destrier and as commanding as a king. He would be a good fellow to lead her own frayed troops, but if she was not mistaken, he would not easily be swayed by her careful charm or her simpering silliness. Perhaps she would be better off with a man less experienced but more easily manipulated. She glanced up through her lashes again at Gilmour's handsome face. "I am such a ninny sometimes," she said. "Will he be accompanying us on the morrow?"

"Nay," Gilmour said. "In truth, he rarely strays far from Mother's side."

"Oh?"

"It seems he feels he failed her in the past and has determined never to do so again."

Loyalty? She forced herself not to scowl as she mulled this over. How was it that a woman obtained such a quality from a man? Could it be that this Bullock was infatuated with Lady MacGowan? Might the two of them be sharing some torrid affair that Roderic merely tolerated? But no. Though the lady of Dun Ard most surely held power in her hand, it did not seem to lessen her laird's strength. There was something between them. Affection, yes. But more a balance of sorts, a trust. Or was it all a facade, a mask they wore as easily as Anora wore her own?

"And the others?" she asked. It was an impressive battalion. The light of the setting sun shone like burnished gold off the tips of their lances, attesting to the workmanship of their forgers, the quality of their steel. "How many will be accompanying us?"

"A dozen. Mayhap a few more."

"A *dozen*?" Her mind raced and her memories soared.

"Lass." He stopped her with a hand on her arm. "You needn't worry."

A dozen against scores of her enemies. But perhaps it would be enough to secure her and hers against the evils of ignorance and aggression. After all, the Mac-Gowans' swords looked to be made of Spanish steel. Their leather crested arrows were cast from two types of bows—mechanical crossbows for power, yew longbows for speed. And their horses! Though they were as large as any native stock, they possessed a certain flair, a sort of high-stepping elegance. How had they obtained such marvelous beasts? Had they crossed the typical war horse with barb blood, or—

"You will be safe," Gilmour said. "This I promise."

"Of course." She lowered her eyes. "I know naught of war or defenses." Or at least she wouldn't if circumstances had not forced her to learn, but with the Mac-Gowans on her side she might yet win the day. After all, they were respected, feared. . . .

"Lass, you're pale as a ghost."

"Nay! No ghost!" she gasped.

"What?" He started back slightly, looking startled.

"I mean, I suppose I am nervous, 'tis all—after . . ." She paused, honing her stricken expression.

"Dear lass." Drawing her hand into his palm, Gilmour covered it with his other. "You mustn't dwell on the past. Please. You are safe now. This I promise for—"

"I will not fail you again."

Anora turned with a start to find Lachlan beside her.

"Brother," Gilmour said, sounding less than thrilled with his company. "I thought you were training with the others."

"And I thought you were overseeing the packing."

Gilmour grinned and lifted a casual shoulder. "The lass was fretting about our journey. I felt it me duty to console her."

"Kind of you. But you needn't bother yourself further, for I am here now."

" 'Tis ever so thoughtful of you—" Gilmour began, then lifted his gaze abruptly from his brother to the distant field and grimaced. "Bugger it! Will Jamie never learn to block an overhand blow?"

Lachlan turned rapidly toward the green. "By the saints, he parries like a limp chicken."

"Aye, 'tis a mockery of the MacGowan name. Would that someone could teach him the proper method."

For a moment Anora thought Lachlan might march straight away to the training field, for she saw the muscles in his broad neck tighten as if he already held a sword. But he remained as he was, a slight scowl stamped upon his face as he eyed his younger brother. "Aye, someone should teach him, indeed. What a pity you're not up to the job, Mour."

"Umm," Gilmour said.

"What is wrong with the way he parries?" Anora asked, gazing toward the battle field.

"He is off balance," Lachlan said. "If he is to stand strong beneath the blow, he must spread his legs thusly and—"

"I doubt the lady is interested in learning how to battle, Lachlan," Gilmour said.

"Nay," she said, and forced a laugh. "I know nothing of the art of defense, of course, but if you say he is inept . . . that is to say, mayhap he would be better suited for staying here whilst we journey—" Her breath stopped abruptly and she turned as a shimmer of white snagged her attention.

"Pearl," she gasped. The mare stepped up beside her. Her foretop, snarled with autumn brambles, fell across her fine dark eyes as her unruly mane brushed Anora's arm. Without another thought, Anora grasped the bridle in her hand and lifted her gaze to the man on the horse nearby.

Ramsay MacGowan stared down at her from a scarred and restive stallion.

"I found this mare in the woods," he said. His expression was unreadable, his eyes as steady as a falcon's. "Might she be yours?"

Anora smoothed her hand down the mare's finely arched neck. A scratch marred the pearly hide of her shoulder, but beyond that she seemed unscathed, and suddenly Anora wanted to cry. But tears were a luxury afforded only by the wealthy and the daft.

"Aye," she said and pursed her lips. "Aye, she is. My thanks for her safe return."

He stared at her hand, and she stopped its movement, curling her fingers subconsciously against Pearl's warm hide.

"I suppose we can hardly let you walk all the way to your father's keep . . . Mary of Levenlair."

He said the name oddly, as if he did not quite associate it with her, but she forced herself to remain calm. It mattered naught what he thought, for the other two brothers were more than willing to believe.

"A fine steed she be," Lachlan said.

"Aye, she is that," Ramsay agreed, and shifted against the high cantle of his saddle. "Finely made, yet tougher than she first appears."

"She's had a hard time of it, I suppose, unaccustomed to fending for herself," Lachlan said.

Aye, it was clear that Pearl had had a difficult time. Her saddle and pad were missing. She had lost some two stone, and her ivory tail, long as a spinster's broom, was knotted with a dozen prickly burrs.

"Aye," Ramsay agreed. "Despite the Munros' bloody nature, 'tis said they treat their mounts well."

Anora stopped her hand in mid air, realizing that she had been petting the mare again. Surely 'twas not a thing a regal lady would do, yet it seemed better to continue than to stare up at him like a cornered hare. She forced her fingers to stroke the mare's rabbit-soft hide.

"The Munros!" Gilmour said. "What the devil do you speak of, Ram? The mare is the lassies'."

"Aye," Ramsay said. "I see that."

She refused to look at him, but kept her hand moving in a slow rhythmic motion.

"What do the Munros have to do with the mare?" Lachlan asked, but when Ramsay said nothing, Anora spoke.

"Your brother thinks I am somehow in league with a clan called the Munros."

"You jest," Lachlan said.

"It happened when he was a wee thing," Gilmour explained, and shook his head as if deeply troubled. " 'Twas the tumble from the rowan tree when he was but two and ten. His mind has not been right since."

She forced a laugh and hoped to God it did not sound like the bray of a nervous ass. "What a pity."

"Aye, 'tis," Gilmour agreed. "He was of quite average intelligence before the fall."

Even without looking, Anora knew that the eldest brother cocked his head in concession to the ribbing. "So the mare is not of Munro stock, Mary of Levenlair?" he asked.

"Not to my knowledge," she said, and looked up at him. She had meant to glance and look away, but suddenly she could not. His sleeves were rolled up above broad wrists and one brawny arm rested almost casually atop the other on the pommel, yet despite his studied nonchalance, there was tension in him. She could tell by the way the tendons were pulled taut in his wide boned wrists, how his mouth, full as a lad's, remained immobile above his hard cut jaw. "But whyever would you think so?" With brutal discipline, she forced her mind back to her subterfuge. She must not falter, not now.

"The Munros ride white steeds," he said. "Did you not know?"

"Nay," she said. "And do they favor green bonnets to match their bonny eyes?"

Lachlan chuckled. Gilmour laughed out loud, but Ramsay's gaze never wavered. "My mistake. You could not have obtained a Munro steed. Not when you do not even know who they are. Is that not so . . . Mary of Levenlair?"

" 'Tis so," she said, and though her knees felt weak and her hands unsteady, her voice sounded blessedly strong.

Ramsay's gaze sprinted from her eyes to her hands, and then, like a scheming devil, one corner of his sensuous mouth quirked upward.

"I leave you to her, then," he said, and releasing his grip, let the reins slip into her hand as he turned his steed away. "There's no need for your thanks."

Perhaps 'twas true. Perhaps the mare was not a Munro mount. After all, that mercenary clan did not own every white steed in Scotland. Perhaps it was merely a coincidence that the Munros had been seen riding through MacGowan land, that the lass had been threatened and wounded, that the girl rode a white steed, that she had whispered the name in her abject fear, that—

Sweet Almighty! Ramsay paced the length of his chambers again—the chambers he shared with his brothers.

Where were they? It was well past nightfall and they would depart from Dun Ard early the next morn. Still, they had not found their beds, which led Ramsay to one logical conclusion: they were with the girl.

He paced again.

Aye, they were with her—flattering her, flirting with her, mooning over her. Even now she was probably glancing up through her lashes and laughing in that way she had. Girlish, yet not quite so. Watching them with sky blue eyes that were worldly wise yet strangely innocent. Touching their arms with bold familiarity while her fingers seemed to tremble at such nearness.

Who was she? What was she really? A child, or a wanton? And why was she here? The story she told was not the true story. At least, not the story she told with her baby soft lips. But what of the story she told with her hands? He had watched them, how they trembled, how they gripped, how they stroked.

If she was the pampered lass of Levenlair, why were there calluses on her petal white hands? If she was the cherished daughter of a wealthy laird, why did she stroke her lost mare as if the steed were her last friend upon earth? When she'd awakened from unconsciousness her words had been harsh enough to peel the hide off a wild warthog, yet his smitten brothers had acted as if her every utterance was the sweetest nectar.

What was it about her that turned their minds to goose down? True, Gilmour had forever been distracted by anything female, but generally Lachlan could keep his wits about him.

What magic did the lass possess that turned their heads? She was not even particularly comely. Ramsay scowled as he paced.

Mayhap he was being less than entirely honest. After all, her skin was like purest cream, and her hair like spun gold. Her eyes were as blue as the heavens and as wide as a child's, but there was nothing childish about her form. No, there she was all but a dream, crafted like a small, luscious goddess, with breasts that . . .

He swore in silence and cleared his head. He wasn't pacing the floor to think about her breasts. There was nothing special about breasts: half the population of Scotland had them, and hers were undoubtedly much like any others. He was pacing the floor because he had to decide why he would be accompanying her tomorrow.

Nay! That was not it at all. He was pacing while he tried to ascertain if he should accompany her. Not that he had any desire whatsoever to spend days and nights by the girl's side; he did not. Even if her lips said she was all confidence while her hands pleaded for help, she didn't need him. Even if her skin begged . . .

Damnation!

His brothers were in trouble. That was the only reason he was considering the journey. Daft as they were, they were still his brothers, and in their present addle-witted state, they could too easily be led astray by a bonny face or a comely figure.

And *her* face and *her* figure . . .

He stopped the thought. He had no interest in either of those mundane characteristics. He had learned that a lovely countenance oft hid an evil heart. It had left a scar and he would not forget. When it came time to take a wife, he would choose one with plain features and average form, one who did not turn men's wits to jelly. One who did not destroy innocent lives while proclaiming everlasting devotion and . . .

Ramsay tightened his fists and closed his eyes to the acid memories. They ate at his innards, threatened his sanity, eroded his peace.

Just as she did. So, 'twould do his brothers no good if he accompanied them. It would only be another lesson in futility, he decided, as he found his bed and forced himself upon its lonely surface.

He would stay at Dun Ard and forget how her chin jutted just so, as haughty as a queen's, while in the depth of her azure eyes there seemed to be an everlasting flicker of fear that—

"Damn!" he muttered, and turning his face into his

pillow, tried to forget all about how her hair gleamed in the firelight, how her delicate body felt against his arm, and how, when they kissed, he felt as if her very soul spoke to his. Not of certainty and pride, but of fears and doubts and a small slip of a lass who needed him like none other.

" 'Twill be monotonous, riding in the midst of the company," Gilmour said. "Please, Lachlan, feel free to lead us. I shall take the tedious task of accompanying the lass." He turned his gaze to Mary, who rode just out of hearing with the maid servant.

"How generous of you." Lachlan settled into his saddle. "But you needn't put yourself out, brother. I'll be riding with—" he began, but suddenly his eyes widened. "Ram," he said, turning toward his elder brother. "Why are you here?"

Ramsay held Gryfon's reins with studied indifference and refused to let his gaze fall to the girl astride the white mare. She wore a velvet cape of emerald green that draped over her steed's ivory croup. Beneath the cape, a sapphire gown with slashed sleeves adorned her small frame. The bright colors made her face look as pale as ivory, framed by the long, loose flow of her golden hair. Like an angel's. But she was no angel, Ramsay thought, and forced himself to see the reality. Near the girl's scruffy shoes, her cloak was stained, and her gown, borrowed from Dun Ard's coffers, was too large for her narrow form. Yet despite all the hardships she had endured, she looked as regal as a queen, as bonny as a—

Ramsay cut short his thoughts, jabbed Gryfon's grinding weight off his toes, and swore in silence. 'Twas hardly the girl's soft gentility that had brought him here. Nay, 'twas the damage she could do amongst his kinsmen.

"I'll be accompanying you," he rumbled, eyeing first Lachlan, then Gilmour.

"Accompanying us?" they asked in unison.

He didn't respond, but mounted instead. Beneath him, Gryfon sidled toward the mare, as if none would recognize his plan if he approached with mincing steps. Ramsay kicked him in the flank, and the stallion halted with a grunt and a irritable flip of his black tail.

"Brother," Gilmour said. "As much as I appreciate your company, I hardly think it necessary."

"You hardly think at all," Lachlan said.

"We cannot all be such scholars as thou, dear brother."

"And we cannot all—"

"Hear me," Ramsay interrupted. His head ached from lack of sleep and every muscle felt as tense as a drawn bow. "I am here merely to see you two dolts safely through this journey and back—naught else. I have no designs on the lass, so you can rest comforted on that account."

"No designs?" It was Lachlan who spoke, though his voice was little above a rumble.

"Nay," he confirmed.

"No interest at all?"

Ramsay said nothing.

"So . . ." Gilmour nudged his mount closer and glanced at the girl. "You do not find her . . ." For a moment he seemed to lose his breath, but finally he sighed, pulled his attention back to his brother, and grinned with foolish enthusiasm. "You do not find her entrancing?"

Ramsay's muscles tightened another notch, like a

crossbow stretched to breaking. Damn it all to hell! He should have stayed in bed, should have ignored the sound of hoofbeats on cobblestones, should have forgotten how she felt in his . . .

"Nay. I do not." Tightening his grip on the reins, he turned Gryfon abruptly away.

Lachlan glowered and Gilmour laughed. "This may prove to be even more fun than I expected."

Chapter 6

The morning was misty, cool, and still. They rode at a steady pace, skirting boulders and ledges, avoiding the numerous rivulets and burns where they could and plowing through when they could not.

By early afternoon the mist had fled, but the clouds had rolled in. They bubbled overhead, casting long shadows and cool sunlight randomly across the evergreen landscape.

Up ahead, Mary's maid servant giggled.

Ramsay frowned at the noise. "Whatever happened to Elspeth?"

"What?" Lachlan seemed distracted, his attention pinned on the group ahead. Gilmour rode beside Mary, and the maid Caraid, only slightly older than the girl she escorted, rode beside her.

"Elspeth," Ramsay repeated. "I thought she had been chosen to see to the lass's well being during this journey."

"Mmmm." Lachlan's gaze never left Mary's back. "It seems there is a bairn that needs birthing. She could not afford to leave Dun Ard."

"A bairn?"

"Aye, Hazel of the Fens' child."

"Ahh."

"Gilmour knows her."

"Of course," Ramsay said. Or at least, Gilmour had thought of that excuse to keep Elspeth close to home. Caraid was young and comely and readily distracted. Elspeth was old, crotchety, and about as easily charmed as cracked shoe leather. And Gilmour was an ass. Beside Ramsay, Lachlan shifted restlessly in his saddle and cast him a jaundiced stare.

"What do you mean, *of course*?"

"Nothing."

"Then why did you say it?"

Ramsay scowled. " 'Twill be a long journey, Lachlan. Do not look for deep meaning where there is none. I was merely trying to keep you entertained with me clever conversation."

"You think it's his?"

"What?"

"Hazel's bairn? Do you think it might be Mour's?"

Ramsay snapped his gaze to Lachlan's, his gut cramping. "Is there a chance of it?"

"A chance?" Lachlan chuckled, but the sound was less than jovial. " 'Tis Mour we speak of here, is it not?"

"Aye." Ramsay scowled. "The lad is . . . wayward at times, but—"

"Wayward!" Lachlan growled. "He's a randy hound

without the scruples of a starved mackerel."

A slow burn began in Ramsay's gut. He tightened his hands on the reins so that the leather bit into his fingers. "Does he have wee ones that we know nothing of?"

"What's that?" Lachlan asked, and turned his scowl from Gilmour to Ramsay.

"Gilmour!" Ramsay gritted. "Has he fathered children?"

Lachlan shifted his gaze away. "Nay," he said sulkily, as if he were loath to admit it. "But he's a lovable bastard, and if he tries any of that charming shit on the lass, he'll be supping on me fist this night."

"Good Christ!" Ramsay wished to God he had stayed home.

It rained that night, not hard, but steady. By morning the road was slippery and the going slow.

Again Gilmour rode beside Mary. Now and then Ramsay heard her golden laughter and his gut would spew out a bit more bile. Ahead of him, Lachlan's stance became stiffer by the hour.

By nightfall Ramsay's stomach was twisted in a tight knot and Lachlan's back looked as unbending as a lance.

Tents were erected, supper prepared and consumed. Near the cook fire, Gilmour wended his way toward his wild tale's dramatic ending. The soldiers listened intently, Caraid gasped, and Gilmour leaned toward his audience, his arm brushing Mary's.

As for Ramsay, he sat in the shadows, keeping his eyes averted from the flame, watching the night.

He was a dolt for coming.

"Nay!" someone said, but not to his own discordant thoughts.

" 'Tis not true," another chimed in.

The clamor of discord yanked Ramsay's attention toward the crowd, but there was no real trouble, only another unbelievable ending to one of Gilmour's unbelievable tales. Of Roderic's five sons, Gilmour was the most like their sire. Long on imagination, longer on charm, but short on any compunction to adhere to the truth when spinning a yarn, especially if there was a bonny lass near at hand.

Ramsay tightened his fist around a branch of prickly gorse and felt better at the bite of thorns.

From the fire beside him the noise dimmed. He heard a rustle of movement but refused to turn toward it. He might be an idiot but he knew enough not to get involved—not with her. He was here only to prevent trouble. Nothing about her fascinated him, not her kitten soft exterior nor her sharp edged attitude. Not her condescending voice nor her fretful hands. Nay, 'twas only for his brothers that he had come. The bastards.

"Mary," said the younger of the two bastards.

"Aye?"

He heard her cool voice as clearly as Gilmour's, though they were hidden from sight by shadows and brush.

"Where do you go?" Gilmour took a few more steps, presumably closing the gap between himself and the girl.

"Sir." Her voice was quiet, with the slightest hint of teasing in it. "I fear 'tis not for you to know."

"Ahh." Another rustle of sound. Was he moving

closer still? The prickly gorse snapped in Ramsay's hand. "Private business."

"You are quite astute, my laird."

Gilmour chuckled. "Astute enough to know that a bonny lass such as yourself should not wander alone in the woods."

There was a moment of silence. "Mayhap you and I have a different meaning for 'private business.' "

He laughed again. "I assure you, Mary mine, I will go only as far as you say. 'Tis your prerogative to call a halt at any time."

Ramsay heard her skirts sigh against unseen underbrush. "Tell me, my laird, do we still talk of my venture into the woods?"

"Most assuredly so. But if you like, we could speak of other things . . . afterward. The moon is quite bonny this night and me legs could use a new form of exercise. Mayhap—"

"Brother!" Lachlan's interruption startled even Ramsay, for the lad could move as silently as a shade when the mood suited him. "Might I have a word with you?"

Ramsay exhaled and dropped the gorse to the ground. A droplet of unnoticed blood followed its descent.

"In truth," Gilmour said, "I was just discussing a matter of some import with the lass."

"And what of your teeth, brother?" Lachlan asked, his tone marvelously level. "Do you feel they have some import?"

There was a slight pause and then Gilmour chuckled. "Mayhap you should see to your business, lass," he said. "It seems me brother wishes to speak to me."

In a moment she was gone, slipping quietly through the darkness of the woods.

"So, brother," Gilmour said, his tone cheery. "You wished to discuss teeth."

"Aye, I did. Where would you like yours?"

"I had rather planned on keeping them where they are." Gilmour's chuckle grated on Ramsay's nerves and was bound to do so three fold on Lachlan, who had never had the patience of a gnat.

"Then you'd best keep your bloody hands off the lady of Levenlair."

" 'Tis exactly what I've been doing."

"But not what you hoped to do, aye?"

Ramsay could almost hear the shrug in Gilmour's tone. "If we have not hope, what have we?"

"All your teeth set firmly in their place."

"It occurs to me," Gilmour said, "that it has been some time since you and I have brawled. As I recall, I was smaller then."

"You imagine your size matters?"

"Mayhap it matters a great deal."

"Are you challenging me, Mour?"

"The lass is not for you," Gilmour said, and spread his stance.

"Tell me, brother, are you that bored or that foolish?"

"Perhaps I am that smitten."

"Smitten!" Lachlan growled. "Randy, more like."

"Is there a difference?"

"There is where she's concerned," Lachlan growled. "You'll take back your words or you'll be eating them for—"

"Oh, for God's sake!" Ramsay said, rising abruptly to his feet. "Shut up, the two of you."

"Ramsay!"

"What are you doing here?"

"Listening to two fools babble in the darkness."

"Out here?"

"Directly in Mary's path to the burn?"

Ramsay snarled a curse. "What the devil's wrong with you? You're acting like a pair of dolts, snarling over her like wolves on fresh carrion."

"Are you calling the lass carrion?" Lachlan asked, his tone disbelieving.

Ramsay swore again, but Lachlan interrupted even that succinct bit of emotion.

"Are you so callous that you do not know, brother?"

"Know?"

"Did you not see her as she lay unconscious? Did you not feel her sweetness? The lass is goodness itself."

Ramsay's snort of laughter echoed in the woods. "Believe this, brother mine. She may be many things, but she is not goodness itself."

"Why do you say so?" Gilmour asked.

"A dozen things. Do you not see it?" Ramsay asked, frustration burning through him. "Never is her story straight. Not when she first came to, not when she awoke in the night, not—"

"When she awoke in what night?" Gilmour asked.

"She said she had a dream," Ramsay said. "That she was all atremble with fear when—"

"She was afraid?"

"When was this?" Lachlan asked.

"Some nights ago. I caught her—"

"You caught her?"

"What were you doing in her room?"

"What was she wearing?"

"What were *you* wearing?"

"If you touched her, I'll break your head."

This last statement was from Lachlan, of course.

Ramsay loosened his fists and exhaled between his teeth. " 'Tis a sad thing."

"What is?"

"That me own brothers be daft as pigeons," Ramsay said, and found, quite suddenly, that he rather favored the idea of a battle, for his muscles were as tight as wagon springs and his mind was boiling like soup stock.

"Daft, are we?" Gilmour asked.

"Aye, you are."

"Because we are not so jaded as you? Because we believe the fairer sex is just that? Because we believe she is good and kind and true?"

"Just so," Ramsay agreed.

"And what do you think she is, brother?"

If they wanted a fight, he would give it to them. Why the hell not? "She is, me wee, naive brothers, a liar."

A growl issued from Lachlan's lips.

"A liar?" Gilmour said. "Did you hear that, Lachlan?"

"Aye," came the snarled response.

"And are we going to stand here and allow him to slander the lassie's name so?"

"Nay, I am not. I fear I am forced to defend her honor."

"*You!*" Gilmour said, glancing at Lachlan. " 'Tis me own place to fight him."

"Think again, brother."

" 'Tis my right. 'Twas I who first knew her for what she was—a gentle lass of unequaled quality."

" 'Twas I who made it so that we were out and about at the outset."

" 'Twas I who—"

"I'm older," Lachlan snarled, and raised his fists to punctuate the depth of his feelings.

"Well . . ." Gilmour shrugged. "You have me there. I cannot argue with God's order of things."

Lachlan stepped forward, and Ramsay saw the lightning quick flash of Gilmour's grin in the moonlight.

"Damn!" Ramsay said and felt the anger rush from him like wind from a bellows. "You're an arse, Gilmour."

Mour almost contained his chuckle. "You'd best save your insults for Lachlan here, brother. He's spoiling for a fight, you know."

"Aye," Ramsay said, "and while we're beating each other senseless, you'll be—" He paused. Within his chest, his heart stopped cold. "Where is she?"

"Who?" Gilmour asked.

"Mary!" Lachlan's voice was low, his hand already on his sword.

Ramsay swore and spun into the darkness.

"Mary?"

"Mary!" Her name rang through the forest.

There was no answer. But somehow Ramsay knew there wouldn't be. Knew it in his soul.

"I'll check camp," Gilmour said, and Ram sprinted into the woods. His heart thumped to life in his chest, kicking hard and fast against his ribs.

"Lass!" Lachlan called, thundering behind him.

A stream glittered in the moonlight. Faint tracks shone in the darkness. Ramsay skidded to a halt.

"Hoofprints!" Lachlan snarled, and fell to his knees. "The same as the warrior's before."

"And the lassie's tracks. She mounted the steed here."

"Can you follow in the dark?"

"Aye. That I can." Lachlan's answer was a growl. He was already trotting along the stream, half crouched like a predator on a scent.

"Go as far as you can. I'll fetch our steeds," Ramsay called as he raced back toward camp.

Swiftly, orders were given, horses saddled, and men armed. They were mounted in moments and riding hard through the woods toward the stream. They met Lachlan near a bend. In seconds he was astride, leaning low in the saddle and leading them pell-mell through the night. Mud flew from his horse's hooves. In the darkness, the faces around Ramsay looked grim. Even Gilmour's expression was dire, for there was no time to lose. It was obvious from the tracks that the horse they followed was running hard, even with a double load. Running hard and taking the shortest route.

Branches scraped leather and flesh, but that didn't slow the riders' pace. Even in the blackness, Lachlan could follow the trail. He had the uncanny instincts of a fox. They would catch up, Ramsay told himself. They would find her. Unless . . .

A thought stabbed through his consciousness. They'd been riding hard for some time, but still no sign of the horse. Was it outdistancing them? With a double load? How—

Ramsay hauled his mount in with a curse. Gryfon half reared, and Gilmour turned in the darkness.

"Ride!" Ramsay ordered. "I'll catch up."

But first he would check the tracks by the burn.

Maybe she *was* racing ahead of them with the mysterious warrior. But then again, maybe nothing was as it seemed.

Chapter 7

The night flashed by in waves of terror and darkness. One moment Anora had been standing beside the burn, and the next she was grabbed from behind and forced onto a horse.

She strained away from the warrior who rode behind her, trying to see his face, but he gave her no quarter. Even if she could see beyond the darkness and his helmet, she was not allowed to turn.

"Stay!" he gritted, and tightened the arm banded around her waist. She froze, her heart striking hard against her ribs.

"Who are you?" Her voice quavered in the darkness, but there was no answer, only the slightest tilt of the arm across her body.

Beneath them, the midnight steed left the water and

leapt, scrambling onto the shore before lurching toward the north at a hard gallop.

Anora hunched forward, snatching for a hank of mane, and the warrior's grip shifted, tightening like death across her bosom. She gasped for breath and bravery, but terror lit anew in her soul. "Why do you do this? What do you want?" she whispered.

'Twas forever before he growled a response. " 'Tis I who should ask that question."

Her mind reeled. He acted as if she had wronged him in some way, but she did not know him. Did not recognize his voice, could not visualize his face, and yet when he spoke, there was something that welled up with the fear, something indefinable, just beyond the reach of her mind. She struggled to see past the barrier.

"So *now* you wish to know me?" he snarled. His breath felt hot against her neck. " 'Tis a bit late for that, me *lady*."

"Who are you? Where are you taking me?"

"Wherever I wish."

"Why?"

"Because I am strong and you are weak. 'Tis the way of the world, is it not?"

Against the horse's flying mane, Anora's hand shook. Miles flew away beneath them. "Please." She whispered the word into the oncoming wind. "Let me go."

No response.

"Why are you doing this?"

The hard muscles of his legs tightened and against her chest his arm crushed her all the more. "Long has the sin gone unpunished."

The sound of distant water splashed against the

edge of her consciousness. Were the MacGowans coming for her? But no. Her captor was ungodly clever. He'd dragged her onto a horse only to dismount in the water moments later. In an instant the horse had disappeared alone, and they had scrambled upstream to another mount and ridden in the opposite direction. No one would find her . . .

From behind, the sound of a hoof on a rock made her catch her breath. She froze, waiting for the warrior to turn and listen, but he did not. Instead, she felt the cold metal of his nose guard bump her skull.

The truth struck her suddenly. His helmet muffled the sounds from behind. 'Twas the helmet and perhaps his inexplicable hatred for her that kept him from hearing the noises that followed them.

Distract him, her mind screamed, but for a moment she could think of nothing. Nothing but the memory of rending fabric, of control being ripped from her by brutal force.

"Sin?" she rasped. "What sin?"

"Methinks you know."

"Know what?"

"Why you must die," he said. The horse lurched around a boulder and in that moment a branch struck her head with dizzying force.

She was thrust from the warrior's grasp. He reached for her, but she kicked with all her might, thrusting her legs out in a desperate attempt to be free, and suddenly she was falling.

She hit the ground hard. Desperation kicked her to her feet and she fled, scampering like a wild hare through the underbrush.

She knew the instant he turned after her. She must find cover! Up ahead, thick woods loomed in a darker shade of black. Her lungs tore as she sprinted toward the forest. Her feet tangled in her skirt, but she managed to stay upright, to keep running. Behind her, heavy hooves thundered against the sod. She heard the horse's snort of exertion, felt its hot breath. Too late, too late! She twisted about, trying to dart away, but in that instant a cry ripped through the darkness. Pivoting wildly, she prepared to meet death, but instead she saw another horse lunge into view.

The warrior turned his destrier to meet him. There was a moment of blinding silence and then his challenge roared through the darkness.

The two horses charged in pounding unison. Sparks flashed in the darkness. Steel crashed against steel. The warrior's blade spun from his hand. He toppled sideways, struck the earth, rolled for an instant, then bounded to his feet.

The mounted man spun his steed toward the other and stopped, and for a moment his face shone in the fleeting moonlight.

"MacGowan." The name left Anora's parched lips like a prayer, but his attention never wavered from his enemy, for the warrior was backing toward his sword.

"Touch her and die." Ramsay's voice was low and steady, echoing in the dark stillness.

"She is mine, MacGowan," rasped her captor. "You have no stake in this."

"What is yours?" Ramsay's bay pranced in place, the sound of his hoof falls solid in the stillness, the jingle of his bit as ghostly as a rattle of chains. "Who are you?"

Silence settled in like doom for an instant. "I am justice."

Ramsay sat perfectly still atop his restive steed. "I have seen the face of justice. It has never before harmed an innocent."

"Innocent!" the warrior snarled, and snatching his sword from the earth, he charged.

Slamming his heels into his steed, Ramsay joined the attack, but an instant before they met, the warrior dropped to the ground and rolled. Gryfon stumbled across his tucked body, and before he found his balance the warrior leapt up and swung.

Caught off balance and unawares, Ramsay ducked beneath the blow and so doing, tumbled from the saddle.

In an instant his horse was gone. There was nothing between the men now but three strides of darkness.

They circled each other in silence, arms stretched wide.

It was the warrior who struck first.

Ramsay parried. Sparks erupted in an arc of gold, then burned to blackness. Their breathing was harsh in the stillness.

"What has she done that you would wish her harm?" Ramsay asked.

" 'Tis none of your concern, MacGowan," said the warrior, and swung again.

Ramsay blocked the blow, advanced a pace, met the other's answered steel and fell back, circling again. "There you are wrong," he said. "For me clan has vowed to keep her safe."

"Then you have vowed foolishly."

"Why?"

"No more words," growled the other, and lunged forward.

Anora cowered in the darkness. Sparks flared in the ebony night and by the slanted moonlight she saw Ramsay fall to his knees.

"Nay!" she screamed.

His face jerked toward her, and amidst the upward thrust he'd planned, his hands faltered. The warrior swung.

She heard Ramsay's hiss of pain, saw him stagger sideways, finally finding his balance.

She whimpered in fear.

The warrior turned toward her, and her mind spun. Who was he? What harm had she done him?

"Think back," he snarled.

Behind him, Ramsay wrenched his sword from the ground.

The warrior glanced at MacGowan, then back at her. *Nay! Please!* her soul whispered, but her lips failed to move.

Still, the warrior turned as if she had spoken. Their gazes met. Recognition almost dawned, and then he shrieked. The sound echoed like the cry of a falcon, and suddenly his black steed thundered out of nowhere.

A lunge, and the warrior was aboard. She knew he would come for her, knew even before he spun his destrier in her direction. She stumbled, trying to escape, but he was already swooping down upon her, his cloak flying behind.

She felt the grip of his hand in her gown and twisted away. A roar bellowed from behind them and he jerked about. Something whistled in the air. For just an instant Anora saw a flash of steel in the darkness. It sang through the night like an angel of death. The warrior screamed as steel struck flesh and flashed past.

His body tilted. His sword clattered to the earth, and then, like a winged host of evil, he set his heels to his mount and was gone.

The world fell silent. Anora turned, then staggered toward Ramsay, drawn irrevocably across the uneven turf until they fell into each other's arms.

"Mary." He whispered her name. "Are you unhurt?"

" 'Tis you. 'Tis you," she murmured, and touched his face, trying to believe that he was real, that all was well. "But . . ." Even in the moonlight, she could see the dark blood on his arm and recoiled in fear. "You are hurt."

"Nay. 'Tis naught."

"You have been wounded," she said, awe in her voice. "For me."

"A scratch, nothing more," he said, and smoothed her hair back from her face. She trembled beneath his touch.

"Why?" she whispered, struggling to understand. He ran his hand down the back of her neck, pulling her gently against his chest. "Why did you risk yourself?"

"You are well," he murmured. His sword arm remained still as he stroked her hair with his other hand, and there, like the breath of a wind, she felt his fingers shiver.

"You tremble," she whispered. "With pain?"

"Nay, lass. Do not fret."

"Why do you tremble?"

"I feared . . ." His fingers tightened momentarily in her hair. "I feared I'd be too late."

"You feared . . ." Against her breast, she could feel the solid beat of his heart. "For me?"

He did not answer, but bent his head. She felt the brush of his lips against her hair.

" 'Tis because you are kind," she breathed.

He stroked her hair again. Dizzy with wonder and speechless hope, she tilted her face upward. She felt safe suddenly, safe and protected in his arms. His fingers slipped beneath her hair, cradling her neck, and slowly, ever so slowly, he kissed her.

Warmth sparked through her as their lips gently met. She trembled with feeling and relief.

"Lass. Me wee, small lass." He breathed the words against her mouth. "I feared I was too late, too foolish."

He had come. Had risked his life. Had found her. She pressed closer, needing to feel his strength. Their mouths joined again. He moaned against the breathy caress and curled his sword arm around her back.

Anora's mind churned. He was cunning and he was kind and he was powerful. Could it be that the prophecy was true? Had he been sent to save her? To save Evermyst?

His arms tightened around her. His kiss hardened. Against her belly she felt his desire burgeon, and with it came fear. But no! He had saved her. He was kind. He was cunning. He was . . .

She pushed against his chest, for the very strength that had soothed her frightening her now.

"Let me go! Let me—" But she was already free, stumbling backward until she found her balance.

"What is it, lass?" His voice was very low, almost hoarse as he stepped forward.

She retreated another pace, trying to still her panic. "I must go."

"Aye." He took a step forward.

A branch crackled behind her. She twisted about only to see his steed step from the woods. It stopped abruptly at her sharp motion, causing its loosed reins to jerk wildly.

"We shall return to camp," Ramsay said. "To await the others' arrival."

"Nay." She stumbled back a step, her breath still painful in her chest. "I cannot."

"Cannot?"

"It will be the first place he looks."

"He?" Ramsay paused, but she said nothing. "The warrior. Who was it, lass? Why does he wish you harm?"

She shook her head, breathless and confused and frightened. "I do not know."

" 'Twas the warrior who attacked you before, was it not?"

"I do not know."

"A Munro, surely."

"Munro?" She felt dizzy and disoriented, torn in two by gnawing uncertainty. In her hazy dream, Munro loomed, and before him knelt . . . Isobel!

"Nay." Anora's breath rattled with her inhalation. "Leave her be!"

"What?" he asked.

She shot her gaze to his. "I must return home."

"At first light—"

"No time. I must leave. Now!"

"Lass," he said and grabbed her arm. She tried to break free, but he held her tight and pulled her closer. "Explain yourself. Tell me of your pact with the Munro."

"I know no Munro."

"You lie."

"You are not kind," she hissed, and grabbing her right hand with her left, twisted sharply upward. His grip broke. Suddenly she was free and running.

'Twas only a few strides to the horse, but MacGowan was right behind her. She knew it as she launched herself toward the saddle, felt the scrape of his fingers on her back as her own caught mane and leather.

The bay pivoted away. Anora held on with desperation, swinging her leg high, but even as she did so, Ramsay snatched her toward the earth. She fell atop him with a shriek and heard the breath fly from his lungs as he struck the turf.

Still, his fingers did not loosen in the back of her gown. "Let me go!" she ordered, terror erupting as she scrambled to be free.

He snatched her back against him, causing his breath to explode from his lungs again, but still he held on. "What frightens you so?"

"Frightens me!" She almost laughed. "Would you not be frightened if someone tried to kill you?"

"Someone did try to kill me," he growled, grabbing her wrist and loosing her gown. "Tell me why."

"You think I know?"

"Aye," he said. "I do."

"Well, you are wrong. All I know is this." She caught him with her gaze, her heart pounding hard in her chest. "I've no time to spare. No time to retrace the miles just trod. I must return home before it's too late."

"Too late for what?"

"For my s . . . For me."

He scowled. "For—"

"My life is in danger," she said. "And if I die . . . 'twill be on your head."

For a moment not a sound broke the silence, and then he swore. "Get on my horse," he said. "We've a long ride ahead of us."

Chapter 8

He night wore on like a mournful dirge.

What the devil had he been thinking? He should never have agreed to her demands. He should have gone to their camp posthaste and waited for his brothers and the others to accompany them north. Or better yet, he should have insisted on returning to the safety of Dun Ard. Or . . . well, there were any number of fine choices he should have made. But what he shouldn't have done was leave his clansmen to go traipsing about into unknown dangers.

Sometime after midnight it began to rain. Softly at first, then harder, biting his face and soaking his doublet. Seated before him on the saddle, bereft of all but her borrowed oversized gown, the girl shivered, but he didn't care. Oh, aye, at the outset he had been terrified that she would be hurt by the mysterious warrior. He had stormed through the night after her, praying with every breath that he would not be too late. But it had been merely reflex that had made him follow her. It certainly was not because he cared for her, but only because she was small and helpless and so innocent . . .

He almost snorted aloud. Innocent, indeed! As he had warned his brothers, she was a liar and probably much worse. All he was certain of was that her name was not Mary. Notmary, he thought, and chuckled briefly. But he'd become somewhat light-headed, so perhaps his sense of humor left a bit to be desired.

She shivered again. He ignored her, though he couldn't help but notice how one bold droplet slid past her proud little chin and beneath the square neckline of her borrowed gown. There it was hidden between her . . .

He snapped his gaze forward, felt her tremble, and reached without thought toward the leather bags secured to his high cantle. In a moment he'd pulled forth his woolen cape.

"Here." He nudged her arm with it. She glanced his way, half reached for it, then drew her hand back and shook her head.

"Nay. 'Tis yours."

He counted patiently to himself in Latin, but still, the thought of throttling her seemed enormously pleasant. "Wear it," he said.

She shook her head again.

He swore, managed to wrestle the thing around his own shoulders, then yanked the edge around her body. His arm brushed her breasts. They were firm and round, with nipples as hard as precious stones, but damned if he cared. She was a liar and a manipulator, a woman who used men for her own ends. Of that he was certain.

Still, she had seemed, for a moment, to be very concerned for him. On her fairy bright lips, his name had sounded like a prayer or a song or . . .

Sweet Almighty, he was an idiot. And it was raining harder still, so that Gryfon laid his ears straight back and tucked his muzzle toward his chest in a hopeless attempt to avoid the pounding rain.

"We'll have to stop," he said into the slanting onslaught. He half expected her to argue, but she remained huddled inside his cape until finally, after what seemed like a drowning eternity, he found a sheltered spot.

It wasn't much, only a stand of rowan which grew in the lea of a hill, but inside the woods the stillness seemed like heaven. Up against a rocky ridge, old leaves were piled in profuse disarray beneath a few sheltering boughs. After turning Gryfon loose in a sheltered area Ramsay finally sank upon his haunches.

"Are you certain your steed won't run off?" Notmary asked from the far side of the rowans.

"Aye."

Even from some distance away, he could sense her raising her chin. "Why?"

"The devil if I know: I've been trying to be rid of him for years."

"Is he so loy—"

Ramsay swore, interrupting the question. "Do you wish to reach Levenlair or not?" he asked.

"Aye," she said simply.

"Alive?"

" 'Tis my preference."

"Then I'd suggest you share me bed."

She stiffened like an offended dowager, and despite the improbability of finding any humor in this horrendous situation, Ramsay felt a chuckle rise up inside him. Perhaps he was losing his mind. "Come," he said, but she shook her head. "Come," he repeated. "Mayhap the rowan will keep you safe even from me."

"The rowan may keep me dry, but naught else."

He squinted at her, trying to read her expression. "You do not believe they bring good luck?"

"No more than wearing one's clothes outside in or the color red or Mondays."

"No faith in any of that time-tested wisdom?" he asked.

"It seems to me that old wives' tales do more harm than good. Thus I have little faith in them and—"

"Men?"

"What?"

"You do not trust men."

"I trust men, if they deserve to be trusted."

"Then come hither."

She didn't move, and he swore out loud. "I am wounded, soaked to the skin, and far beyond exhausted. If you believe me unable to resist your nearness, you either think me a hell of a man or yourself an extraordinary woman."

She said nothing.

He sighed. "Come here," he said. "I'll not touch you."

There was a moment of silence. "Do I have your vow?"

"Aye," he growled.

She came slowly, but when she finally made her way through the sheltering trees, turned her back, and settled in beside him, he felt his arousal rise blunt and hard between them.

Gritting his teeth, he tugged the edge of his cape across her body. Damnation, he had the stupidest wick on earth.

Dawn arrived without fanfare, seeping slowly into Ramsay's consciousness. 'Twas time to break the fast. Past the edge of his sleepy mind he could hear the castle awakening and—

He opened his eyes and his mind yanked him back to reality. No castle. No breakfast. Not even a dawn to speak of, just a lighter shade of murky gray, and . . .

He turned his attention to the woman who shared his pile of leaves. Sometime during the night, his cape had become tangled beneath her body, hugging them together. From so close, her smooth cheek looked ultimately touchable. Her lips were ripe, full, and slightly parted, and the soft hillocks of her breasts rose and fell with mesmerizing regularity when she breathed.

As he watched, she sighed gently and wriggled deeper into the warmth of his cape. Sleeping thus, she looked like a small, frail angel fallen—

He was doing it again. Despite the fact that she had the face of a saint and the form of a goddess . . . regardless of the way her eyes mesmerized him and her hair shone like gold even in the grimmest of weather, she was only a woman. And he had no desire to touch her. Neither body nor soul.

After all, he was no fool. Nay, he was a man who, once testing fire, had no need to feel its burn again. And though he had made a few mistakes since meeting her, he would remedy them now. He would see her safely to Levenlair and be gone, never to think of her again.

With that decision made, he tenaciously ignored the weight in his crotch and reached across her waist to tug his cape from beneath her. Her eyes snapped open instantly. From inches apart, their gazes met. Emotions, unshielded and unexplained, sparked between them. His fingers crept toward her of their own will, but even before he touched her, she was watching him with cool disdain.

He paused for a fraction of an instant, then, grasping the cape, he yanked it from beneath her.

The effort was worth the pain that accompanied it, for with his movement, she was jerked onto her back, gasping.

"What are you doing?"

"Relieving a terrible ache." He rose jerkily to his feet, grimacing at the pain from his injured arm.

"Tell me, Notmary," he said, standing above her. "Whence did your flirtatious ways flee?"

She bounded to her feet, as if she dared not be in so vulnerable position in his presence. When in truth, she had spent most of the night curled like a kitten . . .

Ramsay chopped off his errant thoughts and sharpened his control.

" 'Twas only yestereve that you blatantly baited me brothers," he reminded her.

Raising her chin slightly, she brushed leaves from her skirt without glancing down.

"I did no such thing." Her voice was husky with early morning drowsiness.

"Aye," he said, and tried to ignore how the seductive rasp of her voice thickened the blood in his loins.

"You did. Yet last night you were desperate to leave them."

"I was desperate to save my life."

"Mayhap," he said.

She stared at him. Her pursed lips were impossibly red, her loosed hair littered with leaves. His wick stirred. He'd always had a weakness for loosed hair littered with leaves. It had nothing whatsoever to do with her, he told himself.

" 'Tis time to be going," he said, his voice a husky echo in their little den. "Unless you've an inclination to tell me the truth."

She turned away immediately, as regal as visiting royalty as she made her way from the dripping copse.

They rode all that day, staying to the woods as oft as they could. Ramsay felt like a coward, slinking through the underbrush like a whipped cur, but he had little choice, for with the hours of damp inactivity, his arm felt increasingly stiff. If the Munros found them, he'd be lucky to have enough strength to battle a flea. Hiding was his only option, but the hours droned on forever, and the soggy drizzle only abated long enough to give them hope before starting up again. Notmary shivered against his chest. As for himself, he'd rather keel over in silent death than admit his own discomfort.

It was nearly dusk when they smelled the smoke. The mere tinge of woodsy aroma made his mouth ache with hunger.

"Someone's nearby." Her voice was very quiet.

"Aye." He stared through the close packed tree trunks toward the origin of that heavenly aroma. "So tell me, Notmary, shall we approach them, or do you have enemies that I should know of first? The Munros, mayhap?"

He felt her stiffen. "As I have told you, I know no Munros."

"Aye, you told me. So there's no reason we should not ride directly into their camp, aye?" he said, and nudged Gryfon forward.

Her small body was taut with tension as the trees thinned. Off to the right a trio of shaggy black cows lifted their heads to watch them pass, and from up ahead a bell rang, sounding loud and clear as it floated above a wooden palisade.

"A village!" she gasped.

"Aye," he said, and tapped Gryfon with his heels. "Were you expecting something else? Or someone, mayhap?"

She didn't deign to glance his way, though it was clear that she'd been nervous. Still, she was silent as they made their way across a boggy stretch of fen to the city's front gate and beyond. A young lad with a sagging hat and slanted plaid gazed at them as he guided a herd of swine toward a thicket fence. The squinty eyed pigs grumbled amongst themselves as they went their way.

The city's narrow thoroughfares were a charmless combination of rutted mud and sloping cobblestones, but they didn't have far to go, for fifty rods from the village entrance, Ramsay stopped Gryfon at a wattle and daub inn. It tilted drunkenly toward the grocers on the far side of the street, and above its arched door, a drooping sign displayed a misshapen bottle and faded loaf.

"We're stopping?" Anora asked, scowling at the disreputable looking inn.

"We need a place to spend the night."

"Here?"

"Methinks the king's court may be a bit far."

She ignored his sarcasm. "Perhaps we should push on."

His wound throbbed. "We stop here," he said. "Unless you've an irresistible yearning to spend another night in me arms."

She lifted her chin and brows in regal unison. "In truth, I would far rather be pelted with rotten apples and dragged through the courtyard by my hair," she said.

He snorted, and inadvertently brushing his arm against her breast, refused to apologize as he stiffly dismounted.

"Bonjour," someone said.

Ramsay turned toward the threshold of the inn. A man stood there smiling. How the hell long had he been there? And how much had he heard? He was dark haired and narrow faced, with the kind of combed good looks associated with the French. The roving eye was not lacking either, and as his attention rose to the girl, Ramsay felt his temper stoke even as the other bowed. "I am Leverett de la Court. How may I serve you?" he asked, and managed to drag his gaze back to Ramsay.

"We need a hot meal, a stable for my steed, and a dry place to spend the night," Ramsay said.

"Certainly, monsieur, and since my wife is away on business and the new maid just hired and untrained, I will see to your needs myself," he said, and flashed a toothy leer at Anora.

Something coiled in Ramsay's gut—something that felt nauseatingly akin to jealousy. Just looking at the

Frenchman made him want to shove the girl inside the nearest room and lock the door, but what could he do? Proclaim her to be his wife?

Hah! He'd be dead within seconds if he attempted such a foolish stunt, executed by her scathing hauteur. Better by far to let her fend for herself. After all, she was no innocent babe who must be coddled and pampered. No wounded bird from his youth that must be taken home and nursed back to health.

"We'll have our meal first," Ramsay said, making no explanations as to his relationship with the girl.

"Oui, monsieur."

"And a bath."

The Frenchman's glance slipped with lightning quickness over Notmary's breasts. "The bathing is usually done in the kitchen, my lord."

"Not today," Ramsay growled, and struggled hopelessly with errant feelings that spun in his mind like wind blown leaves—foolish protectiveness, struggling pride. "Send it to the lady's chamber."

"Ahh." The Frenchman's eyes sparkled as he drank in the soggy fabric plastered to the girl's body. " 'Twill be my pleasure to deliver the bathing tub myself," he said, and stepping forward, took her hand in his. "And your name, mademoiselle?" he asked, drawing her fingers toward his lips.

Her eyes widened for a fraction of an instant, and then she snatched her hand from his grip. By the time the innkeeper had raised his wounded gaze to hers, her regal expression was firmly back in place. Her hand, however, was wrapped like a wounded sparrow in Gryfon's black mane. There was a breathless pause, as if the world waited, and then, "Madame," she corrected. Her back was as straight as an arrow and her mouth slightly pursed. "And I shall be sharing a room with my husband, of course."

Ramsay locked his knees to keep from keeling over like a felled oak.

"Of course," said the Frenchman, and turned with slow regret back to Ramsay. "Will you be dining in the common room or in your chamber?"

"We shall dine alone," she said, filling the silence with her regal tone.

"As you will."

"Robbie!" de la Court called, and turned impatiently toward the inn only to collide with a chunky lad who was just scurrying out.

"You called?" asked the boy, stumbling backward as his master found his balance.

De la Court glowered. "See to my lord's steed, then hustle back to the kitchens and tell Farley we'll need a meal for two. Do you hear?"

"Aye."

"Good." The Frenchman turned with a smile to his customers. "If you'll but follow me."

Placing a hand on Gryfon's neck, Ramsay turned toward the lass. Atop the horse, she was in the perfect position to look down her nose at him. How handy.

"So . . ." he said dryly. "You couldn't resist me after all."

She pursed her raspberry lips and glanced at the Frenchman, who had retreated to his doorway. "Merely the lesser of two evils."

Ramsay snorted as he reached up to help her dismount. Gryfon flicked his tail and turned an evil eye toward his master, but the girl set a hand gently to the stallion's russet neck.

"Shall I be flattered?" Ram asked.

"Not unless you're pathetically desperate," she said, and deigned to be lifted down.

The effort jolted a shock of pain through his right arm, but he was not above holding her close in a sort of evil payment. "Mayhap I am desperate," he said.

"You *are* a man," she said.

"Now I *am* flattered."

She arched a brow at him.

"That you noticed," he explained and pulled her marginally closer.

"Beware, or I'll change my mind and choose the Frenchman," she hissed.

He smiled, employing all the besotted adoration of a newly wedded bridegroom. "Surely you do not think I would risk you with a stranger," he said. "Not when you are such an honest innocent."

She opened her mouth to speak, but the innkeeper interjected.

"Is something amiss?"

"Nay," Ramsay said, and turned toward the lad called Robbie. "Give him an extra ration of barley, but be wary," he warned, nodding toward Gryfon. "He can be mean-spirited." Then, turning toward the Frenchman, he tucked Notmary's hand under his arm. "What could possibly be amiss when me bonny bride is by me side?" he asked, and almost laughed as she gave him a sour looking smile.

The common room was fairly crowded. The scent of smoke and stew and hard working bodies filled the place. Laughter erupted, then dwindled as the occupants noticed the new guests. A half score of lusty male faces turned toward them. Notmary glanced at them, her expression aloof, her fingers almost imperceptibly tighter upon Ramsay's arm.

The uncarpeted steps were narrow and steep. Notmary gripped the long sapphire gown in her free hand as they followed their host to the top.

"Here you are, then. Our last room," said de la Court and swung an iron bound door wide. Only inches from Notmary, he turned his gaze toward her. His dark eyes dipped and sparkled as he bowed. "If there is anything you desire, Madame, I will consider it a privilege to serve such a lovely—"

"Me thanks," Ramsay said, and slammed the door behind them.

The girl turned in the silence, her back straight as she glanced about the humble room.

'Twas a narrow space, boasting little more than an ancient leather trunk and a bed that seemed to fill the room like a war horse in a garderobe.

Ramsay cleared his throat. "Well," he said. "Here we be, alone together, and you without a single person to pelt you with rotten fruit."

Chapter 9

"Believe you me," she said, and raising her chin, felt fear fan her belly in a hot wave of feeling. Maybe she would have been safer with the Frenchman after all. At least he didn't have Mac-Gowan's rugged strength, and if it came to a struggle, she might stand a chance, but with Ram ... she skimmed his broad form for an instant, calming her breathing. "Pelted fruit would surely be the lesser of the two evils."

He leaned his back to the wall and crossed his arms against his chest. Dear God, he looked imposing in these narrow confines. "The greater evil being ..."

"You," she said, and paced nervously across the oak slatted floor. The room was small and close, with nowhere to hide and no one to come to her aid. She felt her throat close up and turned away, striving for calm.

"But lass . . ." His tone was perplexed, and though she did not immediately turn to him, she knew he shook his head as if wounded. " 'Twas you who proclaimed us wed. I meself—"

"Would have left me to the Frenchman?"

Had he heard the quaver in her voice? Still facing the wall, she squeezed her eyes shut and wished to hell she hadn't spoken. She was supposed to be haughty, self assured. Impervious. 'Twas the mask she had chosen to wear with this man.

"And what's wrong with the Frenchman, lass? I thought him the type women found appealing."

Opening her eyes, she eased her hand out of her skirt and took a steadying breath. He was probing, trying to find her fear. "I did not say differently."

"Then—"

She turned abruptly toward him, chin raised. "Just because he is appealing does not mean I care for his attentions."

"Unlike me brothers."

"What?"

"Me brothers," he said. "You were eager enough for their attentions. Why is that, Notmary?"

" 'Tis simple," she said. "Your brothers are gentle men."

"Gentle men!" He snorted. "Enamored fools, more like."

She shrugged delicately as she turned to study the window. They were only one floor above the street. Not so far a jump if the worst presented itself. "Is that what you call chivalry, MacGowan?"

"Aye," he said. " 'Tis exactly what I call it."

"Then why did you deign to protect me at all?"

He was silent for a moment, and in that silence, she turned, intrigued.

His scowl was dark as if he himself were uncertain. "Even dolts do not deserve to die."

She raised a questioning brow with superior disdain and stifled a shiver as much for the closeness of the room as for the cloying cold of her garments.

"Me brothers," he explained. "I do not wish for them to be harmed just because they cannot see beyond your bonny face."

She raised both brows now and forced a smile. "So you think me bonny?"

"Not as bonny as you think yourself, lass."

Surprised, she laughed, but the sound quavered slightly. "Ahh, that's right, I cannot have every man swooning at my feet, can I?"

He didn't answer.

"So you resent me for being the fairer of the sexes?" she asked.

"Fairer? Is it fair that women would use men's affections like a sword against an—" He stopped abruptly.

She stared at him. "Against who?" she urged, but a muscle jumped in his jaw and he refused to continue. "I think," she said, "that you are confusing me with another."

He took a step toward her, his gaze as steady as a falcon's. "So you are saying your intentions were true, lass? That you were, in fact, as infatuated with me brothers as they were with you?"

She felt her heart pump faster as he stepped nearer, while the walls seemed to close in like swinging doors.

"They are . . ." She refused to shiver, though his stare added to the cold that stole to her very bones. "They are . . . good men."

"Good men?" He stood only inches from her now. "The truth is, lass, the 'fairer' sex does not become infatuated with 'good men.' "

"Oh? And tell me, Sir Angry—in your vast experience, what does the fairer sex become infatuated with?"

"Power," he said instantly, crowding her slightly toward the window. "Money. A man's ability to heighten her station in life."

"Such a jaded soul," she said, and refused to back away, though her breathing was irregular now and her body stiff.

"Aye, I am that, lass. But I am also the heir to a dukedom. Did you know that?" he asked.

"A dukedom?" She remained where she stood, though they were almost toe to toe now. "How very impressive."

"Aye. Think on it. If you were a duchess, even the Munros would not dare bother you."

"The who?" she said, barely breathing.

"Tell me, lass, is this lying an acquired gift or did you inherit it at birth?"

"Tell me, MacGowan, who wounded you so that you cannot believe a simple truth?"

For a fleeting moment, she thought he might actually answer, but in a instant he turned away. "Take your clothes off."

Her throat closed up, choked with fear. "What?"

"Your clothes," he said, still not turning toward her. "I'll not have your death on me hands. Remove your clothes afore you die of the ague."

"You, sir," she said, "have an astounding sense of the preposterous."

"And you, Notmary, have a grave need to return to

your homeland, though I do not know why. Still, me- thinks your return would be more advantageous if you were alive rather than dead."

"How far sighted of you. But I have no intention of dying just yet."

"Then take off your clothes."

"Are you threatening me?"

He swore with astounding verve. Pivoting toward her, he grabbed her arm.

She gave a squeak of terror and froze.

"Damnation, woman," he said, looking shocked. "What are you so afraid of?"

"N—nothing," she said, and raised her chin, though it bobbled on the lift.

He stared at her in puzzlement for a moment, then snorted. "*Nothing!* You lack the good sense of a goat. I have come through fight and flood to keep you safe, yet you think I would threaten you now?" For an instant his expression softened, but he firmed it with a glare. "Turn around."

She couldn't. Couldn't move, dared not speak, lest her voice betray her yet again.

Their gazes held, but in a second he spun her away with one hand. In an instant she felt his fingers on her laces. Her lungs cramped with fear, and her muscles knotted as her gown loosened. She felt a breath of air on her shoulders and prepared to bolt, but even before she moved, his fingers fell away.

"There you be, then." His tone was oddly hoarse. "I will . . ." She heard him back away and turned, care- fully holding her gown in place. "I will see what keeps your bath," he said.

In a moment, he was gone. The room was empty but for the memory of the warmth of his hand, the deep timbre of his voice. Why had he not pressed his advantage? 'Twas surely not because he lacked the strength. Nor that he lacked the opportunity. She herself had declared him her husband. Therefore, in the eyes of god and king, he had the right to do with her as he would. None would come to her rescue. So why . . .

Kindness!

The word came to her mind unbidden.

Kindness and cunning. Power and peacefulness. Loving and . . .

But no. She pushed the ragged thoughts from her head.

She had no time to consider such girlish ideals. He was a man—selfish, dangerous.

She peeled the wet gown from her skin with some effort. It was heavy, scraping along the gooseflesh that erupted from her arms and chest. Stepping from the sodden pile, she hugged herself as she snatched a blanket from the bed and wrapped it quickly about her frigid body. Then, still freezing cold, she crawled onto the straw stuffed mattress and snuggled beneath the covers.

Minutes ticked away as she warmed slowly. Fatigue slipped in on silent feet. Her eyes dropped closed.

A knock. "Me lady?"

She awoke with a start, unable to guess how long she'd been sleeping. Knuckles rapped at the door once again.

"Who's there?" she called.

" 'Tis the house servants, bearing your bathing tub."

She called them in, and the door creaked open. Two young women, one short and buxom, one tall and handsome, shimmied into the room, carrying a barrel between them. It stood barely two feet wide and three long, but when the maids exited, Anora dropped the blanket and stepped gratefully inside. Warmth rose up her legs like a blessed tide. She lowered herself, filling the tub. The liquid heaven rose higher, covering her breasts, shivering over her shoulders. Reaching for the sliver of soap left by the servants, she washed luxuriously until the water was milky white. It flowed over her shoulders in kindly waves, relaxing her muscles, easing her—

The door opened abruptly.

Anora sank into the vat, splashing water as she went.

"So." Ramsay stood in the doorway. "Your bath arrived."

It took her several seconds to catch her breath. "Why are you here?"

"To assist me bonny bride with her bath, of course."

"Get out," she said, but his dark gaze was steady on her face as he closed the door behind him. Striding to the bed, he tossed a white bundle on the surface and turned. "Not even if you pelted me with rotten apples," he said, and chuckled as he lifted a bottle toward her. "Here, 'twill warm you up the faster."

Sunk to her shoulders in the barrel, she glared at him. "You've been drinking."

He bowed. "Aye, me bonny lass. That I have."

"Leave here."

"You forget, me love. We are wed."

"I'd sooner wed a swine."

"First the fruit and then the swine. Best be cautious, Notmary, or you'll find yourself abed with a boar," he said, and grinned as he took another swig from the bottle.

"Not in this lifetime," she said.

"Not in this lifetime what?"

She didn't answer, but watched him carefully.

"You'll not wed or you'll not wed a bore?"

Silence echoed in the room for a moment.

"Surely every woman wishes to wed," she said.

He studied her in silence, his expression solemn now. "Then why do you tremble when men touch you?"

Her breath caught in her throat, but she refused to look away. Or maybe she could not. "You should not judge my actions by the way I am with you."

"So 'tis just me that you find so objectionable?"

For a moment she saw something in his face, a fleeting emotion she could not quite place. "Surely you cannot blame me for being choosy."

As he stepped closer to the tub, sharp edged scrutiny replaced whatever emotion she had seen in his expression. "Surely not," he said. "You have a right and a duty to be choosy. After all, you are the lady of Levenlair."

Did he say it with sarcasm? "Aye, I am," she said, sinking lower still.

"And therefore you must be cautious not to wed beneath yourself," he added, and rested a hand on the edge of the bathing tub.

She forced herself to keep breathing and refused to look at his fingers, though they were very close and undeniably powerful. "Aye," she agreed.

"But what if you found that you were beneath me?"

She forced a laugh. "Beneath you? Have you any idea the blood that flows through my veins? My mother's kin are—"

"Mayhap I meant it in a more physical sense," he said, and leaned closer.

The breath caught in her throat in a hard knot. "Touch me and I swear you shall regret having ever met me."

He stared at her, unmoving for a moment, and then straightened slowly. "I fear you are too late with that warning, lass. Now, out with you," he said, his tone tired.

"Out?"

"Of the tub."

"You're mad."

"Very possibly true. Get out."

She glanced right and left, found nothing with which to hide herself and turned frantically back toward him. "You'll have to leave first."

"Nay."

"Then—"

"Get out," he repeated calmly.

"Turn . . ." Her voice shook. She calmed it with all the strength that was in her. "Turn your back," she ordered.

He only grinned.

Fear congealed in her stomach. Beneath the water, her hands trembled. "Please," she murmured.

The silence lasted forever, her gut tightened even more, but just when she was certain he would refuse, he turned away.

She didn't delay an instant. Reaching for the towel that hung a few feet away, she rose from the water and covered herself in one fleeting movement. The towel whipped over the surface of her bath, then swept around her body, spraying water as it went. She saw a droplet land on the dark crown of MacGowan's hair and stood frozen for a moment, mesmerized by the sight.

"Can I assume you are decent?"

His words spurred her back into action. Lurching over the edge of the tub, she rushed for the bed . . . and felt her feet slip out from under her. Her stomach jerked, her body tottered, and her feet did a wild little dance of desperation. She tried to stifle her cry of fear, but it slipped out unheeded. He turned with the speed of a giant cat, grasping her by a bare arm and dragging her back to stability.

She found her balance with some difficulty, her heart pounding like a drum in her chest.

"Lass." His voice was low, his lips very near. "Are you quite well?"

"I . . . certainly," she said, and raised her chin a notch though her heart still pounded. "I am fine, and . . ." She chanced a glance at his face. So close. So solemn. "And I had no need of your help."

"Ahh." He drew a deep breath and nodded slightly. "Then I must assume your little dance was enacted solely in the hope of attracting me attention."

She pulled her gaze frantically to his, but he was already laughing. "Have a care, Notmary," he said, and reaching out, casually tucked her drooping towel more firmly between her breasts. "I have no wish to cart an injured lass halfway across Scotland."

Stepping back a pace, he kicked off his boots and let his cloak fall to the floor. Then he lifted his hands to the cat-faced brooch that secured his plaid to his tunic. It came away and in a moment he was tugging the end of the great plaid from beneath his belt. She stared, mesmerized, but then reality cracked into her brain.

"What are you about?" she gasped.

"I am about . . ." He loosened the wide leather band from his waist. "To have meself a bathe."

"What?" For just one moment she feared her eyes might pop like ripe grapes out of their sockets.

"A bath," he said, and let his belt fall to the floor.

She watched it drop, then shifted her gaze with lightning speed back to his face. "You cannot."

"I assure you," he said, and tugged his tartan away from his body, "I can, and I shall." His plaid fell away. He stood in nothing but his tunic now, and though his shirt reached to mid-thigh, she felt her face sizzle at the sight. ". . . Away."

Belatedly realizing he'd been talking, Anora shifted her attention to his face.

He shrugged and reached for the edge of his shirt.

"What! What?" she said, stumbling backward and bumping unceremoniously into the very vessel she had just exited.

He scowled at her as if she were pesky and perhaps somewhat daft. "I said, I am not so selfish with the sight of me own bared body as you. So if you are weak disciplined, you may wish to turn away."

She felt the rough, warm wood of the barrel against her bare calves, but kept her hands clenched in the top of the towel that hugged her body.

He stared at her. "Lass," he said finally, "I fear if I disrobe before your eyes, you may faint dead away, and I must warn you, I'm loath to waste me time on reviving you."

His words seeped slowly into her consciousness. She pursed her lips. "Let me assure you," she said, swallowing and stiffening her spine, "you have naught that would addle my wits."

He opened his mouth as if to speak, then simply bent his arm over his shoulder, grasped the back of his tunic, and whisked it over his head.

Her jaw came unhinged. She bumbled backward and felt the tub teeter with the force of her weight, but couldn't pull her paralyzed gaze from his nether parts.

Only when he took a step forward did her attention snap to his face. She tried to escape, but she was frozen in place, trapped between the tub and his solid weight.

She dared not breathe, dared not move. He loomed over her. But it was neither his height nor his bulk than paralyzed her. It was his arousal.

Long and thick, it reared near the flat expanse of his abdomen.

She had seen that before, had felt the terrible ravages, and fear froze her in place.

His hands closed around her arms.

"Nay!" she cowered away, but he was already pulling her forward, and there was no one to save her.

Chapter 10

His eyes bore into hers. His hands felt like talons around her arms, and against her thigh, she felt the hard crush of his desire.

Panic choked her, cutting off her breath. "Nay!" The single word barely creaked past her lips. Terror burned like bile in her soul, but in that moment he pressed her impatiently aside.

"Damnation!" he growled. "Can I not even bathe without you blocking me way?"

She stared at him as he stepped into the tub. Her heart thumped back into action. Her knees threatened to spill her to the floor.

"Hand me the soap."

It took a moment before her voice would function. "Wh—what?"

"The soap," he said, and dunked his head beneath the water's rippled surface. He reappeared a moment later, seal slick hair washed back from his dark features. Only one narrow, recalcitrant lock dared leave its brethren and brave the hard mass of his chest. Dark as midnight, it curled silkily around the dusky circle of his nipple.

She stared.

He scowled, first at her, then at the soap, and she wrenched her brain back into working order. Trying to disavow the tremor in her hand, she reached for the bar of tallow and lye, but when she handed it over, the missile slipped like a loosed arrow from her fingers and rocketed off his shoulder.

He winced, and though his fingers were working at loosing one narrow braid, his gaze never left her face. "Your intentions may be cruel," he said, "but your aim is fair to middling."

Only then did she notice his wound. It sliced across his bicep in a line of red so angry it was nearly black.

She caught her breath. "Is that from. . . ." Words failed. "From when—"

"From when I saved your hide?" His tone was casual, as if he'd saved women every day of his life since infancy. "Aye," he said, and loosed the other braid before raking his hair back from his hard edged features. The solitary strand of hair skimmed reluctantly away from his chest.

"Oh." Somehow she hadn't thought . . . she hadn't envisioned. In truth, she hadn't realized what a crime it would seem to wound him, to defile such beautiful—

Beautiful what? The thought struck her suddenly, and she stopped all movement, listening to her heart beat like a smithy's rounding hammer against her ribs.

Men were not beautiful. They were cold and selfish—tyrants whom she must outmaneuver at every turn. She glanced at him again, reminding herself that he was not beautiful. She must be deluded, faint, overwrought, she thought, but as her gaze skimmed downward again, she realized her mistake. Even a selfish tyrant could be a thing of physical splendor.

Water lapped at his hard packed belly. Sculpted like an ancient god, he was nearly twice her size, easily able to overpower her, and yet he had not . . .

"Get dressed."

She snapped her attention foggily to his face. "What?"

"There's a gown on the bed." He nodded in that direction. The slick, roguish lock of hair she'd noticed earlier slid from its mates and reached with sultry slyness for his nipple again. "Put it on afore you catch the ague."

She opened her mouth, although she wasn't at all certain what she meant to say. That single lock of hair held her mesmerized, breathless, lost.

"I'll not look."

Not look? As if he expected her to trust him. As if she were so naive that she would believe his words simply because he spoke them. 'Twas ridiculous, of course, and yet when she found his gaze again, she had no strength to insist that he turn aside. Instead, she paced stiffly toward the bed.

The gown was a simple thing. Made of white linen, it was laced at the throat and wrists with blue ribbon. A bed gown. The reality of the situation struck her like a blow. They would be sharing this pallet, forced together like man and wife, with nothing to save her from his advances.

She glanced nervously over her shoulder, and found that despite her own nervous wonderings, his head was back, his eyes closed as he scrubbed his hair with the depleted sliver of soap.

He showed not the least bit of interest in her. Nay, 'twas more than disinterest, she realized. He hated her. Her stomach flipped.

'Twas fear that made her feel so strangely, she thought, but a tiny inkling in her mind wondered. True, she did not like him, yet he made her feel strangely unsteady.

But that was hardly a mystery: it had not been an easy week. Indeed, anyone might become unbalanced. It meant nothing. Nothing had changed. She would return to Evermyst, for she missed everything about it— the dizzying heights, the crumbling towers. But mostly she missed her people; Isobel's soft spoken witticisms, Meara's advice. Even the old women's bickering arguments were missed.

She would return home and do what she must. After all, feelings mattered little to men. Only coupling ... her thoughts crashed to a halt and her stomach fluttered.

Glancing once more in Ramsay's direction, Anora whipped the gown over her head. Then, beneath the security of the floor-length linen, she unwrapped the towel and let it fall to the floor.

One more glance assured her that he still was not looking. She stepped out from the ring of towel, hung in on a nearby peg, and returned silently to the bed.

Nerves jumping, she wrung her hands and paced again, casting wary glances in his direction.

"Ague."

She stopped mid-stride at the sound of his voice, but he had not even turned toward her. Instead, he scrubbed studiously at an underarm. The muscles in his chest danced with the movement. She tore her gaze from them and prepared to ask what he meant, but the truth dawned on her. His one mission in life was to be rid of her. If she became sick with the ague that goal might very well be delayed.

She crawled nervously into bed and dragged the blankets over her bent knees. Only minutes before, this very spot had seemed heavenly, but now the mattress felt lumpy, her nerves stretched tight. She sat very still, trying to breathe normally, but there was nothing to do, nowhere to look . . . except at him.

"Our meal should arrive soon." He didn't glance at her as he spoke. Neither did he wince as he scrubbed at his wound. "Try to sleep until then."

While he was there? In her room, with his clothes lying in a sodden heap and his body bare—

"Will you cease staring at me!" he growled.

She turned jerkily away, but there was nothing else to see. "I . . ." She was out of her depth, shaky and uncertain "I am sorry."

"You're *what?*" The surprise in his voice was clear.

She tucked her knees closer to her chest and scowled at the window as the seconds ticked past. She plucked fretfully at a loose thread in the blanket, then flitted her gaze to his. "I am not without feelings."

He snorted and rubbed absently at his broad chest. "Ahh," he said. "I see. You jest."

The room fell quiet, and in the silence she felt suddenly very alone and weary. She would give much for someone to trust, to share her troubles, to lighten her load. But she had no one. Only she could protect her people—kindly Helena, clumsy but ever loyal Duncan, even poor Deirdre's fate was in her hands. She must be smart, careful. She would use what she could when she must, and waste nothing, especially this man's strength, so long as she had access to it. Aye, she must play her part carefully, lest her people suffer for her failure.

"I can bandage that for you," she said, her voice small and soft.

His glower was daunting. She shifted her gaze breathlessly away.

"Why?" he asked.

"I . . ." She pursed her lips and blinked at the blankets. "I cannot bear to see you hurt."

He laughed. "Why do you offer, Notmary?"

"My name is not Notmary!" Anger mixed with a dozen unknown emotions.

"Could it be that you make the offer because you are attracted to me?" he asked.

Her breathing stopped, but she lifted her chin slowly. " 'Tis yet a far way to me homeland," she said.

"Ahh, so you still need me."

"You'd do me little good dead."

He watched her for a moment, then chuckled. "Honesty. From you," he said and grinned. " 'Tis almost worth the wounding."

She knew she should be insulted. Should, in fact, argue, and yet she could not, for she was mesmerized. Why, she wasn't certain. His teeth were imperfect, his dimples unbalanced. Yet she could not look away, could not draw her gaze from the tilted wonderment of his smile.

A new kind of fear curled in her stomach.

He sobered. "Me arm will be fine," he assured her, his tone low. "You needn't worry. I have no intention of dying. Not before I return you to Levenlair, at the least."

"I . . ." She wrenched her gaze away. "My thanks."

"I'm not planning to survive for your sake alone." Even when he scowled, his eyes were hopelessly entrancing, deep and dark and filled with secrets he did not share.

She fidgeted and forced her gaze to the blankets. It was a strangely difficult task. "I will bind your wound."

Silence. She glanced up, and he shrugged. Muscles, bare and shining wet, bulged and relaxed.

"As you will," he said and placed his hands on the rim of the tub, but there he paused expectantly. She stared at him. "I am about to rise."

"Oh!" she said and froze.

"I would suggest you turn away."

"Oh," she repeated and slipped a shaky palm over her eyes. She heard his splashing exit and kept her gaze carefully averted as he padded across the floor.

"Are you . . . covered?"

"Me plaid is drying," he said.

Did that mean he planned to remain naked? Her heart rate bumped up a pace.

"But fear not. There are extra linens."

She wished to come up with some rejoinder, but found that all words were stuck tight in her throat.

'Twas then that the bed creaked. Yanking her hand from her eyes, Anora found herself staring point blank into his.

He shrugged, so close she could watch the languid progress of one tiny droplet as it made its way between the tightly packed mounds of his chest. "There is nowhere else to sit," he said.

She struggled to breathe.

"Me laird?"

Anora jumped at the sound of the voice from the far side of the door.

"Aye?" He turned with a scowl, his lower body wrapped in a towel.

"Be you ready to sup?"

"Aye," he said. "Come straightaway."

The door creaked open. Two maids stood in the entryway. The nearer bobbed a curtsy. She was small and plump, with pink cheeks and a goodly mass of bosom straining to escape her bodice. "Cheers, me laird. Me lady." She curtsied again. "Me name is Glenna. And this be Mary. Just new to the inn," she said and nodded rather curtly toward the woman behind her. Mary was considerably taller, straight of back and solemn, with strong shoulders and an entrancing face. It was not beautiful, exactly, but fascinating enough to draw Anora's attention from Ramsay for a moment.

"Mary," he mused, glancing momentarily at Anora. "A much revered and oft used name."

"Aye," Anora said, feeling breathless as she glanced back at MacGowan.

He turned his attention slowly from her face. "What have you brought for us, then?" he asked.

Anora noticed that he made no attempt to hide the great length of his muscular thighs from the servants.

She also noticed that Glenna made no pretense of ignoring the display. " 'Tis Farley's best for you, we've brought. Hot pigeon pie and sweet mead."

"Me thanks," he said and stood to receive the meal, but Glenna waved him back even as she advanced.

"Do not disturb yourself, Sir. You've had yourself a hard—oh!" she gasped and bobbled the pitcher in her hand.

Anora held her breath and followed the woman's gaze.

"Your arm, me laird! 'Tis wounded."

He glanced toward it, then gave the maid an encouraging smile. " 'Tis good of you to notice, but not to worry, lass. 'Tis not important."

" 'Tis," she countered, and hurried breathlessly forward. "It must be seen to, and I've some skill at the healing arts."

"You are kind," he said. "But you need not—"

"But I must," she argued, so near now that her bosom bobbled nearly under his very nose. His dark brows rose a fraction of an inch. "I must before—"

" 'Tis his wife's task." 'Twas the tall maid who spoke. They turned in unison to stare at her.

"What?" Glenna asked coolly.

The woman scowled back, looking uncomfortable under their scrutiny. Anora held her breath.

"Surely 'tis the lady's right to see to her husband's wounds."

"Oh. Of course," said Glenna. "I simply thought . . . that is to say . . . some women do not care to be bothered . . ." Her gaze skimmed his bare chest and lower. "I only mean . . . I am available . . . if the lady has no wish to see to your needs."

Silence echoed in the room for a resounding second,

then, "Your food," said the tall maid, and striding forward, shoved a wooden trencher into Ramsay's hands. Honey mead sloshed over the rim of the horn mug as the tray bumped aggressively into his chest. He steadied it absently and raised his gaze, but she was already backing away, wiping her palms hard against her drab skirt as she did so. "Give him the pitcher," she ordered, her tone low, but the other maid just stared, seeming transfixed by a small droplet of ale that slid lazily between his pectorals.

"Now!" Mary ordered, and elbowed the other with some force.

"What? Oh!" said Glenna and jumped, red faced. "Your drink. Of course," she said and thrust the clay vessel toward him. Bobbling the trencher, he took the mead while Glenna wrung her hands and managed to step back a pace. "Might there be anything else you need?"

"Nay." His voice sounded somewhat confused. "I do not think—"

"A larger linen, mayhap?" Glenna's gaze swept longingly downward.

He shifted his leg, managing to hide a few scant inches of bulging thigh from her view.

"More bread? A—"

"We must away," Mary said.

"A change of garments!" Glenna gasped, seeing his wet plaid hanging nearby, but Mary was glowering now.

"Come along," she said.

Glenna turned on her. "You'll not be giving me orders your first day on the job," she snarled, but continued to back from the room. "Please, me laird," she said, sweet faced again, "if you be in need of anything, anything at all, you've but to—"

The door slammed on the last few words, and the room fell into silence.

Ramsay cleared his throat and shifted uncomfortably. "That was . . . unusual."

"Was it?" Anora asked, keeping her voice carefully cool.

He turned his eyes toward her and scowled. "You did not notice?"

"Notice what?"

"The maid, Mary. Did she not seem . . ." He shrugged, looking perplexed. "Familiar?"

Familiar? Nay. But there was something about her . . . something that she could not quite place.

"And the maid, Glenna." He scowled. "Did she not seem somewhat . . ."

"Enamored?"

He stared at her, and then he grinned. It was just the slightest tilting of his lips, but her stomach tightened at the boyish expression. "I am flattered, lass, but I was about to say, confused."

She felt her face warm beneath his perusal, but refused to lower her gaze. "Is there a difference?"

They sat immobile, watching each other from ridiculously close proximity for an endless moment. Then, "Eat," he said, and twisting about, set the trencher on the bed between them.

He didn't have to tell her twice. Reaching for the round loaf of bread, she wrested off a dark piece. Though overdone and somewhat stale, it tasted like heaven when she took a bite. He did the same, then drank a swig from the mug and handed it over.

The mead was gold and mellow, warming her immediately. She reached for the wooden ladle that rested on the trencher. The pie's crust was bubbled and brown, and when she cut into it the scent of the filling wafted upward in a warm cloud that made her lightheaded with hunger. Scooping up a bit of the filling, she tasted the broth. It was rich and warm, a delicious meld of spices and meats.

" 'Tis a strange opinion for one so young."

She paused with her hand midway back to the pie.

He held the mug loosely in one hand, and she noticed how his fingers, though long and powerful, looked as sensitive as a scholar's as they curved around the hollowed horn. "How is it that you know the correlation between being enamored and confused at such a tender age?"

Tension tightened her stomach, pushing hunger aside. " 'Tis not only the passing of time that teaches wisdom," she said, and replaced the ladle on the trencher.

"What, then?"

"Are you not hungry?" she asked.

"Can I not be hungry and curious all at once?"

"Nay." She said the word before she spoke, then scowled and took another hunk of bread, though her own hunger had dulled.

He shrugged, unconcerned. The room fell into silence as he ate. She tasted the pudding again, but it had lost its euphoric flavor, for her mind continued to turn like a burning spit.

"You did not disagree," she said finally, and though she refused to turn toward him, she could feel his gaze on her, dark and moody.

Keep quiet, she told herself, and fiddled with the ladle as she struggled to obey her own commands, but it was no use. "So you think love is naught but foolishness?" she asked.

He lowered the mug and scowled. "I said nothing of love."

"But 'tis true," she said, examining the pie. "You do not believe it exists."

Not a sound echoed in the silence for a moment, but he spoke finally. "You have met the Flame and you have met the Rogue."

She watched him. "Your parents." Something akin to pain tightened around her heart. "They have love?"

He emptied the mug and refilled it from the pitcher. "She lives for him." His tone was matter of fact, but his eyes . . . there was some emotion in his dark, soulful eyes that she could not quite name. "He would die for her."

The words fell like dusk into the quiet of the room.

"Is that love, then?" Her voice was much quieter than she'd intended.

"Is that what you believe?" he asked, and their eyes met.

For a moment it seemed as if her heart were beating in slow motion, as if the entire universe had slowed its daily march. She tore her gaze from his with an effort. "I do not believe in love," she said and forced herself to scoop out a spoonful of meat and broth.

"What do you believe in?"

"Survival." The word came out of its own accord. She knew immediately that she should not have loosed it, for honesty was not a luxury she could afford.

"At all costs?" he asked.

She wanted to lie. But his eyes were so steady on hers. "What else is there?" she asked.

"Some seem to find more."

"I need no more."

He watched her. She could tell without glancing up. "Not even a family?"

Family! Her gut twisted in fear. In her mind's eye she revisited her dream—saw the hulking form of the Munro bent over Isobel. Or was it herself he tormented? Sometimes the dreams were skewed, the meanings uncertain.

"You have you no wish for children?" he asked.

"Children?" She glanced up, surprised from her own tumbling thoughts and he scowled, his mouth tight.

"Some think the need for family is a greater drive than any other."

"And some think to improve their own lot through the sale of their offspring."

"What?"

She berated herself silently. "Here," she said and shoved the trencher toward him. "I have had enough."

"Sale?" he asked, undeterred.

"Why else would a father promise away his daughter?"

"Have you been promised?"

She loosened her muscles with a careful effort. "My own father has been dead for nearly a year, and ill some time afore that. I was speaking of the practice in general."

"Have you been promised?" he asked again, his voice a low monotone.

She couldn't look at him. " 'Twas decided some

time ago that the women of . . . Levenlair . . . would
choose their own mates."

"Decided by whom?"

"The king. It seems he was quite fond of the maid
Mother saved from death."

"Your mother? She is a healer?"

"She was . . . observant." Anora glanced toward the
window. The sky outside was growing dark. "And no
stranger to the sea. 'Twas from the parapet that she noticed the failing ship."

"Ahh." He drank again and bent one knee so that
the linen slipped down his powerful thigh like a slow
tide. "So you are free to marry for love, and yet you
do not believe it exists. There is some irony in that, I
suppose."

"And what of you, Ramsay of Dun Ard? Despite
your parents' affection, you seem no more certain of
love than I."

He shrugged and passed her the mug. "Here.
Drink," he said. Their fingers met for a moment
against the smooth horn before he pulled his away and
she could not help but notice the warmth of his flesh,
could not stop the gossamer shimmer of feeling that
shivered down her spine.

She dropped her gaze with lightning speed. "What
do you believe in, MacGowan?" she asked.

He dropped his dark head against the bed's oaken
frame, exposing the taut tendons in his throat and
seeming to pull her gaze downward, over the hard
muscles of his chest. "Lust," he said quietly. "I am a
true believer in lust."

Chapter 11

"Lust!" Her eyes looked skeptical and cool in her ivory face, but her hand was curled as tight as a frightened child's against the coverlet. "What is there to believe of lust?"

He shrugged, careful to appear as distant as she. "Lust will gain us what we most yearn for. 'Tis the way of man."

"But not the way of women."

"Nay?" He glanced at her. Aye, she was beautiful. Despite the fact that he neither trusted nor liked her, he could no longer deny that. "What do you lust for?"

"There is naught I—" she began, but he interrupted with a snort.

"There is no reason to lie, Notmary. I will see you safely to Levenlair regardless of your answer."

She straightened slightly, and her breasts pressed more firmly against the fortunate fabric of her gown. He scowled and pulled his gaze back to her eyes, for 'twas her eyes that could lie so damnably well. "I lust after nothing," she said.

And not a flicker of discord in her expression, but the tendons in her hands tightened almost imperceptibly.

He almost smiled. "What then brought you to Dun Ard?"

"I believe 'twas you, if your brothers' stories be true."

He canted his head in concession to her answer which was no answer at all. "And what brought you from the north?"

"I told you already. My cousin was with child and needed comforting."

"What cousin was that?"

She paused not for an instant. "Lillias, the Lamonts' middle daughter."

"And?"

"And what?"

"Did she bear the child safely?"

"Oh." She fidgeted with the coverlet for the briefest of moments. "Aye. Thanks be to God. All is well."

"A son or a daughter?"

" 'Tis a girl."

A dozen emotions twisted unexpectedly in his heart, but he shoved them impatiently aside as he delved deeper. "Ahh, a wee lassie. What be her name?"

"I . . ." For a fraction of an instant, her eyes widened and her quick answers ceased.

" 'Tis not Mary, is it?" he asked, keeping his voice innocent.

She dropped her gaze to her hands. "You mock me," she said.

Regret sliced through him, for without her cool eyes and regal expression, she seemed small and afraid. He longed to reach for her, to pull her into his arms and promise to keep her safe from the world. But there was a limit to his foolishness. Still, he could not quite manage to make his voice hard when he next spoke.

"You do not necessarily seem the type to comfort a cousin during her lying in. I am merely curious about your reasons," he said. " 'Twas a long journey from your home in the north just to console your kinswoman."

"Some think the need for family a stronger drive than any other." She quoted him almost exactly.

"But surely your family at Levenlair needs you also. Your sisters or—"

"I have no sister."

He scowled at her speedy answer. "And what of your mother?"

"She . . . drowned . . . some years back."

"Drowned?"

"She was not a witch!"

Sweet Almighty, what was that all about? he wondered, and stared at her in open surprise. Her eyes, for once, were guileless and as wide as forever. "I did not think she—"

"She merely loved the sea. Some do. My maid servant is also quite adept at swimming. There's naught unusual in that, surely." She watched him for an eternal moment, then shifted her gaze back to her hands. "But I fear the sea did not love my mother in return."

"Thus you have no family."

"I have family. Stout Helena was my uncle's wife.

My maid, Isobel, is as dear as a sister to me, and Ailsa, who cares for the goats, is my cousin's—"

"I meant, no immediate family. No siblings or parents."

"Nay."

"Mayhap that is why you do not believe in love."

Her eyes flickered up. "Your brothers . . . do you love them?"

He scowled, searching for an answer that would not undermine any masculinity she might believe him to possess. "In an irritating sort of way, aye."

The beginning of a smile twitched her lips, but she sobered in an instant. "And I, too, care for my own people. Therefore I must reach home. I do not deny that I need your help, MacGowan. Thus, I would bind your wound now so that I can achieve that end sooner."

She reached out and touched his arm. Warmth skittered across his flesh in the wake of her fingertips and all hope of sensible dialogue fled like loosed doves.

"I do not think it requires stitches," she said.

"Nay." He dropped his head back against the bed board again and refused to look at her. Lust was good and well to talk about, but he knew better than to allow such feral emotions into his own life. Better by far to remain distant, controlled, aloof. But maybe he'd drunk a bit much to reach for those lofty standards. 'Twas to be hoped, though, that it was not too late for sanity. "It will heal on its own," he said, and congratulated himself for his outstanding rational.

" 'Tis hot to the touch," she said.

Aye, beneath her fingertips, he did indeed feel warm. He refused to look at her, as part of his bid for sanity. "Do not worry yourself," he said, but she was already rising. For a moment he glimpsed a flash of trim ankle. He'd always had a weakness for trim ankles, but in a moment her gown fell modestly back in place. Still, his wick had a damnably fine memory, and it stood alert, lest she bare the tiniest scrap of skin again, and it be called into emergency service.

Ramsay watched her hurry away from the bed with the remainder of their meal. In a moment she was bending away from him. Her bottom, hugged by her saintly gown, was shown to rounded perfection. His desire swelled to aching proportions. He'd always had a weakness for round bottoms hugged by . . . in that instant she turned, his dirk clasped in her delicate hand.

"What are your plans for me blade?" he asked, keeping his tone level.

"Are you worried?"

"Should I be?"

"Mayhap," she said and eyed his chest for an instant. "If I were the lustful sort."

"Ahh, fortunate I am, then."

"Indeed," she said and putting her knife to a bathing linen, sliced twice into the edge. She ripped off two strips, rolled the cloth into misshapen bundles and retraced her steps to the bed. Retrieving the bottle he'd brought earlier, she doused a rag and settled next to him on the mattress. It sighed happily beneath her tight little bottom. Ramsay gritted his teeth to keep from doing the same.

"Are you well?" she asked, pausing with the cloth only inches from his wound.

"Aye." He exhaled deliberately, tried to relax, and reached, in some desperation, for the bottle. She touched the cloth to his wound just as he took his first sip. It tasted considerably better than it felt, but it was the slow brush of her fingers against his flesh that forced the hiss from his lips.

"I hurt you."

"Nay." He took another drink.

"I am sorry."

"That you did not hurt me?"

"Nay." Retrieving a rolled bandage, she set the edge to his arm. "That you are such a poor liar."

He chuckled, but the mere rasp of her knuckles as they slanted across his chest was almost more than he could bear. Surely mead could drown his desire. 'Twas said to have strong calming powers, but thus far his wick didn't seem the least bit calm.

The silence in the room was smothering.

She cleared her throat. "You are dark."

He could actually feel the tickle of her breath against his shoulder. The linen across his lap strained. "Aye." Her hair was drying to feathery softness. He balled his hands to fists and concentrated on the pain. It was pathetically easy to ignore, so he thought about porridge. He had a strong revulsion for porridge. "I bear French blood on me mother's side."

"And hard," she said.

"What?" He snapped his gaze to hers. She reared back as if struck.

"Scarred!" she said, wide eyed and undeniably startled. "You are scarred."

He glared at her, his torso feeling too tight to accommodate all the necessary organs. "Oh."

She leaned fractionally nearer to continue her job and the backs of her fingers slid languidly against the straining muscles of his side. "How . . ." She cleared her throat again. He couldn't help but notice that her cheeks were pink with color that fingered delicately toward her bosom. He dragged his gaze away and remembered how porridge looked after it had cooled and congealed. "How did you come by the scars?"

Her voice was like nothing he had ever heard. Husky yet soft, and each whispered note seemed to pump his manhood more firmly toward his belly.

"The scars." He dragged his attention back to her question. "I have brothers."

"And I used to resent not having siblings," she said, still bandaging. How damn long were those cloths?

"The scars were not intentional . . . usually," he said.

"That one?" she asked, nodding toward his shoulder.

She was sitting painfully close, and each time she wrapped the cloth, her knee nudged his thigh. Porridge with gizzards! he thought frantically, and took a good long swig from the bottle. Ah, yes, he could remember how it smelled after it had been congealing for a day, but it was difficult to concentrate on it like he should, and if he didn't answer she was likely to believe any sort of outlandish nonsense. Such as, her touch was driving him toward the teetering edge of insanity, and if she didn't stop soon, he would be tempted beyond control to do something truly idiotic.

The back side of her wrist brushed his ribs, but her gaze remained on that half forgotten scar. He gritted his teeth and dredged up a memory. "Lachlan always felt a need to prove himself me equal, even when he was no bigger than a hare."

"He attacked you?" Her eyes were soft and wide, but he refused to notice.

"He hid himself in a tree and planned to land just in front of me as I walked beneath. The element of surprise has always appealed to him."

"But?"

"But he misjudged and landed atop me. Bullock had made him a wee wooden sword which Lachlan always kept strapped to his hip. 'Twas a more effective weapon than any of us suspected," he said.

"And that one?" she asked, staring at a nick on the underside of his forearm. " 'Tis fresh."

"Me brother Iain is still young."

"It should be cleaned."

"I cleaned it."

"With mead," she said, and reached across his body with her doused rag.

He tried to tell her no, to stop her from leaning across him, but he couldn't force out the word. And though her breasts never actually touched him, his lungs compressed as if her bosom were pressed with heartfelt passion against his, as if he could feel the peaked bliss of them against his naked chest. The rich, warm scent of her filled his head, and the innocent brush of her gown against his bare leg was nearly more than he could bear.

Their faces were mere inches apart, the sassy tilt of her lips a breath away.

He hated her! his mind argued, but his doltish desire didn't care a whit. Holding his breath, he reached out, no more able to stop himself than to still the beat of his heart. Her hair felt blissfully soft against his fingertips, and her skin, when he touched it, seemed like heaven. She didn't move, didn't speak. Instead, she sat perfectly still as he skimmed down the delicate length of her throat and curved his hand behind her neck. He gave her one more chance to fly, gave himself one more chance to think, but the only organ that seemed to be functioning properly was insisting that he not think. That he just act.

He leaned closer. At the base of her throat, a pulse thrummed with insistent life. She stared at him, lips parted and so tempting that there was nothing he could do. Nothing but kiss her.

Their lips met softly. Desire roared like fire in his veins, consuming all thought. But he couldn't afford to be consumed. He tried to pull away, to stop such madness, but he had lost all control to his least productive organ. So instead he leaned closer, deepening the kiss, and she moaned against the caress.

It was that single, raspy sound of desire that ripped away all hope of control. He pulled her to him. Her breasts crushed against his bare skin, igniting a thousand fires in his soul. Her waist felt tight against his palm and when he cupped his hand over the delectable curve of her buttocks—

"Nay!" She rasped the word into his mouth.

It took him a moment of hazy pain to realize she was pushing away with both hands pressed against his chest, a moment longer to force himself away.

They sat facing each other. Her breathing was ragged, her eyes impossibly large in the delicate oval of her face.

God, he was a dolt. Once again he'd read her entirely wrong. She did not desire him, did not want him at all. Yet she was not retreating, not flying to the far side of the room. She sat perfectly still, either paralyzed with fear, or . . .

Nay, he would not let himself consider the options. So he balled his hands to fists against the mattress and watched her.

"No lust?" he asked. His voice was so low it was barely audible to his own ears, but she heard him. He knew it by her eyes, and yet, for long breathless seconds she didn't speak, didn't move.

"Mary," he said, and leaned forward again.

"Nay!" she said, and jerked back, breathing hard. "Nay. No lust."

He watched her. Her eyes were as wide as the heavens, and the pulse in her throat thrummed like that of a cornered hare or like that of a woman who desperately wished to be loved. But who was he to call her liar? He was a fool, and probably far worse.

"Well, then," he said, and drawing back, shoved his feet over the edge of the bed. It was immensely difficult to move even that far, but rising was even worse, like thrusting oneself from the edge of a cliff. "I will let you take your rest."

"Where are you going?"

Anywhere but here, so near the flame when he was freezing. "Below stairs."

"In a linen?" she asked.

There was something about the way she spoke— so full of hope and hopelessness all at once that his heart felt as if it had stopped dead in his chest. But no. He would not look for hope where there was only trouble.

Reaching dismally for his plaid, he wrapped it about the towel. There were few things less inviting than five yards of wet wool. Still, its chilly weight would do him good. Belting it sloppily about his waist, he allowed himself one last glance at her. "I go to find dry garments," he said.

"Oh." Her tone was already cool. She drew her knees toward her chest and it suddenly seemed that a thousand rods were placed between them. "Of course."

"Aye. Well, good night to you, then."

"Good night."

He dragged himself toward the door, turned the handle with an effort and stepped into the hall, but as he trod along her words rang in his head.

"*Of course*," she'd said. As if she did not believe him at all. As if he were the liar.

The common room was empty but for a trio of men just finishing up their meals and a pair of serious drinkers who sat near the door. One was balding and squat, the other scrawny and listing haphazardly to the left.

A fire burned in the nearby hearth. It drew Ramsay across the room, for his damp plaid had already cooled his blood. If he was so foolish as to be aroused by a woman whom he didn't like and who didn't like him, soggy clothes had a grand way of chilling his ardor.

Lifting his hands toward the heat, he stared into the flickering flame.

She'd felt so soft in his arms, so tempting, and though she'd pushed away, it almost seemed as if she did not quite want—

Nay, he wouldn't think about that. It didn't matter. Yet her eyes had seemed so unearthly bright, and her mouth . . .

Damn! Her mouth was probably lying. While she told him she didn't want him, it trembled as if she did, while she really didn't. Did that make her a double liar or just a consummate actress?

He ground his teeth. He must have no pride at all. What kind of man made a habit of wanting women who did not want him in return?

"*Of course*," she'd said, in that seductively innocent voice. Of course he was going to find new garments. Why would he not? His own were sodden, yet she seemed to think he would lie. Why? Because 'twas what she herself would do most probably. Or—

"Me laird!"

So deep was he into his own thoughts that he jumped at the interruption.

Glenna dimpled as she curtsied. Her bosom bobbed with a rhythm of its own.

"Good eventide," she said. "I am so pleased you decided to come."

He stared.

She dimpled again. Then, reaching for his arm, she tugged him toward a chair and plopped a mug and a pitcher on the table before him. Ale sloshed over the rim. "Sit. I'll only be a short while. I've little enough to do this eve—since me master hired the new maid."

He scowled as he pulled his gaze from his ale to her face. "I need a change of garments. Mayhap you know where I could acquire a tunic and plaid."

She gave him a slanted smile. "A mite chilly in your room, was it?"

Ahh! Reality struck him somewhat belatedly. She was hoping to seduce him, just as Mary had suspected. 'Twas the very reason she had said "of course." She had expected him to fly from her arms into another's— but had there been disappointment in her voice?

He turned abruptly toward the stairs at the thought. His feet were ready to charge back up toward her, but the maid stood in his way.

"Have a seat, me laird," she purred. " 'Twill only be a few moments afore I am finished for the night."

He dragged his gaze from the stairs. "Mayhap I'll come back later," he said, and moved to step around her, but she turned, blocking his path.

"Don't go, me laird. 'Twill be a lonely night for me, as well. Drink your ale," she urged, and tugged him into the chair so that he was at eye level with her cleavage. It was deep enough to drown in.

"I shall return before you can say Colin McGinny," she said and rushed away.

He stared after her, watching the sway of her generous hips as he tasted his drink.

She was an earthy sort; earthy and honest. If the truth be told, she was the type of woman he preferred. There had once been a time when he imagined he would be one of the lucky few to marry for love. He would find a lass who needed him, who cherished him above all others. She would bear his children and they would cling together for all eternity. But that foolish dream was no more. So why the hell shouldn't he accept this buxom maid's offer?

But if Notmary was so cold—so why was he so damned randy? It wasn't as if her beauty was overwhelming, and her personality left a host of things to be desired. He drank again. Aye, she was a liar and she hoped to manipulate him. Still, he would see her safely home. 'Twas his duty, but he would do no more than that. No matter how soft her skin or how big her eyes or how lost her hands.

"*Of course*," she'd said. Regally, like a queen, yet beneath the cool tone, was there a touch of pain? Was she disappointed?

Ramsay scowled into the fire.

On the far side of the room, the trio of men finally exited quietly. Minutes slipped away, as did the ale.

"Here, then." Glenna was back, refilling his horn. "I'll be with you in a blink."

Ramsay took another swig. What if Notmary was disappointed? 'Twas probably only because she felt her grip on him slipping. Though she sometimes seemed as innocent as a lambkin, she knew he yearned for her. And *he* knew she was not above using that yearning. 'Twas the difference between her and this Glenna.

"I'll be the one to say when I've 'ad enough." The balding man's voice was raised and not entirely happy.

Glenna glanced toward Ramsay and smiled. He lifted his horn and drank to her straightforward ways as she leaned over the table. The balding man's eyes followed her bosom. Ramsay couldn't hear her words, but he thought, with the dim part of his mind that was still functioning, that the bald fellow jumped when she leaned closer.

"All right. As you wish, then," he said, and jerking from his seat, rubbed gingerly at his flat chest.

Glenna glanced toward Ramsay and dimpled another smile before turning back to her patrons and nodding toward the sleeping fellow. Again, he couldn't hear her words, but the balding fellow's were clear.

" 'E ain't my worry."

She stepped closer. The man cringed away, covering his chest with a bony hand.

"All right then. 'Arry. 'Arry, wake up."

After a bit of prodding, the second fellow was on his feet and the pair tottered from the inn.

Glenna was back at Ramsay's table in a moment. "They had to leave."

"All good things must come to an end," he said, and stared dismally at the bottom of the mead pitcher.

" 'Tis only the beginning," she countered.

He glanced up. Aye, she was offering herself, he thought as his eyes fell into her cleavage. And the lovely bit was . . . there was no reason for him to refuse. Certainly not because of Mary. She was the last one to care.

"So . . ." She took the chair next to his and propped her elbows upon the table. "Shall we get you out of that wet plaid?" Her bosom swelled with lively enthusiasm as she squeezed her arms together. He liked bosoms with lively enthusiasm.

His gaze followed its rise and fall. It was a bonny sight, and she was eager, unlike Mary, who had said in so many words that she had no interest at all.

Aye, his mind argued. But her fairy quick hands—

"Your lordship," Glenna crooned, and crushed her breast against his biceps.

Damn her fairy quick hands, Ramsay thought.

"Glenna!"

Ramsay shifted his gaze toward the newcomer as Glenna did the same. It was the tall maid who had brought the meal to his room. The tall maid with the regal bearing and the steely eyes. There was something about her that appealed to him. What was it? Oh yes, she was female. He chuckled quietly at his own razor-sharp wit.

"Mary," Glenna said and shifted her eyes sideways as if looking for something. "What be you doing here so soon?"

"I've come to help you tidy up."

"Tidy up?" she said and snorted. "So he's done with you already, is he? Well, 'tis your own hard luck. This one's mine."

The tall maid straightened with a bewildered scowl. " 'Tis time to bar the doors for the night."

Glenna forced a smile. "Then bar them. I go to find dry garments for me friend here. Come along, me laird," she said and pressing her impressive bosom against his arm, dragged him to his feet. He obliged as best he could, but his stomach sloshed with intoxicants and his feet wandered with a will of their own.

"Glenna," said the maid pointedly.

"Good eventide, Mary."

"Glenna!" Mary said, her tone low as she shifted her gaze to Ramsay for an instant. "I believe de la Court needs your help in the kitchen."

"You did him in the kitchen?" she snarled.

Mary's scowl deepened. "You'd best go straight-away."

"And leave you to the gentleman here? I think not."

"I didn't . . ." The tall maid raised her chin and lowered her voice. "I had no interest in your master's proposal, if that's what you think, but I believe he is hurt."

"Hurt?" Glenna's eyes widened.

"Aye. He asked for you."

The buxom maid stood quickly. "Stay put," she ordered Ramsay. "If she's lying, I shall return in a blink. And you . . ." She grabbed Mary's sleeve. "Come with me."

Ramsay rested his hip precariously against the top rung of a nearby chair as the two hurried away.

From his vantage point, he could see that the pitcher was not quite empty. He remedied that situation and glanced impatiently toward the kitchen.

There was a muffled thud, then nothing.

Maybe the two women were fighting over him, he thought and considered telling them he could handle them both. But upon fuzzy consideration, he decided better of it. There was something about the tall maid that suggested it would take a steadier hand to handle her.

Where was Glenna? he wondered again. Her stallion was waiting. He chuckled quietly at his wit, nearly lost his perch on the back of the chair, and scrambled to stay upright.

"Me laird."

Startled, he twisted toward the voice. The speaker stood nearly eye to eye with him.

"Where's Glenna?" he asked.

Mary's voice was low, her gaze steady. "She has been called away."

"Away?"

"Aye," she said, and followed with no explanation.

"Ahh." He scowled as he turned away. "Well then, I'll be returning to me room."

"I will accompany you."

"What's that?" He glanced hazily through the dimness at her.

"I will accompany you." She repeated her former statement with no more inflection than the first time.

"To me room?"

"Aye."

He pondered this for a moment. "Afeared I will be accosted on the way?"

"Nay."

"Then . . ." Cleverness and patience seemed to have abandoned him completely. "Why?"

"You are besotted with ale."

"I am not."

"You are."

" 'Tis kind of you to offer, but I assure you, lass . . ." It seemed rather odd, calling her by such a gentle endearment when she stood less than a hand's breadth below his own substantial height. "I can reach me room without your help."

"I will—" she began, her voice firm, but a noise from the kitchen interrupted her words. Ducking her head slightly, she glanced up at him through her lashes. "Me apologies, me laird," she murmured shyly.

He stared. What an odd, erratic girl she was.

" 'Tis sorry I be. I . . . have bungled it horribly."

"Bungled what?"

"I . . ." She paused, still staring at the floor. "I like you."

"You—" he began, but realized with breathtaking abruptness that she had just loosened the laces of her gown. Her breasts, high and firm and pale, were just visible above her bodice. "Oh." Perhaps they really had been fighting over him in the kitchens. He glanced distractedly in that direction.

"Please."

"What?" He turned dizzily back toward her.

"Please do not say nay."

"I . . ." Dear God, this was a strange place. "Mayhap you were right," he said and placed a steadying hand on a nearby chair. "I may well be more inebriated than I first suspected."

"Aye."

"What?"

"I . . . would make you very happy," she said, and without glancing up, fingered her bodice open another fraction of an inch.

"I am certain you would," he said, but something about her actions made him feel suddenly old and lecherous. Whatever her reasons for the offer, something about her stiff movements made him doubt that she was overwhelmed with longing for him. "But I fear I am . . . fatigued." It was immensely true. He was tired and confused and though he would not have thought it possible, he was no longer the least bit aroused. "Thus I bid you adieu."

"Adieu?"

"Aye," he said, and turned away.

"But . . ." She was beside him in a moment, grasping his arm as he headed for the stairs. " 'Tis early still."

Her breast pressed against his bare arm, stirring up a bit of faded lust, but the night had been too bizarre for even his wayward wick to maintain much enthusiasm. "Mayhap I shall see you when we break the fast."

"Am I so unattractive?"

He stopped on the stairs, startled by her words. "Nay." Her eyes, he noticed, were an intriguing sort of silver blue and her expression intense. "Not at all, lass. 'Tis simply that . . ." There was something disturbingly familiar about her. Something that he could not quite put his finger on, that grated at his consciousness and confused his already bumbling mind. "You are so young and—"

"I am as old as she."

"Who?"

"Your . . . wife."

His wife! Oh, Notmary. She was in his room. Alone. Lust stirred irrationally. He frowned. God Almighty, he was a dolt for not taking advantage of this opportunity. But this stately lass seemed somehow uneasy about her role of seductress.

"You are bonny and alluring," he said, sobering somewhat. "But I do not think you wish to do this thing. Therefore . . ." Easing her fingers from his arm, he kissed them gently. "I bid you goodnight," he said.

For one prolonged moment she stared at her fingers before lifting her amazed gaze back to his.

He turned to leave, but from the corner of his eye he saw her reach beneath the folds of her gown. His besotted mind was almost lucid enough to sense the danger. Almost.

"Goodnight," she said, and raising an unseen object, struck him soundly on the head.

Chapter 12

Anora's dreams were soft and deep. She lay dozing in a misty glen, cushioned by mosses and serenaded by larks. Not far away, the burn hustled happily toward the sea. The man beside her caused her to moan—but 'twas not a moan of pain, nor of fear. Not this time.

Nay, there was only pleasure here. His hands felt like magic against her skin, and when he spoke, the sound rippled in waves of ecstasy up her arched spine.

"Wake up."

She moaned again, for 'twas so wondrous to lie thus, loving and beloved.

"Awake!"

The mists parted regretfully. "MacGowan?" The name came easily to her lips, but in that same instant she realized her mistake. Her gasp was cut short by the cold touch of steel against her neck.

"Say nothing." The blade nudged her throat. "Rise."

"What—" Her voice shook.

"*Quiet!*"

"The warrior." She whispered the words even as he reached out to drag her to her feet. "What do you want of me?"

"Disrobe," he rasped, and shook her by the arm. Even in the darkness, she could see him glance toward the door. "And be quick about it." The point of his dagger nicked her throat. Fear welled up inside her like a winter wind.

"I—I cannot."

"You can and you shall!" he snarled, and tightened his grip on her arm.

She squeezed her eyes shut, holding back the terror, locking away the memories. But even as she did so, she gripped her gown in trembling fingers. The linen shook as it slid up her legs. Cold air followed in its wake. Goose bumps coursed over her flesh.

"Hurry up!"

She pulled higher. A chill spilled over her breasts. Fabric brushed her face, and then she was naked. She kept her eyes pressed shut, barely feeling the tears that squeezed between her lids.

She felt him step closer, felt his fingers touch her arm, and suddenly she could not bear it, would rather die than endure this again.

"Nay!" She swung wildly at him. Her knuckles connected with his cheek. He stumbled back and she pivoted away, but in that instant his arm locked about her waist.

She tried to scream, but his hand clamped over her mouth, cutting off her air. She clawed desperately, fighting to be free.

No hope. No hope, her mind screamed, but in that instant light streamed into the room. The warrior stumbled and she was tossed free to fall against the bed. Air washed into her lungs.

Sounds boomed around her. Feet scuffled. Men grunted, and then, just as suddenly as it had begun, the noise abated.

Anora remained pressed back against the mattress behind her. Darkness lay like a blanket around her, but through that muffling blanket, she heard a moan. Terrified, she pressed more firmly against the pallet. The moan came again, and now, even in the dimness, she could see a crumpled shape against the far wall.

"Who—who is it?"

"Mary." The shape shifted. "Are you well?"

"MacGowan?" His name sounded breathy to her own ears.

"Are you well?" He tried to rise, then crumpled again.

"MacGowan!" She scurried across the floor on all fours. From somewhere far below she could hear the faint murmur of voices, but they mattered not. "You're wounded."

"Aye, I do believe . . . are you naked?"

Her breath stopped in her throat. She froze where she was, crouched over him, her hands clutched in his tunic.

"Damn him!" The words were low and dark, filled with a deep, unspeakable anger. "Damn him to hell." He shifted, rising unsteadily to his feet. She rose with him. "Bar the door behind me."

"What? Where are you going?"

"Trust no one," he warned, and stumbled toward the door.

Frantic and unthinking, she tightened her fingers, dragging him to a halt. "Nay. Please." They were the only words she could think of for a moment.

She felt him turn toward her.

"Don't go," she whispered.

Even in the darkness, she saw him reach up. His hand felt warm and ultimately strong against her cheek.

"He did me no harm."

"But he meant to." Ramsay turned as if that was all he needed to know, but she tugged him back.

"He is far gone and you are wounded."

From the stairs, they heard an excited rush of voices.

"Get in bed. Draw up the woolens," Ramsay said, and urged her onto the mattress. She did as told, pulling the blankets up to her chin.

"What goes on here?" Light beamed from the doorway, splashing brightness into the room. The proprietor lifted the iron bound lantern he carried, and by that illumination Ramsay saw the Frenchman wince as he flitted his gaze toward Anora. "What has happened?"

Ramsay took one step sideways, blocking the man's view of the bed. "There has been an intruder."

"An intruder! Nay," de la Court said, and grimaced as if in pain. "The doors are barred for the night."

"The maid Mary let him in," Ramsay said.

"Mary?" gasped the Frenchman.

" 'Twas she!" gasped a voice from the hallway.

De la Court turned. Glenna's face gleamed in the

light of the single candle she carried. " 'Twas she who knocked me on the pate," she said, holding a cloth to her head with her free hand.

The Frenchman scowled. " 'Twas also she who kicked . . . who struck me."

"Nay!" Glenna gasped. "She said you were hurt in the kitchen."

"I was indeed hurt, though not in the kitchen," de la Court said, and for just a moment laid his wrist across his crotch. "But why?" he asked, his face twitching. "She was such a comely . . . such an innocent thing."

"Innocent, me arse," Glenna said. "She was a fresh bit of flesh come knocking at your door just this afternoon, is what she was. And me faithful as a hound all these months!"

"Hush, before you wake the whole house," warned the proprietor.

"Afeared your icy-arsed missus will learn the truth?"

" 'Twould do neither of us any good," said the Frenchman, lowering the lantern with a wince. "Come, let us see to each other's wounds."

" 'Tis just like you to worry about me, now that the other maids be out of reach," she pouted.

" 'Tis not true. You know . . ." he murmured, and let his voice slip into a whisper.

Glenna giggled and he glanced past her toward the bed once more, his eyes bright in the lamplight. "My sincerest apologies for the intrusion, madame. Is there aught I can do for you?"

"Nay." Anora felt dizzied and confused, startled by the private drama played out before her. "I am well."

"And my lord?"

"I am well," Ramsay said.

"Then my prayers are answered," de la Court said with pious brevity, and letting his fingertips trail momentarily down Glenna's arm, hung his lantern on the peg beside the door. "Rest assured I shall not sleep until the light of morn." He turned and hobbled away.

The flame flickered as the door closed. The room fell silent as Ramsay turned toward the bed.

Anora drew her knees closer to her chest. "How did you know 'twas the other maid who let him in?"

He scowled at her, saying nothing. In the single flickering light he looked large and formidable. The seconds ticked away as he crossed the room and reached for the bottle he'd left on the floor.

Breathless and taut, Anora stared at him. "Did you bed her?"

He straightened abruptly, his hand wrapped about the neck of the bottle. "Would you care?"

She dropped her gaze. "It seems our lives are enmeshed for a time, Ramsay of Dun Ard." The words were nearly impossible to force out, for a dozen other questions begged to be asked. "I would know what kind of man I am bound to."

He lowered himself slowly to the bed. "And I would know to whom I am bound. Thus I propose an exchange of information."

Her heart did a little trick beat. "What do you mean?"

"I will tell you where I have spent the evening, if you will share a truth with me."

Beneath the blankets, she curled her naked toes. "What truth?"

For a moment he said nothing. His eyes were as

steady and solemn as a falcon's, as mesmerizing as sin itself. "The maid called Mary, have you seen her before?"

"Nay."

"Did she come to the room after me departure?"

"Nay."

He scowled. "The man who came to this room, he came alone?"

"Aye."

"Who was he?"

Raw fear seared her nerves. "I do not know."

"Was he the warrior from before?"

She nodded, barely able to do that much.

"A Munro?"

Tension cranked tighter. Lies lay like rabid hounds before her door. "I know no Munro," she whispered, and tightened her fingers in the blanket.

MacGowan stared at her a moment longer, then his expression changed to one of indifference and he turned away.

"You're wounded." She said the words quickly, foolishly, as if she might want to keep him near. "Again, for me."

He shook his head and moved as if to rise, but her fingers snared his rumpled plaid, and the blankets, set free from her gripping hands, fell away from her body.

Breathless and terrified, she reached to hide herself, but his gaze had already dropped to her breasts. She covered them quickly. His gaze rose more slowly.

"Aye," he said finally, his voice low. "I am wounded. And yet you will not answer me truthfully."

"I do not know the warrior," she whispered.

"Then answer me this: is he the one who causes you to tremble when I am near?"

"I do not tremble."

"Your soul does," he murmured. "Is he the reason?"

There was so little air in the room, almost too little to allow her to shake her head.

"Who then?"

She wanted to hide, to lie, to look away, but she would not. Instead, she raised her chin and held his gaze. "When I was four and ten, my father sent me to court." Against her knuckles, she felt the muscles bunch in his thigh. "I met a baron there. I thought him quite fashionable." Her throat hurt with the effort to talk. "And refined . . . but he was betrothed. Still . . . I thought . . . I thought for love he would surely break the betrothal and wed me. I thought that was why he asked to meet me in the gardens after dark." No more words came for a moment, though she told herself to go on. 'Twas best he knew what he was dealing with. 'Twas best he knew she was no innocent, for once he understood, 'twould be so much easier to turn him aside. "I thought he came to pledge his troth to me." Her throat felt ungodly tight. " 'Twas not the last time I was wrong about a man."

"He raped you." His words were low, almost inaudible, but still she winced at the words.

"I was a fool to—"

"Don't!" he snapped and grabbed her arms in a fierce grip.

She cringed away.

"Don't." His tone was softer now, but just as low, filled with an emotion so deep it needed no inflection.

"Don't . . . what?" she whispered.

"Don't you dare take the bastard's sin upon yourself." A muscle jumped in his jaw. Against her bare arm, his fingers trembled with a terrible strength. " 'Tis his to bear. In this life as well as the next."

She watched him, trying to understand, to define the depth of his emotion.

"Tell me this." He sat perfectly still, as if the slightest motion might push him over the edge of his careful control. "Your father, did he avenge your loss?"

She tried to hold his gaze, but it was impossible. Her eyes flickered to the blankets.

"Did he?" His grip tightened.

"He said . . ." Her throat ached, but she finally forced out the words. They seemed distant from her. "He did not wish for others to know of . . . my shame."

He didn't move, for several moments. "Was there a babe?"

She shook her head. "Nay. No bairn. Only . . ." Emptiness, her soul whispered.

"Emptiness," he said.

The breath stopped in her throat. How did he know? None had read her thoughts before. None but Isobel.

"And fear," he added.

Shaken, she lifted her chin and steadied her hands. "I am not afraid," she said. "And if the truth be told, I learned a valuable lesson."

"Not to trust."

She refused to show her surprise. Instead, she nodded curtly. "Trust is a fool's broken crutch."

"You were a child," he said.

"I was old enough to—"

"To be used?" His voice was hard, his eyes flinty. "Wounded? Terrified?"

"I was not afraid," she said, but her words were no more than a whispered lie. "I was foolish. Old enough to know better than to—"

"You were a child!" he gritted. "Children are supposed to trust." Agony ripped across his stoic features, and he pulled her against his chest, hiding his face from her. "Christ!" he whispered.

She squeezed her eyes shut, every muscle rigid as she fought for strength, but he reached up and stroked her hair, and with each tender caress her control weakened.

"You were but a babe." His hand gently cupped her skull before skimming downward. "An innocent."

She shook her head, denying, fighting the hot wash of emotion. "I was a tease. A—"

"Who said as much?" His fingers tightened for a moment in her hair.

She swallowed hard and gripped his arms for support. "Father thought—"

"Fathers!" he began forcefully, then paused and stroked her hair again, slowly, and on the descent she felt him tremble. "Fathers sometimes fail." He pressed his face to her hair and against her temple, she felt the drop of a single tear. " 'Tis a sin. A crime of the darkest sort. Their first task is to protect, to love, to hold their young ones like precious blossoms in their hands." His own hands were as gentle as a psalm, as warm as a summer breeze, and with the stroking, her defenses crumbled like moldering stone. Tears fell from her eyes onto the bunched muscle of his chest, and her arms crept around him. "You were a bairn, lass. A wee one. 'Twas not your fault, and 'tis not you who should take the blame, nor bear the burden."

He was rocking slightly, swaying gently back and

forth like the rhythm of quiet waves. " 'Tis the bastard who accosted you who shall pay the price for all eternity." She felt him breathe in, then exhale slowly. "And the sire who failed you."

He pressed his cheek against the top of her head. She leaned against him, seeking solace, forgiveness, forgetfulness, and in her tortured mind she again became a little girl.

'Twas early summer and a warm breeze rustled her hair. The pipets were singing, the harebells were in bloom, and she was laughing. Not the cynical laughter of a jaded woman. Not the flirtatious laughter of a manipulator. But laughter of sheer, unadulterated joy, and as the sun shone on her uplifted face and her father crooned to her in tones of unmistakable adoration, she fell asleep.

Chapter 13

Ramsay awoke slowly, yet there was no grogginess. He knew where he was and he knew who he lay with. He knew also that he should leave now, before she awoke, but he could not. For despite every incriminating condemnation he had thrown at himself, he was still weak, and she was so soft in his arms. Like the babe she had once been. Like the babe he himself had failed. Yet even now, even with the guilt he would always bear, he had learned nothing—for the truth was, he wanted her.

Her breasts were bare. Nothing separated him from their beauty, not a hand's breadth, not the merest scrap of cloth. They were small and round, capped with delicate rosy nipples.

She sighed in her sleep, drawing his attention upward. As she shifted, her hair slid across her shoulder, gleaming like ripened wheat in the morning sunlight. Her lips were slightly parted, pink and bowed and hopelessly tempting.

Beneath the blankets, his shameless wick stirred, and as she opened her eyes he realized with chagrin that her thigh rested between his. 'Twas a difficult thing to move away even a fraction of a inch. In fact, he barely managed.

"Oh!" The single word was breathy, frightened. He stopped all movement. 'Twas clear that unlike him, she had forgotten where she was, who she was with. "I . . ." Glancing down, she widened her eyes and tugged a blanket over her nakedness. "I must have . . . fallen asleep."

"Aye." His voice was pitifully low. He could only hope she thought it because of the early hour and not because the sight of her thus had sent all his blood scurrying to his nether parts in a hot rush, like ale down a sailor's gullet. " 'Tis morning."

She cleared her throat and shifted her gaze perfunctorily toward the single narrow window. "Aye."

The silence seemed endless. Now was the time to retreat, of course. Before it was too late. But dear God, she was so soft, like an angel there beside him, and regardless of how hard one might try, 'twas a difficult thing to walk away from an angel when one's soul was on fire.

"Are you well?" Her voice was soft, her expression shy, with none of the hard edged carefulness so frequently displayed.

"Aye," he rumbled.

"You have . . ." She stopped as if uncertain, but in a

moment she reached out and touched his forehead with feather light fingertips. "You have a bruise."

He closed his eyes against her touch, holding himself unmoving before he found enough strength to open his eyes and still not advance. " 'Tis nothing."

Slowly, she smoothed a lock of hair from his temple. "It seems I owe you my thanks yet again."

"Nay." He could barely force out that single word, for her fingers yet remained on his skin. "I did naught."

" 'Tis not true." Her words were a murmur against his soul. "You saved me." She swept her fingers over his ear, sparking off a million frenzied feelings. "Again."

"I did naught but return to me room," he said, fighting for control.

"And what of . . . the warrior?" He felt her shudder to the very ends of her fingertips, but he would not be moved by her feelings. He would not.

"There was not room for him in the bed," he said, fighting for levity.

"He would have—" Her voice broke.

"Nay," he said quickly, and reached out to console her. But despite all previous evidence to the contrary, he still had a modicum of sense, for he drew carefully back. "I don't think he intended rape."

He watched her lips form a circle.

"He brought a gown. 'Tis on the floor behind you. I believe it is the one worn by the maid called Mary. I think he planned for you to wear it as he took you with him."

"Took me . . . where?"

She had dropped her hand between them. It lay mere inches from him, nearly touching his chest.

"I cannot guess. Not without knowing his identity."

She shifted her gaze to the few inches of mattress that lay between them. "You still think I know who he is."

"Do you?"

"Nay."

"But you know why he follows you." He watched her, trying to read her meaning.

"I thought he . . ." She tensed, then forced herself to relax. A lesson in control. He knew it well. "I thought he meant to take what all men want."

Silence stirred between them. He would have given much to convince her that she was wrong, that not all men were groping lechers, but he was not that good a liar.

"Why did you not?" Her voice was little more than a murmur of thought, her eyes twin clouds of blue emotion, pulling him in, pulling him under.

Good Christ, he could not risk the fall again.

"MacGowan?"

He drew himself back to reality with a hard hand. "What is it, lass?"

"Why do you not press your advantage?"

She was the most beautiful sight he had ever seen— delicate, desirable, her defenses down.

"What advantage is it that I have?" he asked.

A frown marked her brow, as if she wrestled with a lifelong mystery. "You are powerful," she said and he almost laughed.

"And what are you, lass? Weak?"

She said nothing, and he turned his gaze carefully away, lest the temptation be too great.

"Aye, I am strong, for I am a man and I am a Mac-Gowan," he said, but even that simple attempt at vanity sounded pathetic to his own ears. "And yet who is it that has brought me brothers clambering to do her bidding?"

She shifted her gaze away and fiddled with her pillow before lifting her eyes fretfully back to his. "I cannot have every man swooning at my feet, aye?"

He winced as he rubbed the bump on his skull. " 'Twas not swooning exactly, was it? More like being thumped on the pate with—"

"Why do you not . . . want me?"

His heart twisted, his stomach jumped, and lower down, hope reared its head. "Do you want . . . me?"

"I . . ." She didn't look at him. "After . . ." She met his gaze for the briefest instant, then skittered hers back to the blankets. " 'Tis . . . unlikely I will ever want anyone," she whispered.

He remained still, letting the emotions rage hopelessly through him. "And if I avenged you?"

"What?"

He should take back the words. But they were out in the open and he could not regret them, though he would have sworn he was not a violent man. "If I found the bastard . . ." The words were hard to force out. "If I made him pay. If he hurt as much as he hurt you . . . could you want then?"

Her lips moved. A breathy gasp was released, then, "You would do that for me?"

"Mayhap I would do it for me."

She shook her head, confused, afraid, though perhaps she did not know it. "Why? He has done nothing to harm you."

"But harming him would surely do me good."

"I think," she began, and ever so slowly reached out. Breath held, he watched her hand draw near. "I think you are very kind," she said, and he closed his eyes at the tender pain of contact.

Against his cheek, her hand felt like magic.

"You are good," she whispered, and skimmed her fingers over the edge of his jaw and onto his throat. Warmth followed its passage onto his shoulder. "And strong." Heat trailed across his chest, caressing his nipple.

"Lass, I—" he began, but when her fingers skimmed onto his belly, he could no longer speak. Every muscle contracted and a hiss of painful desire rasped between his teeth. "Lass, if you do not want this between us . . ." Her hand had crept onto his back and she moved a scant few inches closer. "I think it wise to stop now."

"Is it your goodness that makes me undesirable to you?"

"Undesirable! Nay." He could not resist reaching out. Her skin felt like finest velvet beneath his hand. Her hair was satin soft. "Nay, lass," he breathed, and followed a silken strand down her slim arm. He tried to stop where the blanket was clasped against her breast, but it gaped away from her body, and it was simple, so simple to press it downward, to bare her breasts, to let his breath be drawn from his body in one hard rasp of desire.

He should not touch. He dare not touch, yet he could not stop himself. His fingers skimmed as light as hope over her nipple, cupping gently, before drawing painfully away. "You are not undesirable," he said, his voice finally steady. "You are beauty itself, lass."

She stared at him, her eyes wide as the heavens, and then, like a kindly angel, she kissed him. A thousand feelings smote him at once—hope, pain, need, all crushing in on him with that one feather soft caress. But he remained still, not daring to move, not trusting himself to reach out. She was so close, so soft, so tempting.

He kissed her back, and suddenly there was no return. Curling his arm around her back, he pulled her against him. She came with a moan. He swallowed the tiny sound, drinking in her desire, her need, her femininity. Their kiss deepened, strained. He pressed into her, rolling her onto her back, and suddenly she was beneath him.

Desire roared like an inferno in his head, thrumming like a heartbeat, throbbing in his loins.

"Stop!"

He heard her at the same moment he felt her fists against his chest.

"Nay!"

He rolled rapidly onto his hip. "Lass," he soothed, trying to calm her, but she was already scrambling from the bed. Half falling onto the floor, she struggled to her feet, snagging the night rail to her naked breasts. "What is amiss?" he asked, but she backed away, her eyes consuming her face in a frightened blaze. "Lass." He held out his hand and inched toward the edge of the bed, but she backed away another step. "Did I hurt you? Are you—"

"You are no different!"

He scowled, the dark haze of desire clearing slowly from his mind.

"I thought mayhap the prophecy—" She stopped abruptly, her bosom rising and falling above the scrunched fabric of her borrowed gown. "But nay."

"Lass," he said softly, "I did not mean to frighten—"

"Frighten! Nay, you meant to . . . couple, regardless of my wishes."

"Nay." He shoved his legs over the edge of the bed and rose to his feet. "I tried to—"

"To what?" Her voice was rising toward hysteria. "To rape me?"

He was not a impetuous man, but anger was brewing like a foul tonic in his soul. " 'Twould not have been rape, lass."

"Are you saying 'twas my own fault?"

He stared at her. Dear God in heaven, she was tempting. Even now, when his desire was cooling and his temper rising, he could not deny it. He wanted nothing more than to pull her into his arms and begin anew.

"You did not seem to mind a moment ago."

"Oh. So you can read my thoughts, can you? You can see into my very soul and know my deepest desires."

He shrugged. Pain burned through his wounded arm, but he welcomed it. "You give me too much credit, lassie. 'Twas actually your moans that shaped me thinking. Your moans, and the fact that you lay bare naked in me arms all night, and tried not once to clothe yourself."

"And why was I naked, MacGowan? Was it mayhap because another of your kind forced me at knife point to bare myself?"

The memory sent a hot flame of anger burning through him. He had almost forgotten the fear that had first propelled her into his arms. He scowled, a dozen emotions warring within him.

"You are no different," she said, straightening now and refusing to back farther away. "Mayhap you think

I owe you. That I'll be willing to trade my soul for the safety you can afford me."

Cool rage congealed within him, shaped by a hundred bitter thoughts. "Is that what lying with me would be? Giving up your soul?"

"What else? Might you think you hold some appeal for me? Do you imagine that I want you pawing at me?"

He drew a deep breath and steadied himself. "Aye," he said. " 'Tis, in fact, exactly what I thought."

"Well, you are wrong," she said, and skimmed his half naked body with hot disdain. "You've nothing I want."

"I would be quite wounded, but 'tis obvious that your words and the truth rarely cross paths."

He would not have thought it possible for her to pale further. "I do not want you."

He forced a grin. "So you have said."

"And I shall never say differently."

He stared at her for several seconds, then leaned his bare shoulder against the wall. Rough plaster pressed into his wound, but he reveled in the stab of pain. " 'Twould do you little good to change your mind now, Notmary," he said. "For I will not bed a liar again, no matter how blatantly she offers herself."

Not a bit of color showed in her cheeks. Even her lips seemed to have lost their vivid hue. "And I will not offer," she said. "Not in a thousand lifetimes."

"I fear I do not have that much time to test your resolve," he said, and strode rigidly toward the door. "But please. Try to remain resolute until we reach Levenlair. Or mayhap . . ." He scowled at her. "Mayhap you would prefer to attempt to convince another to escort you home."

"I have no time to waste in search of a more . . . disciplined man."

"Truly?" He stared at her. "If you be willing to travel with the likes of me, there must indeed be a crisis at Levenlair."

She said nothing.

"Still not willing to tell me why you are in such a rush? Well, I suspect I will find out soon enough." Turning abruptly, he left the room.

Chapter 14

It made little difference that the sun shone and the breeze was warm as they journeyed north. The day dragged by in misery.

Ramsay had not purchased another mount, for he had little coin and less to barter, and so they rode double. Of course, it was not the fact that she sat nearly upon his lap and he was unable to allow himself to touch so much as the ends of her wind rustled hair that irritated him. Nay. A dozen other problems worried at his mind.

They'd been riding forever, Gryfon was weary, and despite the sunlight and breeze, Ramsay's damned plaid was still damp. Damp and chafing every time Notmary shifted against him, every time she twisted to find more comfort so that her breast brushed . . .

She turned slightly, and her hair, soft as kitten fur, stroked across his cheek.

He swore under his breath.

"What is it?" she asked. Her tone was worried as she turned slightly and her left breast, determined to cause trouble, pressed more forcefully against his arm.

He stared at her, frantically searching for flaws, but while her personality supplied a host of them, her face revealed pitifully few.

"Did you hear something?" she asked.

He drew himself back to the present. "We'd best stop. The horse is tired."

"Oh." 'Twas very nearly the first word she had uttered all day, and it turned out to be the last.

The night was damp, fitful, unfulfilling. The next day was no better, and his mood not the least improved.

By the following evening, he was all but insane and found himself gritting his teeth each time the girl twisted or straightened . . . or breathed.

"Sit!" He barked the word without meaning to, then glared at her when she turned toward him. For one fleeting moment, her expression was fearful, but she remedied that in an instant.

"What is amiss?" Her tone now was perfectly modulated, like that of a duchess speaking to her serfs.

"Nothing," he said, and counted to twelve in Latin. 'Twas after all a godly language. " 'Twould simply be appreciated if you would sit still."

She stared at him, so irritatingly cool that he wanted to shake her. "So you have changed your mind, have you?" she asked, her voice level.

Ramsay yanked his gaze from hers and stared out into the gathering darkness. "I've not the haziest idea what you speak of."

"Truly?"

Good God, she was maddening. He shifted his gaze back to her face and scowled. "I am not a liar."

"Nay." The smallest corner of a superior smile lifted her lips. " 'Tis I who am the liar and I who am the tease. Is that not what you were thinking?"

"Nay." He shifted his gaze toward the horizon. "I was thinking you are a tremendous pain in the arse."

"Do not worry. 'Tis not too late to take back your vow to extract revenge on my behalf."

"What the devil are you talking about?"

She glanced up through her lashes, as if surprised at his naïveté. "I am a tease, a wanton. Therefore it was my own fault, was it not, MacGowan?"

"If you have something to say, don't waste me time, lassie, for me patience is a bit short just now."

" 'Tis just this: you think 'twas my own fault that I was raped."

His stomach cramped with emotion. The last thing he wished to think about just now was her stolen innocence. Far better to hate her than to ache for her.

She was still watching him. "If you cannot lie, you cannot deny it, can you?" She cocked her head saucily, but her voice was muted. "You blame me."

Darkness fell in dusky mist around them. She felt small but staunchly stiff in his arms.

"Is that what you want me to do?" he asked. "Blame you?"

"Nay," she said. "What reason could I have to wish that?"

" 'Twould give you a likely reason to hate me, would it not?"

She wasn't breathing. He could tell by the cessation of motion of her ribs against his arm as he held the reins. "I do not need another reason to hate you, Mac-Gowan."

He held her gaze. "Good," he said finally, and leaned forward so that their faces were mere inches apart. "For this I know, lass: you were a child when your innocence was stolen from you, a babe to be protected and cherished. 'Twas not your sin, no matter how much you wish me to believe the opposite."

For a moment she stared at him unspeaking, and then she turned stiffly away to look between Gryfon's truncated ears.

The night was long again and quiet, but when Ramsay glanced up it seemed that she was forever watching him. Every time, though, her eyes flickered away. Even after they had eaten their simple fare and found their respective pallets, he could feel her eyes on him.

Morning dawned. Ramsay ate sparingly, then saddled their mount. Gryfon, true to his usual bad nature, managed to step on his master's foot twice before the girth was tightened. Not so merry himself, Ramsay kneed the steed in the barrel and was repaid with a stinging slap from Gryfon's tail across his cheek. Glaring then, they called a silent truce.

Nursing his bruised foot, Ramsay mounted gingerly, then bent to assist the lass. The night had been miserable and his sleep poor. Still, as she settled before him in the saddle, he felt his wick nudge toward his belt, and he scowled.

Miles slipped away beneath the stallion's hooves. Sometime before noon, clouds gathered over the western hills and boiled overhead.

"Why do you keep him?" Notmary asked, not turning toward Ramsay when she spoke.

"Who?"

"Gryfon," she said. "I saw Dun Ard's stable. 'Tis not for lack of mounts that you ride this one. I but wondered why."

"Why?" His mood had not improved in the least.

" 'Tis simply conversation," she said, still facing forward. "Did his ears freeze?"

"Aye," he said, loath to participate in this particular topic. It could do him no good.

"How?"

"He was too damned stubborn to be born in the spring like any other self respecting horse."

"A winter bairn?"

"Aye."

"His ears were already frozen when you found him?"

"He was already *dead* when I found him."

Her brows rose and she turned partially toward him, punishing him with a slight brush of her breast.

He steeled himself against the sensation and concentrated on talking. "As it turns out, I only thought he was dead. Once we were rid of the wolves, we were able to get him to his feet. 'Twas then that he first kicked me."

"But you brought him home. Nursed him back to health."

"He was the last foal from wee Lochan Gorm, Mother's favorite, and she was loath to lose his final colt. 'Tis the only reason."

"I have a feeling there might be more to it."

"Well, your feeling is wrong."

"So you did not care for him? Pity him? Cherish him?"

"Cherish him!" Ramsay said and snorted as he

glowered at the stallion's flattened ears. "I don't even *like* the damned horse."

"I see," Notmary said, and they fell back into silence.

By evening, thunder rumbled ominously and the wind picked up, blowing the first droplets of rain into their faces.

Just before darkness obliterated the countryside, they came to a sheltered spot by a burn. Surrounded by a thick copse of horse chestnuts, it looked to be a dry enough spot to hide from the elements. It even seemed safe to chance a fire here, and by its heat they ate the last of the bread and cheese they'd brought from the inn. Sitting with their backs against the rough trunks of a twin pair of chestnut trees, they watched the erratic flicker of flame.

"If we follow the burn we will reach my home late on the morrow."

Ramsay glanced up, surprised from his reverie. "You know the country round about?"

"Aye." Again silence. She cleared her throat and watched the flame again. "There is something I would say before we reach the journey's end."

If he dared glance her way he would see the golden sketch of her profile limned by firelight—as delicate as a memory, as indelible as a stone carving.

"I am . . ." She paused and fiddled with a fold in her gown.

He waited. Around them, the wind howled like a banshee, but hidden away in their little copse they were dry and cozy.

"I am grateful for all you have done."

He almost smiled as he poked a faggot back into the

fire with a crooked branch. "I hope it did not reveal too much of yourself to say so, lass."

She stared at him, wide eyed.

"Never have I met a woman so sparse with details of herself."

"And what of you, Ramsay of Dun Ard?" she asked. "What have you revealed of yourself?"

He shouldn't have started down this path, he realized belatedly, and shrugged as if the subject held no interest for him. "There is little to tell that you cannot see with your own eyes."

"Truly?"

"Aye."

"So you are an uncomplicated man."

"Aye."

"Who lived an idyllic childhood and has floated into manhood without a care."

"I am impressed by your perceptiveness."

She watched him for an instant. "Tell me again that you do not lie."

"I do not lie." It was more difficult to force out the words than he had expected, even though it was not an outright lie. A shadowed truth, perhaps, but not a lie.

"Tell me, Ramsay of the MacGowans," she said. "Why have you never wed?"

The flame was fascinating, or at least it was a good excuse not to look at her, to keep his expressions hidden from her too-sharp gaze. "Mayhap I had hoped for the same freedom you have."

She laughed a little, though the sound was forced. "Do I have some freedom I have forgot?"

"To marry for reasons other than duty. Is that not what you told me?"

"Aye." She glanced away. " 'Tis true."

"And yet you are not wed."

She sat very still. "Could it be that you intentionally turn the conversation away from yourself?"

"There are no dark mysteries hidden away in my soul. Not like you, Notmary."

"Truly?"

"Truly."

"Who, then, is Lorna?"

Every muscle cranked up tight at the sound of her name, but Ramsay relaxed them carefully one by one and took his time before turning back to her. "Why do you ask?"

"Why do you not tell me?"

He shrugged. " 'Tis no great secret. She was a . . . lady I met at court."

The silence seemed hopelessly hard, but he refused to shift like a recalcitrant lad under her gaze.

"She was no one you held dear, then?"

He gritted his teeth and debated another lie. "Where did you hear her name?"

"From Gilmour."

He nodded. "Me brother has been known to talk too much on occasion." He wished Gilmour were there so he could discuss the matter with him in person. "On *all* occasions," he added ruefully.

"He said you were besotted."

Ramsay wished for the life of him that he could deny it, but his propensity for creative lying was just about at its finish.

"Is she comely?"

"Aye." He did his best to sound casual, as if the matter was of no great importance to him. "Aye, she was that."

"Was?"

"I suspect she is still."

"You no longer see her?"

"She married another."

"Why?" There was something in her tone that made him glance her way. Awe, perhaps—or at least an honest lack of understanding, and though her feelings should not matter, he felt an aching need to determine what they were.

"Mayhap she was hopelessly enamored," Ramsay said.

"With him but not with you?" Her voice was feather soft. "I do not think so."

"Then why?" he asked, almost able to keep the emotion from his voice.

"I would guess her chosen bridegroom was not a common cotter."

"The Saxon king's second cousin."

She smiled a little and glanced down at her clasped hands. "Power and wealth. I would guess that there lies your answer."

"And for that she would . . ." He paused, fighting for calm, for the careful reserve he had learned to build around himself.

"What?"

He clasped the answer firmly into silence. The wind shifted, swirling hard-driven rain drops into their tiny camp. "We had best seek some sleep."

"What would she do?"

He stared at her, almost tempted to tell her the story he had shared with no other.

" 'Twill be fairly dry beneath those branches," he said, and rose, glancing at the small bower created by the sheltering chestnuts. "I will make me bed out here."

"And if it rains?"

He scowled. " 'Twill keep me alert, lest we be discovered." Sweet Almighty, what a marvelous martyr he had become.

She shifted her gaze toward the alcove then back to him. " 'Twould surely do you no good to be drenched again."

But it would do him a world of good to hold her, for she looked so small and soft that his arms ached to—

Amazing. While Lorna had taught him much of pain, it seemed he had learned little of common sense.

"I remain here," he said, thinking that martyrdom was surely much safer than idiocy.

She watched him for a long, silent moment, then said, "About the night at the inn, I—"

"Go to sleep, lass," he said quietly.

She opened her mouth as if to speak, but he refused to allow it, interrupting once again.

"I am hoping to be canonized soon," he assured her.

"After you die of the ague?"

"I do not think martyrs are allowed to die of something so mundane."

She smiled a little, and he forced himself to keep breathing. 'Twas only a smile, after all, the slightest tilt of the lips. "You will find shelter if the rain worsens?"

He stared at her for a moment, knowing he should say no. Agreeing to spend the night near her was foolishness, and standing here arguing with her, merely seeing her hair glimmer in the firelight, watching the flash of her eyes, was nearly his undoing. He pulled his gaze back toward the fire.

"MacGowan." Her voice was very small. "I am sorry."

When he glanced at her, he saw that her face looked so tragic and solemn and sweet that his heart wrenched at the sight of it.

"For . . ." She seemed to wrestle with herself for a moment, but finally she spoke again. "Your loss."

"Loss?" he repeated and curled his hands into tense fists.

"For losing Lorna."

"Oh. Aye." He relaxed marginally. "Good night, lass," he said, and fetching Gryfon, found him a sheltered spot where grass grew in abundance.

The night was endless. The wind moaned, rain drops slashed at unexpected intervals into his face, and beneath him the earth felt as hard and unforgiving as old sins.

Ramsay sat up with an irritated snarl and stared with longing at the hidden alcove. The wind cursed at him and spat wet leaves into his face.

Enough was enough, he thought, and jerked to his feet. So what if he was a fool? So what if he was weak where she was concerned? At this juncture he was surely too exhausted and too damned cantankerous to be aroused by her.

Besides, if he tried anything idiotic, she would most likely dismember him.

Scraping the branches aside, he crouched low and entered. It was smaller even than he had thought, but there was just enough space to crawl in behind her. Still, there was no place to put his arms—no place but around her.

"MacGowan?" Her voice was drowsy, but no note of panic evidenced the tone as he settled his arm cautiously across her waist.

"Aye." His own voice was gruff, low, foolish. " 'Tis I. Go to sleep. You are safe."

"I know," she breathed and slipped back into her dreams.

When morning dawned, Ramsay awoke slowly. She lay against his body, her hair scattered like living gold across his arm, her buttocks pressed snugly against his erection.

He swore in silence and arose with a start.

"MacGowan?" She sat up just as quickly, her sleepy eyes wide. "Is something amiss?"

"Nay! Nay," he said, smoothing his tone. "All is well."

"It is time to leave?" she asked, and brushed a scattered lock from her face with the back of her hand.

Ramsay held his breath as he watched. He'd always had a weakness for women who brushed scattered locks from their faces with . . . oh, what the hell—she made him randy as a hound. "Aye. 'Tis well past time to leave. I will fetch our mount," he said.

In a hopeless attempt to save his failing peace of mind, Ramsay insisted she sit behind him today. It should have been safer than having her perching atop his manhood. Out of sight, out of mind, after all. But even after plaiting her hair into a long fat braid that morn, soft wisps of it were wont to flow against his neck, and now and again her breasts would bump against his back, joggling his mind and hardening his body. He gritted his teeth against the temptation and faced resolutely forward.

Beneath them the miles wore away, bearing them closer and closer to their destination, to the time when he would no longer be tormented by her nearness. 'Twas surely a good thing, he told himself as they traversed a burn. Water splashed up around Gryfon's high-stepping legs.

Then he heard Notmary gasp. "Nay!"

"What is it?"

"Go!" she said, and slipped sideways. He gripped her arm frantically.

"Mary!"

"Let me go!"

"Why?"

"You must—" she began hastily, but at that instant, the sound of hoofbeats reached his ears.

Jerking about, he faced uphill.

Mounted soldiers galloped down upon them. There were a dozen at least, and each one rode a white horse.

"Stay seated!" Ramsay jerked the dirk from his boot.

"Nay!" she gasped, and grabbed his hand. "Nay, Ramsay."

Their eyes met. There he saw the lies laid bare like fallow ground, and when next he glanced up, the first of the warriors was already upon them, then off his horse and down on one knee, his head bowed in deference.

"Lady Anora," he said, his voice filled with boundless gratitude. "You have returned."

She pulled her gaze away from Ramsay. "Caird," she said. "Why are you here?"

"Me lady." He rose abruptly to his feet. "When your escort returned, saying you had been lost, our troops were sent far afield to search for you. Our laird has been horribly . . . worried."

"Where is he?"

"He camps just outside of Evermyst."

Ramsay sat very still, his gaze never leaving the girl's pale face. "Your laird?" he asked.

She did not look at him, did not speak, and Ramsay shifted his gaze down to the warrior. "Tell me," he said, "who is your laird?"

The warrior straightened with a scowl. "He is called Innes Munro," he said, as if there should be none who was not aware. "The Munro of the Munros, and the lady's betrothed."

Chapter 15

The world swirled dizzily around Anora. Banners waved, men yelled, horses galloped. Fears and dreams scattered and melded in her mind, making her want to scream, to escape, but they were already crossing the valley toward home, and with that simple, steady movement, her mind began to clear. MacGowan sat stiff and silent before her, but she dared not look at him. Indeed, she dare not think about him, for she had to concentrate, to consider what must be done.

She had not expected the Munro to send his troops so far afield; she'd thought she'd have more time. She had known, of course, that he would stake his claim, but she had hoped, had believed, that he would remain at Windemoor. That would have given her a chance to reach Evermyst unmolested, to steady her nerves, refine her plans. But now there was no time, for from the top of the next hillock she could see not only the high, crumbling turrets of Evermyst, but the brightly colored pavilions of Munro's camp. Fear clawed at her belly.

Below her, horses whickered. Men pointed, and then a huge man ducked from the largest tent and approached with long-strided purpose.

Around them, their escorts grew silent as their leader drew closer. Tension cranked up like a loaded crossbow until he stood only inches away.

Anora lifted her chin, but let her eyes widen with fear.

His nod was curt, his voice as guttural as she remembered. "You had me worried."

Her heart was beating overtime. "I have told you before, my laird, you needn't concern yourself on my account."

"Oh, but I must. 'Tis me duty," he countered, and stepping toward her, raised his arms. "Come down, now."

She struggled with her fear, pushing it away like a threatening tide before sliding stiffly into his arms. He stood very close, too close, smothering her, but she stifled her fear and kept her movements slow as she pulled out of his arms.

He held her a second longer, then released all but one arm. " 'Tis good to have you home, lady. But I wonder . . ." His eyes were as small and sharp as a ferret's. "Who is this fellow with you?"

She could not speak, could not bear to look at Ramsay, to see the condemnation in his eyes.

"The lady seems to have lost her tongue for a moment," Munro said, shifting his gaze upward, "so I ask you, laddie, what be your name?"

There was a prolonged moment of silence, then, "I am called Ramsay. Of the MacGowans."

"The MacGowans." Anora felt the Munro stiffen, saw his giant hand settle with almost casual ease on the bone handled dirk at his side. "And what might you be doing this far north, MacGowan?"

It was difficult to breathe, more difficult still to raise her gaze to Ramsay's impassive face.

"Last I heard, 'twas not the Munros' task to decide where a man travels."

The Munro grinned, showing the gap where a molar was missing. "It could be you have heard wrong, lad. Why are you here?" he asked, and pulled his dirk from its sheath.

Fear exploded in Anora's gut. "He saved me!" she blurted.

Munro turned slowly toward her, like a bear considering his next meal. "Saved you, lady?"

"Aye. Were it not for him, I might well have perished far from my homeland and . . . you . . . my laird."

"Well, then, I owe him a great debt of gratitude. Come, MacGowan, you will be our guest this night," said the Munro, and tightening his grip on Anora's arm, turned to go.

"I fear I cannot." Ramsay's words were measured.

Munro turned slowly back, his entire body tense. "What is that you say, lad?"

" 'Tis just this—lad," he said evenly. "I must return home this night."

"But I insist that you stay," Munro said, and glanced almost casually at the guards who rode nearby. Immediately they tightened their circle around him. "To accept me gratitude."

Ramsay glanced about him. The suggestion of a grim smile shadowed his face, and then he settled his hand on his sword. "As much as I would like to—"

"Please!" Anora rasped, then calmed her voice with a hard won effort and tried to smile. "Please stay, sir."

He turned toward her, his expression flat, his eyes unreadable. Still she held his gaze.

"Please stay," she repeated, and forced herself to relax. He would be safe; she would make certain of that. "I owe you much."

"Aye," the Munro agreed. "And the lady's debts are me own. You must join us for a homecoming feast. Caird, have me mount brought up."

"Aye, me laird."

"And now, me dearest," Munro said, turning to her again. "You must tell me why you escaped me men?"

"Escaped them!" She glanced fearfully up into his broad face. "Nay. 'Twas simply that the mare you gave me became startled and fled into the woods. I could not stop her."

He scowled. "She bolted?"

"Aye."

"Caird," he snarled, lifting his gaze from her face. "The mare has displeased me lady. Send a man to the south in search of her. When we find her . . ." He returned his attention to Anora, his scowl harder than ever as he nodded. "We shall feast on her carcass and you shall have the first morsel."

"Nay!" Her heart jammed in her chest as words lodged in her throat. "Please. 'Tis not necessary, my laird."

He watched her closely. "The beast endangered you," he rumbled.

"Aye. But . . . 'twas my own fault. As you well know, I am not very strong, and when she took the bit in her teeth . . ."

"So you do not want her slaughtered?"

"Nay," she murmured.

He nodded once. "You have bought the beast's life for a while longer—but tell me, lass, why did you not return to the protection of me men?"

Anora lowered her face, her heart beating hard and fast against her ribs. " 'Tis embarrassed I am to tell you."

"Embarrassed?" He narrowed his eyes and tightened his fist on his dirk again. "Was there one who compromised you?"

"Nay!" She quelled her nervousness, lest he sense it but mistake the reason. People had died for less. "Your men were naught but courteous."

"Good." He glowered at his men, then turned to mount the gigantic stallion just brought to him. From his steed's great height he reached down for Anora's hand.

She shook her head, trying to stand her ground, but she felt light-headed and nauseated. "If it pleases you, me laird, I will walk."

For just a moment, his gaze swept to Ramsay.

"You rode on that wee horse. It would please me if you rode on mine," he rumbled.

She acquiesced without a word, giving him her hand and settling stiffly in front of him.

"Come along, MacGowan," Munro said. "Mayhap you can assist me lady with her story."

The men around Ramsay urged him forward, and he came, riding alongside them.

"She was just about to tell me why she did not return to her escort."

"I fear . . ." She wrapped her fingers in the stallion's mane for strength and concentrated on the verdant country. There, atop a high, flat sided hill, perched Evermyst, fifty rods above the restless sea. Her home. Her sanctuary. She would *not* live in fear here. She would be safe again, as would her people. Of that, she would make certain. 'Twas all that mattered.

"You fear what?" Munro rumbled.

It did not matter what the MacGowan thought. It did not matter how he felt or what he did, she reminded herself. All that mattered were her people, her home, her freedom.

"Lady," Munro said.

Anora snapped her mind back to the matter at hand. "I became turned about in the woods. I tried to find my way back to the safety of your escort, but the mare had run long and hard, and I . . ." She let her voice drift away.

"You should have called out."

"I did. I called and . . ." She swallowed hard. "Indeed, I fear 'twas my own voice that brought the warrior upon me."

"Warrior?"

His huge arm tightened like a vise about her waist. Fear rose in her throat. It took all her strength to keep from attempting to fight free.

"My laird," she whispered, "I cannot breathe."

"Oh." He loosened his grip a mite. "What of this warrior?"

"He came out of nowhere." She kept her voice low, her eyes averted. "Galloping toward me, and I was afraid."

"Who was he?"

She did not need to see his face to feel his anger. The Munro did not like others to challenge what he had claimed for his own. "I do not know."

"Did he harm you?" The words were gritted, his right arm, as thick around as her leg, tightened dangerously again.

"Nay. Indeed, 'twas then that MacGowan found me."

"Ahh." His grip loosened a little. They were climbing, ascending the nearly vertical slope that led to Evermyst's all but unbreachable heights. From beyond the rocky slopes that acted as natural walls about the path, she could hear the rhythmic wash of the waves against the castle's very roots. "So you saw this mysterious warrior, MacGowan?"

For a moment he did not answer, then, "We caught a glimpse of him."

"We?"

"Me brothers were with me."

"The brother rogues. I have heard of you."

Ramsay held his gaze. "And we of you."

Munro grinned, showing the gap in his teeth. "So the tales of me prowess spreads."

"I have heard tales; that I will say."

"They all be true."

"I never doubted it."

Munro stared for a moment, then grinned as if he'd decided to accept the words as a compliment. "So you and your brothers saved me wee lady."

"We took her to Dun Ard."

"Did you, now?" His tone was careful; his small eyes, were narrowed. "And what happened there?"

Memories burned through Anora's mind like a thousand blazing candles. Ramsay's touch, his kiss, his—

"There was little time for aught," Ramsay said, his tone even, "for from the first moment she awoke, she wished to return to . . . her home."

He had almost said "to Levenlair," Anora thought, and realized she'd been holding her breath.

"Awoke?" The heavy timbre of the Munro's voice echoed as they passed through the stone arch of Evermyst's outer curtain, and for an instant, he shifted his eyes suspiciously around him as if the very walls contained unseen foes. But to her it was naught but home.

Ailsa, Anora's second cousin by marriage, stood beside the worn path, her back to the rock behind her. Her breasts, full and pale in the morning light, were all but bare to the world. Grazing on the uneven turf, her goats chewed rapidly as they cocked their heads at the passing riders. "I thank God you have found her," said Ailsa, but her buxom presence did nothing to distract the Munro.

"Awoke?" he growled again. "You were with her when she awoke, MacGowan?"

Ramsay said nothing.

"I was unconscious when the MacGowans found me," Anora explained.

"What's this?" Munro leaned closer, pressing his heavy chest against her back.

"I fell from Pearl, and—"

"Slow down there, lass. It seems this tale gets the

more interesting as it unravels. Methinks we'd best sit and discuss it at length. MacGowan, you will join us, of course."

"Nay," Anora said.

"What?"

"I would like some time to rest, me laird, afore—"

"Lassie," someone crooned.

Anora jerked her attention to the doorway of the keep where an ancient woman stood bent and scowling over a black walnut staff. "Meara," she breathed. "You are well?"

"Aye, lassie. Aye."

"And Isobel?" she asked, barely able to force out the question.

"Aye."

"What of Deirdre and Clarinda?"

"All are safe. And what of you?" The old woman took a feeble step toward them. "You are well?"

"Aye, she be fine," said the Munro. "And you will speak with her soon enough. But for now she is recounting the tale of her adventures to her betrothed."

Ignoring the Munro, Meara scuttled forward a few steps. "You are well?" she asked again, her gaze pinned on Anora's face.

"I am fine," she answered and held the old woman's gaze for a moment, longing for . . . nay, *needing* her ancient wisdom to see her through. She pulled her gaze from Meara's and lifted it to the huge man behind her. "But I am tired. Mayhap we could speak later, me laird."

"I will hear the tale—"

"Surely even *you* can see that the lass is exhausted, Munro!" Meara croaked.

He tightened his arm about Anora's ribs and

straightened. "Methinks it would be wise of you to treat your laird with some respect, old woman."

Meara drew herself up to her full and astoundingly unimpressive height. "And methinks *you* are a—"

Anora gave a quiet sigh and forced herself to go limp in his arms.

"Anora!" Meara croaked.

"Lady," Munro rumbled and shook her roughly. "Lady."

"What have you done to her?"

"I've done nothing."

"By the saints," Meara swore, hobbling forward, "if you've hurt her, you'll be supping with her grandmother this very night."

" 'Tis nothing," Munro rumbled, but a note of uncertainty had crept into his tone. "She's but fainted."

"Fainted!" Meara turned her attention aside to skim the faces around them and returned to MacGowan with a jolt. "You! What's your name?"

"I am called Ramsay."

"Come hither and catch the lass."

He remained as he was. "That would be her betrothed's—"

"Come!" Meara ordered.

Apparently he did so, for despite the fact that she lay slumped against the Munro's chest, Anora could hear the creak of his saddle as he dismounted.

"Let her go," Meara insisted.

"She is mine to—"

"Release her!" Meara ordered. "Or you'll not have to worry on her ancestors' wrath, for me own will be vicious enough."

He loosened his meaty grip. Anora felt herself slipping, but in a moment she was caught in Ramsay's arms. It took all her concentration to remain relaxed as he bore her to his chest.

"Inside!" Meara ordered. "Up the stairs."

A half dozen voices murmured around her as servants and kinsmen drew close.

"Me lady!"

"She is returned!"

"What happened?" Isobel's worried voice joined the throng.

"She fainted," Meara said.

"Fainted!" Isobel's eyes widened.

"Hush now, child. Up the stairs, lad."

MacGowan's footfalls were steady and sure, and in a moment she was laid upon her own bed. It sighed beneath her back. Ramsay drew his arms slowly away. Meara took her hand.

"Is she well?" Ramsay asked.

"What concern is it of yours, laddie?" Munro's voice was strangely silky.

"Mayhap the lad has a heart," Meara said, "unlike some others in this room. Isobel, fetch a mug of ale for your lady."

Feather-light footsteps skittered away and heavy ones paced closer. "So I have no heart, old woman?"

"I've not had the pleasure to check," said Meara. "But 'tis possible, I suspect."

"And 'tis *just* as possible that yours will be forfeited as soon as—"

"What say you, laddie?" Meara asked, interrupting brusquely. "Do you think the Munro here has a heart?"

The room went silent.

"I've been told all have one," Ramsay said finally. " 'Tis simply that some use them more effectively than others."

Meara laughed, but her mirth was interrupted by the sound of the Munro's dirk slicing from its scabbard.

"I hate to kill a guest!" Munro rumbled.

"Aye," Ramsay continued. "All have a heart, but a mind . . ."

There was a growl of rumbling rage.

"Munro!" Meara snapped. "Remember the prophecy or share your sire's fate."

There was deadly silence for a moment, followed by the sound of a razor-edged dirk meeting its sheath again. "Surely not," Munro rumbled, "for me own motives are naught but generous. Indeed, 'tis only me tender mercies I wish to bestow upon the lady—naught else."

Meara opened her mouth to retort, but Anora squeezed her hand and the old woman's face fell back into a scowl. "Then get yourself gone from here," she said. "And let the lass rest."

"You will tell me when she awakens."

Anora squeezed again, and the old woman paused. "I would be pleased as always to serve me laird."

There was a moment of tense silence as if he pondered her words. " 'Tis good. And now for you, MacGowan. Come." His voice held that frightening silkiness again. "We shall share a mug while you regale me with stories of the time you spent with me bride-to-be."

Footsteps crossed the floor. The door closed with resounding finality, then silence filled the room. Anora waited, breath held as she listened to the sounds of nothing, but in a moment the silence was broken by the creak of the door again.

"Forget something, me laird?" Meara asked.

"Aye." Munro's voice was deep with disappointment as though he thought to find her already awake. "Care for her well, old woman, or 'twill be you who haunts this keep." With that he turned and made his way heavily down the wooden stairs.

"Lassie!" Helena hustled in, tears already brimming in her faded green eyes as she clasped Anora in her plump arms. "I was worried sick. Where have you been? Are you well? You can't imagine—"

"Don't tax the girl with your feeble questions," Meara said, prodding the other aside with the tip of her gnarled cane. "What happened with your uncle, lass?"

Anora scooted upward to prop her back against the headboard wall behind her. "He did not come."

"Well, hell's belfry, I can see that," Meara scolded. "But why? He is your father's kin. 'Tis his duty to see to your well being."

"He was more than willing, until he realized 'twas the Munro who had claimed my hand in marriage."

"Did you not tell him of the prophecy? Did you not tell him that Evermyst must be mastered by the proper man, lest blood flow and—"

"Aye. I told him. But he did not care, so long as the blood was not his own."

"Then we are left to our own devices." Meara's voice was low.

"Me lady," Isobel whispered, entering the room with a mug clasped between her narrow hands. In a moment she knelt beside the bed, the drink abandoned on the floor. "You are returned, hale and healthy." Reaching out, she folded Anora's hand in her own. "I feared the worst."

"Isobel." Anora grasped the maid's grubby hand and drew in the sight of her, the stodgy coif, the elfin face. "You are well?"

"Aye."

"I dreamed that you—" She lost her voice for a moment.

Their gazes met and melded, blue on blue.

"Nay," Isobel whispered. "I am well. It has not come to pass. Not—"

"Stout Helena!" Meara said. "Can't you see the lass is faint with hunger?"

Helena speared a glare at the elder woman, then lowered her gaze to Anora and smiled mistily. "Is there aught I can fetch for you, lass?"

Anora reached out with her free hand, grasping the other's dimpled fingers. " 'Tis wondrous to see you, Helena. I missed you so."

The matron hugged Anora's fingers to her plump bosom for a moment. "And I you, lass. And I you," she said, then released Anora's fingers and wiped her nose with her apron. "Now I go to prepare a feast."

The door closed soundly behind her.

"Finally!" Meara said. "Now, tell me, lass—what has not passed? What did you dream?"

Isobel spoke. "That the Munro learned the truth."

"Lord save us! Nay!" Meara pleaded.

"It has not happened!" Isobel whispered. "And it will not. I will not let it."

"You cannot prevent it," Meara said, and turned herself creakily from the bed. "You think yourselves the clever ones, the pair of you, but the Munro is not as foolish as he appears, and—"

" 'Twould nearly defy the impossible," Isobel finished. And though the world lay like a horrible weight on Anora's shoulders, she could not help but smile, for she was home, among her people.

" 'Tis not a matter for mirth," Meara warned her.

"Eventually even that great hulking oaf will see through your weak-kneed demonstrations, just as he will see through Isobel's cloying filth. And as for ghosts—" She snorted, a harsh sound in the grim silence.

"What about ghosts?" Anora asked.

No one spoke.

"What of ghosts?" she asked again. "Was it Senga? Did she make herself known?"

"What did you think would happen if the Munro moved himself into her home?"

"He didn't."

"Aye," Meara agreed. "Moved into your own chamber he did, lass."

"And Senga?"

" 'Twas nothing much," Isobel said.

"Nothing much," Meara agreed. "If you do not think it strange to awaken to find your throat cut!"

"Throat—"

" 'Twas not cut," Isobel soothed. " 'Twas only blood."

"Aye!" Meara glared at Isobel. "A stripe across the Munro's neck just so." She made a swipe with one bent finger across her own neck. "As if it had been cut with a knife. 'Twas his scream that woke me in the early morn."

The corner of a grin lifted Isobel's mobile mouth. "He screams like a house maid."

"Nay," Anora breathed.

" 'Tis no laughing matter!" Meara snarled. "Although . . ." For a moment her face evidenced an expression that could almost be considered a smile. "It did me old heart good to see his broad backside hustling out of our keep. Still . . ." The scowl was firmly

back in place. "He is not his father, lassies. Mark me
words. He will not fear the spirits forever, nor did he
inherit his sire's weak heart."

"Mayhap 'twas not a weak heart that killed his da at
all," Isobel said. "But a visit from Senga, just as is
said."

"Or mayhap 'twas justice for what they did to your
dear mother," Meara hissed, her voice low. "But whatever the cause, 'tis his younger son we must worry on
now. And this much I know: he'll not stay gone, not so
long as Evermyst overlooks the very waters he longs
to control. He means to take our home, and if he must
bed a Fraser to take hold of it, so much the better."

"I cannot wed him," Anora whispered.

"Mayhap his fear of Senga—" Isobel began, but
Meara interrupted.

"We cannot depend on the spirits to protect us. We
must think of another means."

"It seems a vast waste of a perfectly good ghost,"
Isobel murmured.

"Hush, now. I'm thinking," Meara said, and in a
moment, slanted her narrow eyes toward Anora. "This
MacGowan—tell me of him."

Anora held her breath. "Why?"

Meara stopped. "Why do you not tell me?"

A hundred potent memories stormed through her
mind. "Because he has naught to do with this matter."

"Naught to do? Do you forget where your loyalties
lie?"

"Nay, I do not. But neither do I trust a stranger to
right my troubles."

"So that's what he is to you, lass? Naught but a
stranger?" The old woman's eyes were as bright as
river pebbles.

Anora nearly squirmed under her gaze, like a small girl caught with her embroidery not done. "We traveled together, nothing more."

"You allowed a man to travel with you?"

"I had little choice."

"One always has a choice, lassie, and 'tis foolish of you to pretend otherwise. Why did you ride with him?"

Anora said nothing.

"Tell me, lass. Was he kind? Is he cunning?"

"He—"

"Are you fond of him?"

"Nay!" Anora hissed. "He is a man."

The room went silent.

"So you have noticed," Meara said quietly. "And not only a man, but a MacGowan. Powerful, wealthy, and by the looks of him . . ." She almost grinned. "Fit and willing to come to your aid. Surely you have considered what this means."

"Aye." Something twisted in her stomach. "I considered it. In truth, at first I thought 'twas the answer to my prayers. I planned to return here with a score of trained warriors at my beck and call. But 'twas not to be. We became separated from the others, and he . . ." She scowled, remembering the tremble of his hand after the warrior's retreat. Had he really worried for her?

"He what, lassie?" Meara's gaze was as sharp as a well-stropped dirk.

Anora lowered her eyes to where her hand gripped Isobel's. "He is only one man. Hardly enough to fight the strength of the Munros."

"Who is speaking of fighting? I only—"

"Nay!" Anora's heart bumped hard in her chest. "He will not become involved."

"So you care more for him than for your own, lass?"

"Surely you know me better than that."

"Do I?"

"Aye," she whispered. " 'Tis not in me to care for a man."

The room was silent; then, " 'Tis good, lassie," Meara said, her voice a rough whisper in the quiet. "For you know what you must do."

Chapter 16

Every word she'd ever uttered was a lie.

Ramsay sat very still, letting his mind burn while keeping his face absolutely impassive.

She was not named Mary. She was not the lady of Levenlair, and she was not free to marry where she would. She was betrothed! Ramsay stared across the wooden trestle table at the laird of the Munros. Big as a bull, he swallowed a hunk of cold pork, quaffed beer, then wiped his mouth with the back side of an enormous hairy-knuckled hand. Loathing rose in Ramsay's gut, but he stamped it down. She deserved the hulking clod. And he her.

Munro raised a horn to his thick lips once again. They sat in Evermyst's great hall, surrounded by a dozen Munro warriors. Beyond them, servants hovered nervously. Only one maid, heavy with child, dared to come close, her mouth open as she watched in slumped awe.

Ramsay lowered his gaze to his drink again. Thus far not a word had been spoken, and he would just as soon it continued that way. He was a peaceable man by nature, with little use for the kind of emotions that made fools of men.

"So, laddie . . ."

But if that hulking piece of horse shit called him laddie one more time, he'd shove the word down his cavern-sized throat.

"You've spent some time with me betrothed, huh?" Beer foam was already stuck to Munro's beard, but he took another swig and licked his lips. The foam remained with annoying tenacity.

Ramsay said nothing.

"Saved her, did you? Carried her to your keep?"

Christ, his damned jaw was as wide a mule's ass.

"Or was it one of your brothers who carried her?"

Funny thing, he just didn't feel like conversing with the jawbone of an ass just now.

"The MacGowan rogues." The huge man nodded as if unconcerned with his companion's laconic nature. "I have heard tales of your way with women, and I wonder if they be true."

Ramsay took a drink from his horn and silently considered its golden contents.

"Damn it!" The table reverberated beneath the Munro's gargantuan fist.

Ramsay glanced up, careful to look just short of bored.

"I asked you a question, laddie!" The words were growled into a room that had gone absolutely silent.

Behind the Munro, the pregnant woman cackled an eerie laugh.

"Aye. You did that." Ramsay held his gaze. The man was as big as a tower wall and looked twice as solid, but damned if it wouldn't feel fine to get off one clean punch. Of course, he would probably die then, which would be something of a drawback.

Munro glared, shifted, glared again, then drew slowly back. "Ahh, but now you got me wondering, lad. Are you so brave that you do not care that you've pissed me off?" Reaching casually toward a pewter candleholder, he drew it into his hands, then, tilting it slightly, bent it with slow but steady pressure in two. "Or could it be that you're so daft, you do not know the consequences?"

Ramsay shifted his gaze from the candlestick to Munro's face, then shook his head slightly as if attempting to clear it. "Me apologies," he said. "Me mind wandered. What did you say?"

For a moment Ramsay thought the great bull might charge, and indeed, maybe deep inside his soul, Ramsay hoped he would. But the Munro reared back and laughed, throwing his bellowing glee toward the high, smoky rafters.

'Twas the perfect opportunity for an undercut to the chin. And so damned tempting.

"I like your grit, laddie. That I do," Munro said, settling back to stare again. "But you see, the thing is this." He leaned closer, lowering his voice. "Me future bride has left the escort I provided for her, gotten herself lost, and been brought home, unchaperoned and unwed, by a MacGowan rogue. Now, for meself, I am a tolerant man by nature, and I like you, but I am the Munro of the Munros and I would not have me men thinking poorly of me bride."

"Poorly?" Ramsay asked, keeping his tone even.

"She seems the regal lady, too good for the likes of any man, huh? But sometimes I wonder, is she saint or is she whore?"

"You've narrowed it down to one or the other, have you, Munro?" he asked, and drank again, forcing himself to swallow. After all, 'twas hardly his place to guard the girl's reputation. Below the table, he carefully loosened his fist.

The Munro watched him like an eagle on a rat and leaned closer so that he all but whispered his next words. " 'Tis said by some that she whored for the laird of Tytherleigh nearly a decade ago."

Ramsay held himself very still. Though he tried to shut out the memories, he could not forget the sound of her voice as she had told him her story. Could not forget the bottomless sadness in her eyes nor the sight of her restless hands. "A decade," he said softly. "It seems to me she would have been only a child then, Munro."

"Aye." He leaned back a few inches and shrugged. "And all the better broke in early, huh?"

Ramsay took another swig and waited for calm to descend, but he could think of little except how it would feel to drive his fist into the other man's belly. Maybe he could get in a few good blows before the Munro's warriors overtook him.

"Have I surprised you, MacGowan? Mayhap you thought me the jealous sort. The kind to avenge her honor." He laughed again and shook his giant head. "First off, Richard of Tytherleigh died some years ago, the bastard, and second, me old da taught me not to be a fool over a maid, no matter how . . ." He paused and shifted his gaze toward the stairway and back. "I will share a secret with you, laddie," he said. " 'Tis hardly the thought of that wee scrawny thing in me bed that brings me here." He drank and scowled. "She's likely to break like a twig beneath me weight."

One clean blow to his nose—that was all Ramsay asked.

"So you wonder. What stirs the Munro's blood?"

Ramsay watched him for a prolonged moment, then glanced at the warriors who occupied the table not far away. "I would say the fellow in the green tam. The one with the bonny eyes."

The Munro jerked, then curled a lip at the jest. "You have a clever tongue, laddie. I'd hate to cut it out."

Ramsay raised his horn in silent agreement.

"Why, I wonder, are you in such a rush to die?" Munro mused, and sat back again, cradling his drinking horn against his barrel-like chest.

"In truth, I am in no great hurry."

"Nay?"

"No more than the average man."

"But 'twas not the average man who escorted me betrothed back to her homeland. 'Twas you," Munro said, stabbing a blunt finger toward Ramsay's chest. "And were you an average man, I might think you had fallen under her spell."

Ramsay's stomach cramped.

"There are such men," Munro continued. "Those who grow weak at the sight of a wench. Addled at the touch of her wee fingers." He placed a broad and filthy hand almost reverently against his chest, reminding Ramsay of seeing Anora's hand just so not many minutes before. He scowled.

"But not you," Ramsay said. "You are unaffected."

"Me?" Munro barked a laugh and wrenched his hand into a fist. "Do I look like a milksop lassie to you, MacGowan?"

A dozen possible answers swooped through Ramsay's mind. Some were quite clever; all of them were likely to get him killed. He peered into his brew. "I can honestly say, Munro, you do not look like any lassie I've ever seen." It was debatable, in fact, whether he was actually human.

" 'Tis true," growled Munro. "Though I profess to cherish the lass, I am not so foolish as to let meself become enamored. Still, if I thought you hoped to win her hand, I'd take you apart piece by scrawny piece."

"Then you can rest easy." Though Ramsay raised his mug to his lips, he was unable to swallow. "The maid's hand holds no interest for me."

The Munro lunged from his chair, snatching Ramsay's tunic just below his cat-eyed brooch. "What the devil do you mean by that?"

Ramsay glanced up, and though his nostrils flared and his oh-so-tolerant disposition threatened to burn a hole clean through his chest, he remained unmoving. "It only means that I have no interest in the lass at all."

"Damn you!" Munro snarled, and shoved against Ramsay's chest so that he threatened to topple over backward. " 'Tis the Myst you've got your eye on, then."

Ramsay attempted to locate some sort of logic in the other's words, but try as he might, he could find none.

"Tell me, MacGowan, did your sire send you here? And what of your brothers and clansmen? Might they be hidden in the forest roundabout? Is that why you be so smug?"

Ramsay's mind spun.

"Well, you needn't be so sure, me young cockerel, for I'll tell you now: Evermyst has never been taken, and won't be by the likes of you."

Finally Munro's logic dawned on Ramsay. " 'Tis the castle you covet."

Munro scowled. "What else?"

The image of Anora's firelit figure shone in Ramsay's memory. Her hair was gilded, her eyes alight, and through the gossamer fabric of her night rail he could see every heavenly curve of her body. "You jest," he said, momentarily forgetting himself, but he could see no sign of humor in the Munro's low-browed expression. Indeed, he watched Ramsay as if trying to read his very thoughts.

"Could it be that you *are* enamored with her? A MacGowan!" he said, as if the idea was ludicrous.

Was he joking? Was he insane? It was impossible to guess.

"I've no wish to insult your lady," Ramsay said, his tone carefully casual.

"Speak your mind before I stick you to the wall for sport," Munro growled.

Ramsay practiced his Latin. Unus, duo, tres . . . "The old woman seemed to think that unwise," Ramsay said, finding his patience.

"I am no more concerned with the crone than with the shade," Munro grunted, but even as he said it his eyes shifted toward the stairs.

"Shade?" Ramsay asked, but Munro ignored him.

"Answer me question, MacGowan, for I fear I am losing me wondrous good humor."

"And the question again . . ."

"Are you enamored with her?" he growled.

"In truth," Ramsay held the Minotaur's gaze with his own, "I, too, favor more robust women."

Munro's palm slammed against the table top. "Evermyst is mine!"

It seemed there was no way to make this man happy.

"Mayhap I escorted the lady simply because she needed me assistance," Ramsay suggested.

"So you do not care that from this very stronghold, you can see for ten leagues in every direction. All but impenetrable it is, but you have no interest in Evermyst. Is that it, laddie?"

"You plan to take the maid's home for your fortress?"

" 'Tis *not* hers!" Munro snarled. " 'Tis mine! Won for me by me sire."

"Old Ironfist," Ramsay mused, and a dozen half-forgotten stories rose in his memories.

"Aye." Munro drank again. "Strong as a stallion, he was. 'Twas more than once that he tossed me into the moat, arse and armor and all."

"Aye." Ramsay nodded, remembering the tales. " 'Tis clear he was a fine father to you."

Munro narrowed his eyes. "He was a bastard by all accounts, but he knew the play of war." His horn was apparently empty, for he lifted it imperiously and the maid scrambled up from behind to refill it. For a moment her hand lingered on his, causing him to glower at her in some surprise until she cowered away. He raised the horn again, sloshing beer over the rim. "Aye, a bastard he was. Yet even he could not take this place—though he thought he had won the day. Came in peace, he did, or so he said. But once inside the gates . . ." He made a slicing motion across his own throat and drank again. "Just the guards. Not the old laird, of course, though he was a sniveling cur if the truth be told. 'Twas the old woman who had the grit." He glanced toward the stairs again and scowled. "She all but spat fire. Railed at him, she did, and with his own dirk tried to cut his throat as she laid curses on him." He snorted. "Ironfist thought it all foolishness. Threw her and the old laird out in the stable while he claimed their chambers and barred the door behind him." He glanced covertly about the hall as if searching the shadowy corners. "Still, on the morn he spoke of seeing a wee maid all in white in his room. A maid come to find a real man, he said. And then, as though he'd been stuck through the heart with a pig pole, he fell face forward onto his trencher. 'Twas the last breath he took. And yet there was not a mark on him, but for the nick on his neck from his own blade." He scowled. "What have you to say of that, MacGowan?"

Ramsay drank, his mind scurrying off in a thousand directions at once. "Some curses be more effective than others."

"Aye." Munro leaned close. "But I will not share me father's fate. It has taken planning and time, but in the end, Evermyst's old laird was willing to offer his daughter for a few well placed favors."

Ramsay's stomach curdled. "He promised his own daughter to the one who had slaughtered his people?"

" 'Twas not me who did the deed," Munro said, scowling.

"And what of the curse?" Ramsay asked.

"As powerful as he is peaceable. As cunning as he is kind, as loving as he is loved." He carved off a slice of cold roasted boar, then stabbed his knife into the table. It hummed like an arrow in the wood. " 'Tis the very picture of me."

Ramsay watched the shivering hilt for a moment before raising his gaze to Munro's face. "I am somewhat confused."

"The curse!" Munro growled. "There will be death to any who master these halls unless he possesses the necessary qualities."

"Power and cunning and—"

"Aye!"

"Ahh. And you possess those qualities."

"That I do, laddie, or at least, 'tis what I've made the lass believe. But mayhap the lass's time with you has caused her to forget me fine attributes."

"You've nothing to worry about on that account."

"Do I not?" The giant's eyes were narrowed again. "She is a spindly thing. Barely a mouthful, 'tis true, but her eyes . . . well, some may think her bonny in a weakling sort of way. I wonder now, rogue, what of you?"

She'd lied to him since the first, threatened to have him emasculated and eviscerated, and endangered his life at every turn. "As I have said, you needn't worry. Unless . . ." He paused as if just considering an unthought-of possibility. "Unless, mayhap, she does not *wish* to marry you."

"Are you saying I am not everything a woman might want?" Munro growled, and thrust out his gargantuan chest.

"Women are strange, sometimes."

Munro scowled, seeming to deflate somehow. "That they are, and I'll admit I've not had much association with them, but I know none could wish for more than me."

He was like a little boy in a huge man's body. " 'Tis simply that I once heard that the lady of the Frasers could choose her own husband," he said.

"What fool would grant a woman such a privilege?"

Could it be there was some truth to it? "I believe 'twas the king himself."

"It matters not," Munro said, "for the lass has chosen me."

"At her father's insistence."

"He knew what was good for her."

"Or what was good for himself," Ramsay guessed mildly. "What did you offer him, Munro?"

The huge man shifted uncomfortably on his wooden seat. Guilt? Ramsay wondered, but at that moment the Minotaur leaned forward with a snarl.

" 'Tis I who'll ask the questions here, and I will know, did you take her?"

"I beg—"

"You'll beg for mercy if you've stolen her affections," he growled. "Did you swive her or nay?"

Beneath the table, Ramsay's hands formed into fists. He kept them still, though he could not manage the same with his voice. "You have the mind of a sewer rat, Munro."

"Aye. And the strength of a bear," he snarled, and with that statement a thousand emotions seemed to storm across his face. Guilt, regret, anger . . . "Did you lie with her or did you not?"

Guilt? Might it be that this hulking beast regretted his barbaric heritage and his own past actions? Why not probe a bit and see what happened? " 'Tis not a question a gentle man answers," Ramsay said mildly.

Munro rose with a start, nearly overturning the table in his haste. "Nay?" he stormed. "Then I shall ask the maid. But I warn you—" He leaned down, his teeth gritted. "I am *not* a gentle man," he said, and turned away.

Ramsay sat unmoving for a fraction of a second. "Munro."

The huge man stopped and turned slowly. "You've something to say, laddie?"

Ramsay nodded to the nearby soldiers. "Not to them."

The Minotaur paced slowly back, his head lowered into his neck, then he sat down, his mouth tilted down in the chaos of his beard. "Between us, then."

Ramsay held his gaze. "She refused me."

Munro's eyes widened, then narrowed. "You lie."

"I do not."

"You are the Rogue's son."

Christ. What kinds of daft idiocy did people believe about them? "Aye, I am that."

"And yet she said nay?"

"She did."

Munro glanced toward the stairs, his expression a mask of confusion, but in a moment he turned back to Ramsay with a scowl. "If you lie . . ." He shrugged. "I shall have to kill you."

Ramsay raised his brows. "Have you forgot me reputation so soon, Munro?"

The Munro stared for a moment, and then he threw his head back and laughed before leaning close. "Your reputation as a lover holds little fear for me, MacGowan, and now I find even that—"

His statement was cut short by the sound of someone clearing her throat.

Munro swung his huge head to the rear, glaring as

he did so, but in a second his expression changed. "Me lady! You've awakened."

"Aye." Anora's narrow hands were clasped, her face as pale as winter, and it took all Ramsay's control to keep from leaping to his feet to support her. "I . . . have something I must tell you, my laird."

"Tell me?" Munro's brows were scrunched like woolly caterpillars above his narrow eyes.

"Not now, lass," hissed Meara, who stood beside her like a withered gnome.

"It cannot wait," Anora argued, and lifted her chin.

"What cannot—" Munro began, but in that instant a whispered sigh issued over the hall on the wings of a wispy draft. "What the devil was that?"

Near the stairs, a fat friar crossed himself.

Anora winced. " 'Tis naught," she said, but Meara scowled.

" 'Tis Senga!" she whispered. "Your grandmother is restless. 'Tis not the time for this, lass."

" 'Tis the only time."

"She senses trouble."

"Hush, Meara."

"He who spills blood within these walls—" the old woman began.

"No blood will spill," Anora murmured, but her knees buckled slightly before she stood upright again.

"Why would I spill blood?" Munro snarled.

A ghostly sigh washed through the hall again, bringing the last of the soldiers to his feet and causing the Munro to shift his eyes nervously from side to side.

"Have a care, Innes," croaked the old woman, "or you shall surely die."

"Meara!" Anora's voice was strained. "This is difficult enough."

"What is difficult?"

"My laird," Anora said, and grasped the old woman's sleeve for support. "Because of my respect for you, I must tell you the truth."

Ramsay glared hard at her, trying to read her mind, but not for an instant did she turn her gaze on him.

"Tell me," Munro said.

"I cannot marry you, my laird, for I cherish another."

Not a whisper of noise sounded in the hall, and in that silence she turned her impossibly wide eyes to Ramsay.

"Aye," she whispered. "I love him."

Chapter 17

Hell exploded.

Munro yanked his dirk from the wooden plank as he jerked to his feet. A table crashed to the floor. A dozen soldiers rushed forward.

Meara screamed, "No blood! No blood!"

"Lord have mercy," the friar intoned.

Ramsay remained exactly where he was, his gaze pinned on Anora. She stared back in breathless silence.

"MacGowan!" Munro growled and, gripping Ramsay's tunic in his oversized fist, pressed the tip of his dirk to his throat. "Is it true?" he snarled, but Ramsay never shifted his gaze from Anora.

Terror blended with guilt, swirling chaotically through her mind.

"Is it true?" Munro snarled.

"Would the lady lie?" Ramsay asked, and ever so slowly pulled his gaze from her face.

The Munro drew back. "I have never killed a Mac-Gowan," he intoned.

"How fortunate for you," Ramsay said.

"Shed blood in this hall and bear the consequences," Meara warned.

Munro tilted his large head in concession. "You will accompany me outside, MacGowan?"

"Nay!" Anora hissed. "You cannot kill him."

The Munro turned slowly toward her. "I assure you, me lady, I can."

"But you must *not*."

"On the contrary. I must."

"Surely you would not . . ." She paused, floundering wildly. "Surely you would not be so cruel as to sacrifice my babe's sire."

Ramsay started. Munro paled.

"You carry his child?" he growled.

"Aye." Her voice quivered.

"Then you shall surely die!" Munro jerked Ramsay toward him, but just then Meara stepped forward and smacked him with her staff.

"You are a liar, Munro!" she croaked.

The huge man turned to her with a snarl, his fist still twisted in Ramsay's tunic.

"Aye. You are a liar," she repeated, glaring up at him. "For you have proclaimed your love for the maid, yet you move to slay the one she adores."

Munro scowled. His grip loosened.

" 'Tis his right. Indeed, 'tis his duty," Ramsay said.

Anora gasped.

"As your betrothed," he added, holding her gaze.

"Don't," she whispered.

"Aye," Ramsay said, and rose slowly to his feet.

Munro dropped his fist from Ramsay's tunic and stepped back one pace. "You *wish* to fight me, Mac-Gowan?"

"Nay!" Anora gasped, and jerked forward. "He does not."

"Be gone, lady!" Munro snarled.

"You cannot fight him, for he is my chosen one."

"I am your chosen one."

"I never said so."

The Munro seemed even paler now, but he tightened his fist on his dirk. "Your sire did."

" 'Twas not his right to decide. 'Twas mine, given to me by the king himself."

"The king has troubles of his own, girl, and they do not include a disloyal maid on a crumbling piece of rock."

Panic welled up like freezing waves, and Anora's lungs felt crushed beneath the pressure. "And what of the MacGowans?" she asked. "Do you think they will sacrifice their first-born son so that you might have your revenge?"

"The lass is right," Meara said over the friar's droning prayers. "Think on it well, Innes. The MacGowans are as powerful as they are wealthy, and they do indeed have the ear of the king. What will they do when they hear that you have slaughtered their son?"

"Slaughter?" He shook his meaty head, grinning darkly. "I will give him a fair fight."

Meara snorted. "What chance does he have against—"

"He is hurt!" Anora gasped.

"Hurt?" The big man narrowed his eyes. "Is this true, MacGowan?"

"I bound the wound myself," Anora said. " 'Tis in his shoulder."

Munro snarled and stepped forward, but Anora lunged between them.

"Would you have your own men think you a coward, Munro?"

His head was pushed down between his shoulders like a charging bull's, but he was listening.

" 'Tis what they will surely believe, and what of my own clansmen?" She swept a shaky hand sideways to include the onlookers. "What will they think when they learn that you could not challenge a MacGowan when he was hale?"

The hall went silent. Not a soul spoke for an aching eternity.

"I've no wish to battle a weakling," Munro said. "When will you be prepared to fight me, MacGowan?"

Ramsay remained motionless. "I've got nothing planned for the morrow."

Munro barked a laugh. "Spoken like a hero . . . or a fool. Tomorrow, then."

"Nay!" Anora gasped.

"Use your time wisely, MacGowan," Munro warned. "For just past dawn I will return to—"

A whisper crept through the hall like a chill and eerie wind. The place went silent.

Munro shifted his gaze from right to left.

"Senga is unhappy," Meara whispered.

The Munro straightened. "Shade or no, I will meet you," he said. Sheathing his dirk, he ordered his men from the hall.

When Anora glanced at Ramsay, she found that his gaze was pinned to her.

"You must not fight him," she whispered.

He smiled, but there was no warmth, only a cold loathing. "But 'tis me right and me duty to fight for you—and the babe."

"Nay!" she gasped, but Ramsay ignored her as he turned away.

"I shall need a resting place," he said.

She felt the blood drain from her face. "Don't say that."

"Did I say resting place?" he asked, and smiled grimly as he looked at her again. "I meant, I shall need a place to rest. The morrow may be a trying day."

"Meara!" Anora begged. "Do something.

But the old woman's gaze was locked on Ramsay's. "I can show you to a chamber, me laird."

Ramsay followed her and Anora stumbled up after them, her heart beating frantically.

"Here you be, lad." Meara swung open the arched door at the top of the stairs. "Is there anything you might be needing?"

"A eulogy?" he said, and stepped inside.

Meara stared at him and then laughed.

" 'Tis not funny," Anora murmured.

"Nay?" Ramsay shifted his gaze slowly to hers. "I would have thought you would be the most amused, lass. After all, 'tis you who stand to gain the most."

"You must not fight him," she repeated.

"Think on it, *Notmary*. You cannot lose, for if I win the bout, you are out from under the thumb of the Munro. And if I lose . . ." He shrugged. "As you said, me kinsmen will not take it kindly. They will come. All you need do is hold back the Munros for a fortnight, maybe less. When me father hears me fate . . ." He took one step toward her. "But I don't have to explain it to you, do I, lass? For I am certain you thought this all out long ago, did you not?"

She tightened her grip on the door jamb.

"Tell me," he said, never taking his gaze from her. "That morning we found you, were you truly unconscious, or did you plan even that?"

"I—"

"And the warrior," he said. "Who was he? An accomplice?"

"You must leave this night," she hissed.

"What I do not understand is this—why did you separate me from me brothers? Surely we would have been more powerful together. True, the three of us may have been killed, but I hardly think that would have concerned you."

"By morn you shall be far gone," she insisted.

"Gone?" he gritted. "Do you forget that the Munro guards the gate?"

"There is a way," Meara said.

Ramsay shifted his gaze toward the old woman, half forgotten in her spot beside the door.

"What way?" he asked.

"Deep in the roots of Evermyst there is a path that leads to the sea. A boat waits at its mouth."

"In the dark of the night you shall take that boat, and you shall escape," Anora said.

Ramsay narrowed his eyes at her. "Escape?" he said finally. "From me love and her child?"

"There is no child, and you well know it," she hissed.

"How would I know?" he gritted, stepping closer. "How would I know when everything you've told me is a lie? When I cannot believe the simplest word you say?"

She held her ground, forcing herself to meet his eyes. "This you can believe, MacGowan," she said. "On the morrow the Munro will kill you unless you are far gone."

"Then prepare me a stone now, Notmary, for tomorrow will be me last day upon this earth."

"You will—" Anora began, but Meara's harsh voice interrupted.

"Why would you risk your life, laddie?"

He scowled. "There is none who calls a MacGowan a coward."

"You would rather be called a corpse?" Meara croaked.

He turned abruptly toward the window at the far side of the bed chamber. "I stay," he said.

"Nay!" Anora's voice was shrill and high pitched in the narrow room. "You cannot—"

"I can," he countered evenly. "Now be gone, so that I may rest."

"You'll not—"

" 'Tis his decision to make," Meara interrupted.

"Are you mad?"

"Mayhap," Meara said, and urged her toward the door. "But this I know—the lad must sleep."

"Sleep!" They were insane—the both of them.

"Or pray," Meara said, and grinned as she closed the door behind them.

" 'Tis no laughing matter," Anora rasped.

"Isn't it?" Meara asked, and taking her arm, urged her down the hallway. "And why is that, lass? Is he not the answer to our prayers?"

"The answer—" She reared back, appalled and sickened. "I never asked for a sacrificial lamb."

"Didn't you? Remember the stakes: the Munros burn witches."

"I am no witch," she hissed.

"I was not speaking of you, lass. You are the lady here."

Anora winced.

"You said he would leave if others believed that I bore another man's child. You said his pride would make him go as surely as his fear would keep Mac-Gowan safe."

"I said 'twas the only way to keep you and yours free. That is what you wished for, is it not?"

"Aye, but—"

"Then sacrifices must be made. Why would you care if the sacrifices are MacGowan's?" Meara's gaze was hawkishly sharp.

"I've no wish to see a man die," she whispered.

"So you have no special feelings for him?"

Anora gripped her skirt in a trembling hand. "Little difference would it make. I had feelings for Lord Richard. Remember?"

Meara ignored the goad. "Might MacGowan be the one? Is that why you care for him?"

"I do *not* care for him. 'Tis simply that I've no wish to have his death on my head."

Meara pulled her to a halt. " 'Tis the lad's own choice to stay. You've no say in it. You can but pray he has the power and the cunning to overcome the Munro."

"You know what the outcome will be!"

"Do I?" Meara asked.

"The Munros are naught but killers."

"And what is MacGowan? Peaceable? Kind? Cunning? Do not fret, lass. 'Tis not your place to decide whether the lad fights or nay, no matter how much you love him."

"Love him! I do not love him," Anora whispered, but Meara turned away, leaving Anora alone by her bed chamber door.

She opened it in a daze. Her room was broad and barren. Not a single rug softened the cold wooden floor. Only a faded tapestry adorned the far wall. Still, she was home. Exhaustion flooded her. She needed sleep, forgetfulness, but at that moment a rap sounded at her door.

"Me lady?" Isobel's voice was soft.

"Come in," Anora called.

"Good eventide," Isobel said, and curtsied so that her weathered coif flopped over her brow. Tucked into the rope that secured her gown to her waist was a slingshot made of wood and leather—to teach Jamie's geese some respect for her herb garden, she often said. "Is there aught I can fetch for you before you seek your bed?"

"Nay." Anora kept her tone cool. "But come hither. You may help me with my hair."

"As you wish, me lady," Isobel said, and closed the door behind her.

For a moment they stared at each other, then Anora entwined her fingers and turned her back. Taking the few steps between them, Isobel set her hands to her mistress' plaited hair.

"Who listens in?" Anora asked, her voice little more than a whisper.

"None that I know of." Isobel's words were just as soft, her fingers quick as they loosened Anora's braid and spread the hair across her shoulders. "But there are surely those who would resent you if they knew you had no intention of wedding the Munro."

"Do they forget what they have done to our clansmen? To Mother?"

"There are those amongst us who bear more Munro blood than Fraser."

"And mayhap their heritage is the very reason they resent my delay in marrying the Munro. They see nothing but the Munros' power and think an alliance with that clan can do us only good. But they are fools!" Still, uncertainty and guilt gnawed at Anora's gut like wild hounds. "The Munros care not for the Frasers, and they never shall. This last laird is no different from the others. He has no intention of bettering our lot. Indeed, he has no use for us at all. We only take up space that he might use for—"

"Do you hear me arguing, Nora?"

Anora let her shoulders droop. "I cannot wed him," she breathed.

"I will be the first to agree."

"And if MacGowan wishes to fight him . . ." She remembered how he had looked at her with such loathing. She turned stiffly, finding Isobel's hands with her own. Their gazes met with solemn consideration. "Mayhap he will win," she whispered.

Isobel tightened her grip on Anora's hands. "And what if he does win? You have said you carry his child."

"He knows 'tis not true."

"Still, what's to keep him from claiming you as his own?"

She shook her head. "He will not."

"How can you be certain?"

"I have a feeling," Anora said, and Isobel smiled at the statement they both used quite often.

"Truly," Isobel said, "how do you know whether the MacGowan will claim you for his own?"

"He despises me," Anora murmured.

"Then why did he vow to fight for you?"

"I do not know. To punish me, mayhap."

"To punish *you*! It seems he will be the one being punished."

"Don't say that!"

Isobel scowled. "If I left—"

"Nay!" Anora gasped, and crushed the small maid's hands in her own. "Nay, you must not leave me, Isobel. I have only just found you."

"But what of MacGowan?"

She refused to think of him. "What Meara said is true. 'Tis his choice to make, and 'tis like a man to choose to fight when there is another way."

"And what if he dies?"

Anora tightened her grip and her resolve. "Then 'tis God's will."

"You think he is the—" Isobel began, but Anora jerked up her chin, employing that regal demeanor that had served her for so many years.

"I am fatigued," she said. "And do not wish to speak of it any further."

"Nora—"

"Nay!" Turning, she paced to the foot of her bed. Beneath her fretful fingers, the loose corner-post threatened to abandon the bed's frame. "I've no more need of your assistance this night. You may leave."

The room went silent for a moment. Anora pulled her grip carefully from the shaky post and half glanced over her shoulder.

"Might it be true?" Isobel's voice was no more than a murmur in the dimness.

"What?"

"*Do* you carry his child?"

She spun around. "You know better."

"But you wish you did."

"Nay!"

"Then what are these feelings you—"

"I am tired," Anora repeated, unable to maintain her mask any longer. "Please, Isobel. Do not go dredging about in me thoughts just now."

The girl's sky blue eyes drilled into hers for a moment longer, then she nodded. "As you will then . . . me lady," she murmured in her baby soft voice. "Sleep well."

Anora said nothing, but watched the other turn silently away. The door closed with a creak of leather and wood, but Isobel's question was all she heard.

What if he wins?

Anora paced fretfully. It would be his right to claim her. Emotion, unnamed and unwanted, sparked in her chest, but she doused it. He could not win against the Munro. Therefore he must escape now, while he could. But he refused.

She paced again, feeling restless.

What could she do? Meara was right; it was his choice, his alone. But why did he insist on this battle?

It did not matter. Her shoes rapped against the floor boards as she tread the same tired route. It did not matter why he chose this course, for she could not change his mind. It was out of her hands, and if he died—

At the thought, her knees buckled. She grabbed the

bed's corner-post to pull herself upright, and it came away in her fingers.

She stared at it in mute surprise. Perhaps it wasn't out of her hands, after all.

Chapter 18

Outside Ramsay's high window, the world was black, but not half so black as his thoughts.

He is me love.

Remembering Anora's words, he ground his hands into fists. She loved no one, least of all him. 'Twas clear enough, for surely she had known how the Munro would react to her words, and just as surely she expected Ramsay to lose the battle, else she would not have suggested that he leave.

But there was the mystery. Why had she insisted that he go, when she did not care whether he lived or died?

It made no sense. Could it be that she cared just—

"Nay!" He said the word out loud and turned restlessly from the window.

Damn her! She did not care. She was incapable of caring, therefore . . .

The knock on his door was so soft that for a moment he thought he imagined it, but it came again.

He glared at the portal. "What do you want?" His tone was uninviting.

No response was forthcoming.

"Who's there?" he asked again, and in a second a small voice answered.

" 'Tis me, good sir, Isobel, sent to see to your needs."

"I have no needs."

"But Meara insisted that I bring you this cup of ale, and she shall be angry if I fail in me mission." Silence for a moment. "Please, Master MacGowan, if you have a heart—"

Grinding his teeth, he strode across the floor and jerked the bar from the door. "Come in," he snapped, but in that second his eyes narrowed.

"You!"

"Aye." Notmary stepped quickly inside and pushed the door shut behind her.

"Tell me, lass, is it simply that you habitually forget your name, or are you so very fond of lying?"

She turned stiffly toward him, her narrow hands clasped. "I thought you might not grant me entry."

"At times you are surprisingly astute for a deluded liar."

She pursed her lips. "I did not come to spar with you."

"Then you'll be leaving?" He glared at her, but even now, he could not help but notice how her hair spread like spun gold over her shoulders, squared as they were like a small soldier's. As if she faced the world alone and dared not admit her fear.

Christ, surely one as foolish as himself deserved to die at the hands of a man who was built like a bad tempered bull and smelled like a rotting seal.

"I cannot leave until . . ." She kept her hands twisted in the folds of her skirt.

"Until what? You've destroyed me life completely?"

"Until I thank you."

He stared at her for a moment, then paced the length of the room, watching her. "For what," he glowered. "For not telling the raging bull that you lied? That you do not carry me child? That you have no feelings for me or any other? That you are willing to see me die to avoid marrying him?"

" 'Tis not true." Her words were weak.

"What is untrue?" he asked. "That you are willing to see me die, or that you wish to avoid marrying him?"

"I asked you to leave."

"Aye, you did that. Which makes me curious, lass. Why set up this wee charade in the first place? Why set forth the events to ensure this battle, only to try to stall it?"

"I cannot wed a Munro."

"And why is that? Because they do not so readily believe your lies as some? Because you cannot manipulate—"

"Because they killed my mother."

The air left his lungs in a painful rush, but he kept his head, forcing himself to remember their past. "You lie," he said.

She didn't respond.

"She was alive when Ironfist took Evermyst."

"Aye, she was alive then. And she was alive later. But after he died . . ." She turned away. "Some blamed his death on a weak heart, some on our ghost. But the

Munro's eldest son, Cuthbert, did not agreed. He was certain his sire was killed by the curses my mother threw at him. She was declared a witch."

Ramsay almost reached for her, but surely 'twas time he learned that a wounded creature was not necessarily one without teeth.

She said nothing, merely stared at him, and finally he forced himself to pull his gaze from her tortured eyes.

"So you want the Munros to suffer."

"She was my mother," she whispered.

"I am sorry." He spoke to the wall, for he couldn't trust himself to look at her.

"I did not come for your sympathy." Her voice was little more than a breath of pain. She was close now, so close that he could feel the whisper of her words against his hair, could imagine once again how she would feel in his arms.

"Why then?" he asked.

"I only wanted to thank you."

Don't believe her, his mind railed, but he could feel her emotions like an open wound. He turned, needing to hold her, and in that instant, she swung.

Sheer instinct made him duck and grab. The oaken post grazed the top of his head, but already he had his hands on her.

She squawked as he jerked her close, and the bed post fell harmlessly to the floor.

"What the devil are you doing?"

"Let me go!" she hissed.

"Why would you want to hurry the Munro's task?" he asked, squeezing harder.

"Leave off!" she rasped again and squirmed wildly in his arms.

"I will have the truth, lass. Why did you come here?"

"I told you."

"Most maids do not try to kill the man they mean to thank."

"I did not plan to kill you."

"What then?"

She opened her mouth, but he squeezed harder, threatening her breathing.

"The truth," he suggested.

"The boat waits."

"Boat?"

"No one wins against the Munro."

Surprise ripped through him. "You hoped to force me to leave?"

Her silence was more convincing than her words would ever have been.

He loosed her so suddenly, that she stumbled backward a pace. "Why?" he asked.

"I'll not have your blood on my hands."

"Why," he asked again, "when your own mother was—" He stopped, watching her with narrowed eyes. "Tell me, lass, were these all lies, too? Did you even have a mother?"

"Of course I had a mother."

"But she was not murdered by the man I am to fight on the morrow."

She jerked her gaze away. "I never said as much."

"You said she was burned—"

"I said they declared her a witch, and if they thought her a sorceress surely they would believe . . ." She stopped suddenly, breathing hard.

"What would they believe?"

She raised her chin. "That I, too, am a witch."

"Are you?"

He saw the fear in her eyes—honest emotion—and the sight of it soothed him somehow.

"Nay, I am not," she whispered. "I've done nothing but attempt to keep me and mine safe, to fight for what is right and just. 'Tis no more than you would do. But because I am a woman—"

"You rail at the wrong man, lass. For in truth, I do not believe witches exist."

He could hear her intake of breath and watched her closely.

"There have been whisperings about me own mother," he explained. "And about me uncle's wife, the Lady Fiona—'tis said her healing skills be ungodly. But I ask you, lass, what sense does that make? None that I can see. It seems the only ones convicted as witches are those who have neither the funds nor the strength to keep their own for themselves."

If she had heard a word of his explanation she showed no signs. "You do not think witches exist?" she asked.

"Is there not enough evil amongst us, without searching for something that lives only in frightened men's minds?"

"And what if there is evidence?"

"Such as?"

She shrugged tightly. "Conversations with animals."

He shrugged. "I meself talk to me steed. Granted, 'tis mostly swearing, but—"

"Reading another's thoughts."

"Me aunts have the gift."

"Babes born together?" Her delicate body was tense, her slim hands clasped.

"Twins?" he questioned, eyeing her carefully.

" 'Tis said they are of the devil."

"Then half our lambkins are Satan's own."

"I do not speak of sheep." Her tone was terse, though she tried to soothe it. "I speak of people."

"Is it not God's place to judge souls?"

"You . . . do not believe twins are evil?"

"Why do you care what I believe, lass?"

She stared at him, her eyes unearthly wide.

"Why?" he asked again.

"Because I . . . do not believe that my mother was a witch."

"She was a twin?"

She delayed just a moment, as if scared to share the truth, then, "Aye," she said. "But since her wee brother died at birth, they hushed the news, for they had no wish to start the rumors."

"Of incest in the womb?"

She wrung her hands. " 'Tis surely a lie spread by folk with evil minds. And just as surely, twins are not born to different sires. It cannot be true, for then they would not look so much the same."

"Whether 'tis true or not, lass, it has naught to do with you."

"Have you yet informed the Munro?"

Ramsay narrowed his eyes. "He plans to wed you, lass, not—"

"Not kill me?" she asked. "Are you certain of that, MacGowan? And if not me, who then? The Munros are ungodly superstitious, believing any sort of fool-ishness about those who displease them. Worse yet, they live by the sword. War is in their blood. Who will die? Someone I cherish, of that I am certain." Her voice was ghostly soft, a whisper of fear in the flickering light.

"This boat—the Munros do not know of it?" he asked.

"Nay. 'Tis well hidden. You would be safe." Her words were quick and breathy, and her eyes shone in the candlelight. With hope? he wondered, but he squelched the thought.

"Deep within the rock it lies, and when it launches, 'tis near impossible to see for several leagues," she said.

"Then *you* shall be on that boat."

Anora straightened. The light died in her eyes, snuffed out by some indefinable emotion. "And leave my people to fend for themselves?"

"Aye."

"Nay, I will not."

Anger welled up inside him. He tightened his fists and stepped forward. " 'Tis your fault I am here, lass. 'Tis you who have lied and manipulated from the first. 'Tis you who owe me. And 'tis you who shall be on that boat."

"You have no say in this."

"Aye, I do," he said, and reaching out, suddenly snatched her by the arm. "I meself will put you on the water. And there is naught you can do to stop me."

She struggled wildly against him. "Do you disremember!" she hissed. "I am a witch."

He pulled her closer until she stilled in his hands, holding her gaze with his own. "You are many things," he said. "A liar. A fighter." They were very close now. Indeed, below their waists, their bodies touched, though she bent away from him. "A seductress . . ."

His whispered words fell into the void of the night, and it seemed that the air was sucked from his very lungs, for suddenly the world was filled with naught but her.

"Do not fight him," she whispered.

"Take the boat."

"I will not, and you cannot make me, for 'tis one of my own who guards the entrance, and he will not follow your orders."

He closed his eyes in burning frustration for an instant, fighting anger, fatigue, her closeness. "Then you will remain within these walls whilst the battle rages, and if the Munro yet lives at the contest's end, you will take your secret passage to safety."

"Nay."

"Aye!" he stormed. "You shall."

"I—"

"Promise me! Or I swear by all that is holy, I will drag you onto your boat with me bare hands." He paused, fighting for blessed calm. "I vow I will, lass."

"As you will, then," she said softly.

He loosened his grip, forcing his fingers to ease on her arms, but it took longer still to drop his hands from her flesh. "This oarsman, you can trust him?"

"Aye."

He nodded, holding a tight rein on himself, but she was so close, so small and delicate and brave. The very scent of her skin seemed to fill his senses. He ground his teeth and stepped back a pace.

"If the Munro yet lives, you will go to Dun Ard," he said. "Tell me father what has happened. He will keep you safe."

"MacGowan . . ." she said, but he dared not let her

speak, for just the sight of her hands clasped in silent supplication was nearly more than he could withstand.

He hardened his resolve. "I have your vow?"

"Aye." Her voice was low, reverent. "You do."

Chapter 19

Ramsay stood on Evermyst's highest tower and watched the sun rise out of the sea. The light caught the tips of the waves, casting them in heavenly hues of gold and sapphire. Behind him, somewhere in the bailey, a lark burst into song. So sweet it sounded, so fresh, as if it was the first thrush ever to greet the glory of a new day.

"Me laird." A young man appeared beside him. Though he had surely not seen more than six and ten years, he was both taller and broader than Ramsay. Christened Duncan, he was more oft simply called Tree. He and his elders had tried to pack Ramsay into armor earlier that morning, but Ramsay had found it too confining. Thus he wore nothing more than a stitched vest made of double thick bear hide.

"I am come to assist you," said young Duncan.

"Did you bring an army, then?"

The lad shook his head, showing no sign if he appreciated the jest. " 'Tis nearly time," he said. "The Munros awake. Already they crowd about Myst Vale, where you will battle."

From the southern tower, Ramsay had seen their camp in the valley, but he had no wish to watch them prepare for the battle. He knew the Munro would be ready, and that was enough.

"Me laird?"

"Aye." Ramsay pulled his attention back to the lad. He had hands the size of masonry shovels and feet that promised more growth.

" 'Tis time to break the fast."

How had he come to this? Ramsay wondered. 'Twas a twisted path indeed that had led him here, but he would not think of that now. Nay, he would empty his mind and break the fast, though he was not hungry. "Aye, lad, I come," he said, and eyed the boy. Strength showed in every inch of his form and loyalty in his eyes. "But first I would ask you a favor."

"You've but to name it," Duncan said, and Ramsay nodded as they walked toward the stairs together.

In the end, it was not such a simple task to procure a promise from the boy, but finally he did. They fell silent as they rounded the last flight of steps.

The stone felt solid beneath Ramsay's feet. From far ahead he heard a child laugh. The sound seemed to sparkle in the morning air, lighting the very world, but when he stepped into the hall silence followed, and it seemed to him a terrible pity that his arrival would forestall a bairn's happy laughter. His footfalls rang in the stillness, and he found a seat.

Every eye in the hall seemed to watch him.

"Me laird." He turned toward the soft voice, dwelling for a moment on its delicate tone, for this was a morn to savor every moment. The maid named Isobel stood beside the table. On her head she had the same worn coif as the day before. It drooped drunkenly over her temple, hiding her hair, but it could not distract from her eyes. They were immensely blue, he noticed, though she did not look directly at him. "A cup of spirits," she said, "to aid you in your noble—"

"See to the others," said a voice. Glancing up, Ramsay saw the woman called Ailsa push Isobel aside. "Take me own mead, me laird?" she said, bending low to display what she had to offer.

"Me thanks, but—"

"Nay!" shrieked a guttural voice. He glanced up. 'Twas the pregnant woman who shambled toward them. She was shabbily dressed, her dirty gown stretched tight over her protruding belly. "Nay," she repeated, and grabbing the mug from Ailsa's hand, drank it down in one fell swoop. It dribbled past the edges of her twisted mouth, falling on her gown, but she seemed not to notice. Instead, she splayed her fingers across her vast belly and belched. " 'Twould be a sin to waste good brew on a corpse, and that is surely what you will be in a few hours' time. Just a corpse that will rot—"

"Leave off, Deirdre!" ordered a stout, matronly woman who stood nearby. "He's done you no harm."

"No harm. No harm," the woman growled, and turned away, but as she glanced about, all eyes but the boldest and the youngest avoided hers. Even Evermyst's soldiers pulled cautiously aside when she limped past.

"Me apologies, me laird. She is mad," said Ailsa, offering the mug again, but Ramsay's attention was caught on the pregnant woman's stumbling exit.

"Look away," whispered Duncan. " 'Tis an ill omen for you to dwell on the likes of her."

"Drink, me laird," urged Ailsa.

He turned his attention to the serving woman. "Me thanks," he said, "But I'll be needing me full wits about me today. Only food for me this morn, if you please."

"As you wish, me—"

"MacGowan!" Though the sound bellowed up from far below in Evermyst's broad vale, Munro's voice rose as loud and raucous as a black crow's hoarse challenge. "MacGowan, I wait."

Whispers followed the words. Ramsay ignored the noise, speared himself a piece of venison from a nearby platter, and ate it slowly. Then Anora descended the stairs, and suddenly he could do nothing but watch her, for every detail of her seemed indescribably poignant. The blue of her eyes, the lift of her lips, the graceful flutter of her hands.

Ramsay pulled his gaze away with an effort. "You know your task, Duncan?" he asked, without turning to the boy.

"Aye, sir, I do."

"All of Evermyst depends on you. You'll not fail me, will you lad?"

He straightened slightly. "Nay, me laird, I will not."

" 'Tis good." Reaching for a round loaf of coarse bread, Ramsay broke it in half and rose to his feet. "I go, then."

"Me laird." Anora stood not far away. "I beg a moment."

When he turned toward her, the sight of her was nearly overwhelming—a delicate thing of beauty so fragile and fine that she took his breath away.

"I would have a word," she murmured.

He should not let her speak, he knew, but on this particular morn when life seemed so sharply precious, he longed to hear her voice. Yet, she merely stood in silence, watching him.

"MacGowan!" The challenge rang up from the valley again.

She caught his sleeve in fingers strangely powerful for her fragile form. Her eyes were as wide as the heavens and vividly bright, as though tears waited to be shed. Yet he must ignore that fact. He must.

"You'll stay put inside these walls," he said.

"MacGowan." Her voice was a whisper, and yet it seemed to echo through the silent hall.

"You'll stay inside," he repeated, and steeling himself, he lowered his voice. "And honor your vow."

"I cannot—"

"You would lie to me again?" he asked. "On this, of all days?"

He watched her lips part, but he spoke first.

"Swear you will honor your vow. Swear it on your mother's grave, or I will announce to all present that you are a liar."

Anora's lips trembled. Ramsay scowled, forcing himself to keep from touching her, from pulling her up against him.

"Swear it!" he ordered.

"I swear." Her back was as straight as a lance, her chin squared.

By sheer force of will, he turned away. The crowd

was silent as he passed through. The flagstones in the bailey rang as he stepped onto them.

Gryfon tucked his hirsute head, half dragging his groom across the worn turf.

"He is eager," panted the lad.

"Aye."

"MacGowan!" The challenge roared up from the valley again.

"He and the Munro," said Ramsay, and wished to hell that he felt some semblance of that same eagerness. But whatever hot-blooded foolishness had urged him into this battle was long gone now, leaving him cool-headed and introspective. Nevertheless, there was nothing he could do but mount his steed and pray. Beside him, Duncan mounted a dappled gelding and accompanied him from the courtyard. The portcullis moaned rustily as it was hauled up, but behind that was silence, as if all the world already mourned his demise.

All the world but Gryfon, who champed at the bit and pranced forward when the iron gate was barely above his withers, threatening to decapitate his rider before the Munro had a chance. Ramsay swore with feeling and tightened the reins, but it did little to slow the bay's eager pace.

Not far past the portcullis, the land fell sharply away. Ramsay leaned against the bit and swayed to Gryfon's sliding descent, until suddenly, and far too soon, they had reached the valley.

"So . . ." The Munro sat astride a gigantic destrier on the bald knob of a flat topped hill. "You have finally come."

Good Christ, the man looked to be as big as

Evermyst itself, and his steed stood a good eighteen hands at the withers. Half covered in metal, it appeared as indestructible as a mountain, and upon its back the Munro rode with massive arrogance, his chest garbed in black iron but his head bare, showing his grizzly beard and jutting forehead.

"So you haven't lost your nerve, have you?"

Nay, only his sanity, Ramsay thought, eyeing his huge opponent. " 'Tis not too late to change your mind, Munro," he said, hoping he sounded casual, as if battling this beast of a man would be no great feat.

"Change me mind?" The beast shifted in his saddle, wrapped in iron and mounted on a battering ram. "And why would I be doing that, laddie?"

"Mayhap you've no wish to die this day." As threats went, that one wasn't too bad. 'Twas even spoken with some bravado.

Munro grinned, an evil slant of crooked teeth in the mess of his beard. " 'Tis you who will die, MacGowan, for you've made a whore of the woman I chose for me own."

Whore! He'd never liked the sound of that word, and hearing it in association with Notmary made anger seep with insidious heat through his system.

"Come now, do not disappoint me, laddie. You talked so grand and brawny in the hall. I hoped you might prove something of a challenge. After all, I've not had a rousing good fight in some days. If you put up a decent fight I'll not tell the lady what a coward you were in the end. Come now, boy, 'tis a good day to die."

"Feel free, then," Ramsay said.

Munro laughed. "Let the battle be joined," he rumbled, and reached down to pull his sword from its sheath beside his pommel. "There would be little sport in killing you where you stand."

It seemed their charming dialogue was at an end. Ramsay loosened Gryfon's reins. The bay pranced forward like a princeling on parade, snorting a guttural challenge at the larger stallion as they went.

The Murno's steed reared, pawing at them with a giant hoof before dropping to the ground. So it would not be merely a battle between men, Ramsay deduced, but a battle of horses as well.

Munro scowled as he watched them come. "It will not look good if I kill you on such a wee small steed, MacGowan. Come, I will mount you on one of me own before we begin."

The black struck out viciously, slamming an iron-shod forefoot against Gryfon's chest.

"I would ask another favor instead," Ramsay said, holding back his own vengeful steed. "Keep this battle between you and me. None will come to me aid. Thus none should come to yours."

"Agreed," Munro said.

"And when quiet has settled on the hills, I will have paid the debt in full. No one else shall suffer."

"No one?" Munro lowered his gorse bush brows. "By that you mean me betrothed."

Ramsay said nothing, but glanced forward. The hills that encompassed the small glen were steep, covered in verdant turf and kissed with dew. A trio of boulders stood halfway up the eastern hillock, casting long shadows before them, and the sun, just now cresting the trees, shone with brilliance on the world.

Ramsay locked each detail away in his mind.

"So you care for her, do you?" Munro growled. "But does she care for you?"

Munro's destrier, though surely as powerful as his immense size and bad temper promised, bobbed his head ever so slightly when it walked. A bruise in its left forefoot mayhap, Ramsay mused.

"MacGowan!"

Ramsay turned coolly toward his opponent.

" 'Twould be a pity to kill you where you sit and deprive me men of their sport," Munro said. "Hence you will answer me question and grant yourself a few more breaths. Did she go to you in hopes of vying us against each other, or does she care for you?"

Ramsay stared point blank at the huge warrior. "If I win, the lass will never be yours," he said evenly. "And if I lose, you shall treat her well and know that I have paid the price for her sins against you, imagined or otherwise."

"Damn you to hell!" Munro rasped, his veins popping swollen and reddened from his neck. "Answer me straight and true. Does she cherish you?"

Jealousy! So obvious now, it steamed from him in waves. Why hadn't he seen it before, Ramsay wondered, and felt a moment of giddiness for the arrival of such a mind-fogging emotion.

"Speak!" Munro growled, and reaching out, twisted a fist into Ramsay's tunic. "Or before this day is done you will surely beg to die."

"If it's the truth you want, 'tis the truth you'll get," Ramsay said, and let just a dram of anger seep into his tone. "She lay with me so that when she must do the same with you, she could forever pretend she was back in me arms and not with the animal who would take her against her will."

Munro dropped his fist away. "You lie like an Englishman."

Ramsay grinned. "And you stink like a swine."

Munro roared in rage and lashed with his sword, but Ramsay had already tapped his steed's barrel. With the speed of the desert horse, Gryfon pivoted away. Munro's blade swept past his back, but Ramsay was already turning and arced his own blade toward Munro's ribs.

Metal clanged against metal.

Fool! Avoid the armor—aim for the legs or the arms. But there was no time for self recrimination, for Munro was already charging.

Gryfon swung away at the last instant. The black thundered past, slid to a halt, and spun, but Munro's reach was ungodly long. He chopped sideways. Ramsay parried, knocking the blade downward, then hissed as it skimmed across his thigh.

Munro roared and leapt forward, but Gryfon turned away on his own as Ramsay grappled for balance. Munro was closing in. No time! No time!

Ramsay grasped the reins in tight desperation, fighting to cue his mount. For the briefest moment Gryfon faltered, but then he leapt—straight into the air, striking out behind him.

Ramsay heard the thud of hooves against flesh, but when he turned it was clear that the black had taken the blows. Stunned, the big horse halted for a moment.

"So, MacGowan." Munro's voice rumbled in the glen. "Your wee mount has a bit of training, does he? And you are neither so eager to die as you seemed yesterday nor so weak livered as you seemed this morn."

Ramsay gritted his teeth against the pain of his wound. "Why the talk now, Munro? Could it be that you are scared?"

Munro charged with a roar. Ramsay slammed the

other's blade away and sliced sideways, cutting the huge man's arm, but not for a moment did he hesitate. Bellowing with rage, he hacked with the frenzied strength of a madman. Ramsay parried. The huge horse leapt forward, pushing Gryfon beneath his immense weight.

They were forced off balance, and Gryfon scrambled for footing under the black steed's onslaught. Ramsay faltered and Munro struck, sweeping his blade in a wide arc.

Pain sliced through Ramsay's chest. Beneath him, Gryfon stumbled to his feet and lunged uphill. Ramsay tried to tighten his hand around the hilt of his sword, but the world spun around him. His blade tilted and dropped from numb fingers.

'Twas over. Over. Yet his fingers dipped to the sheath in his boot. He was barely able to pull the dirk free.

· "Not ready to give up yet, MacGowan?" Munro's voice seemed to come from a thousand misty leagues away. Ramsay turned his steed with shaky hands. A half dozen rods of downhill slope lay between them. So little room, so little time. But if Munro was badly wounded, Anora could yet escape.

Ramsay straightened with an effort. "Are you going to fight me, Munro," he asked, "or will you simply kill me with your stench?"

Munro's war-cry seemed muffled, but even through his haze, Ramsay realized he was charging. He never knew if he cued his own mount, only knew that they were galloping madly, charging downhill, away from the sun, straight toward the enormous black.

Pain pulsed at every step. Hold on! Hold on!

They were about to collide. For the briefest moment, he saw Munro squint against the sun, saw light reflect against his bloodied sword, and then, "Up!" Ramsay yelled. Gryfon gathered himself and leapt.

Munro's lips moved and he slashed out with his sword, but suddenly Ramsay was soaring, flying like a dove. Then just as suddenly the world jolted and they were spilling downward. He tried to stay astride, but the earth spiraled toward his face. Something struck him. Hooves churned past. Gryfon's. Another's. And then the world went quiet.

Eternity settled softly in.

"Ramsay." He heard Anora's voice from his dream—like a prayer, like a psalm. 'Twas that dream that made him recall his mission.

Munro! He remembered the giant with a jerk and raised himself to one elbow. Beneath him, the earth felt slippery and warm, but when he glanced up he saw his goal.

Munro—on the ground. A gash stretched from his brow to his hairline, but even now he was struggling to rise.

"Nay." Ramsay could not hear his own voice, though he knew he had spoken. "You'll not have her," he whispered, and pushed himself to his knees. The world spun like a top, sucking him in, but Munro rose to his feet and staggered forward.

"Damn you," Ramsay growled. He struggled to stand, and teetered toward the giant. The earth slanted away, tripping him up, but finally Munro loomed before him.

"Come on then. Come on," Ramsay challenged, and waved his dirk, but when he glanced down he noticed that his hand was empty.

Munro grinned, lifted his sword—and toppled like a gargantuan oak to the earth.

Ramsay watched and realized rather belatedly that he himself was staring at the sky.

Fluffy clouds adorned the blueness like woolly lambs at play.

"Ramsay, my beloved," whispered his dreams.

Anora—as he imagined her. Soft, trusting. Beautiful. No fear, no doubt, just love shining from her angelic face. He would not see her again, for he was dying. But at least she was safe, even now traveling away from Munro. She had promised. And he had made certain of it.

"MacGowan!"

She would not be his, but neither would she be the Munro's.

"Wake up, MacGowan!"

He groaned as pain wracked his body, then opened his eyes with aching effort and focused.

She was there, pressing a cloth to his chest and yelling orders over her shoulder.

"Damn it to hell!" he murmured groggily. "You lied again."

Chapter 20

Ramsay was vaguely aware of a crowd arguing loudly around the Munro.

"To Evermyst. We'll nurse him there."

"Be you daft? 'Tis Evermyst what has bested him. We—"

The voices faded to mist. Faces blurred. But Ramsay dared not die now, for the Munros were still in the valley. Bloody bastards! And Anora, damn her, was not yet safe. He struggled to rise.

"Me apologies!" Duncan's voice pierced the haze for a moment. "She—"

"Why is she here?" Ramsay growled. He fought to sit up, but a half dozen hands held him down.

"Me laird." Duncan's tone was wheedling. "She did not wish to go."

"Did not wish—" In that instant, he recognized the round bruise on the lad's temple. "The bed post?"

"Aye, sir. She is quite mean."

"Quiet now!" Anora ordered. She was nearby, stealing his breath. There was strength in her voice, beauty in her face. But what the lad said was true, he realized numbly—she *was* quite mean.

"You swore on your mother's grave," he intoned, his voice weary.

Her eyes caught his, bursting with emotion on his aching soul. Around them the bustle of the world hushed.

"My mother has no grave," she said.

He tried to make sense of her words, but there seemed to be none. "Why—"

"Quiet! This will hurt," she said, and stood abruptly. "Take him now."

"Why does she—" he began, but suddenly the world exploded. Pain crashed through him, stopping his heart, mangling his leg, and on the wings of that agony came blessed blackness.

Pain throbbed through Ramsay like wild, pounding hooves, thrumming, insistent. 'Twas that alone that awakened him. He opened his eyes slowly. A ceiling appeared with lethargic slowness. It was gray, distant, braced with wooden beams as big around as his aching thigh.

"You have returned."

Ramsay shifted his gaze sideways. Anora stood near the wall. Her hands were clasped, her knuckles white, her face the same.

"I knew you would."

His mind drifted dizzily for a moment, dredging up

hard memories. Blood, pain, galloping hooves, horrible bravery. He winced. "Gryfon, is he—"

"Your steed is fine," she said, then, "Though you do not even like him."

He scowled and remembered to smooth his expression into one of unconcern. "Aye, well, I'm not particularly thrilled with you, either."

"As you said, I cannot have every man swooning at my feet."

The ceiling swam momentarily. "I fear I did not realize your methods when first I said that, Notmary."

"My name is Anora. Anora of the Frasers."

There was something in her voice. Something that drew him in. Vulnerability? Softness? Nay, he would be a fool to believe it, and he was rather tired of playing the fool. "A bit damned late to tell me now." He struggled to sit up.

"What have you done to me?" he asked, and glanced toward his chest. It was bound beneath his arms in a long strip of white. He reached for the knot that held it in place. "I cannot breathe trussed like a Michaelmas goose."

"Or mayhap 'tis because the Munro tried to skewer you," she said and, stepping quickly forward, pushed his hands aside. "Leave off or I'll call Tree to keep you out of trouble."

"Tree!" Ramsay snorted, but he left his hands where they fell. It took entirely too much energy to try to move anyway. "He could not keep a boulder on the ground."

" 'Tis not true," she said, and fussed for a moment with his blanket. "He is not called Tree for no reason."

"Aye. 'Tis either his strength or his intellect."

She smiled the slightest amount. Ramsay's breathing stopped, but in an instant she sobered and straightened, her fingers still fretful. "Why did you do it?"

Dear God, she was beautiful, and sad, so sad, but 'twas not his concern, he reminded himself, and harshly drew breath into his starving lungs. "Listen, Notmary," he said, forcing his voice into gravelly depths. "I've recently been used as a target for a mounted Minotaur. Mayhap you could simply say what you mean this once."

"Why did you tell Tree to take me away?"

Something dangerously fragile fluttered in his stomach. He would not let her know the truth. Indeed, he barely shared the truth with himself. "Because I knew you lied," he said.

Her hands twisted about themselves. "And why do you care?"

"Mayhap you have not noticed, lass, but Munro is a wee bit irritating. I had no wish to see him take Evermyst."

She watched him. "Meara said 'twas because you are kind."

His gut twisted up tighter. "I am not foolish enough to be kind, lass. On that you can depend."

"Then why did you fight the battle? If not for kindness' sake."

Because he could not bear to think of her in Munro's filthy hands. "As I said, I do not like the man."

"And so you wished to kill him?"

"As soon as look at him," he said, and realized a bit belatedly that that last statement might have benefited if he'd put a bit of emotion into his tone.

She pulled her gaze away and paced quietly toward the room's narrow window.

"I heard that you offered him a chance to quit the

battle," she said finally. "Why would you do that if you wished to kill him?"

She was limned by the fading light from the window, her hair ablaze and her mouth pinkened by the setting sun. Beneath the blankets, his desire hardened.

Christ!

"Why?" she said again.

Ramsay snagged his attention back to the conversation and snorted. "You jest," he said. "The man is as big as a bloody ox. 'Twas no way in hell I would be able to best him."

"And yet you did," she murmured.

"Aye. I bested him," he said. "By knocking him over the head with me horse."

"By causing him to underestimate both you and your steed. By using every possible advantage against him. By cunning." Her voice was as soft as a velvet sleeve. "Kindness and cunning. Power and peacefulness."

The prophecy—mayhap she believed he was the one. Hope leapt inside him. He strangled it without a shred of mercy. " 'Tis not like you, Notmary, to look for virtue where there is none. 'Twas luck and desperation that won me the day. Nothing else, and you well know it. But then, you are none to call the kettle black, aye? For you would lie to Saint Peter himself."

She actually blanched. "I would do no such thing," she whispered.

He snorted derisively and shook his head. It hurt. "You swore on your mother's grave you would stay inside these walls, and that should Munro survive the battle, you would leave."

She merely stared at him.

"What, lass? Do you disremember, or—"

"I told you, my mother has no grave, therefore the vow was null and void."

"How in heaven's name—"

"She had no wish to be burned as a witch. Thus she chose her own course. 'Tis a long and deadly drop from Myst's uppermost tower to the sea."

He wished now that he could believe she was lying, but the horror in her eyes made it impossible.

"The waters never gave her back. More proof of her sins, I suspect. So you see why I lie, MacGowan?" she said. "Innes Munro has no more love for the Frasers than did his brother. How simple it would be for him to find a reason to believe that others are witches. And what then?" Her voice was a whisper as she turned back toward the window.

"Who? Who might he think is a witch?"

She gazed down at the bailey below. "Myself, of course," she said. "And I may not have my mother's courage."

"You . . ." he began, but stopped himself, his mind spinning. " 'Tis not what you meant," he said. "You wondered what would happen to your people."

She turned back, the glimmer of a smile on her lips. "Now who looks for virtue where there is none?"

"Do not try to lie about this truth," he said. "For this I know—you care for your people's welfare."

"They are all I have. We Frasers were once a great force, and Evermyst a grand fortress. Is it wrong of me to dream of seeing such days again?"

He mulled a dozen old conversations over in his mind. "Is that why you went to court, then? To find a wealthy nobleman?"

She held his gaze. " 'Twas my father's hope to marry me well," she said. " 'Tis why he sent me to Edinburgh. Indeed, even after . . ." She faltered, but in a moment, she went on. "Even afterward, he hoped Laird Tytherleigh would wish to marry me."

Something akin to rage boiled inside him, but he kept his expression stoic. "And what of the prophecy?"

"Father didn't think the viscount's actions negated the possibility of him possessing the required attributes."

Damn it to hell! "So when your father died, you hoped to choose your own mate, as the king had promised."

"Nay. I hoped to have no mate a tall, despite his promise to Munro. Hence my journey to my cousins."

He canted his head.

"I appealed to them for assistance. But once I mentioned the name Munro, there was little hope of help from that front."

"And what of your betrothed's escort?"

"I left them before we reached my cousins, and hurried from there to the MacAras. But they were no more help than my kinsmen."

"Thus you left there, too."

"I still had hopes of finding assistance elsewhere."

"With the MacGowans?"

She shrugged. "I learned at an early age not to be choosy."

"And to lie."

"And what should I have done? Spilled the entire truth and hoped that someone I had never met, someone who owed me naught, would risk his own life for a maid who could offer him nothing?" She twisted her hands together. "It would not have happened. Not until the sun fell into the sea. Not until the seasons ceased—"

"You are right," he said. "Only a fool would see himself wounded for naught."

She drew herself up, and the cool veneer settled back over her features. "So what is it that *you* wanted, MacGowan?"

He dared not think what he wished from her. The road to hell was paved with a woman's charms. "Do you forget, lass? You said you were the lady of the great fortress of Levenlair. Surely there be vast opportunity there."

She stood very still, thinking, and in a moment she spoke again, though it seemed she forced out the words. "You told me you did not believe I was Mary of Levenlair."

" 'Twas only so me brothers would not," he lied.

"So you hoped to win my hand and thereby gain Levenlair's fortune."

He forced a laugh. "I fear I be not as greedy as some, lass. I only hoped for a bit of coin."

"Then why, after you arrived here and saw that we had nothing . . . why did you still battle the Munro?"

"I told you. I did not like the look of him."

"So it was not for me?" she murmured.

Had he wounded her? Did she care? Might it be that . . .

He swore silently and set his jaw. "In truth, you are not the sort to make me risk death, Notmary."

"Then you do not . . . you are not . . . attracted to me?"

Her expression was so sincere, so melancholy. He was beginning to sweat and attempted to lift his leg just to feel the edge of pain skitter across his flesh. "Nay," he said. "No more than average."

"So why, at the inn—"

" 'Twas nothing!" He spat out the words before she could go on, before she could remind him how she had felt in his arms, how her skin smelled, how her breath felt against—God help him, he was a daft prick! " 'Twas naught but a base reaction. Surely you, of all people, know better than to expect more from a man."

"So you do not care for me? 'Twas only . . . desire for coin that brought you here?"

He tried to grin, but the expression felt hideously ghoulish. "You make me sound very mercenary, lass."

"And now I owe you."

"You owe me nothing!" He immediately regretted the words. He had to act cool and self interested, lest his heart be wrenched from his chest yet again. "Unless you're offering," he corrected, and eyed her with what he hoped was lascivious interest.

"And if I offered . . ." She took a trio of quick steps toward him. "You would accept?"

His leer disintegrated into a scowl. "Mayhap you are too naive to understand what a leg injury does to a man." Now he was the liar, for already his idiotic wick was lifting toward her, begging shamelessly for attention.

"I noticed nothing more than a wound on your thigh and chest," she said.

"What?" he rasped.

She straightened even more, though her cheeks were slightly reddened. "Poor we may be, but still I am lady of this keep. 'Tis my duty to—"

"You saw me in the whole?"

"You are not the first, but as I said, I saw nothing amiss . . . in that region."

"Christ!" He'd been naked, and wounded, and unconscious, and in plain view of her and God knew who else. "Christ!" he said again and beneath the blankets his manhood jerked with inappropriate enthusiasm. "You cannot tell just by looking. I am most probably irreparably damaged."

"I've not known a man to say such a thing," she murmured. "Unless he was trying to make me feel pity. To trick me into his bed."

Good Lord! He forced a grin. His face was getting tired. "You've found me out, lass."

She took another two steps toward him. "So that's it, then? You be still attempting to . . . couple with me?"

"You may not be me type, lass, but . . ." God, she was beautiful. "It has been some time for me. You can hardly blame me for trying."

Her expression was disturbingly somber. What would it take to make her smile, he wondered, and found that despite everything—her lunacy, her deceit, the irritating pain that throbbed through him, he still longed with hopeless fervency to take her into his arms.

"Nay, I do not blame you," she said, and taking one more step, perched cautiously on the edge of his mattress.

"You don't?" His words sounded as weak as a girl child's.

"The truth is, MacGowan, I owe you."

He tried to speak. Nothing came out.

"But I have little to offer," she said, and reaching out, set her palm upon his arm. Flesh against flesh. "Thus . . ." she began.

There was no air in the room. No air—and he realized that he had forgotten to inhale. He did so now.

"Thus I propose a solution."

"Solution?"

"I do not like to owe men."

He wanted to assure her that she owed him nothing, but he was wracked with a fear that if he spoke, the truth would spill out like a break-tide. He wanted her with such intensity that he ached with the longing; he could think of nothing else, and yes, though he knew he was a fool, he would die to keep her safe.

"Neither do I like to fear them," she said, "and since I am indebted . . ."

Breathe. Breathe.

"And you are injured, mayhap 'twould be wise for me to . . ." Her hand slid up his arm and onto his chest, and suddenly he was breathing too fast. "To repay you, and mayhap overcome my fear at the same time."

'Twas lunacy! And yet his body screamed for her. Willing . . . nay, eager to have her at any price, for however long she offered. So what if she had no feelings for him? It mattered little. Surely he had learned not to care. But . . . to have her and lose her . . .

"What say you?" she whispered.

"Nay." The refusal was so low Ramsay himself could barely believe it had left his lips.

"What?" Her voice was breathy, close, shivering up his spine like magic.

"I fear I am more grievously injured than I suspected," he said, forgetting where he had ended with his lies, and no longer caring to work out the tangled snarl.

"No interest?"

He swallowed. "Nay. None at all."

She leaned slowly forward. He watched her lips until he could no longer see them, and then they touched his. Desire burned hot as a poker, and he trembled like a leaf beneath its heat.

"Still nothing?" she whispered.

He managed somehow to shake his head.

She drew her hand carefully from his chest and rose to her feet. "You are a liar." She said the words softly but with absolute conviction.

"Me!" Air rushed back into his lungs. " 'Tis *you* who is the liar!"

"Aye. But at least I am good at it," she said, and turning toward the door, left without another word.

Chapter 21

"**N**aught has changed. 'Tis the same as before the Munro came to Evermyst," Anora began, but Meara was already shaking her head. Flickering candlelight chased shadows across the oil portraits that adorned the walls of the solar.

"All has changed and you well know it, lass. The Munro is injured but not dead. Do you think he will take that defeat kindly? Nay, he shall redouble his efforts to have this place."

"Then we shall redouble our efforts to keep it from him," Anora said.

"Aye." Isobel's eyes glittered in the candlelight. "Senga may well be feeling restless."

"Hush," Meara scolded. "This is not a game, and I do not wish to play." She turned her attention on

Anora and scowled. "Long ago, I made a vow to keep you safe. Mayhap I have already compromised that vow. But . . ." Her expression softened and her rheumy eyes grew misty as she glanced again at Isobel. "When I saw her face . . ." The room went silent. She cleared her throat. "Still, I will not worsen the condition by acting as if all is well when it is not. The Munro is angry and he is yet powerful."

"Senga—"

"And he is no fool!" Meara snarled. "He is not his sire."

"Neither was his brother," Anora said. "And yet that one is dead."

"Cuthbert was all cruelty. The devil's own, but none too cunning. His younger brother may seem the same sort, but do not underestimate him. He is not so dim as he appears."

"So what would you have me do?" Anora asked. "Give myself to my mother's killers? Become a Munro so that—"

"I would have you be wise!" Meara warned. "Not a foolish girl bound by old wounds."

"You would call me foolish for struggling to keep my own?"

"Nay, for turning aside those who can help you."

"I will help myself and my people."

"And what of the prophecy?"

Anora shifted her eyes away. "What of it?"

"The lad challenged the bull in his own valley, lass."

"What has that to do with me?"

"Save your foolish act for someone stupid enough to be fooled by it," Meara growled. "You know exactly what I speak of. A veritable stranger championed you. What does that say to you?"

"It means nothing," Anora said. "He did it for naught but personal reasons."

"Oh. And how do you know that, lass?"

It was never good to give Meara too much information. Already her ancient eyes were gleaming.

"He told me himself," Anora said, and clasped her hands lest she fidget.

"And what else did he say?"

"It matters little," she insisted. "He fought for the glory of fighting. He is not peaceable."

"Oh? And what of powerful?"

"The Munro would have surely killed him were it not for MacGowan's—"

"Cunning?" Meara finished.

"Steed," Anora countered.

"Ahh. So 'tis the horse that is cunning. How interesting. Is it the horse that is kind, also?"

"I've no reason to believe either of them is kind."

"Then you must carry his child in truth."

She felt herself pale. "Why do you say such a thing?"

"Because I can think of no other reason he might risk his life. Can you?"

"I've no way of knowing the man's mind."

" 'Tis true, lass, for you do not even know your own."

"I know my mind well and good," she argued. " 'Tis in my mind to care for my own people. 'Tis in my mind to believe that none has the right to take me against my own will."

"Or with your will."

"What does that mean?"

"Just this, lass," Meara said, and took a few scraping steps toward her. "There is only one test that the lad has yet to prove."

Her throat felt tight. "He's proved none of them."

"Aye, he has, and you well know it. 'Tis only the love that is yet unproved."

"Love!" Anora said, panic welling inside her. "I fear you've gone as daft as Deirdre. Mayhap—"

"Why not admit your true feelings?"

Anora flickered her gaze away, settling on Isobel's wide eyes for just a moment before yanking it aside. "Because there are no true feelings to admit."

Meara stared at her, then nodded once. "Then you'd best let another see to his wounds, lass. For you've surely got other things to worry on."

Anora's stomach flopped. " 'Tis my place to see to Evermyst's guests lest—"

"I'm certain I can find another to care for the Mac-Gowan. Indeed, he will probably flourish beneath a hand that does not find his company so onerous."

A dozen arguments came to mind, but before she could herd one off from the others, Meara spoke again.

"He is not so hard to look upon, aye? What say you, Isobel? Might you find the time to look after the braw lad?"

"I—" The maid speared her gaze to Anora's, but Meara drew her attention back.

"Come now, lass, Evermyst owes him a great debt, and since you are now one of Evermyst's own . . ." She shrugged.

Anora wrung her hands. Isobel watched the nervous movement with a scowl, then nodded once to Meara.

"Aye, I can see to him."

"Good, then," Meara said, and shuffled toward Isobel. "You're a fine child, lass. Now go, see if there is aught he needs."

"But he is most probably asleep, and—"

"He is awake," Meara said, and ushered the girl toward the door.

"How do you know?"

"I know something of men, lass, unlike some others here. The lad is yet awake, for he has things on his mind. Go to him," she said slyly. "See what needs he may have."

Anora almost called them back, but in a moment the door had closed and she was alone.

Ramsay lay awake in the narrow room. His chest hurt and his leg felt stiff, but 'twas not the pain that kept him from sleep. Questions and worries and roiling memories gnawed at him.

Why was he here? Why was he such a dolt? Why—

A soft knock sounded at the door. His breath stopped. Anora?

"Who is it?"

The silence seemed to last forever, broken only by the throbbing of his heart against his bandaged ribs.

" 'Tis the maid Isobel. May I enter?"

Was she lying yet again? Was it Anora come to see him at this late hour? Clenching the blankets in his fists, he called out, "Aye. Come hither."

The door opened with a soft creak, and Isobel stepped inside. She wore the same droopy coif as he had seen before, and her gown had gone unchanged. But in the flickering light of the single candle, her eyes were bright blue and strangely familiar, as if he had seen them in a dream.

"You are Lady Anora's maid servant," he said.

She bobbed a nervous curtsy. "Aye, sir. I am that." Her voice was little above a whisper. "Come to see to your needs before you find sleep."

"Me needs?" His breath stopped again. What needs? Could it be that Anora had sent this lass to lie with him? 'Twas obvious enough that he had not fooled her. She knew that, despite his words to the contrary, he yearned for her with a pathetic longing. Could it be that she had sent this lass to take her place in his arms, to—

"You have done much to help us, me laird," she murmured. She stood some distance from the candle, looking drab and hunched and rumpled, as though she would rather crawl into a hole than be there in his chamber. Yet strangely there was something about her that intrigued him, something he couldn't quite name. "And I wonder why."

"What?"

"That is to say . . . 'twas very kind of you to champion me lady, especially since she is betrothed to another."

He frowned. "The Munro challenged me. I could not, with good conscience, run away."

"So that was your reasoning, was it, me laird?"

He stared at her. Even Dun Ard's outspoken servants were not usually so forthright. "I am weary, lass," he said. "Mayhap you could tell me your true purpose for being here and we could both save ourselves some sleep."

Her eyes widened. She glanced sideways, her mobile mouth a pink bow. "Me apologies, me laird. 'Twas not me mission to be impertinent."

He exhaled. "And 'twas not mine to be an ass." His

head seemed heavy suddenly. He leaned it back
against the wall and wished to hell that he had never
laid eyes on Anora Fraser, never been captured by her
wiles. "What were you sent to do, lass?"

She blinked at him, then lowered her eyes, but even
so, it felt like she watched him. "Me lady is worried for
your well being."

"How so?"

The flicker of a frown skittered across the girl's elfin
face. "She is grateful for your help . . ." She paused and
wrung her narrow hands. "Even though . . ."

"Even though?"

"Me lady . . ." Her voice trailed away yet again.
"She does not . . . trust men."

Ramsay tried to keep the emotion from his face, but
try as he might, he could not forget the night in the inn.
Could not forget the aching, doltish need to make the
world right for her, to soothe her fears and hold her forever with nothing between them but warmth and peace.

"Me laird?"

He glanced up with a scowl. "What?"

"I said, I hope you will not hold her . . . lack of interest against her."

"Lack of interest?"

"In you."

Painful honesty. How agonizingly refreshing in this
place of lies. "I only fought the Munro because he challenged me," Ramsay said, his voice carefully level. "I
believe I already explained that."

"Of course," she said, and bobbed a nervous curtsy.
"Me apologies. Then I suppose . . . I suppose there be
nothing holding you here."

He scowled. "Other than the fact that me leg's been
hacked in two."

She skittered her eyes sideways, swallowed, and stepped forward. "You've been lucky thus far, and better your leg than your head."

"I didn't know there were designs on me head."

"Have you not heard of the shade?"

"Evermyst's ghost?"

"Aye." Another quick glance sideways, as if she feared the spirit might come through the very walls around her. "Senga."

"She has a name?"

"Doesn't *your* grandmother?"

He scowled. "Were we not just talking of a ghost?"

"Aye." She bobbed a nod. " 'Tis me lady's grandmother."

"Oh?"

" 'Tis said her husband strangled her in a jealous rage. Thus she remains in this world, seeking vengeance on any who might harm her kin."

" 'Tis lucky for me, then, that I have no such intentions."

"Neither did her husband when they first wed, but I suspect that being murdered may have made her a bit suspicious."

"I see," he said, keeping his voice even.

She scowled. "Do you disbelieve in ghosts?"

"Thus far, the dead have done me less harm than the living."

"You should not disregard their powers," she whispered.

"Tell me, lass. Why would you care if I do?"

"I've no wish to see you killed, me laird."

"No?"

"Nay." Her voice was breathy with surprise. "Of

course not," she said, and took a few steps forward. "For you are bold and kind and . . ." A smile flickered over her face, but somehow it did not quite reach her lovely eyes. "And bonny. Tell me, me laird," she whispered, and stepped a mite closer. "Do you find me repulsive?"

"Nay." In fact, there was something strangely alluring about her, despite her cowed demeanor and unkempt appearance. Still, his wick, always too enthusiastic for his own good, seemed to be sound asleep. Damnation! 'Twould be just his luck that the one woman who repeatedly threatened his life would be the only woman who stirred his blood. "Hardly that, lass."

"Then you would not mind if I would snuff out the candle and . . ." The room pitched suddenly into darkness. "Join you for a small piece of time?"

He frowned, for to his utter confusion, he found that he wanted nothing more than to lie in the darkness and dream of . . .

"Aye," he said, his voice gruff. "I'd appreciate your company."

"Would you?" The mattress sighed beneath her slight weight. "And what else would you do, me laird?"

There was something about the way she spoke that reminded him of Anora. How she sounded when her guard was down and she was soft and honest and . . .

But suddenly Isobel kissed him, tumbling his thoughts into chaos. He pressed a hand to her shoulder, ready to push her away. Yet Anora didn't want him, didn't care for him in the least. Why should he not take advantage of this maid's offer? Desperately trying for some sort of arousal, he slipped his hand up her throat, sweeping off her coif. Her hair tumbled free, and she shifted back.

A slim ray of moonlight slanted through the window, and in that ray he saw a fragile lass who was small and afraid and hopelessly beautiful.

"Anora," he whispered feverishly.

"Nay!" Her gasp was sharp. She jerked away, stumbling to her feet. "Nay! 'Tis me, Isobel."

His mind spun. Guilt and hopelessness washed him. "Me apologies, lass. I . . . I am sorry." She was beyond the reach of the fickle moonbeams now, but it wouldn't matter if she stood in the full light of day; he would still imagine Anora, would see her figure in every swaying flower, hear her voice in every sparrow's song. Damn him! "Me wounds must have addled me brain," he said. "Forgive me."

"Aye," she said, already backing toward the door, and in a moment she was gone, leaving him alone.

Damn him to hell! He scrubbed his hands dismally over his face. He was an ass and a dolt, desperate and hopeless and idiotic. And one thing was certain. It was time to leave.

Chapter 22

Morning dawned with irritating brightness.

Ramsay gritted his teeth as he pulled his tunic over his head, groaned as he adjusted his plaid, and swore out loud as he belted it in place. No use suffering in silence. After all, there was no one here he was trying to impress. Nay, all he was trying to do was leave. His injuries were hardly life threatening.

Opening the chamber door was something of a challenge, but he managed it, then the few steps across the hallway, reminding himself every second that his wounds were just superficial. By the time he reached the stairs, his head felt light and his knees a bit unsteady. Then he remembered the night before, and pushed resolutely onward. The steps beneath his boots seemed to be a thousand leagues away.

Below, faces turned to stare up at him—a plump, graying matron, a scarred soldier, a buxom dark haired maid with a basket of cheese. The great hall gradually grew silent, but in a moment a small figure parted a crowd, and Anora stood before him.

"MacGowan." Clothed in a worn violet gown, she seemed unusually pale this morn. He kept silent, merely giving her a nod. "You should not be up and about."

He mustered a smile. Even that much effort threatened to rip his chest in two, but he reminded himself that he did not like her, and sharpened his roguish grin. "I am flattered that you wish to keep me in your bed, lass, but I fear I cannot stay there."

She scowled. "Are you feeling feverish?"

Apparently she wasn't accustomed to his ready wit. "Nay," he said and returned a scowl for her lack of appreciation. "I am returning home."

"Home!" The word skittered from her lips. "You jest," she said, and even her little cherry mouth seemed pale.

He stared at it.

"MacGowan!" she rasped.

"Your pardon?" he said, finding her eyes.

"I said you will return to your bed this instant."

"I cannot," he said, and refused to allow his gaze to slip to her mouth again, for it was too soft. But neither could he look into her eyes, for they had an unhappy tendency to pull him in. Even her hands were not safe, for they were so fragile and expressive that after one glance he found he wanted nothing more than to cradle them in his own and promise her his everlasting protection.

Christ! If he stayed until sunset, he'd be able to look

at nothing past the toes of her shoes—which were damnably small.

"There are deeds that need doing," he said, and shuffled his gaze toward the distant window where the woman called Ailsa hovered, listening intently.

"You are not ready to leave here, MacGowan. You are too weak."

Aye, he was weak, and how well she knew it. That was the very reason he must go, to send his clansmen to keep her safe. "I request that you see me horse readied," he said and, employing all his strength, managed to ease down the final two steps.

"You cannot leave." Her words sounded tortured. He raised his eyes to hers, and for once, he saw a tangle of uncertain emotions there. Regret? Sadness? Fear? Loneliness?

But nay, he was being the fool again. Whatever she felt, it was not loss for his departure.

"You need not worry," he said, forcing himself past her. "When I reach Dun Ard, I will send word to the king and tell him of your troubles here. There is no love lost between the Stuarts and the Munros. He will set all to—"

"MacGowan—" Her voice was low, breathy, and though he did his best to be strong, he could not resist her eyes.

"Aye?"

"Please . . . I . . ." She gazed up at him. The great hall was as silent as nightfall, as if every ear strained to hear their words. "I will see that your breakfast is readied," she said, and turned abruptly away.

His knees almost buckled, but he forced himself across the floor to the nearest table and lowered himself gratefully to its bench. The walls dipped, but he remained very still until they steadied. Gradually, the volume grew around him again.

"Me laird."

Ramsay turned carefully, lest pieces of his anatomy fall from his body like autumn leaves. Duncan's young face was hopelessly earnest.

"Tell me 'tis not true. You are not leaving."

"Aye, I am, thus I would appreciate it if you would ready me—"

"But you cannot. You have been badly wounded. What if you weaken?"

If he was any weaker, his head would fall straight from his neck onto his—

A scream sounded nearly in his ear, and he twisted about. Pain sliced his arm, then his attacker was upon him, slashing again. He reacted out of instinct, catching the arm and holding it away from his chest.

"Bastard!" The insult shrieked through the hall. Ramsay jerked his gaze to his attacker's face. Deirdre! Surprise and pain weakened his grip and in that instant she jerked her knee wildly upward.

Agony shot through his thigh, burning like hot iron. Letting go, he staggered backward, barely finding his feet. She launched herself at him with a scream. He managed to catch her wrist, but the force of her impetus knocked him backward. She landed atop him, pounding the breath from his body, but he twisted desperately, flipping her over as he did so. Her hand cracked against the floor, and the blade tumbled from her fingers.

She screamed something harsh and inarticulate, and then, in wriggling frustration, she spat in his face. Her knees scrambled, trying to strike him.

"Still! Be still," he ordered, and though she finally

quieted, her crazed eyes bore into him with scalding hatred.

"Coward!" she screamed. "Kill me, then! And kill the babe, since you were too much the woman to kill the sire."

Her words filtered slowly into his consciousness, and as reality came home to him, he slid off her and skimmed his gaze down her soiled form. Her gown was bunched between her thighs, and her swollen belly rose like a melon from her middle.

"What now, MacGowan?" she sneered, spread on the floor like a victim of war. "Has the battle got you randy?"

He pulled his hands away in horror, and in that instant she snatched up her knife.

Anora screamed, a man cursed, and then Deirdre was pulled away to wriggle in a soldier's capable hands.

Ramsay lay on his back, dazed and aching.

"MacGowan." Anora was beside him in an instant. "Are you hurt?"

He considered her question for an instant, then let his eyes fall closed. "I think so."

"You're bleeding. He's bleeding!" she called out. "Tree, David, take him back to his room."

Pain sliced him as hands the size of mallets bore him away. Far above, the smoke-darkened beams swayed hazily.

"Carefully," he groaned.

"What?" Anora leaned close, trying to hear.

"I said . . ." He could barely manage a whisper. "Carefully."

"Careful," she breathed to his bearers. "Be—"

But her words were cut short by cackling laughter.

"That's right. Take him away," Deirdre screamed. "Coddle him. But 'twill do no good."

The journey up the stairs hurt like hell.

"Hide beneath the lady's skirts, MacGowan!" screamed the crazed voice. "Use your feeble wick whilst you can, for Munro will come soon enough, and then it will be gone. Mayhap I'll use it as a bottle stop."

"Sweet Almighty!" Ramsay rasped, jostled between his two bearers.

Anora swung the door open and they hustled him inside. Ramsay moaned as they eased him back onto the pillows.

"I do not think this Deirdre likes me."

"How badly are you hurt?" Anora's face was pale, her fingers unsteady as she wrestled with his belt buckle.

"I'm not about to die, if that's what you're thinking."

"You're not?"

He hoped not. "Nay," he said. " 'Twould be horribly embarrassing." His belt fell open. "What are you doing?"

"Tree, find out what's keeping Meara. David, take Deirdre . . . to the dungeon."

They departed in an instant. Anora set her fingers to the brooch that held Ramsay's plaid crossed against his chest. For a moment the emerald cat eyes flashed against her hand, then she tugged his tunic upward. The process seemed entirely unrelated to him.

"I've done nothing to her," he said. His own voice seemed entirely unrelated to him. "And yet she hates me."

"Quiet now. Meara will be here soon."

"Women usually do not detest me until they get to know me. Except for you, of course. Yet she does. Why is that?"

"I fear it will hurt if I remove your tunic."

"It hurts already."

"I could cut it off."

"You could leave it be."

"MacGowan—"

"Leave it be, Notmary. I've worse troubles than that, just now."

"You vowed not to die. You'll not be going back on your promise." Emotion quivered in her voice.

"As you will, then." Refusing to try to read her feelings, he leaned his head back against the wall.

"I will cut it off," she said, and reaching for the sheath in his boot, pulled out his dirk by its antler handle. It sliced easily through his shirt. In a moment she was tugging the fabric away from his right arm. He heard the soft intake of her breath and turned hazily to stare at the wound himself.

"Humnph." It was all he could think to say.

"She opened your old wound."

"I see that."

"Helena, get Meara," she said, as a stout maid hurried in with a bowl.

"Why does this Deirdre hate me so?"

The maid hustled out.

"Some say she is possessed. Some say the ghost has made her mad."

Tearing a square from his shirt, she dipped it into the nearby bowl and carefully washed the blood from his flesh. The fingers of her left hand were wrapped gently about his elbow. They looked slim and fragile against the darker flesh of his arm, and he pulled his attention away with some difficulty.

"And what of you?" he asked. "Do you think she is possessed by the shade?"

"Nay! Senga is not evil. She would never harm one of her own."

"One of her own?"

"Deirdre is a Fraser."

"Then why her attachment to the Munros?"

Her fingers tightened slightly on his arm. The feelings smoked through his system, easing the pain like a draught of wine.

"She says the babe is the Munro's seed."

"Is it?"

"I know not. Perhaps she lies, or perhaps . . ." She shrugged. "Her memory is a chancy thing, but he has not claimed it. Nor will another, for she is . . ." Her voice broke. "I am sorry." Her voice broke. "I did not believe she was a danger. But recently her behavior has been . . ." She shook her head. "I fear her condition worsens."

"She has not always been like this?"

"Nay. Before her fall she was a gentle soul, though she . . . she liked the lads."

He said nothing.

"Ailsa was bringing in her goats when she found Deirdre at the bottom of Potter's Crag. Unconscious, and pale as death."

"And you do not know how it happened?"

"Your chest is bleeding again." Anora's voice was very small, her hand unutterably soft when it stroked his shoulder. He pulled his gaze away and concentrated on the far wall. A crack ran diagonally from the corner.

"It will heal. And what of Deirdre?" he asked.

"She had not a scratch on her, yet she was unconscious for some time. When she awoke..." She shrugged. "She suffers from headaches. Some days she is docile and kind, sometimes she is frightening. There are those who think that she should be put away before she hurts another. But I could not..." Her words faded to a halt. "Too many mistakes," she whispered. "I should not have let you come here."

There was such hurt in her voice, a world of aching regret.

"You could not stop me. I came of me own free will," he said.

"And you have lived to regret it," she whispered.

If only he could regret meeting her, but even now he was trapped in her eyes. He kept his hands carefully at his sides, refusing to let them reach for her.

"You cannot be expected to withstand the Munro alone," he said. "There was naught you could do but seek help."

"I could have wed him."

Ramsay's stomach clenched.

"He is the Munro," she said. "Powerful, wealthy. Many of my own people think me foolish for rejecting him. Some simply think me weak, afraid of men."

"Who thinks so?"

"Ailsa, for one."

He thought back. An image of a buxom woman with dark hair came to mind. He motioned toward his own chest. "The maid with the—"

"Aye," she interrupted.

"And what do you think?"

"Mayhap she is right."

"If that is case, why did you refuse him?"

"Because the Munro is cruel. Barbaric. He cannot be trusted, yet I dared not tell him nay. Thus I pretended to honor my father's wishes until I could find help. But the more I came to know him, the more certain I was that he would mistreat my people." Her voice was soft as evening shade. "But mayhap 'tis only myself I worry for. I could not bear the thought of . . ."

Her fingers slipped with silken thoughtfulness over his bandage and onto his belly. It contracted with agonizing excitement beneath her touch, but he gritted his teeth and didn't move. "Of what?" he asked.

"Of being touched. Of touching." She raised her gaze, catching his. "But now . . ." Her voice was a whisper.

"What?" His own was nearly too low to hear.

"I find I can think of little else."

He could think of nothing to say. Could think of nothing at all, in fact, but that her lips were too bright, her eyes too wide, her touch too soft to resist. He should say *nay* now, save himself from the misery she was sure to cause him, but she was leaning closer and God help him, one kiss might well be worth death.

He held his breath, waiting. Her hand felt like heaven and hell against his abdomen, her eyes shone in the morning light, and his heart, damn it, was squeezed like a bellows in his chest.

"MacGowan," she whispered.

"Notmary," he hissed, and then she kissed him.

Feelings exploded like fireworks inside him. Pleasure and pain all mixed in a—

"What's this, then?"

At the sound of Meara's voice, Anora jerked away and launched to her feet. The old woman stood in the doorway with Isobel behind.

"Have you got your own way of healing then, lass?"

"Meara." Her voice was breathy, panicked. Ramsay's heart commenced beating again, though he had thought it might not. "I thought mayhap you weren't coming."

"I see that."

"Well, I . . ." She stopped, snapping her gaze to Isobel, who stared back, her gaze just as wide. "I leave him in your hands, Meara." Sparing one rapid fire glance for Ramsay, she rushed out the door.

Meara's eyes were as dark and inscrutable as she approached the bed. It creaked beneath her weight.

Ramsay's tunic lay in tatters upon the mattress and his heart was still doing a wild fling in his chest, but he forced himself to remain stoically still beneath her stare.

"The lassie's been hurt enough without the likes of you, MacGowan," she said.

He scowled. "I've no intention of hurting her."

"And mayhap you be too wounded to know how to do anything else just now," she said.

A crash of memories smote him. Pain, guilt, fear.

She was right. Even if Anora cared for him, he had no caring to give back.

"I will leave on the morrow," he said.

For a moment the old woman stared at him, and then she snorted. "You're not good enough for the likes of her and never will be, but if you leave tomorrow, laddie, I'll kill you meself."

Chapter 23

"He is handsome." Isobel's voice was soft.

Anora snapped her gaze to the girl's. Had the maid read her thoughts? "Who?" she asked, but if Isobel was fooled she did not show it.

"The MacGowan."

"Oh." Anora fiddled with the linen on her lap. Embroidery had always seemed a frivolous thing to her, but for years frivolity had been one of her masks, and now she found it helped her relax after scampering from the infirmary like a scared rabbit. It had been a long day, filled with grinding doubts and crumbling discipline. "So you think him bonny, do you?"

"Aye. Who would not?"

She shrugged, but the movement felt stiff. 'Twas not like her to lie to Isobel. In fact, she didn't know if it was possible, but the feelings inside her were so raw, so fresh and roiling and uncertain, that she dared not expose them to the light of scrutiny, lest her world crumble to ashes around her. A noise caught her attention. 'Twas faint but disturbing, like the shadow of a scream.

"What was that?" Anora asked.

"I know not. Mayhap 'twas Senga," Isobel murmured. "Who would not think the MacGowan handsome?" she repeated.

Anora glanced up. "Mayhap someone who cannot trust men."

" 'Twas a long while ago, Anora."

"But still fresh in my mind." She stood abruptly to pace, her embroidery forgotten.

"Then you have no feelings for him?"

She should say no, yet she could not quite manage the words. "What if he learns the truth, Isobel? I cannot risk it."

"Then what shall you do?"

"I need do nothing. He'll be leaving soon."

"Will he?" Isobel's tone was uncertain.

"Of course. There is naught keeping him here."

Anora waited for Isobel to respond, to argue, to say nay, there was every reason for MacGowan to stay, for 'twas obvious he had lost his heart to the lady of the keep. But she said no such thing.

"You will not miss him?"

"Of course not. When he leaves, things will be as they were."

"And the Munro?"

"He has been bested, weakened. Betweenst the two of us, we can be rid of him forever."

Isobel grinned, that slight tilt of mischief that Anora

had known since long before she'd met the girl. "The three of us," Isobel corrected. "Betweenst the three of us we shall—"

"Me lady!" The words were accompanied by a loud rap at the door. "Me lady, a word, please."

"Enter."

Helena pressed the door open, her expression worried, her hands clasped. "Me lady, Deirdre has begun her travail."

"Now?"

"Aye."

"In the dungeon?"

She nodded. "Meara is with her, but I fear 'tis not going well. She thinks the babe might be turned about."

"Dear God! 'Twas her scream I heard."

"Aye." Helena wrung her hands. "She is being difficult."

"I'd best go to her."

"Nay, me lady," said the matron, and paused, her expression pained. " 'Tis you she curses."

"Me?"

"For bringing the MacGowan amongst us."

"She maintains her devotion for Munro?"

"Aye."

"Is there truth in it?" Anora asked. "Is the babe his?"

Helena shook her head. "I do not know."

" 'Tis possible she does not, either," Isobel said. "I have seen this sort of madness before."

"I must go to her," Anora said, and swept past Helena's protests and down the stairs. Another scream sounded, filled with pain and rage and certain madness. In the great hall, folk were gathered in uneasy groups. Their voices were hushed, and as Anora passed by, she noticed more than one invoking the sign of the cross. Whispers of ghosts and devils sneaked about the room like an evil wind, but she continued on, hurrying down the spiraled stairs to the rocky room below.

As she reached the dungeon's doorway another scream tore forth, echoing against the stone walls. Anora faltered, and Isobel, beside her now, wrapped her arm protectively about her waist.

"I cannot leave," Anora said. " 'Tis my duty to care for her."

"Then we shall see this through together," Isobel whispered.

They entered the room side by side. Deirdre lay on her back on a lumpy cot. The smell of blood and sweat was nearly overwhelming.

Meara glanced up, her creased face bleak as she shook her head.

"What can I—"

A bellowing scream cut her words short as Deirdre shoved herself to her elbows.

" 'Tis you!" The woman's face was red, her eyes shot with blood.

"Deirdre." Despite herself, Anora's voice shook. "Lie back. Let us help you."

Deirdre stared in bewilderment, and for a moment Anora hoped that the kindly maid of old had returned.

"Let us—" she began again, but in that instant Deirdre launched from the bed with a feral shriek of rage.

Anora stumbled back. Meara yelled an order, and from the far side of the dungeon, two men rushed forward to snatch her back.

"Help me?" Deirdre snarled. Veins throbbed in her

neck and her hair was a mass of sweaty snarls. But
'twas her eyes that held Anora captive. Insane, helpless, hateful. She laughed, throwing back her head,
then cut the sound short. " 'Tis you who are killing
me."

"Nay," Anora gasped.

Deirdre struggled wildly, then stilled to glare. " 'Tis
you who stole him from me," she said.

"Who?" Anora asked, but Deirdre screamed again
and doubled up, falling hard to her knees.

"Get her back on the bed," Meara ordered.

The men lifted her away.

"You'd best go, me lady." Meara's voice was
strained. "You'll do no good here."

Anora began to protest, but Meara shook her head
and turned wearily away. There was naught to do but
find her way back up the stairs with Isobel.

From the great hall she could hear the murmur of a
hundred voices, but she could not go there. Not yet, so
she escaped outside.

The sky was as black as tar, but the air felt cool
against her face.

"I'd best hurry back to the kitchen," Isobel said.
"Stout Helena asked me to fetch the marjoram."

Anora turned to her. "I am sorry."

"For what?"

She shrugged. A whisper of a cry reached her ears
and she shuddered. "For everything."

Isobel smiled. "You imagine I would ever have
learned to swim the firth or filch a purse if I had spent
me days at court?"

A rustle of noise sounded from the darkness and a
dark haired lad appeared, a basket dangling from his
frail arm.

"Oh! Me lady," he said. "I did not see you there."

"Jamie," Anora said, turning nervously. "How fares your mother?"

"She is well, me lady," he said, and bobbing, ducked inside.

The night went silent.

"They fear me," Anora whispered.

"Nay, they fear hunger," Isobel said. "Naught else."

"There is a ghost howling in their keep and a madwoman calling me a witch. You do not think they fear that?"

"Keep the hounds of hunger from their bellies and the fear of brigands from their gates, and they shall not care if you be witch or saint."

"Isobel—"

" 'Tis true," she said. "You do not know the power of satiety until you feel the bite of hunger. Make Evermyst great, and they shall kiss your hem all the days of their pathetically easy lives."

Another noise shuffled from the darkness.

Isobel glanced toward the source, immediately rounding her shoulders and dropping her face. "I go now, me lady," she murmured. "Unless you have further need of me."

"Nay, see to your tasks," Anora said, and in a moment she was alone.

Make Evermyst great. The words echoed in her mind, but how could she do that when her walls were crumbling, Munro controlled their borders, and—

A whispering shriek found her ears again, and she turned abruptly away, striding through the shadows. The kindly darkness swallowed her. Through the misty night, she could barely make out the mill, the cobbler's shop, the herb garden.

From the kennel, a hound whimpered, and Anora turned toward it. Inside the low building, the dogs rose to meet her, and there, amidst the wagging acceptance of the hounds, she settled onto the straw.

She didn't know how much time had passed when she awoke, but she felt a sudden jolt of panic. She should not have left the keep. She should have been there with her people, keeping vigil and praying.

Stumbling out of the kennel, Anora hurried across the bailey. When she entered the great hall she heard a moan issue from below and she faltered, wanting more than anything to rush back out into the darkness. But her people were here. She straightened her back and stepped toward the tables.

"Lady Anora."

She turned with a start. "MacGowan!" He stood nearby, his face drawn but his back unbowed. "You should be abed."

He didn't acknowledge her order. "Where have you been?"

"I do not think—" she began, but the sound came again, so soft now that she had to strain to hear it.

"Drink."

The noise continued on, a tortured whisper of sound.

"Drink, Notmary," Ramsay said, and nudged her arm with his mug. "Unless 'tis your wish to faint dead away before your clansmen's eyes."

She took the mug, and realized suddenly that she'd been holding her breath. The mead ran warm and soothing into her stomach.

"Come," MacGowan said, and taking her arm, led her to a table.

"You're limping," she said, and felt strangely disembodied, as if she were not herself at all, but another.

"And you're shaking. You should not have left."

She turned toward him, anger brewing. "What should I have done? She does not want me with her."

"You went below?"

" 'Tis my responsibility to—"

He swore quietly, his fist whitening against the edge of the table. "She might have killed you. You should not have—"

"Who are you to tell me where to go and—"

"One of those who do not depend on you," he said, his voice low. "Unlike these others here." He turned abruptly away, his expression hard. "You have a duty to them."

"And pray, MacGowan, what is that duty?"

"To stay alive." His voice was nearly silent, and when he turned back to her, his eyes were as steady as stone. "Do you have some aversion to that, lass?"

Her world was crumbling, and she found, to her horror, that she wanted more than anything to fall into his arms. "Deirdre . . ." Her voice was a tortured rasp. "She blames me."

"She is mad."

"She is a Fraser."

"And what of the others, Notmary? Are they not Frasers, too?"

"Aye."

"Then stay alive for them. Be strong for them."

She skimmed the crowd. "And what if I am not strong?" she whispered.

He almost smiled, and it seemed that he nearly reached out to touch her.

"You challenged the Munro, lass."

"I am a fool."

An expression of regret crossed his face, but in a moment it was gone. " 'Tis too late to change your course now. You have set yourself against the bull."

"And for that me own people hate me."

"Only if you are wrong. You cannot permit your own people to side with your enemy, 'twill weaken your cause."

A moan sounded again.

Anora shivered. "Deirdre has sided with them," she whispered. "What would you do, MacGowan? Slit her throat afore she can damage another—"

A low wail echoed through the hall, ending on a quivering gasp.

A silent eternity passed, then footsteps sounded on the stairs. Anora turned, her breath held.

The two soldiers entered. Scratches ran the length of one's cheek. "She is gone, me lady," he said.

"The devil has her now," someone murmured.

Anora's head felt light. "And the babe?" she asked, just as Meara stepped into the hall.

In her arms she held a bundle of cloth, and from that cloth one tiny fist waved amidst a sporadic mewling.

The old woman's eyes were as hard as chiseled brownstone. "I would know this!" Her ancient voice boomed above the baby's lament. Every face turned to her, every breath stilled. "Who has fathered this child?"

A whisper of voices murmured amongst themselves.

"Speak!" she stormed.

"Mayhap 'twas a Munro," Malcolm said. "She was enamored with them."

"She was mad," Meara said.

"Or possessed. 'Tis best she is gone."

"And what of the babe?" Meara asked. No one answered. "Will her passing be a blessing, also?"

"Perhaps it will. Maybe she is the devil's own."

"Damn you, Malcolm," Meara said. " 'Tis because of men like you I have seen babes lost before. 'Twill not happen this time." She turned, eyeing the throng before her. "If the father of this bairn stands amongst us, he will step forward now and claim his own."

Not a soul spoke.

"Who?" Meara demanded.

" 'Tis me." The voice was not loud, and yet it resonated in the great hall like the toll of a heavy bell.

The room turned in breathless awe and watched as Ramsay MacGowan stepped forward.

"The child," he said quietly, "is mine."

Chapter 24

Not a whisper of breath filled the hall. Every eye was trained on Ramsay, but he kept his gaze on the bundle in Meara's arms. Transfixed, he was. Mesmerized, for there, within those rags, lay his redemption.

"What say you, MacGowan?" The old woman's head was tilted, as though she had misheard him.

"I said the child is mine."

Murmuring started afresh, buzzing like hornets about the great, echoing hall, but he let them buzz, feeling no need to swat at their passing. "You've been here but a few days, MacGowan," Meara said. "How can this be?"

Ramsay shrugged, and for the first time let himself consider the consequences of his actions. But he had no desire to turn back. Instead, he was pulled irresistibly toward that wee, small bundle until he stood directly before it.

For a moment he held Meara's bead-bright gaze, and then he shifted his attention and breathlessly brushed the blanket aside.

The babe's tiny head turned restlessly. Her skin was blotchy, as wrinkled as old parchment and as ugly as sin.

"Is she . . ." Ramsay paused and kept his words for Meara alone. "Is she deformed?"

"And what if she is, MacGowan?" asked the old woman. "Is she then yours no longer?"

For a moment he faltered. Surely he was a fool, insisted his better sense—but in that instant the babe opened her eyes. Blue as purest cobalt, they found his face with unerring, unblinking accuracy. The freed tiny fist curled tight around the edge of the blanket, but he noticed neither her unyielding grip nor her sudden stillness, for he was trapped in her gaze, captured by a thousand emotions that gripped his heart with deadly ferocity. "She is mine," he breathed.

Meara nodded, then straightened to her meager height and glanced about the hall, her eyes snapping. "If any would challenge the MacGowan's claim, speak now or forever be silent."

Not a sound whispered through the room, as though none dared breathe until this crisis was past. The old woman nodded tightly. "Come along," she said and ambled toward the stairs. The wooden steps creaked beneath her feeble weight, but no other sound followed their ascent. When they reached the chamber where Ramsay slept she turned, her wizened face somber as she faced him. "If you hope to win her heart with this, you are even more the fool than I first thought," she said.

Ramsay pulled his gaze from the babe in her arms. "I am tired and I am wounded," he said. "Speak plain or leave the bairn and go."

The faintest grin lifted Meara's rumpled face, but in an instant it was gone, replaced by her usual glower. "And if I leave the bairn and go, MacGowan, what then? You are poorly equipped to feed her."

He returned her scowl. The babe was beginning to yowl. "Methinks you have little more to offer her, old woman."

She actually laughed, then put the babe to her shoulder, rocking as she did so. "If I did not hate you I might be tempted to like you, MacGowan."

He ignored her statement, grateful that the babe was already quieting. "She will need a nursemaid," he said.

"You are wiser than I suspected," said the old woman. "Do you happen to know of any who might be up for the task?"

"Surely there is someone who could nurse her here at—" he began, but the old woman was already interrupting.

"There are none. Seonag's babe is the youngest, but not so wee as to still suckle."

"Then beyond Evermyst. A crofter's wife, or—"

"The Frasers have fallen on hard times, MacGowan. 'Twill be no simple task for you to care for this small one."

Worry and guilt gnawed at him.

"So what now? Shall I send the babe to the Munros?" she asked.

Suddenly he was overwhelmed by reality, by duty, by the thought of binding himself to such a helpless life.

Meara nodded. "Mayhap 'tis best," she said, and stepped toward the door. "The Munros be superstitious and cruel, but—"

Ramsay caught her by the arm. "I have me faults, old woman," he said. "But what I say I'll do, I do."

The ancient eyes flickered to his face. "Then the babe is yours," she said, and handing him the bundle, grinned mischievously. "And mayhap something more."

The baby wriggled like a puppy in his hands. He pulled it cautiously against his chest, and the tiny, scrunched face turned immediately, searching for sustenance.

"Why?" said a breathless voice.

He turned instantly toward the source, and there he found Anora, her hands clasped. He dragged his gaze back to the red face hidden within the gray blanket's warmth. The scarlet mouth closed on the blanket, then bellowed in frustration.

"Might it be that you hope to avenge yourself on Deirdre in this way?" Anora asked.

Ramsay shifted the infant a bit farther up his chest.

"Is that it, MacGowan?" Anora asked. "Do you plan to watch the babe die and know that you have had your revenge for the humiliation caused by the mother?"

He jerked his gaze to her face, momentarily ignoring the fact that the child was attempting to nurse on his tunic. "Is that what you think of me?"

The baby mewled, but no other sound broke the silence. Anora shifted her attention to the wriggling bundle and back.

"I know not what to think," she murmured. "Each time I believe I understand your motives, I find . . ." She paused. "Tell me why."

For a moment he was tempted to do as she asked, but he had not trusted even his brothers with the truth. Surely he would not be so foolish as to start with her.

"She will need a nursemaid soon," he said.

"There is none."

The baby complained more insistently. Ramsay's mind spun. "What of the goat herder?"

Anora scowled. "Not all things are as they seem."

"What?"

"Ailsa only looks as though she is nursing."

"I did not mean . . ." Ramsay shook his head, and realized Meara was long gone. "I wish to get milk from her beasts."

"Will a babe drink goats' milk?"

"We have little choice but to find out." Stepping forward, he lifted the baby toward her.

She backed abruptly away. "What are you doing?"

"Trying to save the child's life," he said and pushed the bundle toward her again.

She retreated another several steps.

He scowled. "Are you afraid of her?"

"Certainly not."

"Then take her."

"I am lady of this keep. 'Tis not my place to care for an infant." She lifted her peaked chin, but glanced nervously toward the door as if longing to escape.

"You would rather appeal to this Ailsa?"

She winced. "I know little of bairns!"

Ramsay's heart jerked, but he had no time to waste.

"Come, lass. 'Twill do you no harm to care for the babe for a wee span of time. Indeed, 'twill do you naught but good," he said, and pressed the wriggling bundle into her arms.

She took it with breathless terror, holding it away from her body as if it were a serpent. The baby squawked and the fear on Anora's face sharpened.

"Hold her close," he said, and nudged the babe toward her bosom. "She, too, is afraid."

For an instant he thought she might deny her own fear, but instead she nodded and straightened, bearing the babe to her shoulder.

The tender image seared its way into his heart, but he didn't allow himself to move closer. 'Twas far too dangerous, so he turned with careful disipline and left the chamber.

Outside, the air felt fresh and revitalizing. He drew it into his lungs, grateful for this time to think. By the time he reached his destination, his leg ached, but his mind felt clearer. His knock sounded against the cottage's weathered door, and in a moment it opened.

The widow Ailsa stood in the doorway. Her dark hair was loosed and fell about her shoulders in waves, but it was her breasts that drew his attention. Pale and round as rising loaves of bread, they greeted him from above her bodice.

"Well!" Her voice sounded surprised but hardly displeased. "Me laird MacGowan." She smiled and shifted her weight slightly, showing her incredible wares from a different angle. "You have finally come."

"Aye," he said, and resolutely kept his gaze from

straying south. "But mayhap for a different purpose than you suppose."

"MacGowan, I have—" Meara's words stopped as she shuffled into Ramsay's chamber. "Lass, what be you doing here?"

Anora held her breath for an instant. "MacGowan went to the cheese maker's."

"The . . . Ah!" Meara said and grinned. "To fetch milk."

"So he said."

"But you do not believe him."

"He is a man." Anora paced the floor again, the babe cuddled to her shoulder.

"Aye," Meara said, watching her. "He is that, and the father of this child, I believe he said."

Anora sent her a scowl. "I am no fool, Meara."

"Then pray tell, why did he claim it?"

Anora tightened her grip on the tiny bundle. It felt heavy and limp and ultimately helpless against her bosom. "To win some hold on Evermyst."

"You *are* a fool," Meara said, and turned toward the door. "Tell the MacGowan there may yet be a nursemaid to be found. I have sent Cant to inquire about it."

"Where do you go now?"

"To find a milk bladder." She turned toward the door.

"Surely some other can do that so that you can care for this babe," Anora said, but the old woman had already turned away and seemed suddenly quite deaf.

"Meara!" Anora called.

"What is it you want?"

"Send Helena up to care for the bairn."

"Of course, me lady," Meara agreed with all due

subservience and creakily closed the door behind her.

The baby mewled. Anora paced again and again. Minutes slipped away beneath the tread of her slippers, and fatigue set in. Where was Helena? Against her shoulder, the baby was silent. Trying to see past the concealing blanket, Anora walked to the bed and leaned carefully over the mattress, but with the cessation of movement, the infant awoke with a jerk. Anora straightened, and paced again, back and forth, until the tiny thing was again a limp bundle against her chest.

Fatigue wore at her. Anora paced to the bed again, and this time she slipped onto the pallet herself, careful not to disturb the babe. Propping her back against a pillow, she lifted her legs onto the bed and waited breathlessly for the child to complain, but she did not awaken.

Anora closed her eyes. Against her breast, she could feel the steady beat of the tiny infant's heart, and upon her neck, the babe's soft exhalations brushed her skin like the fluttering beat of a butterfly's wing. Silence settled softly in, and in that gentle frame of mind, Anora fell asleep.

Ramsay hurried back up the steps toward his chamber. His leg ached and his chest wound complained, but with surprisingly little verve. Inside his tunic, the bottle of milk felt warm and smooth against his skin. How he was going to feed it, he wasn't sure. The door opened silently beneath his fingers. Mayhap he could soak a cloth with it and—

His thoughts stopped as abruptly as his feet, for there upon his bed was Anora. The babe slept against her soft bosom. Her lashes looked downy fine against her ivory skin, and in slumber, her face looked as young and vulnerable as a child's. Gone was the harsh aloofness, replaced by naught but beauty and—

"MacGowan."

Ramsay jerked at the hiss of Meara's voice. She stood hunched nearly double behind him in the hallway, bent over a wooden cradle almost as large as herself.

"What are you doing?" he asked, hurrying toward her. "Did you carry that yourself?"

"Pipe down," she ordered. Glancing through the doorway toward the bed, she straightened creakily and lowered her voice even more. "I commissioned the leather wright to craft a milk bladder. You'll find it inside the cradle." One more quick glance at the bed, then, "Good luck to—"

"Me laird!" The woman called Helena rushed around the corner, her expression worried. "I just heard of your sojourn to obtain milk. 'Tis surely a kindly thing you have done. Still, 'tis a woman's task to care for—"

Upon the bed, Anora stirred.

Helena jerked her gaze in that direction and gasped. "What be me lady doing here?"

Meara scowled. "She appears to be sleeping."

The younger woman mouthed something indiscernible and stared at Meara again. "Surely 'tis not proper for her to—"

" 'Tis none of your concern, Stout Helena. I've seen to the lassie's care since the day she was birthed, and—"

"You! 'Twas I who nursed her through her infancy."

"And you've stuck your nose into her life ever since. But I've no time for your meddling now."

"Meddling!" Helena gasped, puffing out her chest

once more. "I only came to help me laird with the babe."

"He doesn't need your help."

Ramsay scowled. "In truth, I could use—"

"Hush!" snapped Meara, and glanced darkly past him toward the bed. "Or you'll wake the lass."

Helena pursed her lips and crossed her arms against her immense bosom. "I know what you're up to, Meara of the Fold, and—"

"And if you care for the lass, you'll not interfere," hissed the old woman.

Helena scowled, first at Meara, then at Anora. "If gossip starts, there'll be no stopping—"

"Then it had best not start," Meara said. "And if it does, I shall know who to blame."

"I only came to assist with the babe's—"

" 'Tis the duty of the lady of the keep to care for the orphaned and unfortunate," Meara said.

"Surely you would not deny me the right to—"

"Leave be!" Meara glared with such ferocious intensity that even Helena quailed as the old woman turned her toward the stairs, her voice lowered to a whisper. "If we are careful and wise, this keep may yet have more bairns than . . ." Her words faded away as they went down the stairs.

Ramsay closed the door with a bemused scowl, then heard the baby rousing.

Setting the bottle of milk on the floor, he approached the bed. The babe stirred restlessly in her cocoon. Reaching out, he drew her carefully from Anora's arms, but the maid awoke.

Her eyes, sleepy for only a fraction of a moment, snapped open, and her gasp was hollow with fear as she scrambled up against the pillows. "Why are you here?"

Ramsay straightened slowly. " 'Tis the room I was given."

She glanced about. "Oh. My apologies. I must have . . ." She licked her lips and watched him draw the baby to his chest. "I must have fallen asleep."

"Aye." Something ached inside him. She feared him still. After all they had endured together. But nay, they had not really been together. Since the first they had been apart, for she could not even trust him with her name.

She cleared her throat and pressed back a few gossamer strands of hair from her elfin face. "Ailsa gave you milk?"

"Aye."

"In exchange for what?"

He glanced at her, wondering momentarily at her suspicious tone, but there were no clues to be found in her alabaster face. "We made a barter of sorts," he said, and pulling his gaze from her, bent to remove the bladder from the cradle and put the baby in its place. She started whimpering immediately, waving her arms in protest and scrunching her reddening face.

Lifting the bottle of milk and the bladder, Ramsay turned to Anora. She hurried over and together they managed to pour the milk into the supple dispenser, but by then, the baby had set to howling.

Tension cranked up inside Ramsay as thoughts of his past failures gnawed at him. "I've not fed a bairn before," he admitted, and bent to lift the babe from her bed. She turned her face immediately, searching for food, and Ramsay, stiff with fear, set the bladder to her lips. She brushed impatiently past it, still searching. He shifted his weight onto his hale leg and tried again.

Anora motioned toward the bed. "Sit. 'Tis enough

that you hold the child. I will manage the bladder."

He considered refusing, but the babe was crying and his leg aching, and there was little room for pride.

The mattress ropes groaned as he eased himself against the pillows. Anora took the bladder and leaned down, coaxing the babe to take what she so badly needed.

Minutes ticked by. Minutes filled with worry, hope, and howling frustration as the baby refused the bladder.

Anora straightened her back as if it were sore, then hurried around the mattress to crawl across the bed. In a moment their attempts began anew. Ramsay cradled, Anora coaxed, until finally, after what seemed a grinding eternity, the baby began to suckle.

Ramsay remained absolutely still, holding his breath as he listened to the babe slurp and swallow. His heart leapt, and lifting his gaze, he found himself staring point blank into Anora's eyes. They shone in the candlelight like liquid sapphire. Were there tears in her eyes, he wondered—but in an instant her lashes swept downward, hiding her thoughts. Against his chest, though, where her arm rested, he felt her tremble with emotion.

The babe lost her grip on the bladder's nipple, recovered it, and suckled again, until finally, sated and limp, she fell back asleep. Anora eased the nipple from between her parted lips and straightened. Against his hip, Ramsay felt her thigh shift away, and with that simple movement his heart twisted with regret.

"She sleeps," he said, trying to fill the void. Anora nodded wordlessly as he lifted the small bundle carefully to his shoulder. His chest ached dully with the pressure, but somehow it felt right. Rising carefully to his feet, he closed his eyes for a moment and let the soft weight of the babe ease his soul. Aye, he had failed in the past, but mayhap with this babe he might put his guilt to rest. Bending slowly, he placed the wee child inside the cradle, then wrapped the blanket more snugly around her. She wriggled momentarily and her hand, perfectly formed and impossibly small, curled softly around his finger.

Ramsay's throat tightened with emotion. New life, innocent life, and damned if he wouldn't protect it. The thoughts clogged in his throat, and he swallowed.

"She is well?" Anora whispered beside him.

"Aye." The single word cracked oddly, and he cleared his throat. "She is well."

"And you?" Her voice was velvet soft.

"What?" he asked, making certain his tone was deep with masculine composure.

"Are you well?" she asked.

He turned toward her with a scowl. She didn't move away, didn't avert her eyes, so he lifted one hand to his chest and rubbed with absent annoyance. "Aye. I am healing fine."

Atop an iron clasped trunk, the single candle sputtered, tossing fickle shadows about the room.

"I was not speaking of your wounds."

But his wounds were a relatively innocuous topic, while other subjects—

"I wish to know why," she said, and caused his hand to pause its fretful motion on his chest.

"Why what?"

Her eyes were as steady and bright as twin sapphires, glowing with candlelight and unspoken thoughts. "There were three score of men in the hall," she said. "None stepped forward but you. Why?"

He shrugged, trying to look casual, but fearing with a terrible fear that even that simple motion told the tale of his sins. "As I said, I am the bairn's f—"

"Please!" The word was sharp. "I would rather not hear that lie just now."

"At Dun Ard," he said, "there be many babes about. 'Twill be no great difficulty to take her there and give her into the care of a nursemaid."

Her expression didn't change a whit. "So you say that you claimed her because it was the simple thing to do."

Her explanation, though obviously foolish, was far better than the truth.

"That though you are wounded in a distant land," she continued, "it will be no hardship to travel alone to your home and there give her to another."

He scowled and glanced toward the cradle. Even with the blanket wrapped tightly about the bairn, he could see her tiny face, her minuscule mouth, slightly parted, her perfect fingers, placed just so at the blanket's edge. " 'Tis not . . . natural for a man to raise a babe. She will need a mother, of course. I am certain I shall find a woman who yearns for a child."

"So you will give her up."

From the cradle he heard a tiny sigh, and knew that despite his determination to cease being foolish, he'd be dead and damned before he'd let another have her. She was too tiny, too innocent, too fragile—a wee bundle of life that needed him and was not afraid to admit it.

"You will give her up?" Anora asked again.

"Of course."

"You lie," she said, and in that moment he saw her eyes fill with tears. "You will raise her as your own."

"Nay, I—"

"You will keep her," Anora whispered. "You shall fawn over her and adore her, and make her believe that the sun cannot rise without her consent. Already you adore her. I see it in your eyes."

He cleared his throat and loosened his fists. "I fear you are shortsighted, lass."

"Nay." Her voice was infinitely soft. "This once I see clearly, MacGowan. You cherish the child. I but wonder why."

Looking into her eyes, he saw the hopelessness of arguing. "Cannot a man wish for a child?" He paced toward the window. "Must he always be embattled and wounded and . . ." He swung his arm in a hopeless gesture to include the world at large. "Cannot he hope to right the wrongs he has—" He realized with belated panic what he had been about to say.

Anora's shadow flickered, slim and willowy against the far wall. "What wrong have you done, MacGowan?" she murmured.

"I would begin a list, lass," he said, "if I were not so in need of sleep."

"So there are many?"

"Beyond count."

"More than one that involves a child?"

He pivoted toward her without realizing he had moved. "What do you know of the child?"

She held his gaze, unblinking. "What child?"

Ramsay squeezed his eyes closed and blocked away a thousand grinding memories. "I claimed this babe because there was none other to do so. 'Tis the only reason."

"You lie, MacGowan. You think you have done

some horrid wrong. And I wonder, what terrible things do you imagine you have—"

"I do not imagine them." The words came out of their own accord, though he knew better than to loose them.

"What are they, then?" she whispered.

Ramsay tightened his jaw, holding his swirling emotions at bay. "A child is dead because of me."

"Whose child?"

"Me own. I was the sire!" he growled. "But I was not . . ." His throat ached. "I was not its father."

"How—"

"I had not wed the mother," he said, his voice hollow and empty.

"Lorna," she guessed, then, very softly. "You loved her?"

"I . . ." He thought he had. Nay, he had been certain he had. She'd made him wild with burning emotions, and when she gave herself to him he could think of nothing else. "I planned to wed her, but circumstances . . ." He paused, reliving the past with aching accuracy. "There was trouble with a neighboring clan and I returned home. 'Twas there that I received her missive."

She watched him with solemn, unblinking eyes.

"It said that she carried me child. That she was sick with loneliness and would surely perish if I did not return to marry her." He paced across the room, watching the shadows swell and die away before him.

"She died?"

"Nay. It seems that a grand title is a wondrous healer."

Anora shook her head in bemusement.

"It took some time to receive the missive, but when I did, I returned posthaste to Edinburgh. 'Twas then that I learned she had wed a fat marquis with a fatter purse."

"And the babe?"

Beyond the window, the night was blacker than hell. "The wealthy marquis did not wish to raise another man's child. Lorna wished for a wealthy marquis." He loosened his fists. "She was not one to do without what she wanted."

"She . . . killed the babe afore it was birthed?"

"Nay." He turned slowly toward her. "I killed the babe. 'Twas I who created it and I who failed to protect it."

Anora shook her head. " 'Tis not your fault that she would—" she began, but Ramsay stopped her.

"Who shall I blame, then? The lass who thought she would have to go into travail unwed? The lass who would bear the brunt of people's scorn while I took her innocence and walked away unblamed? Aye." He nodded once. " 'Twas me own fault."

"So 'twas against her will that you took her, Mac-Gowan?"

"I—" Nay. She had come to him, seeming so sweet, so soft and innocent, with whispered words that made his young blood run hot and wild in his veins. "It matters little if she wanted me or nay. Only that I failed in the end."

"Even if she created a child to lure you into wedlock."

There it was. That terrible possibility back again to haunt him, but he did not want it. "Is it so hard to believe that she lay with me merely because she desired me, Notmary?"

She stood very still, her hands clasped before her. "Things are not always as they seem, MacGowan. You would not be the first man to be fooled by a bonny face and a tearful word. You can take my word on that."

The possibilities stared at him like grinning gargoyles, demanding that he look them square in the face. "In truth," he murmured, " 'tis bad enough to know I failed without knowing that I am also a fool."

"You are no fool," she whispered. "You are only tenderhearted."

"I am many things, but I am not tenderhearted. I am jaded and hardened and—"

"Is that why you've told no one of Lorna's horrid deeds? Is that why you've left her in peace with her fat marquis? Is that why she could be certain you would do just that?"

He deepened his scowl.

"Is that why you accompanied me here? Is that why you claimed the babe?"

"I claimed the bairn to assuage me own guilt, and you damn well know it."

She took a single step toward him. "So I should be adding selfish to your lists of undesirable attributes, should I?"

"I *am* selfish," he said.

"Are you?" she asked, and closed the small distance between them.

"Aye." It was difficult to speak with her so close, for raw memories made him long for solace, made him ache to pull her against him, to lose himself in her softness. "Aye," he said again, "for even now, with all that is behind me . . ." 'Twas the devil's own task to face his weaknesses. "I long to bury me sins in your purity."

He waited for her to turn and run, but she didn't.

"I am not pure," she whispered. "I lost that long ago."

"Nay. You have not lost it, lass. You shall always be pure, for 'tis in your very soul, and none can take that from you."

For a moment all was still, then her palm was a soft atonement against his cheek, and her voice was as gentle as a psalm.

"How can you be so kind, MacGowan?"

He squeezed his eyes shut. "I am not kind, lass. No matter what other lies you choose to believe, do not trust that one."

"Ahh, I remember," she whispered. "You are selfish."

God, yes—for even now he ached to hold her, to kiss her, to claim her for his own, when 'twas that very act that had caused such pain before.

"And you are not cunning," she murmured and slipped her fingers ever so gently across his lips.

He swallowed hard and tightened his hands into fists.

"Nor are you powerful," she said, and slid her fingers across the bunched muscles of his shoulder. "Nor peaceable." Her hand skimmed the bandages that covered his chest. From the cradle, the baby sighed. "Nor loving," she whispered. "And yet . . ." She drew closer, and he ceased to breath, to think, to function. All he could do was wait, to watch her move nearer. "I still want you," she whispered, and pressed her lips to his.

Chapter 25

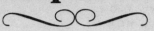

"Lass." Ramsay's voice was low and raspy, shivering up her spine as he pushed himself away. "You have forgotten one attribute: I am damnably weak."

"Are you?"

"Aye."

Her heart was pounding like a rounding hammer in her chest. " 'Tis good, then. A fine match. You are weak and I am a coward."

"You are many things, lass. But a coward—"

"I am afraid of men."

"You have challenged the Munro."

"I have challenged every man, for I cannot wed. I cannot allow them to touch me, to see what I truly am. But when I am near you, I find I long to . . ." She stopped, frozen by fears so old they had etched themselves into her very soul. "Mayhap this one night we could help each other."

"I cannot help you."

"Because you are weak?"

"Aye."

"And you would . . . hurt me?"

For a moment she thought he would lie, would say that yes, he would harm her, but his expression twisted into one of deepest regret.

"Do you not see the problem? Yonder lies a babe, unwanted and uncherished—"

"You cherish her," she whispered.

He shoved splayed fingers through his hair with frustrated impatience. " 'Tis not the point and you well know it, lass. I dare not bring another unwanted life into being."

"Is there no means of . . ." She swallowed, chilled with fear, yet hot with an indefinable longing. "Of coupling without creating a child?"

"Anora . . ." It was the first time he'd spoken her Christian name, and the sound traveled through her like mulled wine.

"I need your help," she whispered, and wondered, quite suddenly, if perhaps he needed, just as much, to be needed. "I cannot rule Evermyst alone forever. That I see, now. I must take a husband. But how can I, when I am afraid to . . ." She stepped cautiously forward, feeling as if the earth might crumble beneath her very feet. "To do this," she said, and raising her face, kissed him again.

Feelings as hot as sunlight rushed through her. For a moment she feared he would draw back, but he did not. Instead, he tilted his head ever so slightly and returned her kiss with slow, aching tenderness. It was she who drew back, trembling, though not for fear. Nay, 'twas because the feelings were so strong, so intense, that she felt she would surely burn to ash if she did not stop.

"You have come to your senses and decided against such foolishness?" His voice was deeper than the shadows beyond the window.

Her own was the smallest of whispers. "Aye. I have come to my senses."

A muscle jumped in his jaw. The shadow of his braid fell across his lean cheek, and his eyes were intense. "Then you have changed your mind?"

"Nay," she murmured.

"Then I will do as you ask."

The breath froze in her throat. She managed a nod and reached for his hand. It felt unearthly strong and warm beneath her fingers, but when she tugged him toward the bed, he resisted.

"It has been . . ." He cleared his throat. ". . . A long while for me, lass."

Her mind scrambled. "Then you and Ailsa did not . . . couple?"

"Is that what you thought? That I could take another when you are . . ."

"When I am what?"

"In the world." He said the words with weary resignation. "Still, being with the milk maid might have made this situation simpler."

She forced herself not to wince. "It will be difficult with me?"

"To wait," he said. " 'Twill be difficult to wait, lass. Thus, I think it best if we begin here."

"Here?" Her heart kicked back into gear.

"You might disrobe me," he suggested, and her heart threatened to leap from her chest.

"I do not think—"

"Control," he said. A muscle bunched in his jaw again as if every fiber of his being was already straining. " 'Tis what the bastard took from you those years ago, lass. He could not take your virtue, nor tame your wilding spirit. Thus he took your control. 'Tis what I would give back to you."

"But I have never . . . I do not know how."

"It takes no scholar," he said, and lifted his own hands to his chest as if to begin the process, but the cat pin was not there.

"Your brooch," she murmured. " 'Tis gone."

" 'Twas a good exchange," he said, and reaching out, took her hand in his.

"Ailsa has—" she began, but in that instant he drew her palm to his lips. Desire arced like summer lightning up her arm. ". . . It?" she breathed.

"Lass, I do not think I can discuss the milk maid just now," he said huskily, and kissed the heel of her hand.

She jerked beneath the onslaught of unknown feelings, already breathing hard. "MacGowan!"

"Aye, lass?" He raised his head slowly, and in the candlelight his eyes tore at her very soul.

"I feel . . . strangely unbalanced."

"Do you?"

"Aye."

" 'Tis a good thing," he said, and kissed her wrist.

She yanked her hand away, ready to flee, but he made no move to follow, no move to stop her. He stood as still as stone with his back against the wall.

She worried at her lip. "Where do I begin?"

He shrugged, the movement slow. " 'Tis your choice, lass. I merely wait."

" 'Twould be easier if you . . . did more."

He nodded. "Aye."

"But you will not."

"I have before," he said, and she could not help but remember the inn—the rush of hot feelings, the need, the consuming panic. "It did little but grant you a reason to hate me."

She winced. " 'Twas not my plan."

"I believe it was, lass. A simple way to keep yourself safe from men. From me."

She considered denying his words, but his gaze was steady and sure. "How is it that you know me so well?"

"I do not. Not half so well as I would. Time wears on, lass."

She wanted to reach for his belt but she could not, so she knelt and untied his garters from below his knees. It should have been a simple task—mundane, even—but her fingers faltered, so he nudged off his boots himself.

She stood finally, glanced briefly at his face, then lowered her eyes. Best to get this over with quickly, like any onerous task, she told herself. But the trembling in her hands was not from loathing. Still, it took all her will power to reach for his belt. She tugged at it, felt it loosen, and pulled it away. She dropped the belt and reached cautiously for his plaid. It eased away from his hips, its great length falling to the floor until he stood in naught but his tunic. Although his shirt nearly reached his knees, she dared not look down. Butterflies fluttered in her stomach. 'Twas foolishness, she told herself. Then she noticed that his hands were clenched to fists, causing the corded muscles of his forearms to stand out in hardened ridges beneath his sun browned flesh.

"Are you . . ." She raised her gaze fleetingly to his. "Nervous?"

"Nervous! Nay!" he began, but then their gazes met and melded and he let out his air in one hard breath. "I am bloody terrified."

"You?" The word trembled when she said it. *Don't talk! Just act. Get it done with.* But he fascinated her, entranced her. "Why?"

He didn't answer immediately. "Me brother Gilmour, 'tis he who gained our da's smooth ways."

She stared at him without understanding.

"With the lassies," he finished.

"You're afraid of being unable to . . . couple?"

"Will you cease calling it that? Like two boars in rut! Nay," he said, and relaxed a smidgen. " 'Tis not me fear, for just looking at you, with your hair all aglow and . . . there is not a man alive who would not be moved. 'Tis simply that . . ." He exhaled slowly and loosened his fists. "I would have you enjoy this."

"Enjoy it! I'm but hoping to survive it."

He chuckled. The sound was full and low and somehow made her stomach flip foolishly. " 'Tis good to know you expect so little of me, but I had rather hoped for more."

She had no idea why she felt like crying, but suddenly she did, so much so that she had to bite her lip in an attempt to hold back the tears. "You're afraid of disappointing me?"

He winced. "It sounds worse when said aloud."

"Why?"

He shrugged. " 'Tis simpler to ignore one's weaknesses if they are not spoken."

"I mean . . . why do you care?"

"Surely you know, lass."

"Nay," she whispered. "I do not."

"If we do not hurry, we shall surely be found out. Or is that your hope?"

It should be, of course. She should be searching for an excuse to stop this lunacy, but . . . he was so beautiful, so bonny and manly and powerfully alluring. Her hand reached out of its own accord to touch his cheek. His eyes closed. Muscles coiled beneath her fingers, as if it took all his considerable control to keep himself from reaching back, and somehow that knowledge was more sensuous than all his other enticing attributes. So enticing, in fact, that she could not help but rise on her toes to kiss him. Their lips met in trembling intimacy. Her hand slipped over the taut muscle of his shoulder, then down the tight mound of chest. A gravelly noise issued from his throat, but he did nothing, not until her fingers slipped with tremulous curiosity onto his abdomen.

The muscles jumped beneath her hand. Startled, Anora almost fled, but again he made no move to seize her. She tightened her resolve and sidled closer until their bodies were nearly touching. Fascinated, she placed her palm against the hard muscles of his belly. Craning up on her toes, she kissed his chin, his cheek, the corner of his mouth.

He turned to her like a starving man, kissing her with a hunger so ferocious that it almost drove her away, but somehow the fear was not enough to drown the desire that raged through her. His tongue brushed her lips, seeking entry, and she gave way, letting him in. Hot longing scorched her. She drew back, breathless and dizzy, and found to her surprise that her fist was bunched in his tunic near one lean hip. Their gazes met in a flash of scalding desire, and then, like an amateur's marionette, she lifted the tunic.

Beneath her bent fingers, she felt his muscles coil, but he made no move toward her. Finally, with breathless anticipation, she raised the shirt farther. His every muscle was frozen to rock hard immobility as the fabric slipped up his body. She didn't look down. Indeed, she couldn't. Instead, she held his gaze, watched the expressions mirror her own—desire, impatience, and maybe, if she let herself admit the truth—fear.

Nearing his chest, the tunic's hem scraped his bandage. Anora slipped her left hand beneath the bunched cloth.

His flesh was warm, firm, crisscrossed with undulating muscle that stretched from his belly to his throat, and suddenly she wanted to feel every inch of it. Her fingers skimmed over the lean ridges of his ribs, up the sloping underside of his mounded pectorals and onto his nipple.

"Sweet Almighty!"

Anora jumped, but he remained where he was, breathing hard, his shoulders pressed against the wall behind.

"Did I hurt you?"

"Nay."

His voice was raspy, low, little more than a rough whisper of sound.

"Then why—" she began. He leaned forward and kissed her.

His longing seared her like a flame, and when he

drew back, her knees felt weak and her lungs over-taxed.

She took a steadying breath and leaned into him. "Oh," she said.

"I long to love you," he murmured. "To fill you with my desire and feel you climb the summit of pleasure."

"Oh!" Against her hip she could feel the hard evidence of his longing, but suddenly it held no fear for her, only an aching kind of indescribable need. Her hands moved slowly but surely over the sculpted ridges of his belly, up his mounded chest. He raised his arms without taking his gaze from her hers, and she slid her hands breathlessly over the dancing muscles of his triceps. His throat corded as he bent his head, and finally the shirt dropped from her tingling fingers to the floor.

He was naked. Bigger than life. Powerful as a destrier, he stood before her, and finally fear coiled in her belly.

She took a step back and skimmed his body with her gaze. His chest was broad, sweeping down to a narrow waist and hips only the slightest bit wider. And between those hips . . .

Her breath caught in her throat, for despite his immobility, his manhood was intimidating. It rose bold and restless from a nest of dark hair, as if reaching for her.

She backed away. His muscles bunched as if he would follow her, but he did not. Instead, he reached up to grasp the bed frame with one hand and the window shutter with the other. The muscles in his chest and arms coiled as if he held himself there by hard-won will power alone.

Candlelight flickered across his bare skin, casting shadows beneath his powerful arms and thighs, and at the apex of his legs, his desire stirred again.

Her lungs felt strangely tight within her chest and desire hung heavy in her gut, but she dared not step forward. She longed for a word of comfort, of assurance, of admiration. 'Twas what other men would do: coax, cajole. But he said nothing, as if challenging her courage with his very reticence. It disturbed her somehow, irritated her.

"You will not . . ." She let her gaze slide downward again, felt the breath halt in her lungs, and sprinted her attention back to his face. "You'll not hurt me?"

It seemed like forever before he spoke, and when he did his chest swelled slightly. She could not help but notice every flex of muscle, every lift of a limb. "What I say matters little, lass. 'Tis what you believe that counts."

"I believe . . ." What—that he would sooner die than harm her? 'Twas foolishness. Men were cruel, hard, undisciplined. Life had taught her that. "You are a man," she said, lifting her chin.

He raised one brow. "Had you decided the opposite, I would be sorely wounded, lass." Good Lord, he was conversing with her as if he had just met her on the streets of Edinburgh, instead of standing spread before her like a pagan gift of war. "Indeed, I am a man. 'Tis your choice now what you will do with me."

"I do not trust men," she whispered.

"So I have noticed."

"For they are cruel."

"I cannot deny it."

Frustration exploded within her. "Not even to say that you are different?"

"Nay."

"Mayhap 'tis because you are not. Because you are just like the others, selfish and . . ." Her words stuttered to a halt.

"And what?" he asked.

"And yet I want you," she whispered.

The tightening cords in his wrists were the only evidence of any emotion. "Where?" His voice was incredibly low. She swallowed hard, glanced sideways and wrapped her hands about each other in an effort to keep them from shaking.

"On the bed."

He said nothing but dropped his arms to his sides and placed a bent knee on the mattress. He looked like a great lionlike creature with his most private parts just nudging past the powerful bulge of his bandaged thigh. She watched in breathless awe as he stretched out on his side, then reminded herself to breathe and searched for something to say.

There was nothing. So she tried to take a step forward. That was only marginally more successful, for her legs felt as stiff as stone block. "I do not . . . know if I can do this, MacGowan."

He looked up at her with half masked eyes. "Do not play me for a fool, Notmary. You can do whatever it is you wish to do."

She winced. "You'll . . . show me how?"

"Aye." The single word was as deep as the night.

"What do I do now?"

He didn't speak for a moment, as if a hundred possibilities were running through his mind, then, " 'Twould be much appreciated if you would disrobe."

Fear skittered up her spine. "Is that necessary?" she whispered.

"Nay." He cleared his throat, looking rather sheepish. "Nay. Only preferable. Being naked alone is . . ."

"Too intimidating for me."

He raised his brows. "Too humiliating for me."

"Nay." That could surely not be true, for he looked like a god of fertility, stretched powerful and confident before her.

"Lass, I do not know how you think I spend me nights. But this is not the usual."

"So this . . . so you are doing this just for me?"

"Nay." He grinned, a slanted flash of white in the dimness. " 'Tis for entirely selfish reasons that I am thus."

His words sent a warm rush of feelings through her, feelings that urged her fingers slowly to the laces at her back. But the knots were high up and hard tied.

"I need . . . help." She made it to the bed and turned slowly, presenting her back to him.

His fingers never so much as brushed her skin. Even when he swiped her hair over her shoulder, he did not touch her, yet it seemed that they were flesh to flesh, so strong were the feelings. The laces eased. She felt his breath against her neck and remained frozen as his lips touched her there, just below her ear. Gooseflesh shivered down her arms. She felt the rough brush of a day's beard graze her shoulder, and somehow, like magic, the gown slipped lower. His kisses followed, down her neck, along her spine. Her head fell back as she drowned in the heady feelings. She arched her back, driven with a consuming need to be nearer until her thighs were pressed up against the mattress. His kisses ran lower, and her gown fell away. But there was still the underskirt, drawn tight at her waist.

'Twas along that barrier that he kissed her now. 'Twas along that barrier that she felt the rasp of tongue.

She gasped, but when she jerked, she found that she had moved only marginally away, and indeed, when he did not follow, she closed her eyes and leaned back against the bed. Kisses again, hot and sexy, skimming up her spine, nipping at her waist, caressing her shoulders until her hands trembled to loosen the last of her garments. They fell away with a sigh of satisfaction, and though she dared not turn, she could hear his exhalation, could feel it brush her skin, and then, like a forbidden dream, his lips touched her buttocks. Shards of desire stabbed her with primitive need, and she grasped the bed post in one hand, holding herself upright as his kisses skimmed downward, over the underside of her bottom, grazing her thighs. She spread them without thinking. He kissed higher. She felt his hair brush her buttocks, felt his tongue lick her wetness.

She jerked about, tripping in her skirts as she did so. The floor tilted toward her face, but his hand snapped out to catch her wrist and pull her easily to her feet.

Their eyes met. He was wounded, without his full strength, yet his hand felt as unflinching as a vise around her arm. And she was naked, vulnerable. Helpless. Panic skittered up her spine.

Yet . . . he hadn't forced her, hadn't rushed her. Indeed, 'twas she who felt impatient, who felt desperate and driven. She who finally leaned forward and felt her nipple caress his as she kissed him.

Something akin to a growl sounded in his chest. She felt his great body tremble and he dropped her arm, giving her every chance to back away. Despite the bitter residue of fear, she had no wish to do so. Deep inside she ached with longing, not just for release from her physical yearnings, but for something more—for peace, for understanding, for touch, which suddenly seemed as necessary as the very air she breathed.

She touched his face, watched him close his eyes, then ran her palm slowly over his brawny shoulder and down his muscular back. His manhood nudged her hip impatiently, but still he did not rush her. Instead, when she stroked her palm around to his abdomen, he leaned back onto his heels, breaking off the kiss.

In the flickering candlelight, he looked like a primitive warrior, naked to the world, his member hard and ready. And like a primitive maiden, she went to him. Slipping with quaking trepidation onto the bed, she kissed him again, until, as if by some unearthly magic, they were stretched out on the mattress, her body pressed tight and hot against his.

His kisses were everywhere, warm and needy, and their bodies had begun some sort of timeless rhythm that she failed to understand or control. His hardness pressed against her wetness just so, and her hiss of pleasure melded with his groan.

Their movement ceased. Their eyes met. 'Twas not too late to quit—but her body insisted otherwise. And when he kissed her, there was nothing she could do but grip his arms and skim her knees up the length of his powerful thighs. There, poised above his manhood, she eased around him. Heat filled her, spread her, enlightened her. She gasped at the raw, aching pleasure and pushed tentatively against him. Feelings sprang through her like hunting beasts, pressing her on, but he pushed his head backward and remained as he was, unmoving, every sinew tight as a bowstring. She moved again. More feelings, wilder yet, crowded in on her. She eased up on her knees, her hands still clasped around his arms as she arched into him, squeezing hard.

Then he began to move, rocking into her with a careful pressure that heightened the feelings a hundred-fold. She moaned at the rush of need and pleasure, and he raised himself up on his elbows, changing the pressure slightly. She panted with longing, pushing harder still, and suddenly felt his mouth upon her nipple.

She could take no more. Feelings burst inside her like artillery fire. Lights danced. Her head swam, and in that swimming state of utopia she felt his hands touch her for the first time. Felt them wrap about her waist, felt them lift her away.

She wanted to complain, to insist that she stay just as she was, wrapped with cocooning warmth about him, but in an instant, he settled her against his throbbing heat. She pressed against it, seeking the final dregs of pleasure and feeling his seed pulse out in a hot rush.

Their groans combined, and then, like a found waif, she rested her head upon his chest, listening to the steady beat of his heart until sleep took her.

Chapter 26

◦⟩⟨◦

"Anora."

Her dreams were warm and comforting, her haven hard to leave, and she awoke slowly, opened her eyes in the flickering candlelight, then jerked in surprise.

"MacGowan!" It wasn't exactly that she had forgotten he was there. In fact, she could remember every moment before she fell asleep. Yet it seemed far less real than the dreams from which she had just extracted herself. "Did . . . did you wake me?"

"Aye." He moved his hand as if he would reach out, then curled his fingers against the mattress and remained as he was, his torso naked but for the bandage that crisscrossed his hardened chest. "Are you well?"

Memories bloomed in her mind like spring cro-

326

cuses. Memories of hot flesh and aching need and gentle euphoria. "Aye," she murmured. Residual desire curled in her stomach like a haunting wisp of wood smoke. She too was naked, her breasts exposed to the nipples above the comforting blankets. She could pull the woolens higher, but 'twas surely a bit late to lock the stable door now. His gaze felt hot and nerve-wracking, but strangely exhilarating. "Did you . . ." His eyes were as bright as the moon, intense, and as hopelessly mesmerizing as everything about him. "Did you need something?"

His nostrils flared like a stallion's, and for a moment she hoped that he would reach for her again. "The babe wakes," he said instead. "I will need to fetch fresh milk."

"From . . ." Her stomach fluttered. "Ailsa?"

"Nay. Her lad will bring it by."

"Oh. Oh!" she said, and grasping the blankets to her chest, abruptly sat upright. "I must go."

"Aye," he said, and swinging his feet off the bed, stood up.

His back was to her, and the muscles between his shoulders flexed with captivating beauty, while his—

He turned and she dragged her gaze to the blankets scrunched in her hands and forced herself to breathe. In and out, in and out, as if her world hadn't been turned inside out by this god of a man who had just wrapped a cloth around his hips. Though it covered his loins, it cracked open at one hip, showing the entire length of one powerful thigh. The muscles there bunched and flexed as he stepped forward and stood with her garments clasped in his outstretched hand.

Oh! She was supposed to take them. "Thank you,"

she said, and dropping the blankets, reached for her gown.

"Do you need assistance?"

His voice was deep and strangely entrancing, while his eyes—

"Anora?" he said.

She jerked. "What say you?"

"Do you need me help?"

"Oh. Nay, I can . . ." Thoughts, set to swirling like frenzied grains of sand by her embattled senses, scrambled to make some sense of her uncertain emotions. "Well, aye. I could use your help. If you . . ." She swallowed. "Don't mind."

A muscle jumped in his jaw as he stepped back, giving her room to exit the bed. But he was naked, or very nearly naked, and for a moment she couldn't quite remember what to do.

"Please, lass . . ." He lowered his gaze to her breasts, then clenched his jaw as if he waged some internal battle. "I will avoid gossip if I can, but if you do not dress soon . . ."

"What?" she murmured. She was frozen to the bed, waiting breathlessly for him to finish. Their gazes caught fire, and he stepped forward. His lips crashed against hers in a kiss of searing intensity, burning all thought to ash.

"Oh," she breathed as he drew away.

"And we wouldn't want that," he murmured.

From the cradle, the baby complained softly.

"Nay. Nay, of course not," Anora said, and stepping from the bed like one in a dream, stood on unsteady legs before him.

"Mayhap you should put it on."

"What?"

"The gown," he said. "You'd best put it on."

"Oh." She nodded, but failed to do more. "Aye."

In the end, he all but dressed her. His fingers fumbled a few times and once he kissed her again, but finally she was clothed and heading like a demented sleepwalker toward the door.

"Will you be safe?"

"What?"

"Shall I see you to your chambers?" he asked.

She glanced down the length of his fabulous form and back to his eyes. "Like that?"

"I could don me clothes."

"Nay. I wish to remember . . ." She paused and swallowed. She had truly lost her mind. "Nay. I shall be fine."

From the wooden cradle, the baby mewled softly.

"You'd best go then, lass, before the castle awakes," he said, and opened the door.

"MacGowan." His name escaped her lips, though she knew better than to loose it.

"Aye?"

She swallowed hard. "When can we . . ." She glanced hopelessly toward the bed, trying to find words for what they had done. But there were none, and in that moment he kissed her.

Tenderness and longing and a dozen unnamed emotions sizzled between them until she was breathless and weak kneed.

"I am here until I am gone," he said, and suddenly she found herself on the far side of the door.

Her journey down the dark hallways seemed strange and dreamlike, but she arrived finally at her own door. It opened with a low groan. The sound conjured a memory of Ramsay's quiet—

"She is well?"

Anora stumbled backward, bumping into the door. "Isobel!"

The girl watched her, her gaze steady. "Is something amiss?"

"Nay! Nay. All is well."

"Then she yet lives?"

Anora's brain scrambled.

"The babe," Isobel said. "Meara said you were tending the babe. That it was your right and your duty, and that all should leave you to the task."

"Oh! Aye. The babe." Her face felt hot and her hands unsteady. "She is well."

" 'Tis good. Then she will soon be strong enough to travel."

"Travel?"

"If MacGowan calls her his own, surely he will wish to take her with him when he goes?"

Anora felt her throat close up, as if she were sinking beneath icy waves. "He is wounded."

Isobel scowled. "Because he is a man. You said yourself, 'twas because he chose to battle."

"In our defense."

The room went silent. "Might it be that you want him to stay?"

She saw the emotions in Isobel's eyes and recognized each one as her own. Fear. Jealousy. Guilt. "Nay, of course not."

Their gazes met, but Anora could not hold hers steady. "I'd . . . best find me bed," she said. "It has been a long night."

"Aye," Isobel said, and turned solemnly away. "That it has."

* * *

Anora knew she should be tired, but when the sun rose, she did the same. 'Twas not the fact that Ramsay would be breaking the fast that made her rush through her toilet. Nay. She had duties to see to, she told herself. But when she entered the hall her breath stopped in her throat, for he was there, looking so much the bonny rogue that she could not take her eyes from him.

"Me lady." Cant approached rapidly from her right, interrupting her view of Ramsay. "I've a matter of some importance I would discuss with you."

And thus the morning began. Duties and decisions kept Anora busy throughout the day, broken now and again only by a glimpse of Ramsay from the corner of her eye. But even that much sent hot blood spilling into her cheeks, and she was forced to look away, lest others guess the wild bent of her imaginings.

Not until evening did she find a chance to settle into her chair upon the dais in the great hall. Ramsay was seated at another table and her heart twisted with disappointment at the seemingly vast distance between them.

Immediate self incriminations followed. She was no foolish twit, set aflutter by his mere presence. She had used him on the previous night, had employed his body in an attempt to . . . better herself. She was, after all, the lady of this keep, with responsibilities and—

"Anora." Meara sat not far from her, her dried apple face disapproving. "Surely Evermyst's champion should sup at the high table. We've no wish to seem ungrateful, do we?"

Anora turned her gaze breathlessly toward the old

woman, and for a fleeting heartbeat of time, she thought she saw a gleam in the old woman's eye. Then it was gone, replaced by bland disapproval.

"Would we?" she asked again.

"Nay! Of course not," Anora breathed. "Clarinda," she said, turning to the nearest server. "Tell the Mac-Gowan that I request his presence at my table."

In a moment he was there, bowing slightly at the waist. The movement seared a thousand memories through her mind, but she held his gaze and tried not to blush.

'Twas a task that did not become easier throughout the meal, for whenever their gazes met, she remembered the night before—the heat of his kisses, the strength of his—

"More mead, me lady?" Isobel asked from beside her elbow.

"Oh!" Anora jumped. "Aye. 'Tis . . . rather warm in here."

"And you, me laird?" 'Twas Ailsa who spoke from beside his elbow, and 'twas Ailsa whose bosom threatened to fall into his mug. Anora stiffened.

Glancing up, Ramsay allowed the dark widow to fill his horn to the brim.

"Me thanks," he said.

"Is there anything else I can do for you this eve?" she asked, still bending low.

Ramsay shifted his gaze to Anora, his eyes gleaming. "Nay. That will be all," he said.

"More mead here," called someone from the table, but Ailsa ignored him.

"Are you certain?" she asked.

"Aye. Quite," he said, and Ailsa departed with a scowl.

Anora turned her attention to her grouse pudding and tried not to look giddy.

"The babe is doing well, then?" she asked, not glancing up immediately.

"Aye." There was something about his voice that made it difficult to breathe. "Helena is seeing to her care whilst I sup."

"Ahh." There was so little to say and so much she wished to do. "And your wounds? I trust they are mending well."

"Unusually quickly. I feel quite hale. Mayhap 'tis the air here at Evermyst that makes me feel so fit."

She lowered her eyes to her plate and hoped with all her soul that Meara could not hear the wild hammering of her heart. But there was little hope of hiding the blush of her cheeks.

"You must make certain to get enough rest," she murmured to her pudding.

"Not to worry," he said. "I am very fond of me bed . . . now."

She all but squirmed beneath his hot gaze and struggled to speak with some semblance of normalcy. "The babe was not fitful, then?"

The slightest corner of a smile lifted his lips. It captivated her, pulling her gently under his power. " 'Twas not the babe so much as another who kept me awake," he said softly.

Suddenly her mouth felt hopelessly dry.

"Mayhap, if you have a moment this eve, you could come by and see wee Mary."

"Mary?" she whispered.

"Aye. I have named her after a bonny lass I once knew. Should you have a moment, you might grant her your blessing."

Say no! her conscience warned. "When?" she breathed.

"I but wait," he said, leaning closer.

"More mead, me laird?" 'Twas Ailsa, determined to try again.

"Nay." He drew his gaze from Anora and stood. "Me bed waits. Good eventide to you, Ailsa. Me lady."

"Good eventide," Anora said, and refused to look at either his retreating back or Ailsa's peeved expression.

Neither did she look directly at Isobel when the girl came to her chambers some time later.

"Me apologies for me lateness," she said, but Anora brushed away her regrets as Isobel helped unlace her gown.

"Do not trouble yourself, Isobel. In truth, I am so tired I could sleep fully clothed."

"Mayhap you will not require me presence again tonight, then. Seonag's babe has a bit of a fever. She asked me to help see to him."

Hope leapt in Anora's heart. "By all means, Isobel. See to your duties elsewhere."

In just a few minutes, Anora was alone in her night rail. She paced the floor with bare feet, impatience burning at her, but she must wait until the castle slept.

Hidden away in a small alcove, another woman waited. In her hand she held a clay vessel, and in the vessel was a small amount of pig's blood. Seduction had not been successful in manipulating MacGowan, but the blood would do the trick. It had worked on the Munro and it would work again. But for now, she must wait until the castle slept.

Chapter 27

Ramsay opened his eyes. What had awakened him? The babe? Anora? Had she come?

He sat up swiftly. Morning light streamed through the narrow window. He scowled at it. Morning? Already? And wee Mary hadn't cried? He turned nervously toward the cradle only to find it empty.

His gut twisted as he sprang out of bed and glanced wildly about the room, but logic seeped slowly into his groggy mind. Someone had come to feed her. Surely that was it. Still, he swept his plaid about his bare waist and rushed down the stairs. One glance about the hall told him the babe wasn't there. It took him a few minutes to reach the kitchens, but even before he arrived, he heard the baby's cry.

Although he slowed his steps, he could not do the

same with his heartbeat, but when he passed beneath the kitchens' mortared arch he immediately saw the infant's wizened face peering over Stout Helena's shoulder.

'Twas a cozy scene that met him. A homely fire crackled in the gigantic hearth. The soothing scents of warm bread and saffron filled the air. A trio of maids had abandoned their cutting board to croon over Mary while Tree swiped a fritter from a scolding matron, and the friar filled his mouth with the same.

At the first sight of the babe's rumpled face, relief swamped him in a frantic tide. He shushed it with manly stoicism. 'Twould not, after all, be terribly impressive if he burst into tears at the sight of the wee lass.

"So, Helena," he said, making certain his tone was firm, "you be the one who filched me bairn."

A handful of women stopped their cooing long enough to glance toward him. Stout Helena turned with a sheepish smile.

And Clarinda screamed. A dish shattered against the stone floor.

"Merciful Jesus!" Helena gasped and clutched the babe to her bosom as if to ward off a ghost.

"What is it?" Ramsay rasped.

"Senga," Clarinda whispered.

"She is angry."

"What's that?" he growled.

"Your throat, me laird," Helena gasped. "It has been cut."

"The devil it—" he began, but as he raised his hand to his neck, he felt a line of dried liquid stretched across his flesh. When he brought his fingers away, he saw that they were dark with . . . "Blood," he whispered.

Near the far side of the room, Tree stumbled abruptly backward as Isobel crossed herself and Anora rushed into the chamber.

"What's happened? What is—" Her gaze grew wide as it fell on him. Her hair was a wild cascade of gold about her shoulders. "MacGowan!"

"Senga has visited him," Clarinda whispered.

Ramsay scowled at the speaker and rubbed his fingers absently together. " 'Tis not me own blood," he soothed, and Anora's gaze went to his face as her delicate hand fluttered to her own neck.

The babe squawked once.

"He is chosen to die," someone whispered.

"Nay!" Anora's tone was sure, her expression hard. "No one shall die; 'tis naught but dried blood. Helena, see to the babe. Tree, take a basin of water to Mac-Gowan's chamber."

"You are right," Ramsay said. " 'Tis naught but a wee bit of dried blood, easily remedied. No need to bother Tree—"

" 'Twas superstition that took my mother," she said. Her gaze caressed him for the briefest of moments. "I'll not have it take you. Go, please, be rid of the evidence before others see."

He nodded once. "If you wish it, me lady."

She turned slowly away. "Isobel . . ." Her gaze met the maid's. "Come with me," she said, and in an instant they were gone.

Ramsay watched the empty doorway in bemusement. A dozen odd nigglings tickled his mind, but in a moment they vanished, folded beneath a score of others.

What went on here? Did someone mean to frighten him off? Had an intruder breached his quarters and somehow streaked his throat with blood? Certainly he would have awakened. Then again, he had not awakened at all during the night, and surely the babe had cried. Why had he slept so soundly? The previous night in Anora's arms had been wondrously wearing, but that hardly explained the situation.

"Helena," he said, and watched her faded eyes widen as he turned toward her. "I'd have a word, if I may. In me quarters."

She pulled her brows high with obvious misgivings, but nodded just the same.

They walked side by side up the stairs in silence while the baby mewled a half complaint. He reached for her, and though he thought for a moment that the stout matron would not relinquish her hold, she finally did, handing him the babe with obvious regret.

Ramsay snuggled the child against his chest, hiding the blood on his neck as he glanced toward the other.

"Do I frighten you, Helena?"

She pursed her pale lips and thrust out her impressive bosom. "No man frightens me, me laird. Only the devil himself . . . and . . ." She stopped and glanced sidewise at him, past the babe's small bundled form.

"Senga?"

"Aye," she said, nodding her gray head.

" 'Tis the shade I wish to learn about," he said. "Do you think it was she who left this blood upon me?"

She crossed herself nervously. " 'Tis her mark."

"She left it on the Munro."

"On the Munros," she corrected. "First the old man. Then the sons."

"*Sons?*"

"Aye. 'Twas the elder of the two who first became . . . enamored with me lady. She wanted naught to do with him, what with the cruelty he had shown her mother, but her father . . ." She shrugged as if loath to say ill of the dead. "You must understand, the Munros be powerful neighbors. 'Twas little more than a year past that they invited me lady and her sire to their keep. He'd been ill for some time by then. Mayhap that made it even more difficult for him to remain unimpressed by their strength and wealth. Feasts fit for the king, they had. A hundred candelabras made of gold. A host of soldiers, each brawnier than the last. Still . . ." She sighed. "The lass could not forget her mother and turned aside Cuthbert's suit.

"Raids followed. Sheep were slaughtered, cattle stolen, and . . . well, 'twas then that Deirdre fell and not much later that we learned she was with child.

" 'Twas drunk, Cuthbert was, when he arrived on the firth that cold winter's day. Drunk and declaring that he would have our Anora, whether she be witch or saint." Helena shook her head, her expression solemn. " 'Twas a fool's errand to try to climb the Myst to her chambers, but a fool he was, and as a fool he died."

"And he was marked with the blood?"

"None here saw the body, but 'tis rumored that he was."

"And Innes Munro?"

"While me lady was gone, he moved into her chambers and awoke with the same stripe of blood."

"But he is not dead."

"Nay, for he was wise enough to leave."

They stood in Ramsay's room in silence for a moment. "Do you think I will die, Helena?"

She raised her solid jaw and looked him square in

the eye. "When you first came, I knew there would be trouble."

"Why is that?"

"At the start I thought 'twas because of the prophecy. I was sure that you, like the others, did not have the required attributes. But then you bested the Munro. Power, you had. But peace also. And cunning. But kindness?" She paused, and when she turned her gaze on the bundle in Ramsay's arms, her old eyes filled with tears. "Well, mayhap you have that too, and if you are loved by none other . . ." She tightened her mouth and lifted her plump bosom even more. "Well, the babe will surely remember your deeds."

He smiled a little for her pride, then lifted his hand to his throat. "Who has done this?"

"Senga—"

"Let us assume that 'twas not a spirit, but a person of flesh and blood."

The old matron scowled. "Think you that someone here wishes you harm?"

He shrugged, glanced at the babe's sleeping face, and bent slowly to place her in her cradle. "When did you fetch wee Mary?"

She looked a bit sheepish. "I am surely not the type to interfere," she said. "But she was crying, and you were fast asleep."

"At what hour?"

" 'Twas some hours afore dawn. I had not yet heard the third bell of nocturne. When I reached your room, the cradle was still rocking, so I knew you must have just seen to her, yet she was still hungry and you were fast asleep, so I took her to me own chamber to care for her. I meant to replace wee Mary in her cradle, but when I returned to her room, you seemed so exhausted, and she was so peaceful in me arms—"

"And you saw nothing amiss? No one in me chambers? No one in the hallways?"

"Nay. Who would wish you harm?"

"I was about to ask that very question of you."

"You've bested the Munro. Who here will mourn that?"

"Surely Deirdre was not alone in her adoration of them."

"Deirdre's mind had turned septic."

"She hated me. Who else might feel the same?"

She shook her head.

"Another of Anora's suitors, mayhap?"

"I know of none."

"No one who adores her?"

"In truth, me laird, you'll find no dearth of folk at Evermyst who adore—hey now!" she said, turning her attention toward Tree as he sloshed water out of the rim of the basin he carried. "Mind the floor."

"Me apologies," Tree said, skittering his gaze to Ramsay's throat, then darting it away.

Ramsay scowled at the lad's nervousness and cleared the room as quickly as possible. He needed to be alone to ponder, to unlock the mysteries of Anora and her Evermyst.

Despite the morn's odd opening, the day passed without mishap. Evening came, and though some turned spooked eyes on Ramsay, none spoke to him. He cared not, for it gave him time to observe and contemplate.

The serving maids avoided him, and Isobel seemed to shrink into her drab oversized gown anytime he happened to glance in her direction. Even Ailsa seemed leery, though she finally ventured near.

"Mead, me laird?"

"Me thanks," he said, lifting his mug. "I've a question for you, Ailsa."

She started slightly, her dark brows drawn together. "What's that, me laird?"

"Have you lived here all your life?"

"Why do you ask?"

He smiled, hoping to put her at ease. " 'Tis just this," he said, and leaned slightly closer, "I fear the folk of Evermyst think me destined to die by a ghostly hand. I was hoping one who had been birthed elsewhere might not share those same beliefs."

"I am not a Fraser by birth."

"Oh?"

"Nay, I married into this clan when I was but—"

"MacGowan."

He turned breathlessly at the sound of Anora's voice. Ailsa curtsied briefly and hurried away.

"You are well?" Anora asked. She spoke softly, but there was no need, for he sat virtually alone at this table.

"I am well," he replied, his voice just as quiet. "And you?"

"I need to speak to you. Alone. Wait a while, then meet me in the solar," she said, and was quickly gone.

Ramsay remained in the great hall for a time, sipping his mead and watching, until finally, when he thought none would connect his departure with Anora's, he left.

The solar was a high chamber with an iron bound door that stood open. On fine afternoons, sunlight bathed the room in golden hues, but it was dim now. Yet when Anora turned and the candlelight glistened off her gilded hair, the chamber seemed bright as midday.

"Ramsay." His name sounded like a prayer on her lips, so sweet and breathy that for a moment he could not move. 'Twas Anora who rushed across the floor to close the door and press her back to its heavy timbers. "I feared . . ."

Sweet Almighty, she was beautiful, small and fragile and lovely—yet not fragile at all, and she cared for him. He could see it in her sapphire eyes. "Feared what?" he asked, and allowed himself one step closer. He would not rush her, would not undo any small trust he might have gained.

She stilled her expressive hands and raised her small chin. Her lips, bright as holly berries, were already pursed, and her expression suddenly aloof. "I asked you here to request that you leave Evermyst."

He hurried to match her cool change of moods. "May I ask why?"

"You do not belong here. You are not a Fraser."

He said nothing.

"My people—they fear you. You are disrupting the order of things." Even her hands were perfectly poised now, and he found, to his consternation, that he could not possibly play the game so well as she. For despite everything, he could not see her without thinking of her naked.

"And what order is that, Notmary?"

She paused for a moment, then said, "You must leave."

"Because you do not want me here?" he asked, stepping forward. "Or because you are worried for me?" He was close enough now to see the cobalt flecks in her eyes.

"I do not want—" she whispered, but in that moment he kissed her. When he drew back, she was pale and shaken.

"Please." Her voice was naught but a sliver of sound, and he gloried in her lack of composure. "You must leave."

"Because of the spirit?"

"I . . . I do not know. I thought 'twas . . ." She paused, looking frantic.

"You thought it was who?" he asked, but she shook her head.

"There is none here who would harm you," she whispered. "None who is living, at least."

"I've found little reason to believe in spirits, lass."

She turned away. "Evermyst is haunted. All know that."

"And that has stood you in good stead, has it not? After all, if the spirit can best the Munro, what enemy would be safe?"

"Regardless of what you think, no living soul killed the Munros."

"Thus 'twas this Senga?"

"I have no other explanation."

"And now she is bent on killing me?"

She shook her head as if her thoughts were boiling in her mind. "I do not know. I only know that you must leave before 'tis too—"

"Anora." He grasped her arms in a steady grip. "Who is it who wants me gone?"

Her face was as pale as death. "I know of no one. No one of flesh and blood."

"Then I cannot leave."

She turned her hands so that she grasped his sleeves in desperate fingers. "Why? To prove yourself yet again? To make me love you only to lose you?"

His heart tripped in his chest, and for a moment he could not breathe. "Do you love me?"

"I will not if you die! I swear it, MacGowan! If you—"

He kissed her thoroughly, only drawing back when she felt limp in his arms. "I have no intention of dying, lass."

"Then you will leave?"

"I cannot."

She drew slowly away, her expression suddenly blank and her back very stiff. "Then I'll not mourn your death."

He wanted to pull her close and lose himself in her, but her nearness jumbled his thoughts—and just now he needed a clear head. "Why are you so certain I will die?"

Her eyes gleamed with wetness. " 'Tis what happens to those . . ." She halted, her lips pursed and her chin high.

"To those you love?" he asked.

"I'll *not* mourn you," she said, and yanking the door open, rushed into the night.

Chapter 28

Ramsay lay in the darkness. Sleep, dark and seductive, called to him, but he dared not let it in, for he waited. Someone wanted him gone, but did they also want him dead? And if so, why? Fuzzy half-formed questions smothered him. Fatigue wore at him. It would have been simpler if he could leave his bed, if he could pace, but he could not—for whoever had breached the sanctity of his room would only do so again if they thought him unconscious. And so he lay fighting sleep, counting off the hours with the toll of the friar's small bell.

Some distance from the door, the cradle was silent, empty but for the blankets that lay in a bundle there, since things were so uncertain. What if the grudge held against him extended to the babe? What if her

346

wee life was in danger? His heart contracted, and for a moment he was tempted to race out of his room to check on the babe's well being. But she was safer with Helena than with him. Mary was safe. Anora was safe. 'Twas his own life that was vulnerable, or so the miscreant must think. For miscreant it surely was. A person of flesh and blood, and a person he could best.

Yet how had any person been so silent as to sneak into his chambers unnoticed?

He imagined a shadow falling across his door. It paused and then, like a wisp of smoke, it slipped beneath his portal and flowed toward the cradle. He heard it rock gently, but in a moment the quiet noise ceased. He felt the shadow turn, felt its coolness fall across his bed, but no evil seemed forthcoming, only a calm sort of consideration, as if someone was watching him sleep. Yes, that was it. She wished him no harm. She was a kindly soul, after all. Small and fragile, she only worried for her kin. Thus she stood at the foot of his bed and—

Christ! He sat up with a jerk and glanced frantically about the room. It was empty. He was alone, and yet— did the cradle still rock slightly? Nay, 'twas his imagination, he assured himself. His heart raced and his head felt woolly, but all was well. No brigands had interrupted his solitude. No spirit had invaded his chambers. It was nothing more than a dream, no matter how tangible the presence had seemed.

Cautious, stiff, he lay back down. Minutes ticked away. Shadowy thoughts crept back into his mind with insidious softness, soothing, lulling. Somewhere in the darkness a dove sang. Its sweet voice reminded him of Anora. How she spoke. How she felt in his arms, in his bed.

He murmured her name like a dream, and then, in the deepest recesses of his mind, he sensed a movement.

Someone in his room—near the cradle! He jerked to a sitting position and a white figure spun toward him with a gasp. A ray of light from the window slanted across her face.

"Anora!" Her name rasped from his lips. She leapt toward the door, but he was closer. He stumbled out of bed. Blankets tangled and knotted around him, but he wrestled free, blocking her path. "Anora," he whispered again.

She backed away, a pale, ghostly form in the darkness.

"Why?" he whispered, but in that instant she pivoted away. 'Twas then he noticed the open window.

She flew toward it, while he, mired in sleep and blankets, stumbled after. For a fraction of a moment she paused on the windowsill. He saw her pale face turn toward him for an instant, and then, like a freed lark, she soared into the inky sky. The moonlight shone on her pale billowing gown for a frozen moment, and then she was gone.

He couldn't move, couldn't speak. Then, broken free from immobility, he dove for the window. "Anora!" he yelled. Panic washed him in cold waves. "Nay!" he cried, and scrambled frantically onto the ledge to search for her, but she was gone. Disappeared. Broken on the rocks below. He knew it, and with that knowledge, his will to live was also broken.

"Anora," he whispered and leaned into the wind.

"MacGowan!"

He turned with a start, nearly falling as he did so.

"MacGowan, what are you doing?" Anora raced

forward. Her pale gown, made diaphanous by her lantern, billowed behind her.

"Lass." He whispered the word and stepped, entranced, from the window. "You were just . . ." He glanced sideways, into the endless darkness. "Here."

"What has happened? What is wrong?"

"You . . ." He scowled, lost in his dreams, in his misty uncertainties. "Someone . . . was here."

"Senga?" she whispered, her tone awed. "In truth?"

He shook his head, disoriented and baffled. The room danced. "Through the wall?"

"What?"

"If she is not flesh, why not go through the wall?" he asked, and turned toward the door. The floor seemed to tilt beneath him, but he remained upright. " 'Twas not a ghost. 'Twas a person, and we shall find her body down below."

"Nay!"

Ramsay turned, trying to read her tone, but she was already racing to the door, lantern held high. She did not fly down the steps, as he had expected, but rushed toward her chambers. Once there, she pulled aside a hanging tapestry and wrenched a wooden panel from the wall. Ducking into the dark passageway, she hurried down into the heart of Evermyst.

Ramsay followed, down, down into darkness, until he saw the slightest glimmer of light shining around a bend.

"Who goes there?"

" 'Tis your mistress." Anora's voice was breathy. "Ready the boat."

Someone stepped out of the darkness. "Is that you, me lady?"

"Aye."

"You have need of the boat? At this hour?"

"Now!" she snapped.

They were in the water in a minute. Glancing up the sheer face of the rock, Ramsay calculated the location of his window, and there they searched, up and down the precipitous shoreline. But they found nothing.

Finally, strangely exhausted and confused, Ramsay followed the lantern light up the tunnel toward Anora's chambers once more. In the circle of light her face was as pale as death. The panel creaked open and they stepped into the flickering light of the room.

"Me lady!" Anora's maid stood beside the bed, one narrow hand sheltering a feeble flame. "I heard your door open and came to make certain all was well. I have been worried sick. Where have you been?"

"Isobel!" Anora whispered, and as she stepped forward, the lantern wobbled in her slim hand. "You are . . ." She paused inches from the maid. "There is no cause for worry. The MacGowan thought someone was in his chamber."

"His chamber?" the girl asked, turning wide eyes to Ramsay.

"Aye. He thought 'twas a woman, and that she . . . dove from the window toward the sea."

Isobel blanched and stumbled back a step, crossing herself as she did so. "Lord save us."

"You heard nothing from his room?" Anora asked. Ramsay concentrated on the conversation, trying to decipher her hard tone of voice, but it was strangely difficult, as if his mind still slept.

"Nay," Isobel gasped. "Do you suppose it was Senga, warning him away?"

"Nay!" Anora's voice was hoarse. "Why would she?"

The women's gazes met and locked. "I know not,"

Isobel whispered, wide eyed. "But 'twould be a pity and a shame if your champion met the same fate as the Munros. Dead before their time."

"What do you think killed Ironfist Munro, Isobel?" Ramsay asked, but the girl only shrugged. She looked paler than ever tonight, her lips so light they held almost the hue of lavender.

"I know not what killed the Munro." Isobel ducked her head. Her ugly cap shadowed her face, and her baggy gown seemed more drab than ever in the gloomy darkness. "But 'tis said it was by Senga's hand."

"Senga." He did not believe in ghosts, yet when he said her name it was little more than a whisper. "Have you seen her?"

"Nay, but I have felt her," Isobel murmured.

The whisper of a shiver breezed up Ramsay's spine, weakening his knees, but he locked them hard and focused on the moment. "So you know not how she looks?" he asked.

Isobel flickered her gaze nervously to Anora and away. "In truth, me laird, all know how she looks."

He turned, concentrating hard. Sleep crowded in on his senses. "How?" he asked, and in one hazy moment, Anora turned away, bidding him to follow.

'Twas not far that they went, just down the darkened hall to the solar. There, beside the far wall, Anora lifted her lantern. The circle of light rose until, looking down at him from a gilded frame, was Anora in her youth—her golden hair loosed, her blue eyes alight. But there was something different. Gone was Anora's aloof nature. In its place was a gentleness, a carefree happiness. It drew him in, transfixed him, for it seemed almost that she smiled for him alone, for him and the future they held together.

"When was this commissioned?" he murmured, still falling into the glistening eyes.

"A hundred years ago."

Ramsay's dreamy thoughts crumbled. "What?"

She lifted her chin slightly. " 'Tis not me, but Senga," she said, and Ramsay, feeling the earth give way under his feet, toppled to the floor.

He was waking! Anora held her breath. Of course he awoke. He was strong. Invincible. He had bested the Munro; surely he would awake. Yet her hands still shook as she watched his eyes open.

His lashes, ridiculously long and full, lifted like the rising sun. His dark gaze roamed the room for an instant, then settled on her face. "What happened?"

She tightened her hands in her skirt, careful not to let them caress his rough cheek, to feel the pulse that thrummed in his broad throat. "You swooned."

"Swooned?"

His tone was dry, but devoid of the haziness and uttered delusions of the previous night. It had been almost as if he were drugged. But surely she wouldn't have . . . Anora clamped down on the thought. " 'Tis not uncommon when one has been wounded."

He watched her in silence for a moment, his dark eyes steady. "You think 'twere me wounds that caused me to lose consciousness?"

"Of course." She tried not to look at him, but God help her, she could not stop herself. "What else?"

"A sleeping potion, mayhap?"

She jerked involuntarily. "What?"

His eyes were deadly level. "Someone wished me to sleep soundly."

Though she tried to drag her gaze away, she could not.

"Someone poisoned me mead," he said. "I should have realized it earlier."

Fear knotted her belly. "Nay."

"Who was it?"

" 'Twas no one. You are deluded."

"Was it you?"

"Nay!" She leapt to her feet, but his hand clasped her wrist, pulling her back down.

"How did you do it?" he asked, his face inches from her. "How did you exit by the window, then enter by the door? Why are you not dead?"

She said nothing, fear clogging the words in her throat.

"Are you a witch?" he whispered.

Panic erupted inside her. "Nay!" she gasped, and jerking from his grip, stumbled backward. "You may stay the day while I ready your entourage. But on the morrow you will leave," she said, and turned shakily toward the door.

"Anora," he said, and though she knew better, she turned toward him, her breath stopped in her throat.

"I'll not be leaving, lass. On that you can depend."

For a moment she feared that she, too, might faint, but she steadied her nerves and raised her chin. "Then you may die like the others."

"I may indeed," he said, and she forced herself to leave.

Ramsay spent most of that morning in bed, yet despite his lack of activity, the hours sped by, for his mind was spinning. That evening, in the great hall once again, he said little and observed much—how Helena poured the ale, how Meara watched everything, how Isobel kept her eyes averted, and how Anora, looking pale in her crimson gown, could almost hide the fear in her eyes, but not quite. When the meal was ended and the keep had been given time to settle into silence, he left the hall and strode down toward the kitchens.

Isobel should yet be there. Isobel with the narrow hands and bird quick glances.

"Ramsay."

He turned with a start, and there, just rounding the corner from his right, was Anora. The crimson gown made her appear more fragile than ever and her wide eyes were bright with a terrible anxiety.

"I thought you had retired to your chambers," he said.

She glanced sideways and wrung her slim hands together. "I've only a moment, but I must speak to you," she said, for once not attempting to hide her fear.

Worry cut at him. "What is it? What's wrong?" he asked, and strode toward her. Her eyes widened still more and she stepped quickly back.

"I cannot speak here. There are ears everywhere. Meet me at Myst Vale—where you battled," she whispered, and turned to leave.

"Anora." He grabbed her arm. "What is amiss?"

They were inches apart, her eyes as wide as bluebells, her lips like scarlet bows, and already he felt himself pulled closer, longing with a terrible need to draw her close.

"Nay!" She pulled free and backed away. "I cannot. Meet me at the vale."

"Why must—" he began, but she cut him off.

"If you love me, you will meet me, and you will tell no one," she said, and fled.

"If you love me, you will meet me . . . If you love me you will meet me . . ."

Her words ran through Ramsay's mind like a litany. It had not been a difficult task to escape the keep without being seen, though the precipitous descent from Myst had caused his thigh to throb as his scabbard pressed into it. Beyond the castle's feeble lantern light, the night was quiet, the air cool. Mist curled like forgotten souls from the lowlands, and high above, tattered clouds whispered past a grinning moon.

"If you love me you will meet me." And so he came, for he could no longer deny the truth. It burned at his soul like a Candlemas flame, consuming him. Aye, God help him, he loved her.

He slipped across the open moor and into the trees beyond. Branches rustled, whispering secrets that made him turn and glance behind, but no one followed, so he hurried on, his mind churning.

The moon slid beneath a wisp of a cloud, and the midnight wind whispered his name. He turned back again. Nothing but darkness.

"So you have come."

Ramsay jerked forward, and there, standing before him, was the Munro. The moon skidded clear of the clouds, shining its silver light on the giant's broad scarred face.

Then the final puzzle pieces clicked together in

Ramsay's mind. He straightened, glad that he had come, happy to pay the consequences to know the truth. "So Isobel told you I would be here."

Even in the darkness, the surprise was evident on the Minotaur's face. "In truth the maid told another, someone she calls a friend, but my spies are many. So you knew the lass planned to betray you?"

Ramsay shrugged.

"I meself was surprised that she wanted you gone, for I thought surely all of Evermyst worshiped you as their champion. But it seems me lady's maid thought you were putting her mistress in grave danger."

"Did she say how?"

"How?" The Munro grinned as he pulled his sword from its sheath. "In truth, laddie, I care only that you are here."

"So you have come to be rid of me."

" 'Twas the lassie's wish, even if she planned for another to do the deed," he said, and took a scant step forward. "And how can I resist? She loves her mistress so."

"Aye," Ramsay agreed, "she does that. Like a sister. But I fear I've no wish to die this night, Munro."

The grin broadened. " 'Tis damnably bad luck for you then, isn't it, laddie," Munro said, and lunged.

Ramsay danced backward, arms flung wide. "Mayhap we should discuss this first."

"I do not hate you as I'd prefer, MacGowan, but we've nothing to talk about," Munro said, and slashed again. Just as Ramsay leapt backward a second time, a woman shouted and a missile whizzed out of the darkness. The Munro stumbled back with a grunt.

"Run, MacGowan!" she yelled.

Munro's men streamed out of the woods, but Ramsay was busy searching behind him. And then he saw her, her face pale in the moonlight as she stood amidst the ghostly trees.

"Anora!" he yelled, but just at that moment Gryfon raced up from behind him, and on his back was another lass. "Anora?" Ramsay gasped, gazing in confusion at the pale oval of her face. He glanced at her, then at the woman behind, terror alive in his mind. Which one was she? "Get back!" he yelled, desperate to save them both. He finally whipped his sword from its scabbard. "Back to the—"

Then Munro's men fell upon him. He slashed at the closest two. They parried and fell back, but there were a dozen more, pressing up from behind. The closest raised his sword, but again something whirred out of the darkness, slamming him aside. Rocks! They were rocks, thrown from the woods like well placed arrows. But other warriors pressed past their fallen leader, and in that moment Gryfon leapt forward.

"Nay!" Ramsay yelled, but the rider pressed the bay onward, plowing into the nearest two soldiers. They stumbled aside. One stayed down, but the other rose, bringing his sword to bear. "Get back, lass!" Ramsay shrieked.

"Take her!" Munro roared, stumbling to his feet. "Take her unhurt."

"To the castle!" Ramsay yelled as he parried, but the rider was already aiming Gryfon toward an advancing swordsman. The warrior went down, but another had come up beside them. "To your left! Your left!" he yelled, but even now Anora was being pulled from the bay's back. Frantic, Ramsay slashed his blade in a hard arc. The closest man hissed in pain. The others retreated only slightly, but it was enough. MacGowan leapt into the opening and rammed his shoulder into Gryfon's barrel.

The stallion stumbled sideways with a grunt. The man on the far side fell with a yell beneath his weight, but refused to let go. Anora was pulled sideways. Ramsay reached to grab her, but too late. She disappeared from view. Gryfon plowed ahead, and Ramsay leapt in, kicking the warrior's sword arm. The soldier yelled as his blade flew into the darkness, and relaxed his grip on the captive's arm.

Grasping Anora's wrist, Ramsay yanked her to her feet. Then they were running, scrambling through the woods as he searched frantically for the other maid, but already they could hear the Munros crashing up from behind. Closer. Closer. Pivoting about, he pulled Anora behind him and raised his sword, arms outstretched.

The Munros streamed at them in a roaring mass. Ramsay struck, parried, and struck again. They fell back, just as a devil's yell rang out. A flash of gold streaked out of the darkness as horses galloped toward them from the woods.

Ramsay's heart sank. They were done. There was no hope.

But a rock flew, striking a rider, and the horseman jerked about, his face visible in the moonlight.

"Gilmour!" Hope flooded Ramsay as his clansmen charged from the darkness. With renewed strength he leapt toward the Munros, but in that instant another missile was loosed. It struck his skull with reverberating force and he dropped, falling quietly at Anora's feet.

Chapter 29

Ramsay groaned as he awoke. His head rang like an iron bell and his leg throbbed with pain that seemed to rumble its way through his entire being.

"You say he swoons often?" asked a familiar voice.

Ramsay cracked one lid open and got an eye full of Gilmour's grinning face. Memories flooded back like a break-tide, and he sat up with a jolt. "Where's Anora?"

"Ahh, so our long-lost brother joins us," Gilmour said. "Welcome to the land of those who stay awake during a battle."

"Where's—"

"MacGowan." She was there, unscathed, unbowed.

"Anora." He whispered her name and she came into his arms. "I feared . . ." he began, but could find no words to complete the aching panic he had felt.

Nothing to explain the empty void he had faced at the thought of losing her. He slipped his hand onto her cheek and drank in the sight of her. "You are well?"

"Of course," she said, but when she covered his hand with her own, her fingers trembled. "And you?"

"I am fine."

"Not to worry, me lady," Lachlan said. "I fear me wee brother has always been wont to swoon like a milk-fed babe. He'll recover."

If Anora heard him she showed no sign. She slid her fingers gently over the bump on Ramsay's skull. "I am sorry." Her face was pale. " 'Tis my own fault. Isobel only meant to save you from—"

"Your sister is a fine aim."

"Sister! I have no sister," she gasped, but for an instant her gaze darted toward the door.

"Aye, you do, lass," he murmured, and followed her gaze. Isobel stood near Meara with her back to the wall. For the first time since his introduction to her, she was dressed in something other than faded, drooping gray. Indeed, the sapphire blue cape wrapped about her slim form and covering her head was just as bright as the colors always worn by her mistress. "Your twin, I believe."

"Twins?" Lachlan said, and rubbed his arm as if nursing a bruise.

Anora shook her head. "We are not—"

"There is no need to lie," Ramsay said. "The truth is out." Anora's lips moved in silent denial for a moment, then, "How did you know?"

"At first 'twas simply her hands," he said, and stroked Anora's gently. "But then there were a dozen wee hints. Her lips were all but blue after she dove from me window into her beloved sea—a fact I failed to see in me drug-induced state. But me conversation with her, when she pretended to be you and sent me out to the vale—that was quite revealing. She called me Ramsay, which you have not to this day, and suggested that I might be in love with you. A dangerous lass, but quite astute. She is the one who pretends to be Senga, who made certain me mead was drugged, who visited me room in the wee hours of the morn, who rocked Mary's cradle, and who dove from me window into the firth."

"Is this true?" Anora asked, her gaze meeting her sister's.

The girl frowned as she stepped forward. "I know naught of rocking a cradle, but as for drugging you . . ." She shook her head. " 'Twas clear Ailsa would keep your mug full of whatever fine herb I dropped in her pitcher."

"Isobel!"

"I am sorry, sister." The whisper was gone from Isobel's voice, replaced by a demeanor as bold as her twin's as she swept back her hood. Golden hair glistened in the candlelight. "I could not bear to lose you."

"Lose me!"

"To MacGowan," she said, and fixed him with her gem bright eyes for a moment.

"And so you would see him killed?" Anora asked. "Delivered to the Munro—"

"The Munro was not to have him," Isobel said, drawing closer. "I have more than one friend who would be willing to see the MacGowan taken from Evermyst until you forgot him, until you remembered that we cannot let another in. Until you remembered our mother."

"But with Ramsay gone, Munro would have only increased his efforts to have me!"

"But do you not see?" Isobel said, her tone softening. "The Munro would never have had you."

"We cannot hold him outside these walls forever."

"Maybe not outside the walls," Isobel agreed. "But outside your heart?" She smiled. The expression was wistful, and Ramsay realized that until that instant he had seen nothing but trepidation on the girl's elfin face. "For a few brief months, you shared your life with me. Indeed, you shared your very soul, for I felt as though we were one. But there is no place for me here now," she said. "Truly though, mayhap 'tis for the best. I tire of playing the soft maid."

"Isobel—" Anora said, but her sister shook her head.

"Me apologies, MacGowan," she said, though there was little remorse in her tone. "When I went to your chambers to test your loyalty and you turned aside me advances, I knew that you truly cared for me sister. Still, I convinced myself that your departure would be the best thing for her. I could not allow you to be killed, though. Not when me sister adores you as she does."

"I do not . . ." Anora began.

"There's little point in denying it," Isobel said, her gaze still on Ramsay. "Though I do not understand the attraction, she cherishes you." She shrugged "I know, just as she knows the truth about me.

"She knew in her heart that I was the one who wished you gone. She knew, yet because she cherishes me, she believed my lies to the contrary. You are blessed among men, MacGowan, for she adores you like none other."

"Do you?" Ramsay asked Anora.

Their eyes met. "I—"

"Hold up!" Gilmour said. "I am utterly flummoxed. How could you not know they be sisters? You've been known to be daft, Ram, but surely none could be so simple as to miss the great beauty they share. Indeed," he said and stepping toward Isobel, took her hand between his. "I am already light-headed from her charms."

Isobel threw back her head and laughed. "Or mayhap 'tis from the rock I hit you with," she said, and pulled her hand from his. "Believe me, MacGowan number two, had I not wished you to know me true identity you would not have known."

" 'Twas you who threw the rock?" Gilmour asked.

"The lass is quite adept with a sling," Lachlan rumbled.

"A maid must have some means of defense when she is born to poverty."

Gilmour scowled, and Isobel smiled, enjoying his bemusement.

"I meself did not know I had a sister," she said. "Not until some months ago when I tried to filch the very turnips the lady of Evermyst was attempting to purchase."

"How can this be?" Lachlan asked.

"Ignorance is an evil thing," Meara said, her voice dry as dust. "Evil and intolerant. Twins are thought to be the devil's work. And triplets . . ."

"Triplets?" Ramsay asked. "There were triplets?"

"Nay, nay, there were not," Meara said quickly. "I only mean that men are fools at times, and their sire, God rest his soul, was no exception. What difference does it make if the womb bears one babe or more? Surely the blessings be only multiplied. The laird of

Evermyst was not an evil man, but ignorance and superstition guided him." She shook her head. "When the lady learned that she was to bear more than one child, she was afraid. 'Tis not unknown for the second bairn to be put to death, so she begged me to hide the weaker of the two. I took Isobel far away and placed her in the care of a merchant's wife." Her ancient face cracked with grief. "I did not know she would fall into harm's way."

"Do not fret," Isobel said. "I am not the lady of Evermyst, but neither am I dead. I have learned many things. Enough to make me own way in this world."

"Your own way," Anora repeated. "Whatever do you mean?"

"Even at our first meeting at the market, we knew the truth. 'Tis not safe for us to be together," Isobel said. "Prejudice and ignorance—"

"Cannot win out over right and strength," Ramsay said.

"What?" asked the sisters in unison.

"If you will be me wife," Ramsay began, his throat aching with emotions as he held Anora's gaze, "I will let no harm befall you or your sister."

"But—" Anora began.

"Nay!" Ramsay said. "Hear me out. I know that you do not trust men, but this I vow: if you will pledge your life to mine, I will keep you safe or die in the effort."

Anora's face was pale. "MacGowan—"

"Do not say nay," he whispered, and Lachlan stepped forward.

" 'Tis not just me brother's might that will protect you, lass," he said. "But all the MacGowan power. We are the brother rogues. Who can best us?"

"I don't know," Isobel said, eyeing Gilmour.

"He gasped like a child when me rock hit him."

"MacGowan." Anora breathed his name and ever so gently caressed his cheek. "There are times when even right and strength cannot best hatred and intolerance. And those who hate me will hate you, also. I could not bear to see you hurt."

"Then marry me," he said. "For nothing could wound me more than being without you."

"I—"

"Marry me," he said, "or I shall befriend Senga and haunt Evermyst meself."

"I fear you will not hear from Senga again once I have departed," Isobel said.

"Aye," Meara agreed, "but if she could, your grandmother would return to meet this man." She nodded firmly. "For he is powerful and peaceable, and cunning and kind. But is he loved, Anora? You alone can answer that."

The room fell into silence.

"Am I loved?" Ramsay whispered.

"Aye," Anora murmured.

Gilmour frowned. "I always suspected God had a fine sense of humor. There is only one mystery left, then," he added. "Who was the warrior who led us here to best the Munros?"

"The same warrior who seized the lass from our very camp," Lachlan said.

"Aye. But who is he, Ram—" Gilmour began, but found his brother locked in Anora's embrace.

"I suspect he's busy," Lachlan said.

"Humph," Gilmour answered.

The wedding took place at Evermyst. The walls of the great hall were festooned with bouquets of dried white heather to bring luck to the newlyweds, and the floor was covered with fresh reeds mixed with sweet strew. A score of clans gathered together to celebrate. Frasers mingled with Forbeses and MacGowans and MacAulays and Munros in a riotous crush of cousins and kinsmen and friends.

Upon the dais, Ramsay stood with his bride, and scores of well wishers drank to their health. Against the far wall, wee Mary lay content in her wooden cradle, and near at hand a dark haired Irishman lifted a mug and a devilish smile.

"I do not understand it, Rachel," said he, speaking loud enough to make certain Ramsay heard every word. "Here's your wee cousin, naught much to look upon and somber as a stone, yet he gains himself this bonny bride. 'Tis a miracle, I say."

"You're not the one to call the kettle black, Liam," said a huge warrior who nudged his way through the crowd.

"Haydan," said the violet eyed woman on Liam's arm. " 'Tis glad I am to see you."

"I only mean," said Liam, not missing a beat, "that wonders will never cease. But then, I've heard this keep is bewitched, so mayhap there lies your answer."

"Nay," said Gilmour, stepping forth. " 'Tis the way Ram swoons that draws the lasses. Prettily, like a fine, delicate maid. Ohhh," he crooned, and lifted the back of his hand feebly to his brow. "I feel weak. Marry me, Anora, or I shall surely faint."

The closest bystanders chuckled and Gilmour grinned.

"I had hoped that her pity would run short before the time of the wedding, but I see that it was me own luck that ran short. Nevertheless . . ." He raised his horn mug. "I congratulate you, brother, and welcome your bonny bride into the clan."

There were shouts of "cheers" and "hear, hear," as Ramsay gazed at his bride's beaming face.

"Tell me, wife," he said, squeezing her hand and looking deep into her smiling eyes. "Did you marry me because of the way I swoon?"

"Is it the truth you want, husband?"

"It might be an interesting change," he said.

She laughed and rose on her toes to whisper her words. "Indeed, I married you because you make *me* swoon."

"Oh," he breathed, and felt his blood rush southward.

Her lips drew closer to his. Ecstasy waited.

"Here now!" someone yelled. "Surely you can wait till you reach her bed, MacGowan."

Ramsay pulled away and raised his mug in an impromptu toast. "May me union with the fair lady of Evermyst forever aid in the peace amongst our clans." As cheers rang through the throng, his gaze fell on the Munro, looming above the heads of his countrymen. "Excuse me, me love," he said, and extracted himself to weave through the crowd, keeping the red curly head in sight like the northern star.

"So you have come," Ramsay said simply.

"Aye." The Munro nodded once. There was a healing bruise on his brow and when he raised his hand to accept the drink he did so slowly, as if he hurt. "Let it not be said that the Munro be not a man of his word. I said I would come and so I have, as a sign of accord between your people and mine. Not that I am afeared of fighting you again."

"Nay," Ramsay said, and rubbed his chest, easing the wound still healing there. "Nay. I too would have no qualms about a battle between us."

" 'Tis for the lady," Munro said and lifted his brooding gaze over Ramsay's head. "For her there shall be peace . . . and for the wee babe."

"Aye." Ramsay scowled. "So you have spoken with Ailsa."

"She came to Windemoor some weeks ago, asking to speak to me." He sighed. "I knew 'twas she who had found the maid called Deirdre after her fall. But I did not know that she had seen Cuthbert and the girl together."

"Maybe she was mistaken," Ramsay said, striving to keep his tone level. "Mayhap the child is not your brother's at all, but—"

"The babe is most probably his. Just as he may be the one who pushed the maid from . . ." He grimaced. "Mayhap 'twas the widow Ailsa's loyalty to me clan that kept her from immediately telling what she knew, but Cuthbert was . . . not as gentle as I."

Ramsay cleared his throat. " 'Tis that very gentleness I would appeal to now."

The Munro's scowl consumed his face. "What's that?"

"About the bairn. She is as much a Fraser as a Munro, and though her mother is gone, the same is true of her father. And while I understand that you might mourn his loss, the truth is—"

"What be you trying to say, MacGowan?"

"I'd like to keep wee Mary."

Munro glared. "Why?"

"I've become somewhat attached."

"You jest."

"Nay, I do not."

"And if I agreed, what would I get in return?"

It was Ramsay's turn to scowl. 'Twas best to drive a hard bargain, of course, but if the truth be told, he would give up much in exchange. Gryfon came to mind. And he had a couple of brothers—

"What would you like?" Ramsay asked.

Munro raised his gaze to the dais. " 'Tis a bride that I need."

Ramsay stiffened. "You'll not lay a hand—"

"Don't get all alather, laddie; I've no intention of taking yours."

"Then what—"

"Though I do not understand it, women seem to find you rogues somewhat..." he narrowed his squinty eyes, "... appealing."

Was he joking? Ramsay wondered. If he had swooned one more time in the past few weeks, he would have been laughed out of Scotland. "So you want—"

"Quiet," Munro warned, still leaning forward. "You may not know it, but maidens of breeding do not always find me ... charming."

"They don't?"

"Your tutelage will be changing that, MacGowan."

Ramsay kept his expression impassive as full understanding dawned. "As you wish, then."

"We are agreed?"

"Aye."

The giant nodded grimly. " 'Tis good," he said. "But I tell you now, if so much as a word of this gets out, I'll tear you limb from limb and—"

"You must be the Munro."

Ramsay turned at the sound of his brother's voice,

but Lachlan didn't shift his gaze from the giant's broad face.

Munro glanced down. "And you must be the brother the wee maid wounded with her rock."

Lachlan's brows lowered and Gilmour appeared beside him just in time to laugh. "I'm certain he meant nothing by it, brother. After all, 'twas a good sized rock, flung by, well, by a braw lass."

The Munro chuckled, and Lachlan's brows lowered more.

"This be me wedding day, brothers," Ramsay warned under his breath. "And I'll not have a fight between—"

"What goes on here?" asked Flanna.

The lads turned in unison. "Nothing, Mother," they said, and Ramsay slipped away with a smile.

Across a sea of heads, he could see his bride. Standing beneath a bower made of dried and twisted flowers, she gazed across the crowd. An expression of concern was on her bonny face. Ramsay hurried through the mob to her side.

"Anora." He stepped up beside her and followed her gaze out over the crowd. "What is amiss?"

"Nothing. 'Tis naught." She looked up at him and smiled, but in that instant, he saw where her attention had been. A solemn faced young man stood at the edge of the crowd with his back to the wall.

He wore a wide brimmed leather hat, a padded doublet of russet hue, and high black boots that rose above the knees of his dark trews. There was a soberness about him, a taut virility that Ramsay almost recognized, as if he had seen him somewhere . . .

"The warrior!" he hissed, and prepared to leap through the crowd, but Anora caught his arm.

"All is well."

"But 'tis he," Ramsay rasped. "The armor is gone, but 'tis he just the same. The one who—"

"The one who made our meeting possible," she said, and moved closer, so that their bodies just brushed.

Ramsay pushed his instant desire aside, for her safety was all that mattered. "I'll question him now, learn the truth before he knows we suspect—"

"I have other things in mind," she said, and slipped her hand into his. "More important things."

"More impor—"

"More enjoyable," she said, and rising on her toes, kissed him.

Ramsay's every nerve sprang to keen edged attention, but he fought for rationality. "You are me wife," he said, letting the meaning of the words slip to the core of his being and brace him with heady protectiveness. "I'll not let anything harm you."

She smiled, dimpling slightly. "You are my beloved," she said, "and he has no wish to harm me."

Beloved. He ached to take her into his arms here and now, but duty came first, and he must be cautious, lest he compromise her safety and make his own life unfit for the living. "How do you know he wishes you no harm?" he asked, shifting his gaze from her face to the warrior by the wall.

"I have a feeling," she said.

"And what if you be wrong?"

"I am not wrong. But if I were, you would save me," she murmured, and laughed.

Ramsay stood transfixed, for in her face there was neither restraint nor fear, just the soft, kindly trust of an angel in love.

"As you have already saved my heart and my soul," she said, and squeezed his hand.

Her fingers were as fragile as a song and when he lifted them to his lips, he knew that his dreams had come true. She was his, forever and always, to protect and nurture and cherish.

Somewhere in the crowd a child laughed. The music of lutes and psalteries filled the air, and near the far wall, wee Mary giggled. An unseen hand rocked her cradle, and as music reached for the high rafters, Senga hummed along and smiled mistily at her granddaughter's burgeoning joy.

The very best in historical romance
By the most talented authors . . .

Coming next month, two spectacular stories that will
make you believe in the timeless power of love . . .

***

THE MACKENZIES: ZACH
Ana Leigh

"One of the most exciting western
romance series of all time."
Romantic Times

He's a rugged undercover Texas ranger—and a MacKenzie
man. She's a beautiful Harvey Girl who thinks he's a dangerous
outlaw. Together, theirs is a love that defies all rules.

• •

THE WARRIOR'S DAMSEL
Denise Hampton

A spectacular new series by a dynamic new author . . .

Sir Rafe Godsol, courageous warrior knight, selects as his
bride the most beautiful—and unattainable—woman he's
ever known, Lady Katherine de Fraisney. She's the daughter
of his most hated foe, but theirs is a love that can overcome
all obstacles . . .

"A wonderfully talented writer!"
Rexanne Becnel

"Enchanting, vivid . . . exciting"
Susan Wiggs

Judith Ivory

"Judith Ivory is irresistible.
Susan Elizabeth Phillips

THE INDISCRETION
0-380-81296-7/$6.50 US/$8.99 Can
Passion flares in Regency England when an
improper millionaire makes an indiscreet proposition
to a straight-laced British beauty.

THE PROPOSITION
0-380-80260-0/$6.50 US/$8.99 Can

SLEEPING BEAUTY
0-380-78645-1/$5.99 US/$7.99 Can

BEAST
0-380-78644-3/$5.99 US/$7.99 Can

....

Available wherever books are sold or please call 1-800-331-3761
order.   JI 0401